FLASHPOINT

MADELAINE DUKE

FLASHPOINT

Michael Joseph
London

First Published in Great Britain by Michael Joseph Ltd
44 Bedford Square, London WC1
1982

ISBN 0 7181 1876 6

Typeset by Granada Graphics, Redhill.
Printed in Great Britain by
Hollen Street Press Ltd at Slough

CONTENTS

FREEDOM FROM FEAR I
Russia to Israel 1944 - 1969   9

VICTIMS OF FREEDOM
Kenya 1962 - 1969   51

FREEDOM TO KILL
America 1968-1969   93

ACADEMIC FREEDOM
England 1970   115

FREE ENTERPRISE
America, Rhodesia, Israel 1973   137

FREE FROM ATTACK
America, South Africa 1974 - 1975   173

FREEDOM OF MOVEMENT
America 1976 - 1977   201

FREE FOR ALL
Europe 1978 - 1981   233

FREEDOM FROM FEAR II
Satellite SRB II 1984   271

From YURYI ANDROPOV, Chairman KGB
To BORIS NIKOLAEVICH PONOMAREV Chairman International
Department of the
COMMUNIST PARTY

Moscow, 6 October 1969

The latest report of the nuclear accident in the Urals, Zone 27, states that the number of casualties has risen to six hundred. The area has been sealed off. My men are enforcing strictest security.

Several thousand inhabitants on the perimeter of Zone 27 are likely to have suffered radiation damage, but they will not know the cause of their health-deterioration. In order to prevent any spread of information all persons aware of the nuclear explosion have been transported to the isolation block of Kamensk Labour Camp and will be kept there until they can be transferred to the new SV security complex in the Western Sayan.

As a precautionary measure we have arrested the most inconvenient dissidents (list appended).

It is regrettable that Military Intelligence was, of necessity, heavily involved in Zone 27. Now all GRU personnel should be withdrawn forthwith. I would be most grateful for your support at this final stage of a military disaster that is liable to cause repercussions abroad unless my Directorate is given a free hand in containing the situation.

From Defense Secretary
To Chairman, Senate Appropriation Committee

Security Rating D-one-6   Washington DC, 3 July 1970

I am receiving reports of a disaster which I consider even more damaging than the nuclear accidents at Palomares, Spain, and Thule, Greenland. For one thing, it is nearer home.

Last night a device exploded in North Dakota, killing one hundred and seventy military personnel and civilians. The long-term radiation damage cannot be assessed but is liable to affect the health of thousands. If this damnable business became public knowledge – I am certain you will agree – it would seriously undermine our nuclear deterrent system and the missile research program. The environmentalists, reds and just about every organisation that makes up the anti-nuclear lobby would retard the effective defense of this country, giving Russia the ultimate nuclear lead.

The Security Forces in North Dakota appear to have acted fast and efficiently. Everyone likely to know the nature of the explosion, between three and four hundred people, has been rounded up for pollution tests. They are being kept under guard at Minot Air Force Base. Obviously this is a short-term solution. If news of the accident is to be kept under wraps permanently – and there is no doubt in my mind that it must be – it will cost money.

To put it bluntly, potential informants will have to be bought. According to initial FBI estimates their silence will cost us between eight and nine hundred million dollars. Such amounts cannot be paid out of the President's special fund without causing accountability problems.

The cost of the accident will have to be absorbed within various departmental allocations and the President will be looking to you for advice and help.

This is all the information I can give you at the moment. You will be asked to attend a meeting at the White House within the next twenty four hours.

FREEDOM FROM FEAR I

Russia to Israel 1944 - 1969

1

The man's gun was pointing at his chest. The gun was an AK47 assault rifle. The man was wearing a sand-coloured cotton suit which might have been made in the 'thirties, especially the baggy trousers. The gunman couldn't have looked more Russian if his bosses had put him in uniform.

'That's a stupid thing to do,' said Samuel, in Russian. 'Do you want to get yourself in trouble, *tovarish*?'

The gun wavered and drooped.

'All right. This time I won't report you.' Samuel turned his back on the man. He wouldn't shoot. Not now. Too unsure of himself.

Samuel had seen some godforsaken places in the past, but this was the worst — this rock-strewn desert, bleached a grubby white by the inexorable sun. He looked upon the dark crater before him — a hole like a gigantic bullet-wound — trying to control his heaving stomach. Why so squeamish now? Seen enough dead bodies before. Yes, but not bodies such as these; thirty or forty of them, recognizably old men, women and children, the expressions on their faces petrified in grimaces of uncontrolled terror.

Approaching the nearest cadaver, a girl of twelve or thirteen, he touched her side with his toe. The faintest tremor. God! She couldn't be alive! Suddenly she caved in on herself and disintegrated. An empty shell, a husk in human shape; now, nothing but a silhouette of black dust. No point of reference; no comparison with anything in his experience — not even the obscene mountain of skeletal dead at Auschwitz concentration camp. They, at least, had been solid enough not to fall apart when the excavators shovelled them up. Don't think of it, you fool! Just take it easy and stay alive.

Samuel turned to the Russian who was still standing around in an agony of indecision; just another Soviet-manufactured Pavlov's dog.

'Where's your commander?'

The man shuffled his feet. 'In Keren . . . *gospodin tovarish*.'

'You're an idiot. Whoever sent *you* to a place like this? I want to know who's in charge of this little party . . . right here.'

'Colonel Alexei Kirov.'

'Who did you say?'

'Colonel Kirov.'

'Good. So there's *something* you know. Where is your colonel?'

The guard grinned with relief. 'In his tent, over there. I take you to the colonel?'

'You're learning.'

'Thank you, *gospodin tovarish*.'

The Russians had made their camp among large boulders, which gave them some shelter from the dehydrating khamsin. Half a dozen light-weight nylon tents of American manufacture. Samuel wondered whether they'd been stolen by guerillas of the Eritrean Liberation Front from the American base at Asmara or whether the United States had sold them to Russia — as obligingly as they sold vast amounts of equipment, from nuclear hardware to computers. There was an astonishing communications gap between American big business and the American military pundits.

The guard lifted the flap of the largest tent, equipped as a laboratory. 'Tovarish Colonel . . .'

'What the hell are you doing here? You're supposed to be . . .' Kirov saw Samuel. 'Who are you?'

'The introductions can wait.' Samuel took in the officer at the paper-strewn folding table. The face, weather-beaten and bloated, still looked somewhat effeminate. Kirov had been fair, tall and lean; now the extra weight made him look much shorter. 'I suggest you send your man back on duty.' Samuel injected irony into his advice. 'Mustn't leave the holocaust out there unattended.'

Recognition came into Kirov's pale eyes. Could it be? The intruder was a head shorter than he . . . built like a wrestler. No fat; dark skinned; bare arms covered with black hair. 'Borodin . . . you haven't changed much.'

'You have, Kirov. Put that moron out of his misery.'

'All right, Kowalski. Back to your post.'

The gunman made a smart exit.

Kirov motioned Samuel to a camp stool. 'Where have you sprung from?'

'Moscow, of course. Someone in the Presidium is interested in this location.'

'The back of beyond in Ethiopia?'

'Eritrea, to be precise. Yes . . . interested.'

'I'm working on the report now,' said Kirov, stiffly.

'Relax, Alexei, relax. Your people will give you credit for your report. We are interested in another angle.'

'Political.'

'Cause and effect, perhaps.'

'That's my business.'

12

'Colonel Kirov, there's no such thing as individual business in Soviet society. You should know by now.'

'Have you come here to remind me . . .'

'Now what would be the point of that? This is 1969. You've become a distinguished officer. I'm proud of you, Alexei.'

'And you? You've become a distinguished commissar?'

'We won't talk about me. There's no time.' Samuel glanced at the papers on the table. 'Are these data complete?'

'Not so fast. Show me your authority.'

Samuel laughed out loud. 'You military boys! How do you get away with such ignorance? You don't imagine that a certain person in the Presidium issues his men with passports, do you?'

'I'm not required to be a political animal.' Kirov was on the defensive.

'Forget it, Alexei. All we want to know is what you and your scientists here are making of this operation.'

'They've reached no satisfactory conclusion. Nor have I. You can pass on to your boss that we're working with our hands tied behind our backs. How are we to evaluate the effects of this . . . this . . .'

'Experiment?'

'Whatever it is . . . if no one will tell us how it was accomplished.' Kirov's frustration was genuine enough.

'I don't know either,' said Samuel, truthfully. 'But, looking at this . . . valley of death, I can't help suspecting a nuclear incident.'

'You can stop suspecting Borodin. Take my word for it; the radiation-level here is normal.'

'Well, one shouldn't impinge on subjects one knows nothing about. I was just remembering that weird picture . . . the imprint of a man on a wall in Hiroshima, after the Americans had dropped the atom bomb.'

'I remember it too.' For a moment Kirov looked almost carefree. 'You're probably right about one thing . . . the husks of people out there are unique. But, according to my team of scientists, they're even more puzzling than the Hiroshima shadow. Something — and we haven't begun to understand — what has gutted them — desiccated their insides and yet preserved and hardened the skin-tissues.'

'It must have been an incredibly fast process.'

'Why do you say that?' Kirov was wary again.

'An impression. Nothing more.'

'Your master may be satisfied with *impressions*. I am not.'

Samuel got up. 'I'll leave you to your work.'

'Where do you think you're going?'

'Where I came from.'

'From this hellish African desert all the way back to Moscow? Like Icarus, I presume.'

'That's right.' Samuel smiled. 'How else?'

'You're not leaving this site. My guards will see to that.' Kirov followed Samuel out of the tent. 'We'll be taking you back to Keren with us. This place is top secret . . . not open to visitors. In Keren we'll be able to establish your credentials . . . I hope.'

'Unsound, politically speaking. But please yourself, Alexei.'

The sight of the amused man made Kirov feel annoyingly uneasy. He remembered Borodin, the boy, cracking walnuts in those strong white teeth of his . . . savage *kulak*.

'When do you propose to leave for Keren?' asked Samuel.

'Tomorrow night.'

'That suits me.'

'We have quite good campbeds. You'll be comfortable.'

So Kirov was hedging his bets . . . making his guest or prisoner, prisoner or guest *comfortable*. 'Thank you for your hospitality, Alexei.'

'If I were you, I wouldn't attempt to leave . . . prematurely.'

Samuel sensed something of the old resentment in Kirov. A weak man doomed to proving himself. A weak man with brains though. He'd probably volunteered for the appalling job out there.

'We understand each other, don't we, Borodin?'

'A bad habit, spelling things out . . . as I told you many times in the past.'

'I'm not spelling out what the position is, Comrade Borodin. But I assure you, my men are remarkably good shots.'

The fast chop on the neck hadn't damaged the guard in his tent. Samuel reckoned he'd wake up in the morning with a mild headache – nothing worse. The other men, guarding the two trucks against marauding guerillas, hadn't seen him; not while he'd been making his way out of the camp. He was clear of it now.

He skirted the steep petrified sand-dunes above the camp and stood up straight beside a thornbush. He wouldn't need his compass; the stars were bright. He identified his old friend Sirius, the little dog-star, harbinger of the dog-days. It certainly was a hellishly hot night for a long trek. And the terrain of thorns, rocks and sand was treacherous. He didn't think he'd make the rendezvous with Joram and the jeep before daybreak. What a revolting mission! What a mess!

For what? Kirov had asked him. Over dinner he'd shown Samuel something of the quixotic character he'd inherited from a long line of ancestors who had been their own masters. Not counting possible consequences Kirov had spoken his mind. What the devil was Russia playing at? Why send technical advisers — don't we know what *that* means — to Egypt and Tanzania, to Afghanistan and bloody Eritrea? Why send *him* here — a senior intelligence officer of the GRU? Was the Kremlin shaping up for the next war? Damned if he wanted to donate his two sons to the paranoiacs in power.

Kirov was a very troubled man — which did not mean that he wouldn't carry out his duties according to the book. He'd spoken like a man and a father of loved sons, but he was as much as ever a Soviet GRU officer. He'd act like one, the pigheaded bastard.

That Kirov had let him read his report didn't surprise Samuel. Why not? His non-findings, summed up in the final paragraph, were of no great scientific value. *The victims of the holocaust were Africans living in an isolated semi-desert village between the inland town of Keren and the Red Sea port of Massawa, an area originally populated by the almost extinct Kuama tribe. On-site investigation has yielded no scientific explanation for the total destruction of the dwellings, undoubtedly the usual mud-huts with thorn roofs, the absence of any normally durable object (e.g., made of metal), or the process responsible for gutting and dehydrating the corpses on the periphery of the crater.*

Samuel fingered the stones in the pocket of his bush-shirt. They were the one negative that might eventually yield a positive answer. One of Kirov's young scientists, interested in the minerals on site, had shown him his boxed collection. Pointing out the smallest set of specimen, he'd observed that they were heavier than pieces of equivalent size in the other boxes. Had these specimen been subjected to treatment in an atomic reactor, which could have changed their molecular structure, the result might well have been what he had picked out of the crater. But the fact that the radiation-levels on site were normal made such a speculation a non-starter. Nor had the young man felt happy about the alternative theory — the bombardment of the place by a meteorite.

Samuel felt satisfied that the information he'd gathered — for what it was worth — couldn't have been more complete at this stage. As to Kirov — he and Alexei had come as close to one another as brothers who had once shared a dreadful period of fear and degredation. But he had no illusions now; when Kirov discovered his absence he'd send out a search-party with orders to bring him back, alive or dead.

By three in the morning he'd reached the gulley parallel to the Keren road, the kind of terrain favoured by the rebels of the Eritrean Liberation Front. Here, among the deep fissures and thorns, ELF men could watch the road, choose their time for laying mines and booby-traps, and withdraw unseen into the wilderness or the safety across the Sudan border.

Samuel backed into a clump of thorns and sat down. He'd heard movements on the road ahead. He'd stay put until he'd identified and placed each sound, no matter how long it took. Computing past experiences on the run, stored memories of similar terrains, and knowledge of the military position in the area built up over the past year, gave him a fair idea of his present situation.

The units of the Imperial Ethiopian Army which had been operating in the district against the ELF rebels belonged to the 2nd Division, commanded by Major General Teshome Erghetu. In recent weeks those units had sustained heavy losses of equipment in ambushes on the Asmara-Keren road. They'd therefore returned to base for retraining with new FN rifles, which meant that they'd withdrawn from the vicinity. Hence the night-operators on the road were bound to be an ELF group. It was likely that they were preparing a trap for Kirov's party. With the Russians dressed in civilian clothes, the Etritrean rebels could hardly be blamed for hitting their allies by mistake.

ELF would be more justified in butchering him, Samuel reflected; but they weren't going to. He might have taken a chance on evading a handful of guerillas, but not with Kirov's men on the prowl. He'd been hearing sounds, unconnected with the Eritreans on the road, north of his position. Perhaps a stray goat was wandering through scrub and dislodging stones, but he wasn't prepared to check. He didn't like the idea of getting sandwiched between two hostile forces, in the dark.

Samuel resigned himself; best stay under cover until daybreak. He made himself comfortable, resting his head on his knees. The worst of it was that he'd miss his rendezvous with the jeep. What a hell of a place to get stuck in!

2

Samuel changed step; slow quick-quick slow, slow quick-quick slow. Alternating one's rhythm was a useful device when one was almost dropping with exhaustion on a long trek through ice or furnace heat. He didn't consider himself an expert in any field except in the art of survival on interminable walks. It was a question of making the best use of all one's built-in defences.

If your circumstances become intolerable in one time-dimension, what is to stop you going into another? The body can function in all time-dimensions, on any terrain. 'Don't live in the past,' Esther was liable to advise. Esther had no imagination, which was good, because it was easy to live with a totally predictable woman. Don't live in the past? What a foolish notion! The past, the present and the future weren't separate entities, like three cabbages. These time-dimensions were a single, indivisible phenomenon of the mind or brain or God-given computer. So — when the heat burns into your body, you might say, 'Oiweh . . . how my muscles ache! How the thirst is making my tongue cleave to the roof of my mouth! Oiweh, Oiweh.' Or you can say to yourself, 'So the sun is trying to eat into the marrow of my bones? Never mind . . . so I go into the frozen wastes of Kazakhstan.' Nobody can stop you. There's no identity problem. You can safely be yourself — Samuel or Shmuel Volatian.

And while your body — a well-tried forty-year-old mechanism in fine fettle — struggles on through this searing alien land, your mind will travel in the safer, more familiar dimension. And no one can stop you . . . no Eritrean, no Russian, nor your Major General . . . the *Rav Aluf*, not even Rabbi Kassim.

Rabbi Kassim had said it on the first of April 1939, when all people in their senses — except the English — had been sure that an all-engulfing war was about to break out. 'It's bad enough to be an Armenian in Russia, but to be an Armenian Jew is a perversity of fate.'

It had been a warning, and it had been a joke. Itzhak and Katarina Volatian had laughed. Shmuel could still see his parents in their little shop, packed with jewel-coloured Armenian carpets, blankets and hand-embroidered shirts, laughing with the high-spirited young rabbi.

The shop had been a small magic cave of beautiful things. In his grandfather's time the Volatians had owned five workshops and employed all Armenian families with the skills of making those masterpieces of silk prayer rugs and hand-woven cloths. But after the pogroms in Odessa, when many Jews had been killed or deported to Siberia, the Volatians had reduced their business interests and their style of living. Shmuel's father had been brought up on a policy of modesty in all but education. He'd become a renowned linguist, and he was striving to turn his son into a scholar. No one could steal what was in your head, he'd reasoned. Jews had been forced into many exiles for many generations; the best gift one could give one's child was the ability to communicate with the people of foreign nations.

By 1939, at the age of ten, Shmuel had acquired a working knowledge of German, English and Hebrew and had read the major Russian classics.

Soon after Rabbi Kassim had made his thoughtful joke, Shmuel's father had moved the family to Moscow. Perhaps life would be safer in a big city where one was unknown. Itzhak had hired a French teacher for his son — the best his savings could buy. Professor Karminski taught at the University. Normally he did not accept private pupils and Shmuel never understood why he'd consented to teach him, except that Karminski obviously found his precociousness entertaining.

It wasn't his brilliance that made Shmuel stand out at school, but another of his family's gifts — music. His mother had taught him to play her mandoline; his father — habitually bellowing at him to use his chest as a soundbox — had badgered him into singing like a professional. At school, his music was the language that helped him communicate with his anti-Semitic Russian mates.

The summer of 1939 was warm and sunny. Shmuel went swimming every day, discovered that he was good at the sport, and felt reluctant to listen to anything not connected with competitions and medals. Why were the adults worrying about politics and war? All right; Russia and Germany had signed a non-aggression pact. There was a picture in *Pravda* of Stalin and Ribbentrop shaking hands. What was wrong with Russia and Germany *not* going to war against one another? A week later Germany attacked Poland, and England declared war on Germany. But what did that have to do with Russia or the Volatian family?

When the Red Army moved west and occupied a large part of eastern Poland, Shmuel began to listen to his father. As Red tanks rumbled into Brest Litovsk, where the Soviets had bowed to Germany twenty years earlier, Itzhak suspected a double double-cross, remembering Alexander I's temporizing deal with Napoleon at Tilsit. Was history repeating itself? Had the Stalin-Hitler deal been a move to gain time and arm for an all-out Russian-German war?

Whatever happened wouldn't be good for Jews, Itzhak told his family. Should they move again? But where? Into the country? It couldn't be done legally. With Russia involved in war, who would bother to issue the necessary permits? On the other hand, in a big city . . . if one lived quietly . . .

Live quietly? wrote Rabbi Kassim from Odessa. What for? Whatever happened wouldn't be good for the Jews. How would a wise man act the day before Armageddon? Think, friend Itzhak, think. Surely he would look at his vanishing world and salute it with a strong heartbeat of joy — joy in all the splendour he'd known. And if one had a son, perhaps a live spark of what had been would survive in him and he'd build Jerusalem anew. So where's the sense in *living quietly,* in effacing yourself? No, no! Live for the day. *Carpe diem!* Take the boy to the grandest restaurants where he'll discover memorable food; never mind whether kosher or not. Go take him to the opera; let him feel the spirit of God in the thunder of superb voices. Let him listen to the orchestras. Show him the treasures in our museums — the Rembrandts and the Botticellis. Is a great painting not the artist's affirmation of continuing life? an act of faith in the future of God's domain on earth? Think of Beethoven's celebration of the Lord's creation; *Joy! Sublime spark! Daughter of Elysium!*

So let your child live in grace, art and joy while there is yet time.

Soon time changed into something without shape, an expanding or contracting mist that shrouded the world like an unwholesome vapour from the marshes.

There was the long, long day when Itzhak and Katarina finished packing their boxes, when the officials came and sealed their two-room apartment, when the truck — already full of scared Jews — took them to the railway station. Why are they taking us away? they asked one another. Because we are guilty, said the Clown. Why are we guilty? Because we are Jews.

Where are you sending us? they asked the young captain who allocated them to the goods-vans. Away from the war, he told them. You wouldn't know how to fight, like real Russians. But don't worry; you'll be given jobs and wages. Where? Where? *Dalyeko*, he said . . . far away. *Dalyeko*, said Shmuel's father, could be five thousand miles from civilization, possibly the homeland of the slit-eyed Mongolian guards who were travelling with them.

There was much work to be done while the vans rolled east. With two hundred people in a confined space it wasn't easy to organize schedules for emptying bladders, defecating, cooking, sleeping and keeping vermin at bay. There were good days, when the train stopped in a station, when they took water aboard and bartered a gold trinket for fresh vegetables. There were bad weeks, when they had to make do with the black bread the Mongolian guards doled out, when they were travelling through frozen wastes which seemed to sustain no form of life at all.

The train crawled on endlessly, past Sverdlovsk and Kurgan, Danilovka and Akmolinsk. At Karaganda the Mongolians made them pack their bags and get out. They didn't want to leave the train. It had been their home; at least the vans had sheltered them from cold and blizzards.

The Mongolians herded them into sheds beside the station. Their leader was a worried man. What had happened to the trucks which were to take these people to their destination? What was he to do with them?

For two long weeks Jews and guards shared hunger and the arctic cold of the derelict sheds. Some of the older people, including the Clown, died. Then, late one night, they saw the dim headlights of a convoy. The truck-drivers were Mongolians unlike the guards, wild-eyed bearded men dressed in wolfskins. In the Volatians' shed the drivers put the women in one corner and extinguished the kerosene lamps. Shmuel heard the heavy breathing of those brutes, the impatient shuffling of the men awaiting their turn. All night long he lay very still and listened to the sounds of rape.

In the morning the guards had gone and the new Mongolians put the Jews in the trucks. No one made an attempt to escape; there was nowhere to escape to. Karaganda was a military base; the commander had told the guards that there was no room for any Jew in his town; there wasn't enough food for his own men; any interloper would be shot. The trucks were as safe as any place could be in that godforsaken wilderness. The Mongolians, quite gentle after the satisfactions of the night, even provided bread and dried fish.

Play the mandoline! Itzhak ordered Shmuel. Sing, child, sing! Remind God that we're still alive. Reach out to the Mongolian animals. And Shmuel struck a chord; he sang and his father sang in harmony.

> *Na Mayoo na maghilkoo*
> *Nikto nye preedyot,*
> *Tol'ka rannyeyoo vyesnoyoo*
> *Salavyey prapayot.*

> *To my grave*
> *None will come,*
> *Only early in the spring*
> *There the nightingale will sing.*

> *A oomru ya, oomru ya . . .*

Singing, they arrived at Murskoye, somewhere south of Semipalatinsk, in Kazakhstan. Murskoye was a huddle of low stone houses in a valley, surrounded by wastelands of rocks and ice. The factory, where the men worked, produced springs for machines which were built in Semipalatinsk. No one knew what kind of machines. The Jews called their new home *Dalyeko*. Far away it was, so far that Shmuel imagined himself outside earth, somewhere in space.

The Volatians were lucky. They had to share their room with only one other family, the silversmith Chernigov, his wife and baby-girl. Between them they made a wooden screen, dividing the room and achieving an illusion of privacy.

In Dalyeko one heard little news of the war, except when the Comrade Engineer in charge of the factory called the workers together and told them that the Soviet army had the Germans on the run. But why did the war drag on, year after year, if the Soviet army was winning?

In the autumn of 1943 fewer and fewer supplies were reaching Dalyeko. No raw materials for the factory, no spare parts for the trucks. Food-stocks had never been lower. There was little that would grow in the poor soil of the valley. In 1944 there weren't even enough potatoes to feed the population of two thousand. That summer Mongolians and Jews alike reached starvation level and there were many deaths. Itzhak stole one of the few remaining goats for his sick wife, but she died . . . she died quietly, while Shmuel sang her favourite song, 'The Red Sarafan'. Then

Itzhak was imprisoned. Perhaps the Chernigovs, who had shared the goat, perhaps someone else in the house who'd smelled cooked meat, had accused Itzhak of theft. While he was in prison, Shmuel became good at stealing for himself and his father.

By the autumn of 1944 Itzhak, wretched without his wife, abandoned life. He'd suddenly become a frail old man. The time has come, he said to Shmuel, when you must take over. Live, boy. You are your parents' future. Leave Dalyeko and turn west. But first, let's have a game of chess. I want you to beat me. The game was a draw. His father was still laughing when Shmuel left the prison. In the morning the jailer found him dead.

Shmuel was fifteen when he collected his inheritance — his father's boots and sheepskin coat and his mother's mandoline — and walked through Dalyeko's only street, past the allotments and the factory, towards the unmarked snow-plains of the Kazakh hinterland.

It would have been less gruelling — Shmuel believed — if he could have played his mandoline. But such was the cold that his hands went stiff and useless within seconds. So he put his mittens on again and sang to himself.

The first twenty-four hours after Dalyeko was the knife-edge of life or death. He trudged on all through the day — the mirage of a hut and a fire before him. By nightfall his body was one great ache. He wanted to stop, make a fire, but there was nothing to burn — not even twigs. The snow and the mountains stretched into an endless, empty eternity. He thought of burying himself in the snow. He might survive. But what if he did? In the morning he'd be that much farther from any shelter, that much weaker.

There was little difference between night and day. If anything the stars were more comforting than the granite-grey light which seemed like the last emanation of a dying universe.

When he saw the wisp of smoke, perhaps on the second, perhaps on the twenty-second day, he believed he was asleep on his feet — dreaming. It turned out to be real; rough stone shelters built in a circle, a blazing fire in the centre, the marvellous smell of meat. For a while he heard his own voice, and then he let himself sink into warm blackness.

He came to on a plank-bed, in the arms of an enormous woman. Days later? Weeks later? He didn't know. All he could think was that his mandoline had gone. Had they burnt it? For the first time in his life he was gripped by fear, sickening, paralyzing fear.

'The mandoline . . .' he cried. 'My mandoline . . .'

The woman held him close. 'There, boy . . . there. I'll give it to you. It's all right. What a funny little man! He comes in from nowhere, half dead. And what does he do? Play and sing his heart out. Sing for food.'

21

Danka got up and made strong hot tea on her little spirit-ring. Then she told him that he was nowhere near a village or town, road or railway. This was a camp of Mongolians, men who'd been treated worse than wild animals in the Soviet army, and who'd deserted into the far-away wastes where no Russian — except one boy — would ever find them. Men needed women, so they'd taken with them three *tovarish polevaya zona* or comrade-battlefield wives, girls who hadn't been moral enough for the high and mighty Communist Party or the Komsomol. Danka laughed. A dozen men and three women . . . it was a sweat. Better though, much better, than sleeping with self-righteous prigs of Soviet European soldiers. And if the boy needed her . . . well, she'd oblige him too.

Shmuel didn't know whether he wanted to be obliged or not. But that night Danka opened her legs to him and he felt tenderness and an immense gratitude. In her arms he sensed in every part of his body and mind that his life had truly begun. He'd reach his destination, wherever it was. He'd again sit in a red plush seat under glittering chandeliers and listen to the glorious voice of Eugene Onegin.

Shmuel played to the men at the campfire. They listened to his deep contralto and learned his songs. In time they sang with him, and their voices rang out across the frozen white plain.

Aral Khan, their leader, was a practical man. He'd stolen the trucks and provisions his people had needed for the long journey, shown them how to build the shelters and taught them to hunt and forage for their survival.

There were wolves, foxes and hares in the mountains. The men knew how to trap the animals, covering great distances on their crude skis and bringing home meat and pelts. There was a good market for the skins in Semipalatinsk. Aral Khan would make his way to the town every two or three months and return with tea, flour, petrol and whatever else his people needed.

For the rest of the winter Shmuel accompanied the men to the hunting grounds and learned their crafts. He would not have recognized the onset of spring if Aral Khan hadn't shown him the first blades of tough steppe grass under the snow and the first fox-cubs in the stony wilderness of the mountains.

Nothing was said when he decided to go on his way. His hosts had sensed his restlessness for some time. Danka and Aral Khan gave him a hat of wolfskin and a pair of skis, and took him by truck as far as the outskirts of Semipalatinsk.

He walked hundreds of miles, and he used his skis wherever the terrain was suitable. As he left the east behind, travelling became faster and easier. Sometimes he managed to jump a train, sometimes soldiers would give him a lift. And food became less of a problem. It was not so scarce, though usually no better than soup, polenta or bread — but there it was, to be stolen or begged for a song or two.

The closer he came to Moscow the more he learned about the war, the murderous battles of Stalingrad and Leningrad, the appalling losses of civilian lives. Now the Soviet armies were in Berlin, the war was almost over, and the people Shmuel met were too poor and exhausted to feel joy. Many soldiers from the east were being sent home; as no one had provided them with a railway warrant or transport they were straggling through the country looting and stealing for survival all the way.

On the river Don, south of Lipetsk, Shmuel met an old countryman in a horse-drawn ladder-cart who offered him a bed for a night or two. Soldatov had lost both his sons in the war — the younger about the same age as Shmuel.

'What good has it done?' he asked. 'Nothing to look after any more . . . not even my own piece of land, which I could pass on to my daughter and her children. When the Communists took over they swallowed up our land and made big communal farms. I'm just a labourer now . . . a nobody. Now we've won the war. So what? Stalin's taken my sons; will he give me back my land? You, young one . . . you too have lost, but you stand at the beginning of life. Don't waste it. If I were your age I would leave Soviet Russia. I'd go somewhere where a man can still own his bit of land and his own soul.'

'Where would you go?' asked Shmuel.

'I'd keep going west . . . perhaps even to Germany. Now things will be bad there. But the Germans will recover. They're hard-working people . . . and they'll never work for the State, not like us blockheaded Russians.'

Plodding along in the creaking cart they came to a line of ornamental iron railings and broken-down gates flanked by stone pillars. On one of them stood a lichen-covered stone eagle.

'What's in there?' asked Shmuel.

'The past, young one . . . the dead past. Marayevo used to be the country mansion of Count Krasnykov. The Communists confiscated it of course. There was talk of making it into a school. But no one bothered in the end. They say the house is falling apart . . . and the trees have grown into the windows. The Count was a private in the army. He was killed in Leningrad. A few weeks ago a woman and a child arrived and went to live at the house. Then some soldiers went in there . . . looters, you understand. A big place like this must be a great temptation to the poor devils. Kolya — the policeman — says they killed the woman. Perhaps she wouldn't share her food with them. Who knows?'

'And the child?'

'Kolya found only the woman. They say she was the Countess Krasnykova.'

Shmuel turned and gazed back at the stone eagle. He made up his mind to go and look at the mansion. Perhaps something had been left . . . a painting, or a beautiful rug of the kind his father had sold in their shop in Odessa.

Shmuel had never been inside a private house as large and imposing as the Krasnykovs'. He stood in the circular entrance hall, gazing at the twin stairways which swept to the first and second floors, at the finely carved convex doors. Superb craftsmanship had gone into making the place, blind brutality into devastating much of it. Wading through the broken glass of mirrors and chandeliers he opened a door at random. He found himself in a ballroom such as he'd once seen in a movie.

Straw and horse-dung on the parquet floor, bullet-holes in the broken stucco ceiling, slashed and broken furniture testified to the mood of the marauders who'd invaded the mansion. What had he hoped to find? The first sign in years that not all beautiful things had been destroyed in the war? Some reassurance that he'd left behind for good the life of a wild animal? He thought of the dead — the old Clown, his mother, the people who'd died of starvation in Dalyeko, his father — and felt immense sadness. This too was death — the destruction of objects which had once given pleasure.

At the far end of the ballroom a shaft of sunlight picked out the bright colours in a large pile of junk. As he approached, the foul smell became worse. He picked up the leg of a gilt chair and a piece of turquoise damask and gently put them aside. Underneath he found a book, bound in green leather — almost undamaged: *The Case of Sergeant Grischa* by Arnold Zweig.

Russia was reshaping, he read, *Russia was awaiting peace with her rifle at her feet. Firing had ceased between the German and Russian trenches: all was brotherhood. As the war must needs end soon, deserters were thronging back to their native villages and towns* . . .

Shmuel tucked the book under his arm . . . a wonderful book in English, and he could still understand the language. He'd read every word, but not here; the smell was too bad. But curiosity made him dig deeper. He uncovered a box of some dark wood inlaid with mother of pearl. Inside were intricately carved ivory chessmen. His hands shook with excitement as he counted them. Miraculously, the set was complete. He worked fast, moving the debris despite the stench. Suddenly he came upon the cause — two dead men in uniform. They were lying on their backs, sunken eyes staring into space; a very young lieutenant and a middle-aged corporal. It was clear from their head injuries that they'd been bludgeoned.

Shmuel assumed that the two of them had pursued the looters and been overpowered by them. He was wondering what he should do about

24

them, if anything, when someone jumped at his back. The person tried to pinion his arms, but Shmuel turned fast and pushed him to the floor. It was easy. When his attacker didn't move he knelt down beside him. The boy was about his own age, as fair as he was dark, and as good-looking as a girl. He was tall but pathetically thin.

'You damned thief!' he spat at Shmuel. 'Go on, finish me off. Killing . . . that's all you're good for.'

'You're sick.' Shmuel touched the boy's forehead. 'Fever.'

'Get on with it.' The voice was arrogant.

'Who are you?'

'Count Krasnykov.'

Shmuel laughed. 'Don't tell anyone else. The age of the aristocracy's been over for a long time.'

'Let me die . . .' the boy looked weak enough to die, 'with my own name.'

'Don't be stupid.' Shmuel lifted him in his arms. 'Got a bed somewhere?'

'Cellar . . . I'm hungry.'

'I'll get you something to eat.' Shmuel carried Krasnykov into the hall.

'Thief . . . scum.'

'Shut up. Where's your room?'

'There.'

'Anyone else around?'

'Our servants.'

'*Tovarish*, this is Soviet Russia. Remember? Don't play games with me. I want to help you. But I'm not going to be jumped by any pal of yours . . . though I don't think you have any pals, or you wouldn't be in such a state. Which door?'

'Back . . . there. Through the kitchen . . .'

Shmuel crunched through charred wood and broken crockery. The mess was worse than in the ballroom, but at least there were no corpses around. He was struggling to open the horseshoe-shaped door at the back, which presumably led to the cellar, when Krasnykov lurched against him. He saw the knife in his fist, felt the sharp point cut into his flesh.

25

3

'Stop!' The Russian's shout sounded unnecessarily loud in the burning stillness of midday. 'Come out or I'll shoot!'

Shmuel grinned. Surely the idiot was thinking back to front; what was the point of shooting if he couldn't see his target? And he'd have to hold his fire if he did show himself, because Colonel Kirov wouldn't be too happy with a dead captive. For one thing, Kirov had no proof that his visitor was not a special envoy sent by the gentleman in the Presidium. Anyone else in Kirov's position would have given up the pursuit by now. Not Alexei. Too arrogant to believe that he might be making trouble for himself. The crazy stubbornness of the weak, obsessed by the need to prove that he was right.

'Come out!' There was hysteria in the guard's voice.

Poor *muzhik*. No fun trudging through this furnace of Eritrean semi-desert. Quite likely that he'd never served anywhere outside Russia. The first confrontation with such heat was terrifying.

Shmuel silently shifted his body to the edge of the thorns. The man was making for the rocks ahead. He appeared to have made up his mind that the fugitive was pressing on in the Keren direction and that he'd have to catch up with him. What would Eritrean guerillas make of this stranger in the absurd civilian city-suit that failed to hide his gun? They wouldn't ask too many questions. Shmuel reckoned that the guard was aware of the danger. The Colonel would have warned him. Did Kirov know any better than he himself what this macabre cat-and-mouse game was all about? Kirov was squeamish; the holocaust had certainly affected him. But by now his priorities would have shifted to the manhunt. Shmuel didn't doubt that — for Kirov — it was mostly a personal matter.

He gave Kirov's man and himself half an hour before he moved. Then, as quietly and smoothly as a leopard, he began to double back. He had enough bitter chocolate and lemon-water to last him another forty-eight hours. It wouldn't take him long to reach the ruins of Debra Sila — the place where the Muslim guerillas had burnt to death fifty-two of their Christian fellow-Eritreans. It would be cooler in that sad little oasis. He'd allow himself a short rest and then take a curved, longer route out of this deathtrap.

If man were a logical animal — as he likes to believe — he and Kirov would now be sitting in the air-conditioned officers' mess in the harbour of Massawa, drinking a cold beer before lunch, watching the ships on the Red Sea, enjoying the view of the sculptured, knife-edged sand dunes of the Yemen across the water. If one lived logically, certain conflicts would never arise. Kirov and he would be on the same side . . . Kirov, the aristocrat, whose age-old way of life had been destroyed by Soviet Communism, and Samuel Volatian — alias Borodin — who had been uprooted by processes of the same revolution.

Once, a quarter of a century ago, Count Alexander Krasnykov — alias Kirov — had tried to stick a knife in him. Poor bastard . . . he'd achieved a scratch, no more, because he'd been too weak even to hold a spoon for a bowl of soup. He'd never again attempted a physical attack, yet he hadn't forgiven Shmuel for the way he'd reacted. Shmuel had laughed, not derisively, but with genuine amusement at the spark of courage that had made the sick boy turn on him. He'd laughed out of affection for the human spirit — and something like admiration for the strange boy. Of course Alexei — pride hurt — had misunderstood; and the misunderstanding had cast an immovable shadow on their relationship.

Within hours of finding Alexei and talking things over with Soldatov, the old farmer, Shmuel was sure that Alexei was suffering from typhoid fever. It was not surprising. The pollution of the river, from which passing bands had been drinking, had caused several outbreaks in the district.

There was nothing Shmuel could do except feed the patient and keep him as clean as possible. Soldatov advised, quite rightly, that Alexei should stay at the mansion. The fewer people who knew of the young Count's existence — especially as a typhoid case — the better.

For days on end Shmuel expected Alexei to die. He sat with the delirious boy, read *The Case of Sergeant Grischa* and learned what political and military hierarchies could do to a man. No book had ever moved him more deeply, yet he couldn't altogether believe that the world was ruled by the devastating self-interest of man, by fear and greed. Surely if there was nothing else, he wouldn't be sitting with this sick stranger when he should be escaping the country where his people had been persecuted and killed for generations.

Then, one morning, Alexei wakened from a long sleep and looked at Shmuel out of clear grey eyes. 'I heard music.'

Shmuel laughed. 'Are you sure?'

'I'm not mad.'

'No, you're not,' said Shmuel, happily. 'Look.' He picked up his mandoline and put it in Alexei's hands.

'You?' He felt the instrument like a small kitten. 'But it was a voice I heard.'

'Very well.' Shmuel retrieved the mandoline and struck a chord.

Na Mayoo na maghilkoo
Nikto nye preedyot,
Tol'ka rannyeyoo vyesnoyoo
Salavyey prapayot.

'Mother of God! What a voice!' There were tears in Alexei's eyes.
'Who are you? Who are you?'

'Not the thief and killer you think I am.'

'Tell me,' demanded Alexei.

Why not? The young Count — the wicked aristocrat — was even more of
a fugitive than he, the Armenian Jew. Shmuel told him of the shop in
Odessa, the brief interlude of opera and concerts in Moscow, the long
dreadful journey in the goods-train. He talked of Dalyeko, the cold, the
starvation, and of his endless trek across Russia.

Alexei listened. Afterwards he made no comment and asked no question. But on the following day he began to speak of the future. They
couldn't hide in the derelict mansion for ever. They should go to Moscow. A city offered more possibilities.

'For what?' asked Shmuel.

'Friends who might help . . . a job. I don't know.'

Shmuel watched Alexei devour the rabbit stew he'd cooked. 'Who's
going to help us? Who's going to give us work? We must be the most
undesirable people in the country . . . an aristocrat and a Jew.
Krasnykov and Volatian beg to apply for the position . . . of what?
Commissar? It's a laugh.'

'What are we going to do?'

'Well, I've thought about it. Remember the corpses in the ballroom? I
went through their pockets and found their papers. The lieutenant was
Alexander Kirov . . . the old man, Misha Borodin. The photo on
Kirov's pass is so bad that it might be a picture of any young male — even
you.'

Alexei thought for a while. 'And you?'

'Oh, I could say that I am the old man's son . . . make up stories as and
when I need them. You'd need the lieutenant's uniform, though I don't
know how we could get it off. He's as stiff as a log.'

'Break his bones.'

Shmuel shivered. Such a solution wouldn't have occurred to him. But
Alexei — the gentleman — had worked it out. 'You seem cut out for a
military career. It's you who could be a killer, not me. Why *not* step
straight into Lieutenant Kirov's shoes?'

'I know nothing about his past.'

'Play the boy-hero who's suffered hell and lost his memory. It's either
that or some labour camp for you.'

'Who are you going to be?'

28

'Myself or Borodin's son, as necessary. I'm leaving Russia, so it hardly matters.'

'Leave Russia?'

'Best I can do . . . travel west. I might even get to England.'

'We'll need money.'

'*You* will need money for a rail-ticket to Moscow.'

'How am I going to get it? It's no use . . . It's hopeless.'

'All right, you weed. You can rot here and wait for the ghosts of your servants to take care of you. I'm going.' The moment he'd said it Shmuel could have bitten off his tongue. The boy had only just recovered from a serious illness. Could he be blamed for his hopelessness and the fear of being left alone?

'Listen, Alexei.' He took the inlaid box from the sack where he kept his few possessions. 'This chess-set is yours . . . carved ivory. It must be worth money . . . enough to get you to Moscow.'

'You keep it. You found it.'

'You need it more than I do. I mean . . . you've been sick. You haven't yet got your strength back.'

Alexei opened the box and set out the pieces. 'Let's play for it.'

'All right.'

Alexei took his time over each move. Perhaps it was still hard for him to concentrate, perhaps he was out of practice. But Shmuel had to acknowledge that he was a good player. They were about level when Alexei moved his queen into a position where Shmuel's knight could have taken her. Shmuel could have warned him, but he knew that it would hurt Alexei's pride to be *given* back his queen.

Shmuel would have liked to keep the beautiful chess-set, but he felt that he had no choice. Ignoring the queen he could have captured he made his next move, aware that he was giving away the game.

'You're good,' said Alexei, as he completed the winning move. 'My chess-set, I'm afraid . . . But where am I going to sell it?'

'I'll take it to Lipetsk for you.'

'Who's going to buy it?'

'Soldatov might know a dealer.'

'That old peasant!'

'You're a fool, Alexei. If you don't get rid of your silly, snobbish ideas you won't survive on your own for five minutes.'

'Then you'd better come with me, hadn't you?'

'Me . . . play nurse to a useless snob who can't even understand that his class has been done for . . . before he was born!'

'What about you, Jew?'

'I never belonged to a class . . . I belong to a minority.'

'Much good has it done you.'

'If nothing else, it's done you some good.'

Alexei held out his hand. 'I'm sorry, Samuel,' he apologized for the first and only time. 'I know what I owe you.'

'You owe me nothing. In this house I received the education which will keep me alive.' He picked up the leather-bound volume of *Sergeant Grischa*. 'This book's given me what I need . . . the knowledge of how authorities work. You might get quite a good price for it. I'll try to sell . . .'

'No, Samuel . . . keep it. Too bad I can't afford to give you the chess-set.'

'Hard luck. I reckon you'll survive . . . Lieutenant Kirov.'

The story of *Sergeant Grischa* 'the soldier ground into the dust by a monstrous war-machine that had assumed a life of its own, prepared Shmuel for some of the sights in Poland. Not for the dead, not for the living skeletons of Auschwitz. There the war-machine had surpassed itself. Shmuel read a neat, efficient ledger that listed the items of prisoners' clothes and the weight of gold fillings pulled out of their teeth — all sent to the Fatherland— and saw before him the respectable administrators who had perpetrated such work for their superiors in Berlin, and striven for promotion.

Shmuel, travelling through foreign country, escaped into a sense of unreality. The trees, glowing in the golden green of spring, looked like beeches and silver birches and yet he could not believe that they were. Nothing seemed quite what it was. Everything was alien.

He passed through the unknown exterior world dissociated from it — yet seeing those mountains of rubble which had once been towns and villages, those shacks the homeless were making from branches, boxes and scraps of armour-plating, the people themselves, so grey and patient and withdrawn.

Women, who had exchanged German for Russian masters, were clearing bombed sites; women were mending the broken roads and working to resurrect the devastated fields — weatherbeaten women of indeterminate age who paid no attention to Shmuel.

He was trudging along a rough road in nowhere when he came across a heavily loaded Russian army lorry. The driver and his mate, standing over the exposed engine, told him that the officer in charge had told them to *sort it out* and driven off with a column headed for Berlin. So much for bloody officers.

Shmuel studied the engine. It wasn't rusty. It wasn't dirty. Someone had certainly looked after it. So why had it suddenly packed up? The answer came to him in a flash.

'Have you got some insulating tape?' he asked the driver.

'So our boy's a mechanic.' The man laughed, but he got out his toolbox and gave Shmuel a roll of black tape.

Shmuel pulled up the electric lead, which was hanging loose, put it into the only socket that didn't seem to serve a purpose and bandaged the joint with tape. 'Try her now,' he told the driver. The pot-holes in the road must have shaken up the electrics.

The man mounted the cab. The engine started up first go. 'He's done it! The kid's done it!'

Sasha naturally offered Shmuel a lift. Poor kid . . . searching for his dad in the chaos that was Berlin. What a hope! trying to find a corporal somewhere in Germany. All the same . . . wouldn't he be proud of his own boy if he'd followed him like that? Sasha wasn't stupid. He knew he'd be taking risks smuggling the boy, who had no papers, through all the Russian army check-points. But what the hell. Stalingrad had been a damned sight worse. The boy had got him out of a hole. He was a comrade and he, Sasha, wasn't going to throw him to those Polish dogs. He'd hide the lad among his load of canned food and trust to luck.

Berlin looked worse than any place Shmuel had seen in Russia or Poland — a great sea of rubble overrun by soldiers and scavengers. The road-map was no help to Sasha, who was trying to find the quarters of his unit. It took him the best part of a day to make the derelict barracks. Hitler, the creator of all the destruction, was dead. The war had been over for weeks, yet Berlin still appeared to be a city under siege. The people, ugly and sick with fear and hatred. Armed Russians everywhere.

While Sasha and his mate went in search of someone to whom they could report their arrival, Shmuel made off through the labyrinth of corridors into the setting sun. He was still on his way west.

It was late in the evening when he found a ruin suitable as a shelter. At least it looked good enough not to collapse on top of him. He'd found water to wash in and a mattress when hunger came upon him. What an idiot he had been! In the lorry food had been all around him. Why hadn't he filled his sack? Too obsessed with the idea of leaving Russia and Russians behind him for ever. Well, there was nothing for it. He'd have to find something to eat, if it took him all night.

Experience had taught him that it was easier to steal if one didn't look like a tramp. He took off his clothes and changed the filthy Russian trousers and tunic for a black suit and striped shirt he'd found in the rubble of a bombed shop in Poland. It was all he had; he'd saved up these clothes for his arrival in the west.

He looked at himself in the cracked mirror of what had once been a bedroom. The trousers were too long, but they covered his shabby boots. Yet the man's jacket fitted well; his shoulders had become wide and strong. The face, still a boy's, wasn't bad: swarthy, with the first shadow of black beard on the square chin and wide jaws; dark eyes, large and alert; blue-black hair combed smooth off his high forehead. He laughed at his reflection. He hadn't looked so respectable since the night he'd listened to *Eugene Onegin* at the Moscow Opera. He most certainly would eat a good supper.

He'd walked for a couple of hours when he saw the bright lights of a big house which might have been a school. Passing the gates he saw a courtyard full of army vehicles and an armed sentry. He circled the place more slowly. Returning to the gates he came across a couple of uniformed men who were talking to one another.

' . . . so I says to 'im, *not me, mate*. If you want to stay in the bleedin' army . . .'

English? Shmuel was almost certain that the man had spoken a form of it. He made for the back of the compound and climbed over the wall, dropping down under a tree. He skirted the wall to the nearest corner of the building and then, fast and silently, ran for an open door. A smell of cabbage told him that he was near a kitchen. Selecting the door opposite, which stood ajar, he slipped inside and turned on the light.

His instinct, developed in times of starvation, hadn't let him down. He was in a store full of canned beef and marmalade, vats of flour and sugar, pots of lard and honey. And then — in the middle of all these riches — he saw something that brought the stupid tears to his eyes, bunches of bananas.

He broke a banana off the stem, peeled it and took a bite. He was back in Odessa, about to go to school for the first time. His mother, on her knees, had straightened his shirt collar and hugged him. Then she'd led him to the door and picked up a small parcel. 'Here are your sandwiches, love . . . No, not in your pocket. We'll put them in the satchel. You're not to eat them until teacher tells you. But if you get hungry . . .' she'd given him the banana, 'you may eat this during the first break. But don't wipe your hands on your trousers.' He'd felt her tenderness as never before; and her concern, for he was a Jewish child going out into a world hostile to his race.

Shmuel was on his third banana when the door was flung open and a huge red-haired man charged in and lifted him off his feet. Shmuel kicked and fought to no avail. Why, in God's name, hadn't he made sure of an exit or — at least — a hiding place? He must have been out of his mind to hang around instead of taking what he needed and making himself scarce.

'Come here, Bill!' bellowed the soldier, in English. 'Would you believe it? I've found a young *Kraut*!'

Understanding the insult, Shmuel squirmed harder. 'I am not . . . a German.'

'You've got an English tongue in your head, have you! Then you'll be able to do some explaining, won't you? Not that it'll do you any good, you thieving *Kraut* bastard.'

32

4

The red-haired captain and Shmuel confronted one another across a table in a makeshift office. When he'd found the intruder, Captain Cohen hadn't foreseen that he'd be faced with a night-long non-interrogation. At times it crossed his mind that the boy was interrogating him.

Shmuel had denied that he was a thief, with burning indignation. 'I do never steal,' he'd flung at Cohen, 'only when I am cold or hungry.'

'One law for you, another for the rest of the world. Is that it?'

'I can pay for the bananas,' Shmuel had told him with naïve dignity.

'How?'

'Listen.' Shmuel lifted his mandoline from the floor.

Captain Cohen had listened. So had most of the people in the building. The voice, which had grown up into a glorious baritone, had begun with a quiet country song and ended with a piece of music so fast and full of life that Cohen felt like dancing to it.

After making his payment, Shmuel had told the Captain his whole life-story, not because he needed to unburden himself, but because he wanted Cohen to send him to England. He wanted a new life, a new country. Obviously the Captain had to know with whom he was dealing.

'Not so fast, little man,' Cohen finally stopped the flow of rapid and wildly inaccurate English.

'I am not little,' objected Shmuel. 'I am the most usual length.'

The boy was right. He was about five-eight.

'And I am strong . . . strong like you.' In one lithe move Shmuel vaulted over the table, put out his arms, and lifted the tall Englishman off his chair.

Cohen burst out laughing. 'Put me down, damn you.'

'Now you will send me to England?'

'Shut up, you! and listen to me for a change.'

Cohen told Shmuel something of what the world in 1945 was really like. Europe, for a start. Thousands and thousands of *displaced persons*, pouring into the British, American and French zones of Germany and Austria; people from Poland, Hungary, Romania, Yugoslavia, Czechoslovakia — fleeing from the engulfing Soviet occupation armies; thousands upon thousands of Jewish survivors, gypsies, slave-workers, all people who had lost their homes and jobs; people who were sick, injured,

33

dying. The hurriedly erected camps were overflowing with them. And there were few indeed who didn't want to emigrate to America or Britain.

How could Britain, poor and bomb-scarred, cope with such an influx of Europe's flotsam and jetsam? It was out of the question. Britain had to find homes for her own people, jobs for her own soldiers. For once Britain had to give herself priority.

Shmuel, completely ignorant of the magnitude of the war, felt that he hadn't begun to live in the real world. He did not interrupt Captain Cohen until he mentioned the *doodlebugs* which had hit London towards the end of the war. What were *doodlebugs*? he asked. Flying bombs. The pilots took the bombs to London and blew themselves up?

'No. They were unmanned rockets,' explained Cohen. 'They were launched mechanically from inside Germany. Not all that many of them got through. Quite a lot were shot down at sea.'

'How did you know they were coming?'

'Technology.' Captain Cohen did not explain radar to Shmuel. But he talked of rudimentary scientific facts. Coal could be converted into electric light, couldn't it? Petrol provided driving power for a bus. Hadn't he used a telephone? Hadn't he listened to a radio? He talked of the conversion of nature's materials into soundwaves, heatwaves, lightwaves. And now there was nuclear power. Had Shmuel not heard that the war with Japan had ended? Well, one bomb had brought about the collapse of Japan — an atomic bomb that had exploded with energy equivalent to 12,500 tons of high explosives and killed 70,000 people. And the basis for the dstructive power of the bomb was a mineral that could be mined like coal — uranium.

Shmuel remained silent for a long time. 'Energy . . .' he said at last. 'Power . . . You don't have to kill people with it, do you? It could work many machines for us. And your flying bomb . . . going from Germany to England. Couldn't you send food from a rich country to a poor country in the same way?'

'Hold on,' Captain Cohen smiled. 'You're going too fast for me. Let's hope atomic power, and other scientific inventions, will eventually help rather than destroy. But we can't go into all that now. Do you know what time it is?'

Shmuel shook his head.

'Five o'clock in the morning. I'd better find you somewhere to sleep . . . and give you a few more bananas.'

'Energy . . .' Shmuel hadn't listened to the Captain. 'One day, at school, our teacher put a mirror in the sun . . . and then he put a piece of paper opposite. It caught fire. He used energy from the sun to burn the paper, didn't he?'

'Yes. How old were you when you left school?'

'Ten. But I had a French teacher. And my father gave me lessons, in

Dalyeko. I want to know about . . . technology. Where can I go?'

The Captain got up and yawned. 'I wouldn't know what to make of you, Master Volatian . . . if I weren't a Jew.' He marched Shmuel into the office of the duty sergeant.

'Bill, think you could find somewhere to lock this young man up?'

'Lock him up? Is he under arrest, sir?'

'Let's say . . . in protective custody. Master Volatian is rather over-endowed with scientific curiosity, and he's just discovered modern technology. It wouldn't be wise to let him loose on the world.'

Shmuel was about to protest at the mockery when the expression in the captain's eyes stopped him. No, it wasn't mockery; more a kind of abrasive irony, a strange form of affection.

It took Shmuel a long time to believe the people who tried to convince him that he had not been caught up in the kind of administrative-political machine which had crushed Sergeant Grischa. What was he to make of the camp in Bavaria, full of Jewish kids who talked of *erez Israel* instead of Palestine, of the youth leaders who made him learn modern Hebrew instead of technology? Had anyone asked him whether he wanted to go to that non-existent Promised Land — Erez Israel? What's more, what was he to make of English soldiers — like Captain Cohen — who served Britain officially, yet unofficially contravened their orders by illegally shipping Jews to Palestine. Plans for setting up a Jewish homeland in Palestine had existed before Shmuel was born. Now Jewish activists in Palestine were fighting and harassing the British troops who were occupying the country. Oh yes, the Jewish guerillas out there were fighting to make a home for the survivors of the holocaust; and illegal Israeli organizations, such as Palmach, were collecting the remnants of European Jewry and smuggling them into Palestine under the noses of the British troops — though frequently with the connivance of Britons such as Captain David Cohen.

Shmuel was all set to escape from the Bavarian camp when Captain Cohen unleashed Rabbi Kassim at him. The cheerful young rabbi from Odessa, who'd warned his parents of Armageddon and advised them to take their son to the opera, had turned into an emaciated middle-aged man. After three years in Belsen concentration camp — still more dead than alive — he'd thrown himself into the work of rehabilitating his fellow-Jews. He didn't spare Shmuel. His horrifying descriptions of how Germany — a reputedly civilized country — had massacred millions of Jews almost convinced Shmuel that Israel was his only solution.

The person who finally convinced him was a British army sergeant whom everyone in the camp called the *Rav Aluf* — by the Hebrew title, Major General. The Rav Aluf was a sinewy little man with absurdly regular features and an unexpected grin. He had amber eyes, full of vitality and mischief, and the quiet voice of a commander accustomed to obedience.

The Rav Aluf let Shmuel have his say and then turned on him. 'All I've heard from you so far is *roh-tzeh, roh-tzeh* . . . I want, I want, and . . .'

'*La-leh-chet.*'

'Yes, to go. Your Hebrew's coming along quite well, but until you've learned to say *I want to serve* you'll be no use to us.'

'I *am* one of you,' Shmuel defied him, 'whether you like it or not. What do you expect? Of course I *want* . . . of course I *want to go*. I want to go where I can learn about such things as radiowaves, lightwaves . . . and the new technology, computers.'

The yellow eyes looked amused. '*Tov*. And if we let you go to Jerusalem University, what will you do with your learning?'

'Use it.'

'How?'

'To make something more useful than flying bombs.'

'Who's going to decide what's needed? You?'

'No. I expect it'll be someone like you, Rav Aluf.'

'What if you disagree with my decision, Shmuel?'

'I'll tell you. And I'll tell you why I disagree. Then we'll have a discussion. Sometimes I'll be right, sometimes wrong.'

The Rav Aluf laughed. 'You'll do for Israel.'

Suddenly Shmuel felt that he'd gained admittance to the one land he had always wanted to enter.

The Rav Aluf shook hands with him. 'I can promise you one thing. We won't allow you to waste what abilities you have.' Then the vigorous grin, 'Who knows? One day we might even send you to England.'

They sent him to Cyprus. Much to his surprise he didn't mind. Swimming in the warm sea was an unforeseen luxury and joy. When they gave him the job of teaching fellow-refugees to swim, he became almost reconciled to camp life.

One of his pupils, a sixteen-year-old like himself, was a petite girl with shining fair hair and dark blue eyes — Esther Levy. As a *displaced person* she was unique. She was American. In the summer of 1939 her parents had taken her on a holiday in Germany. The parents had intended to engineer the escape, from Berlin, of Mr Levy's brother and his family. Instead they'd been overtaken by the war. The whole family, including Esther's parents, had died in the gas-chambers of Buchenwald.

Esther had inherited a fixed idea — her father's dream of a Jewish homeland in Palestine. He'd been a passionate supporter of Theodor Herzl and the early Zionists. Esther never doubted that she was destined for Erez Israel. She was waiting impatiently for the ship that would take her *home*, but those illegal immigrant ships were few and far between.

Some, which had accomplished the voyage, had been caught by British naval vessels and sent back; others had been so derelict that they had sunk.

Shmuel, aware of the uncertain future, did what he could to make Esther live in the present. Relaxed after a day in the water, they'd sit on the beach and lose themselves in his music.

'Sing "Where the Jordan flows",' she'd ask of him.

He'd answer with the *Lorelei*. *'Ich weiss nicht was soll es bedeuten . . . I don't know why it is that I'm so sad. I can't get an ancient fairy-tale out of my head . . .'*

He made such fun of the sentimental German schmaltz that she had to laugh. 'Shmuel, can't you be serious!'

'You don't want me to be like everybody else, do you?'

'You never will be, my crazy Russian *yeh-led.*'

In November the Rav Aluf arrived with the news that Shmuel would be included in the next shipload to Palestine. Shmuel buttonholed the Rav Aluf, after he'd briefed the party.

'Esther Levy must go with me.'

'Must?'

'Yes, sir. You're not supposed to split up families.'

'So you've become a barrack-room lawyer, have you? What relation is Esther to you?'

'She's my *Isha.*'

'Your woman!' The Rav Aluf glared at Shmuel. 'What do you think the ship is? A pleasure cruiser for . . .'

'Families,' Shmuel cut him short. 'We can't help being young. But Esther and I will marry and raise a family. You men of the Palmach keep talking of a future Israel. *We* are the future, Rav Aluf. So you'd better get us to Erez Israel, both of us.'

'I'll look into it.'

'You can save yourself the trouble, sir. Esther has nobody but me.'

The sea-voyage, normally a short one, took eight days. The boat, camouflaged as a fishing vessel, seemed to cruise in ever diminishing circles. It was only at night that it advanced towards the coast of Palestine, mile by slow mile, a blacked-out ghostship evading the vigilant sea and air patrols. What Shmuel found hard to bear was the docility and patience of his fellow passengers — that people who'd suffered the torments of the damned in the death-camps should still be the pawns of politicians.

He felt primitive hatred for the *great* world leaders. They were playing international chess with the survivors of the holocaust. How could they? How could they refuse such people entry to the land they'd been promised in the solemn Balfour Declaration in 1917?

The very thought of killing had always been abhorrent to Shmuel; yet now, faced with those sadly resigned passengers, he realized that there were forces within him that could make him kill . . . kill politicians. He said so to Esther.

'Don't think that,' she begged him.

'What if you were given the chance to exterminate the commandant of Buchenwald? Would you let him go?'

Esther stared into the dark, listening to the unseen ocean. Shmuel put his arms around her — worried, contrite. What a fool he was! He should never have asked her such a question.

She said, 'Yes . . . I would let him go.'

'I don't understand you.'

'You see, Shmuel . . . so many of us in Buchenwald were alive one moment, and nothing the next. It made me feel that being alive was a great miracle. I don't think anyone . . . anyone on earth has the right to destroy the miracle.'

'And yet the little and the big politicians will go on making wars . . . and every war will be a *holy* one.'

'I know.'

'You can accept it?'

'There's no choice. All I can hope for is that I'll stop being afraid. I'll be happy if we find freedom from fear in Israel.'

Early that morning they saw lights like clusters of stars low on the horizon. The passengers were quiet — they'd been asked to keep silent — but their excitement could be felt all through the ship. There, over there, was the Promised Land. Erez Israel, seen at last. Below deck they listened to the drone of a plane overhead. Friend or enemy? *Irgun-zwei-Leumi* — the Zionist freedom-fighters — or the English? Shmuel took Esther by the hand and guided her through the crowd towards the steps up to the deck.

'What is it, Shmuel?'

'Listen.' The sounds of a motor launch getting louder. Patrol boats converging on the ship? 'We've stopped . . . They won't let us land.'

'They must.'

He felt her despair like a pain.

A voice rang across the water, 'Who are you? Identify yourselves . . .'

'Come.' Shmuel pulled Esther to the deck. Now the contours of the shore were clearly visible. He thought he could see movement on the beach. He reckoned they were within a mile.

'We could swim for it.'

'Yes. We must.'

Their captain was answering through the loud-hailer, in a language they couldn't understand. Pretending to be a Liberian ship with a legitimate cargo. One ship had bluffed its way through. Would theirs get away with it?

Shmuel said, 'We've got to make it now . . . before they board us. When you get in the water, wait. I'll find you. Sure you want to risk it?'

'Yes. Let's go.'

The shouts from the patrol boat masked the splash. The water was much colder than he'd anticipated. A moment of panic. Had she passed out? What had become of her? And then he felt her arms about his waist. She was holding on lightly — not scared. Evading the beam of a search-light, he struck out towards the land.

They were clear of the ship when he heard the roar of a motor — another patrol boat approaching fast, bearing down on them.

5

The helicopter beat a slow, stolid path through the night. As Shmuel watched, it performed a tight circle, which it repeated at two-minute intervals. Good timing. In case he missed the rendezvous with Joram's jeep he'd pre-arranged another site, a post the Ethiopian army had abandoned to the Eritrean guerillas. The helicopter was indicating that the post — which was accessible by a rough track — was unoccupied, for the moment. His scouts, men experienced in policing desert country, had done their reconnaissance as efficiently as usual. The transport, which would take him back to the Rav Aluf in Massawa, was no more than three miles ahead.

Shmuel watched the helicopter disappear among the stars, and moved on — a silent shadow in the war-torn stony wilderness. The image of Eritrea's barren five-hundred-mile coast came into his mind. The fact that the Rav Aluf had sent him on this mission proved how valuable this coast was to Israel's security. If the Russians, either directly or through their guerilla allies, ever succeeded in taking control of this coast, Israeli planes would no longer be able to overfly Africa. Israeli aircraft would have to round the Horn of Africa — a bad trip through the narrow Gulf of Aden and a great strategic disadvantage.

He hadn't needed the Rav Aluf's explanations to understand the position. Every move Russia had made since the end of the war had been designed to advance her expansion plans, every shipment of arms to Arab regions, all *financial aid* to the leaders of *underdeveloped* African countries. Was Russia really paranoiac enough to imagine herself encircled by enemies bent on her destruction? It was one theory. Shmuel didn't subscribe to it. Much as he disliked having to agree with the Rav Aluf, he felt convinced that Russia's long-term aims were control of Middle East oil, of Africa's vast mineral resources — not least uranium, of all the oceans. If a lot of little wars, preferably fought by non-Russians, rather than the ultimate atomic bang could defeat the non-Communist world once and for all, so much the better.

Communism's declaration of war on the world wasn't new. Karl Marx had published it in *Das Kapital* in 1867, more than a century ago. What was new was the consciousness in countries such as America and Israel of Russia's inexorable advances since the Second World War, and of the unprecedented horrors of atomic warfare.

Shmuel thought of the holocaust he'd seen at Kirov's camp, of those dreadful, gutted shells of humans. Where did they fit into the advanced science of modern massacres? How had such deaths been accomplished? Who had committed the slaughter? If it had been a Russian operation, why had Alexei Kirov been genuinely puzzled by what he'd found? The Rav Aluf had been called in by the Israeli forces who were helping the Ethiopian army against the Eritrean rebels. An Israeli satellite tracking scanner at Debre Zeyt, South of Addis Ababa, had picked up an inexplicable picture. So the Rav Aluf had sent him into the back of beyond. Soon he'd be before the Rav Aluf once again. What was he to report? That neither the distinguished Russian intelligence officer nor he himself understood who or what had activated the massacre, or why it had been perpetrated in an area so remote from civilization?

Never again, Shmuel promised himself. He'd had his bellyful. The Rav Aluf had singled him out for such missions ever since he and Esther had jumped ship and flopped on the sands at Nahariya. They'd been lucky at that. Other passengers had tried to swim for it and drowned; the rest had been sent back to displaced persons' camps, where they'd vegetated for another two years or more.

Throughout the struggle between the Jewish activists and the British troops the Rav Aluf had made use of him. His knack of moving great distances unnoticed or unseen, developed on the trek across Russia, had served well in the hit-and-run battles which had continued in Palestine until the State of Israel had come into being in 1949.

Early in their working relationship the steely little commander had recognized that Shmuel would never make an ordinary soldier. He abhorred violence — even in wars forced upon Israel — and he rebelled against any organization which threatened to interfere with his academic plans. He therefore, wisely, treated Shmuel as a freelance member of

Mossad, Israel's Intelligence Organization.

After landing in Palestine, Shmuel and Esther had been taken to a kibbutz on the Sea of Galilee. They'd worked on the land until the Rav Aluf had sent them to a school which was to prepare them for university. Esther had studied Arabic and Russian; Shmuel had progressed from electrical engineering to quantum dynamics and the computer sciences.

What energy he'd expended! He didn't think he'd have the stamina now to go through the massive work at university, do his stints as an army reservist and intelligence agent, and live a full family life. He and Esther had married four years after their arrival in Israel. In 1951 David, their only child, had been born. Esther had almost died. There were to be no more children. But when Esther became a teacher there was no lack of young people in their home. David grew up in a large and boisterous family of *sabras* — Israeli children who'd never known a country other than their own and who didn't know the meaning of racial persecution.

There never had been genuine peace between Israel and her Arab neighbours, but Shmuel achieved serenity and contentment in his work, first at the Weizmann Research Institute, later at the Tel Aviv Electrics Company, and — above all — in his family.

In 1965 he bought a small house at Ramat Hasharon. As he explored his garden for the first time he remembered the old Russian farmer who had advised him to go to a country where he'd be allowed to own his land. The intense happiness of owning that small piece of ground was an unexpected gift. He hadn't realized that physical *roots* could mean so much to him.

At the end of the day's work a sense of anticipation would settle in his mind; in the car, on his way home, he'd sing to himself. The orange tree would be flowering. The plumbago would soon be a mass of pale blue blossom. The vine at the back of the house needed pruning; he'd do it tonight. Had Esther remembered to water the begonias?

Life on his sundrenched patch was so perfect that it seemed to him he was having one of his rare nightmares when the first bomb dropped on Tel Aviv.

6

Later they called the fierce battles of June 1967, against the armies of Egypt, Jordan and Syria, the *Six-Day War*. Six days was all it took to kill five of the family's precious children – boys who were just a couple of years older than his son. David – at sixteen – had been too young for the war; Shmuel – not too old at thirty-eight to be called upon once again by the Rav Aluf.

He'd come through the desert battles convinced that the Israelis had won by a miracle, and alert to Israel's need for more sophisticated and scientific military hardware. Israel, surrounded by Arab countries pledged to destroy her, needed better equipment than her hostile neighbours. That was the opinion he'd advocated in the report to his commander.

Early in 1968 the Rav Aluf had called at his house and referred to the report. 'Not everyone agrees with us.' The *us* was his way of telling Shmuel that he was to be involved yet again. 'Some of my colleagues on the general staff are scared of upsetting our American friends. We depend on the States, on France and Britain for certain arms and aircraft; that goes without saying. But how long are we to ignore that Russia is pouring equipment into Egypt? not to speak of *aid* to Marxist guerillas who are trying to overthrow a number of legal governments. The Eritrean Liberation Front for one . . . fighting the Ethiopian army. You know, Shmuel, however American and Russian politicians twist and turn . . . in the final analysis Israel is alone and must be able to stand on her own feet. At this stage we must act as if we didn't have a friend in the world. Do you agree?'

'I'm afraid so.'

'Good. Then there's no problem.'

'In doing what?'

'We must have our own nuclear . . . capacity.'

'Ask for it, and you'll unite the world against us . . . America as well as Russia.'

The Rav Aluf laughed. 'Ask for it? No fear. Don't ask. Develop nuclear power quietly, very quietly and our enemies *and* friends will unite in a conspiracy of silence convenient to us and them. There is a plan . . .' In his quiet voice the Rav Aluf outlined an operation astonishingly outrageous in its conception and audacity.

'Why me?' Shmuel stared at the sun-spots that patterned the cool, tiled floor of his study.

'Isn't it obvious?' asked the Rav Aluf.

Unfortunately it was. Shmuel couldn't pretend that his old taskmaster was wrong. He had the technical knowledge, the training and experience for rapidly changing the plan if necessary, and the essential ability to speak the required languages. Had Father Itzhak Volatian known what he was letting his son in for, he wouldn't have been so dedicated to turning him into a linguist.

The Rav Aluf had already convinced the Prime Minister that it was worth spending precious foreign currency on Operation Plumbat. If Shmuel undertook the assignment of co-ordinating that ambitious project, he'd be backed by unlimited financial resources and a hand-picked team of Mossad agents.

'What do I get out of it?' It was an academic question. Shmuel had no doubt that he'd already been built into the calculations of that phenomenal plan. There was no question of refusing the assignment. But what was the harm of asking?

'What do you want to get out of it . . . Dr Volatian?'

'Peace.'

'Don't we all!'

'I want off the hook, sir. I'm thirty-eight. Isn't it time Mossad found younger men for their adventures abroad?'

'Even Mossad would be hard pushed to find a man with your qualifications . . . tough, fit, and determined enough to survive such adventures abroad.'

'If I do take on Operation Plumbat, I want your assurance that it'll be my last job of this kind.'

'Don't you know better? Who am I to make such promises?'

'Only one of our most important and successful generals.'

'One among others. Don't worry Shmuel. We're not going to waste you on any operation that isn't tailor-made for you.'

'There are too many good tailors in Mossad,' Shmuel capitulated. 'You might at least keep one old promise.'

'What's that?'

'Of sending me to England. Send *us*. Esther hasn't been in an English-speaking country since she left New York as a child. She's not asking to go to the States; but she teaches English and she wants to go to England — her source. And David wants to come with us. He's never been out of Israel.'

'What's England to you?' asked the Rav Aluf.

'Advanced computer sciences.'

'Concerts and opera?'

43

'And Captain David Cohen, who delivered me into your hands. Any objection?'

'No. Why haven't you taken a holiday in England before?'

'You should know, sir. At first we couldn't afford it. Then we weren't allowed foreign currency for junketing abroad. And in the past few years I've had no time for holidays . . . thanks to the chores you have wished on me.'

'So now you're requesting a busman's holiday . . . I expect you know there are plans for an international computer sciences symposium at Cambridge?'

'That won't be until 1970. We don't want to wait . . .'

'Shmuel, this is off the record; you know the Karmel Company near Haifa?'

'I know of it.'

'Well, there are plans for developing it very considerably . . . and for building an important subsidiary at Beersheba. A new technical director will be appointed. You understand?'

'Yes. What a beautiful carrot! But what's it got to do with our trip to England?'

'A good deal. The Karmel appointment won't materialize until 1970-71. A spell of study-leave before you take on the new job would be one hundred per cent justified, wouldn't it? You know, our government departments do have to justify expenditure of that type.'

'How are they going to justify the cost of a gamble like Operation Plumbat which will surely be enormous?'

'It must not be a gamble. And success will be the justification. We will be making a big investment in Israel's future security. Isn't that more or less what you advised in that well-reasoned report of yours?'

'Not quite,' said Shmuel wryly. He hadn't advised an operation that would span Europe, from the giant empire of the Société Générale des Minerais in Belgium to the European Economic Community's organization for the control of nuclear materials in Vienna, from the office of Turkish entrepreneur Yarisal in Italy to an insignificant German soapfactory owned by a former *Luftwaffe* pilot.

No operation as ambitious as Plumbat could have relied on watertight planning. There were too many incalculables, not least the personalities and habits of the *partners* in the enterprise. The co-ordinator had to be an unfailingly good judge of character, flexible enough to change course at any awkward point in the operation, so amiable or dominant that his word would be accepted at all times. Shmuel was well aware what the Rav Aluf and Mossad were asking of him.

The action began with his visit to the attractive village of Hettenhain in Germany, the luxurious home of ex-pilot Schulzen. Schulzen's firm,

44

Asmara Chemie, had done good business with Israeli firms for four or five years — ever since Schulzen had spent an enjoyable holiday in Israel. When Shmuel explained to him that Israel wanted to go into the mass production of petro-chemicals and needed uranium as a catalyst, Schulzen was more than willing to take the business in hand. It would be a profitable transaction. But where was he to lay his hands on two hundred tons of uranium — a nuclear material tightly controlled by Euratom, the EEC's watchdog?

Shmuel told the German that a Belgian company, SGM, had shipped home large quantities of uranium oxide at the end of Belgium's rule over the Congo. That a silo full of uranium, stored near Antwerp, had remained unsold and was something of an embarrassment to SGM.

The next move was Schulzen's offer to the Belgian company. He wished to buy two hundred tons of uranium for his company, as Asmara Chemie was going into the production of petro-chemicals. The offer landed on the desk of Monsieur Denis Dewez, deputy head of SGM's uranium division. M. Dewez had never heard of Schulzen and Asmara Chemie but he agreed to a meeting in Germany.

He was dined and wined at Schulzen's home and reassured by the credentials of several obviously bona fide businessmen, such as Shmuel, who were able to produce references from a Swiss bank and a well-known firm of German lawyers. M. Dewez undertook to draw up a contract and submit it to Euratom for approval and clearance. There was one small snag. The uranium would have to be industrially treated before it could be used as a catalyst. Shmuel said that a firm in Milan would undertake the work. The journey to Italy would not constitute export out of Europe.

Once the wheels had been set in motion Operation Plumbat progressed without too many snags. A Swiss lawyer set up a shipping corporation under a Liberian flag of convenience. A Turkish businessman, Mr Yarisal, resident in Italy, asked a German shipbroker in Hamburg to buy a cargo boat for the company. Moeller, the shipbroker, procured a vessel of 2600 tons — the *Scheersberg A*.

By way of a trial run the *Scheersberg A* sailed from Emden in North Germany to Naples in Southern Italy. After months of running around Europe, Shmuel found the sea voyage enjoyable and relaxing. After a change of crew the *Scheersberg A* sailed to Antwerp. She took on 560 metal drums of uranium and departed for Genoa in Italy. She failed to arrive in Genoa. But on the 2 December 1969 the *Scheersberg A* appeared in the Turkish port of Iskenderun without any cargo whatever. About the same time the uranium arrived in Israel, where it was taken to the Dimona reactor in the Negev desert.

Mossad and the Rav Aluf congratulated Shmuel on a beautiful operation: and as the Rav Aluf had foreseen, Euratom and the European Economic Community maintained unanimous silence about the deal.

The last thing Shmuel expected was that the Rav Aluf would call upon him yet again, within a few months of Operation Plumbat. The trip to Ethiopia and Eritrea sounded downright unattractive.

7

Shmuel let his mind slip into a new time-dimension. The near future looked good. Any moment now he'd be reaching the rendezvous and that would be the end of his desert trek; his last one, he hoped. He'd dig in his heels. If Intelligence were contemplating any more Ethiopian or Eritrean capers they'd have to find themselves another man. In future he'd travel for pleasure. His next destination would be England.

The sky had turned a milky white. Soon the sun would be burning down, punishing what wretched vegetation there was, and the glitter of sand and rocks would make his eyes smart. Not for long. In the Mercedes truck he'd be out of it. This time he'd let one of the boys do the driving. Catch up on sleep. Next stop Massawa. A leisurely bath, clean clothes, and a long cold drink. No reason why he shouldn't be back in Tell Aviv by tomorrow . . . the Sabbath. Esther wouldn't be working; David would be home. They'd pick peaches from their own tree and go for a picnic at Ginnosar . . . swim in the soft waters of the Sea of Galilee . . . talk in the shade of the tamarisks, of everything except the dead in the Eritrean desert.

Shmuel was within sight of the old army post when a loud explosion sent shock-waves along the ground under his feet. The cloud of dust was near but some way east of the route his truck would have to take. He broke into a run. He wanted to be out of this little war, whoever was waging it.

The Mercedes was parked beside a deserted blockhouse, pointing in the get-away direction. The three men beside it looked relaxed, but they had guns in their hands.

'What the devil are you doing here?' Shmuel heard himself say.

The Rav Aluf leaned his gun against the car and went to shake hands with Shmuel. 'I came for the ride.' The bushy white eyebrows lifted. 'Any objection?'

'Yes. This isn't a health resort for generals with itchy feet.'

'Well, the bang we've just heard seems to prove your point. Let's go.'

They piled into the truck. The Rav Aluf took the driver's seat; Shmuel got in beside him. Until they hit the road, progress would be slow — too slow for Shmuel's liking.

'How did it go?' The Rav Aluf made it sound as if Shmuel had just returned from a party.

'Somebody's wiped out a village in a particularly nasty manner. I don't know how. Nor do the Russians.'

'The Russians?'

'They were there . . . I don't have to report now, do I?'

'No . . . though this might interest you. I've been in touch with the American base at Kagnew. Their tracking-scanner picked up much the same mystery as ours.'

'What do they make of it?'

'They've got half a dozen Ph.Ds working on it. At the moment they've got electronic warfare in mind. That's their biggest worry.'

Shmuel shook his head. 'Shouldn't they be thinking of all the atomic junk instead? or the report that Russia's training a hundred thousand men in chemical warfare?'

'Oh, they're thinking. But it's the infinite possibilities of electronic warfare that really stick in their gullets. Atomic or chemical warfare *wastes* populations and countries on this earth only. But potting at one another's satellites in outer space . . . knocking out the spies-in-the-sky . . . that's now considered the ultimate shabby trick.'

'Have any satellites been knocked out?'

'Not yet . . . unless you are bringing relevant news.'

'I am not. The whole thing looked to me like a nauseating non-event. If the Russians or the guerillas had done me in it would have been a complete waste.'

'Yes, it would have been a pity . . . By the way, what do you make of the explosion?'

'An anti-tank mine?'

'Something like that. Best forget about it. Luckily it's off our road.'

'Stop.' Shmuel leaned out of the truck, shielding his eyes. 'We must be within a hundred yards of it. Look! see these rocks? They must have been split apart just now. You can tell by the surfaces. Let's take a look.'

'No. It's none of our business.'

As the Rav Aluf let in the clutch, Shmuel opened the door and jumped out.

'Come back, Volatian!'

Shmuel strode away in the path of the broken rocks. He didn't turn back, but he heard the men behind him. The Rav Aluf had been wrong; so had he. They hadn't taken account of the sharp bend in the road. It was there that the guerillas had laid the mine which had blown up one truck and wrecked the second. There could be no doubt. It was Kirov's party the Eritreans had destroyed. With the Rav Aluf beside him he gazed at the mutilated bodies of the Russians in what was left of their pathetic civilian suits. Friends or enemies. What sickened him was the senseless waste of these poor, helpless puppets. He walked among the debris, picking up a shred of metal, a broken box, staring at the bloody remains of men.

'Come on, Shmuel.' The Rav Aluf took him by the arm. 'What's the point?'

'Two men are missing. We've got to find them.'

Interface I
From YURYI ANDROPOV, Chairman KGB
To BORIS NOKOLAEVICH PONOMAREV, Chairman International
Department of the COMMUNIST PARTY.

Number: KGB/ID 29A67372P367   1 November 1969

While your Directorate's reports on infiltration at the Middle East Soviet
Embassies and in key points in Somalia, Iraq and Iran show some progress
towards the long overdue strengthening of our intelligence operations
against American political advances, the Politburo is repeating its request
for clarification of the Ethiopia/Eritrea incident.

I must remind you that it is the duty of your directorate to keep KGB
informed of experimental operations carried out under GRU auspices. At
the moment you seem to be falling down on your task of co-ordinating the
fragmented operations of the Chief Intelligence Directorate of the Soviet
General Staff and of channelling GRU information to KGB. I cannot
emphasise too strongly that Politburo will not tolerate the continuing split
between the KGB and the GRU, which is most certainly not the fault of
KGB. Comrade Suslov of the Politburo has pointed out, and I concur with
him, the importance of co-ordinating the work of all Intelligence
Directorates.

While I refrain whenever possible from intervening in army intelligence
affairs the Army must not be allowed to run away with the idea that its GRU
is a privileged and autonomous organization. Be good enough to convey
this to GRU. Furthermore I must insist on speedy clarification of the
Ethiopia/Eritrea business.

What happened in the first place? Clearly someone carried out a
modification of Satellite Turgay. Who? When? What type of modification?
Why did you ask GRU to investigate on site instead of referring the matter
to KGB? Having asked GRU to investigate why have I not received a copy
of the GRU team's report? Be good enough to resolve the matter forthwith.

Concerning your CIA intercept, it has made no difference to Politburo
thinking. The work on nuclear, chemical and biological warfare will
continue according to schedule. However, our first priority remains

49

research and development concerned with the elimination of enemy satellites.

There appears to be a certain lack of appreciation of the current tactical position in your Directorate. The war against American imperialism will not end until we have put a stop to America's geopolitical encroachments. When it comes to a shooting war our greatest danger will be the satellite network, especially the weapon-guidance potential which will enable the Americans to fire with unprecedented precision and accuracy.

For this reason KGB can no longer tolerate information gaps like the Ethiopia Eritrea incident. We cannot afford intelligence-fragmentation in the present climate.

While I do not propose to exaggerate the importance of internal opposition, KGB is well aware of the growing dissent against Government. We still cannot estimate the damage done by General Grigorenko's countrywide crusades against our Communist system. But there is no doubt in my mind that disaffection in the Armed Forces and, equally serious, among the most prominent of our scientists is spreading continuously. As fast as we remove the trouble-makers new suicide candidates appear on the scene, their courage equalled only by their political stupidity. Unfortunately the courage is having a worrying effect on large sections of our apolitical population while the stupidity remains ignored.

I hope I have made it clear to you that we expect you to greatly increase your vigilance over GRU. Furthermore, we expect you to accomplish the tightening-up operation on your current financial resources. There is no question of additional funds being made available to you. If your personnel is unequal to the task, the Politburo will undoubtedly direct me to reconstitute the structure of your Department.

VICTIMS OF FREEDOM

Kenya 1962 - 1969

8

A normal day? Was it? According to his kid brother the days in Kenya were normal, in England they were not. John sat up in bed, listening to the stillness. He'd been having nightmares of London: the steel-grey sky caving in on him, disintegrating in an explosion of rocks, not unlike the thunder of traffic. He remembered the moment on the corner of Trafalgar Square and the Strand. Five forty-five in the afternoon; a deluge of people pouring out of the underground, streaming towards Charing Cross Station. Andrew, stopped dead in the middle of the pavement, gazing at the flowing masses with disbelief, compassion and a touch of fear.

'We are not going to live in London,' he'd reassured the thirteen-year-old.

Andrew had shaken his head. 'It's not normal, is it?'

He'd liked Winchester though. The ancient school buildings; nothing of the kind in Kenya.

'Where are you from?' the scholar had asked Andrew.

'Kisumu.'

'Where's that?'

'Nyanza Province.'

'What country?'

'Kenya.'

'Suppose your people have left because of the killings.'

'We haven't left. I'll be going to school here. That's all. Because my brother's going to an English university next year.' A subtle implication that he wouldn't contemplate school in England if he didn't have to look after his brother. Little brat.

Meanwhile they were back at home. Christmas with the parents as usual.

John got out of bed and pulled up the Venetian blinds. In a sense Andrew was right. A normal day. In England the outlines had been blurred. Here the sharp morning light on hills and fields was exactly what one would expect in December — a light so clear that he could recognize each of the blacks working among the coffee plants, even see the red dust on the leaves of the baobab tree between garden and paddock.

On the terrace below Lakomi was laying breakfast. She was wearing the scarf they'd bought for her in London, twisted into a high Luo-style shape that made her look taller than ever. On her way back to the kitchen she leaned over the terrace rails, touched a half-open rose, and stooped to sniff the scent. Aggressive roses, the Princess Elizabeth. They were shooting up as high and strong as yucca weed.

John turned and opened the door of the bathroom between his room and Andrew's. A wet towel on the floor indicated that his brother had taken off in a hurry. He hung it on Andrew's rail and looked into the mirror above. Shaving was becoming a daily chore. Worst of black hair. Cornish looks, according to his mother; fine black hair, dark eyes and a fair skin. As a kid he'd burned easily; but he'd gradually adjusted to the African sun until he'd acquired a permanent light tan. Still, the new beard showed. His father had been right; if he hadn't been in such a hurry to start shaving at sixteen he might have got away with it for another year or so.

John scraped the safety razor over his face, took a shower, and went to put on the freshly laundered clothes Moya had put on his table — a blue Aertex shirt and floppy trousers, both faded. His father's cast-offs. He disliked new clothes. The suits Sarah had made him buy in London would stay in the wardrobe.

Sarah had bought herself those new American jeans — two pairs — and worn them ever since. Andrew approved, but he was not convinced that one's mother should be wearing tight trousers. Not that she wasn't young enough, or that she didn't look good in them. Just that Sarah was his mother. He was too conservative, she'd told him. Well, he wasn't keen on unnecessary changes.

He wasn't sure that his move to England was strictly necessary. Too late. He'd agreed to it. The parents were certainly not forcing him and Andrew to leave Kenya. The four of them had discussed the educational options. Andrew had reckoned that Winchester — his father's old school — might just about satisfy his voracious mind. And John hadn't wanted him to go alone. He didn't think that Grandmother Whitmore, who lived in Sussex, was quite enough family for his adventurous brother, so he'd picked a college that catered for people interested in engineering and technology. The arrangements had been made; that was that.

Nothing wrong with the plan except one thing, a question which had plagued him ever since they'd returned home. Why were the parents so anxious to get him and Andrew out of Kenya? If Charles and Sarah had fled the country in 1952, when he had been six years old and Andrew two, he'd have understood. The Kikuyu campaign of terror against white farmers had been worst in the early 'fifties. Whole families had been butchered, including several children from his school. Yet they, the Whitmores, had stayed. Now, in 1963, the prospects were surely improving. Kenya was on the threshold of independence, the so-called struggle for nationhood was virtually over, and Charles Whitmore had told his family that President Jomo Kenyatta was bound to call off the dogs of war. Even the tensions between the two major tribes, the Kikuyu and the Luo, appeared to have lessened within the past few months.

John wondered whether he was being too suspicious. Perhaps the parents' arguments for persuading him and Andrew to leave the country were exactly what they seemed — a wish to give their sons the best possible education. Perhaps.

John went down the back stairs to the kitchen. He asked Lakomi whether she'd seen Andrew.

She smiled. 'Yes, he go about with Okot.'

He looked into the dining-room, crossed the hall and wandered out on the terrace. That was where the geckos congregated in the early morning but the boys weren't there. John vaulted over the rails and followed the stone-flagged path to the south side of the house. He saw his parents through the French windows. Sarah, pale hair tied back with a white shoe-lace, arranging poinsettias in her big stone vase: Charles locking up the gun cabinet.

John couldn't remember a time when his father hadn't made the rounds with the Smith & Wesson in a holster on his belt. Checking all outhouses, doors and windows at night; on horseback before breakfast, inspecting the whole plantation. He was saying something that made Sarah laugh. They were looking relaxed, the two of them.

John walked on through the garden. Sarah had imported many flowering shrubs from England, but it was the South African protea which made the most spectacular show, their big scarlet and yellow blooms wide open to the sun. There was something animal about their fat fleshy leaves.

Raspar was working in a bed of petunias. He straightened his back and waved to John. 'We had a letter from my father.'

'Good. How is he?'

'The teaching goes well, but without us he's much alone. He hopes he can visit us in the summer . . . if they let him.'

John stopped himself from saying that *they* would. Kenyatta's Kenya-African National Union party were carrying out a punishing africanization policy. KANU was determined to drive out Kenyan Asians such as Lakomi's husband, the father of Raspar, Okot and Naroo. Never mind that there were not enough black doctors, businessmen or teachers to replace those of Asian descent. Get rid of them. Raspar's father had been sacked from the Kisumu high school and considered himself lucky to have got a job in a school for Asians in South Africa. He'd had to leave behind Lakomi, a woman of the Luo tribe, and his sons.

No one knew as yet how free Kenya would deal with the half-Asian half-African boys. Yet Lakomi considered herself lucky; she was the Whitmore's housekeeper, like her mother before her; she had her bungalow on the plantation, a good home for her family and a job for her eldest son Raspar.

'You looking for Andrew?' asked Raspar.

'As usual.'

'Over there, I think.' He laughed, teeth brilliant white in his ebony dark face. 'He and Okot . . . they have the dick-dick on the brain.'

John let himself out into the paddock. It was getting hot; Buster, his father's stallion, and the two mares had crowded into the shade of the eucalyptus trees.

Andrew and Okot had made an enclosure at the back of the stables. John stalked close and watched. Okot was holding on to a dick-dick, the small baby gazelle he'd found abandoned in the bush, while Andrew was treating its left front leg. He'd taped four thin metal strips around the leg and was deftly bandaging over the splint. The dick-dick was keeping surprisingly still.

'You don't know how the baobab tree got upside down, do you?' Andrew's voice soothed the gazelle. 'You don't? Well, I'll tell you. Listen. After God had created the world he was very tired. But he was pleased with all the life He'd put on this planet. He asked everyone whether they were satisfied with the way He'd made them . . . You see, even God likes a bit of appreciation. All the animals praised Him . . . and all the plants and trees, except the baobab. The baobab tree said it didn't like its shape at all, because it looked too much like every other tree. God said it wasn't fair . . . all the trees were different. In fact he'd made the baobab extra useful, 'cause it would provide humans with cream of tartar and bark for making blankets . . . and cavities for sheltering people. But the baobab kept on complaining. So, God said all right, and gave it an extra big crown. And do you know what? The baobab said God had made it look worse than ever. Then God got really cross. He tore up the baobab and stuck it back in the earth head down, with its roots all up in the air . . . And that's why it's such a funny-looking tree. Right, Okot. Let him go.'

The gazelle wobbled, then gingerly stalked away, leaped a few yards and bucked. The splint stayed in position. Andrew picked up a bottle with a teat. Okot caught the deer and pointed it at the milk.

'Come on,' Andrew coaxed. 'Not telling you any more stories.' He put the teat in his mouth and sucked. The gazelle got the idea and went for the milk greedily.

Okot laughed. 'It'll grow up and steal your mother's flowers.'

'If the leg mends.'

'It will.'

'Hope it does before I go to England.'

'Plenty time. It's only a little bone.'

The dick-dick had finished the feed and stalked into the shade of the woven fence.

'Breakfast!' called John.

'Coming.'

The boys climbed out. Okot made for the Luo bungalows in the valley. Andrew trotted ahead of John. Not the shortest way home. Ever since his stay in England he'd climbed the high ridge at the back of the house every morning as if he needed reassurance that nothing had changed in his absence. Nothing had. The acres of coffee stretched into the distance east and west; a rich dark sheen. The house, white and square in the oasis of blossom; the paddock sloping down to the bungalows of the Luo workers. Windows in Kisumu shooting off darts of light. The massive roofs of the native market dark as a beached whale. Beyond, the shimmering line of Lake Victoria.

'The bone hasn't snapped, John . . . not quite apart.'

'Then it should set all right. Where did you get the splints?'

'Didn't find anything in your workshop.'

'Well?'

'Oh . . . I took them out of Sarah's willpower dress.'

'Then willpower won't keep it up any more. Better tell her.'

'She won't notice. I'll put the splints back in . . . You going to Terry's party tonight?'

'I said I would. You?'

'No. I've got things to do.'

'Chicken.'

'Terry's different now.'

True. Theresa was fifteen, two years older than Andrew. She'd still go riding with him by day, but in the evening, in a long dress, she was a young woman and they had nothing to say to each other.

'They're going,' said Andrew. 'The Marsdens are leaving . . . for good.'

'That's an old story.'

'They've sold their plantation to a big American company.'

'Who told you?'

'Okot.'

'How would he know?'

Andrew kicked a stone down the path. 'Erina told Lakomi.'

If the Marsdens' cook had told Lakomi it was probably true. John didn't like the thought of their nearest neighbours leaving. Why now, when Kenyatta had promised not to confiscate the estates of efficient white Kenyans? It was understandable though. The Marsdens would have gone years ago if they'd been able to find a buyer for their plantation. They hadn't been in Kenya as long as the Whitmores, who'd settled three generations ago and cut their farm out of the bush. Unlike Kevin Marsden, Charles Whitmore had maintained — even during the worst terrorist attacks — that his family belonged as much in the Nyanza Province as the Luos whose language they spoke and whose customs they understood and respected.

Breakfast was as much a time of meetings as a meal. Anyone working on the estate, anyone from the town who wanted to discuss something with the Whitmores, could be sure of finding them on the terrace — or in the dining-room during the rainy season — at eight o'clock.

For once John and Andrew found their parents alone. Sarah gave them coffee. Charles passed the dish of kedgeree.

Andrew took some photographs from his shirt pocket and gave them to his mother — pictures of Billy, her King Charles spaniel pup, of geckos on the drawing-room ceiling, and an African starling — cobalt blue against the hot red of the soil.

'They're good . . . very good.' Sarah gave them to Charles. 'I'm glad you didn't buy him a cheap camera.'

'Dad, I need new films,' said Andrew.

Charles laughed. 'You always do.'

'If I had a telephoto lens . . .'

'You'd use even more film. Not making any promises, Andy.'

'There's Christmas . . .'

'I'll think about it when I go to Nairobi.'

John helped himself to toast and marmalade. 'The Patels have had a letter from South Africa. Did Lakomi tell you?'

'Yes. Not much hope of Patel visiting his family.' Charles spoke quietly. 'Tom's been trying to help . . .' Tom M'boya was a young Kisumu politician, the only Luo in Jomo Kenyatta's all-Kikuyu government. 'The upshot was . . . Asians who've left the country are not allowed to return, not even on a visitor's visa.'

'Ridiculous.' Sarah looked exasperated. 'Surely Kenyatta can't exclude all Asians for ever. He'll have to let them come on business and as tourists if nothing else.'

'He's got bigger worries just now . . . such as keeping Mr Odinga and his Communists out of power.'

'That's no comfort to Lakomi.'

'Lakomi's educated, thanks to her husband. She understands what's happening and she isn't giving up hope. Things will get better after independence.'

'These vicious racialist policies?'

'They'll get watered down, Sarah. Kenya needs some whites and some Asians and Kenyatta knows it. He's no fool. Once he's the internationally recognized leader of Kenya the fire in his belly will cool. He'll want a quiet life and good opportunities for lining his pockets.'

Was that what it was all about? John asked himself. Wealth . . . personal wealth? Was that why Kenyatta had whipped up his Kikuyu tribesmen into those obscene, frenzied oathing ceremonies in which they'd pledged themselves to destroy the whites? The murder of white Kenyans would be remembered. But would black Kenyans remember that whole tribal communities had been wiped out because black men had refused to commit murder?

John wasn't sure how much Andrew appreciated Kenya's troubles. Politics, Andrew had told him, was boring. And, as usual when the subject cropped up at breakfast, he'd withdrawn. He seemed absorbed in a book he'd propped up against the coffee pot.

'What are you reading?' John asked him.

'Listen to this . . .' Andrew lifted his face, grey eyes conscious of John's companionship. ' " . . . It is a desert only in the sense that it contains no permanent surface water. Otherwise its deep fertile sands are covered with grass glistening in the wind like fields of gallant corn. It has luxurious bush, clumps of trees and in places great strips of its own dense woods. It is filled too with its own varieties of game, buck of all kinds, birds and lion and leopard. When the rains come it grows sweet-tasting grasses and hangs its bushes with amber berries, glowing raisins and sugared plums . . ." John, lets go on safari there – one day.'

'Where?'

Charles had been listening. '*The Lost World of the Kalahari*. The book's by Laurens van der Post.'

'Have you been there, dad?'

'No. But it's a place I always wanted to see. It must be Africa at its most unspoilt.'

'Must take enough films.'

'Andy, look at a map. The Kalahari desert's a long way from Kisumu. It'll have to be a properly planned safari . . . when you're a bit older.'

'Promise?'

'Promise.'

Lakomi came out with a visitor, her uncle Joshua. The old farmer sat down uninvited, according to Luo good manners. Sarah offered him coffee, which he accepted.

'Your cows and your family look very fine, Bwana,' said Joshua in Luo.

'Yes, we are grateful,' replied Charles. 'How are your cows and family?'

'The animals and the millet are good. I am not complaining about my family, Bwana, but my youngest son upsets the spirits.' The spirits of dead ancestors which dwelt among the living. 'Since his return from the city he wanders in the night and comes home drunk. His wife speaks of returning to her parents.'

Joshua's family would have paid *lobolo,* in cattle, for the bride. If her complaints were justified the young wife and the *lobolo* would be lost. It was a serious matter.

Charles said, 'I share your sorrow, Joshua.'

The old man sipped his coffee. 'I think my son wanders far in the night.'

'Do you wish me to speak to Sergeant Tsuru?'

'Yes, Bwana. It would be wise . . . We have been listening for the drums.'

'You've heard them?'

'The wind comes from the hills, but we hear no drums. We do not understand it. The city has changed my youngest son. He has become a stranger.'

John took the path along the high ridge to the Marsdens' estate. It lengthened his ride by about two miles but he preferred the track through the fields. He listened to the throb of the crickets, syncopated by the baritone croak of frogs. Normal evening sounds. The stars, as Andrew had observed, looked much nearer than in England because Nyanzw Province was close to the equator. Buster put up his ears. John slowed the stallion, staring into the darkness ahead. He felt alert, yet no more wary than usual. Something white came flashing out of the sugar-canes. A stray goat. That was all.

His family had discussed Joshua's information. Charles had talked with his men, dropped in on Sergeant Tsuru and spoken to people in the town. He'd come to the conclusion that no oathing ceremony had taken place and that the excesses of Joshua's youngest son were the result of a new illegal drinking and whoring den where the kaffir beer was cheap and deadly. It wasn't unusual for such places to open up and Sergeant Tsuru soon got rid of them. One thing was certain; if Joshua's news had worried his parents they'd have asked him to stay at home.

John thought of his send-off with amusement. Sarah had given him a box of chocolates as a birthday present for Terry; he'd drawn the line at taking a bunch of roses. She'd looked him over, as usual, making sure that he was wearing a respectable shirt and properly pressed trousers. Wonder in her eyes. It still surprised her that he was a foot taller than her. Then a kiss. She wouldn't forgo the physical contact; he was glad he'd outgrown the tough-guy period when her kisses had embarrassed him.

As the lights of the Marsdens' house came into view the rhythm of dance music drowned the natural night sounds. He wished they weren't using amplifiers. Unacceptable noise-levels, Andrew would say. The twist was all right though. Nothing to it; everyone doing his own thing.

He rode Buster through the open gates into the yard and gave the reins to Ndole.

'What are you doing here?' John asked him in Luo. They'd been at high school together.

'Holiday job,' said Ndole. 'In the new year I'll be going on a government course.'

'You'll be our future district commissioner.'

Ndole laughed. 'Who knows? If Tom M'boya becomes minister for home affairs.' He sniffed the air. 'They've started roasting the pig.'

Fifty odd people were crowded together on the patio, some tending the barbecue, most of them dancing to the music of the Beatles. Terry, in a long black dress meant to make her look grown up and sophisticated, was in the thick of it. Her round face with the wide mouth and small nose was attractive — John could see that — but it was also uncommonly immature; unlike her body.

Mr Marsden gave him a chunk of pork and a baked potato and Terry came to sit with him on the low wall by the barbecue.

'John, we're leaving.' She was obviously happy about it. 'Father's bought a farm in South Africa . . . in the Cape. We're going in March. Will you stay with us . . . you and Andrew?'

'We'll be in England.'

'I might see you in England in the summer, before I have to go back to school. I want to see London.'

'You've got it all planned, Terry.'

'Yes. Don't tell my father. Why didn't Andrew come?'

'He's got things to do.'

'Rats. He's silly about dancing. He'll never learn if he doesn't try. He's a bit young, I suppose. The trouble with Kisumu is . . . there aren't enough men; not real men.'

'Come on, let's dance.'

'Later. I want a drink.'

John took her glass. 'I'll get it.'

'Not the fruit-cup. Father's got super whisky.'

'Not for you, Terry.'

'Oh! go and play with the kids.'

There were relays of food all evening; steaks, sausages, kebabs. John did a stint at the barbecue with Terry's father.

'Got a good crowd after all.' Mr Marsden, his big face lit by the charcoal glow, watched the jiving, twisting dancers. 'Glad we didn't cancel the party.'

'You wanted to?'

'Well . . . We thought a lot of Terry's friends wouldn't be allowed to come. People are a bit on edge. Can't tell how the Kikuyu will react to independence.'

61

'My father says things will get better.'

'Yes, eventually. But the Kikuyu might decide on a show of strength in the last days of British rule . . . just to remind us and the Luos who's top dog. Well . . . I daresay I've been too nervous all along. Worrying about my women, you know.'

It was well past midnight before John saw Terry again. She was seeing off a mob who were squeezing into a Mini Traveller. They were laughing at her; she was reeling drunk. John hoped she'd have a hang-over she'd never forget.

It was quiet at the back of the house. Even the crickets and frogs had given up. A solitary firefly, bright as a fallen star, drifted past and disappeared into the bougainvillaea. John knew that something was wrong as he walked into the yard. Ndole had saddled his horse. He was talking to Raspar, who'd come on his bicycle. When they saw him the two black boys fell silent.

He asked, 'What is it, Raspar?'

'Bwana, there's been a raid.'

He wasn't Bwana. His father was the master. No one on their estate called *him* Bwana. Suddenly it seemed that Raspar had been speaking to a stranger. A raid? Presumably it concerned John Whitmore. But John Whitmore was merely a name, a convenient label for someone unknown to him . . . a form of life which pretended to an identity which never existed.

'Bwana . . .' Raspar put something in his hand.

There was nothing unreal about the gun.

9

Lakomi had waited for them in the copse, a mile from the plantation. She'd pleaded with John. What was the use of going to the house? It was dangerous. The raiders had withdrawn, but they were still in the grounds. She'd heard them. They might run out of liquor and return. They weren't human . . . they were devils . . . evil . . . evil. She was positive; Andrew had not been in. Okot and Naroo were looking for him. There'd be no help until they reached Kisumu. The raiders had cut the telephone. Best go at once . . . to her people. They'd be safe there. The Kikuyu wouldn't dare attack such a big village.

He left her with Raspar and rode Buster into the paddock. Andrew might have been with the injured gazelle, but he wasn't. John ran along the fence and entered the garden from the back. The house was blazing light out of every room. The scullery door was hanging off one hinge. The stillness was stifling.

His parents were in the drawing-room, Charles hanging over the arm of a chair with a knife in his back, Sarah on the floor. He saw her slight body, one leg straight, the other bent at the knee in the posture of a dancer. He had to move; if he could bring himself to move he'd wake up and the nightmare would be over. As he dropped to the floor beside her the pain and horror of the destruction paralyzed him. Sarah's head lay on her shoulder, almost severed. He might have squatted beside her for minutes or hours. Only *they* were real people, Sarah and Charles. He was nothing . . . a husk . . . empty . . . useless.

Suddenly he heard high-pitched cries. Billy came creeping from under the sofa. Andrew. He picked up the puppy without thinking. Andrew. He ran up the stairs and flung open door after door. Then, forcing himself to function, he searched each room, each possible hiding place until he was convinced that his brother was not in the house.

. He pulled the patchwork cover off his parents' bed and took it to the drawing-room. It was intolerable to leave his parents exposed in their helplessness. He put down the puppy and lifted his father to the floor beside Sarah. Then, as devoid of feeling as if he'd been drugged, he closed the eyes of the dead and covered the bodies.

Now he knew where he'd find Andrew. With the dog in his arms he walked out of the house and through the garden. It was obvious; Andrew had waited until Sarah had paid her nightly visit to his room and then slipped out of the house by way of the terrace. He'd wanted to make sure that his gazelle was not in pain and had settled for the night. On the way back he'd noticed the lights, including the blaze from his own window, and realized that something was wrong. He'd been trained to keep out of sight if he suspected a raid.

John walked straight up to the baobab tree and climbed inside the hollow trunk. Andrew was lying on the dead leaves, asleep.

John walked his brother to the stable block and got out the Land-Rover.

'What are you doing?' asked Andrew drowsily.

'It's two in the morning, Andy. Go back to sleep.' He reckoned that Okot and Naroo would be in the copse with Lakomi and Raspar.

'The raid . . . Is it all over?'

'Yes, it's over.'

In the kraal of Lakomi's father, John and Andrew were never alone. By day dozens of silent grieving Luos would walk into the small brick bungalow where Lakomi had made their beds; by night her three sons would stay with them.

Helen McGregor, Sarah's sister, and her husband Angus came from Rhodesia and took over. At the funeral service the Anglican church was packed with Luos and the few white Kenyans who hadn't yet left the country. The vicar was a Kikuyu trained in England.

The prayers meant nothing to John. Who were they praying to? A remote old gentleman with a white beard? or an egomaniac so indifferent to people that he made or destroyed them for his amusement? In the flower-decked coffins lay two of them whose voices would never be heard again, who'd never again love and think and take care of the land. Sarah and Charles, aged thirty-eight and forty; still young; cheated of the pleasures of watching Andrew grow up.

The vicar's tone of voice had changed. ' . . . and when we celebrate our country's independence let us remember them as Kenyans who became victims of freedom . . . valuable Kenyans. In the words of Dean Swift . . . *whoever could make two ears of corn and two blades of grass grow upon a spot of ground where only one grew before, would deserve better of mankind, and do more essential service to his country, than the whole race of politicians put together.'*

John felt ill with hatred. The *race* of politicians. Yes, it had been politicians who'd killed his parents, as surely as if they'd committed murder with their own hands. Parasites. Vermin that should be exterminated before the whole living world fell victim to their futile, facile promises of freedom — whatever that meant — and prosperity.

But for once the politicians acted fast. The Whitmore killings had come at a highly inexpedient time, within days of Kenya's becoming an independent black state. It was incumbent upon Jomo Kenyatta to present to the world the image of a democratic, just and impartial president. Conveniently Joshua's youngest son turned Queen's evidence and was given a light sentence in return for information that led to the arrest of the men who'd killed the Whitmores. The raiders — seven Kikuyu — were executed. Kenyatta in person pledged safety for Charles Whitmore's sons, or full compensation if they decided to sell the plantation.

John and Andrew, with Helen and Angus McGregor, left for Rhodesia without having decided the future of the plantation. In the plane John found an American science journal which a previous passenger had left with the travel-sickness bag and the lifebelt instructions.

He began to read, and for the first time since the death of his parents he found himself concentrating. The article on space exploration recalled the first manned orbital flight by Russian cosmonaut Yuri Gagarin on 12 April 1961 and the first American manned suborbital flight by Alan Shepard on 5 May 1961. In the two years that had passed since then space technology had advanced considerably. President Kennedy had challenged the country to put a man on the moon by 1970 and, as a result, the National Aeronautics and Space Administration, NASA, had launched the Gemini Programme as a bridge between the Mercury and Apollo projects.

The facts and figures in the article fascinated John. The spacecraft were becoming successively more complex. For instance, in the Mercury spacecraft there were seven miles of wiring, in the Gemini ten and a half miles; the Mercury spacecraft consisted of 750,000 parts, the Gemini spacecraft of 1,320,000 parts. And he had been proud of himself when he'd repaired the wiring in his father's old jeep . . . real genius that.

Then there was the computer story. The first modern computer had been built in 1944; it was 51ft long and 8ft wide and it took four and a half seconds to multiply two numbers. The computers made for space research now were no larger than an average suitcase and could carry out difficult mathematical calculations in split seconds.

John told Andrew what he'd been reading.

'Yes.' Andrew seemed unimpressed. 'In Kenya one's out of it . . . The laser's more interesting, I think.'

'What's a laser?' John challenged him.

'It's an acronym for *light amplification by stimulated emmission of radiation*. Basically it's a device for generating lightwaves. You see, one can organize the vibrations of these lightwaves and make a powerful beam . . . any size, from a pinhead to St Paul's Cathedral.'

'What's the use of it?'

'Well . . . the laser can be coded and channelled, so you can direct it anywhere. It can convey messages which can be gathered by a particular receiver. It can be used in industry . . . for cutting metal, for instance . . . or in surgery where it might do a sort of welding job.'

'I didn't know you're interested in technology, Andy.'

'I'm not. I can't even mend a fuse. I just read about lasers in Uncle Angus's medical journal. If things like lasers and computers are going to be used in treating people or animals one will have to understand them.'

Suddenly John knew without a doubt that they'd have to let the plantation go. Andrew had chosen to go to an English school because he'd understood instinctively that Britain was his gateway into the twenty-first century. Andrew had a hunger for knowledge, and he'd eventually apply his knowledge to some form of life. His own interests were less clearly defined. He supposed it was objects that intrigued him, and how to make them function. He might have applied the skills learned in England to farm machinery and to modernizing the plantation. If his parents had lived. Not now. Andrew would make himself at home in many places — anywhere in the living world. John recognized that the family's house and land had already become alien territory to both of them.

The plane was flying through a spectacular sunset. Clusters of clouds passed by, like those pink balls of cotton wool his mother had used for cleaning her face.

'Shall we let them have the estate?' asked Andrew.

'Is that what you want?'

'No use hanging on. Not now. Lakomi will never work there again . . . nor Raspar. John, what'll happen to her?'

'She'll stay with her family. She is a Luo.'

'Think Mr Patel will ever get her and the boys into South Africa?'

'He'll keep trying.'

'And Tom M'boya will keep trying to get him back his old job in Kisumu,' said Andrew, with a tone of disillusionment mature for his years. 'I wish they'd come with us.'

'Lakomi told us . . . She and the boys belong with her own people.'

'What about us, John? The English aren't our people. We're Africans.'

'With an English skin.'

'That's about all.' Andrew immersed himself in his book, still *The Lost World of the Kalahari*.

John read over his shoulder. *We have forgotten the art of our legitimate beginnings. We no longer know how to close the gap between the far past and the immediate present in ourselves. We need primitive nature, the First Man in ourselves . . .*

Andrew looked up. 'John, I think he's really saying something about time. There are different kinds of time.'

'What do you mean?'

'When this plane arrives in Salisbury, Rhodesia, everyone on it will know exactly where he is . . . and the time of arrival: the date and the time on watches and clocks. But it won't be the same as time in the universe . . . where worlds are separated from one another by millions of light years. Perhaps that concerns no one but space experts. The third time's something that most people must have . . . and I don't really understand it; the time inside one's head. Everything's there and I can move fast from one to the other . . . Mother trying on jeans in Harrods; our first holiday in Rhodesia — I was three then and I remember Uncle Angus showing me his surgical instruments; finishing school in four or five years' time and being back in Kisumu.'

'Andy, that's stretching it.'

'But it's all in my head . . . and a lot more.'

'You're just telling yourself that you want to go back one day.'

'Don't know that I want to. I want it in my head that our parents will be there to meet us in Salisbury. But I can't have it. I can't.

66

10

There were moments during their first couple of years in England when John had the impression that Andrew was rejecting his new environment. On the other hand he made friends at Winchester, boys he invited home to his grandmother's cottage, and masters who had a genuine regard for his lively mind.

In 1965 the Rhodesia controversy sharpened and John, at his college in Cambridge, found little understanding when he supported Ian Smith's stand against a black majority government. When Smith's Rhodesia made her Unilateral Declaration of Independence his fellow students — with the exception of one black Rhodesian — were entirely in favour of imposing sanctions which would economically isolate Rhodesia from the rest of the world. They listened to Kole Okango in the Students' Union because he was a black man, but when he explained to them the complexities of tribal society, the never-ending dangers of tribal conflicts, and the need for a white administration until such time when there'd be sufficient blacks of statesman-quality, the students argued back with bland incomprehension.

'Not that all whites are statesmen,' Kole Okango said to John after the meeting. 'But on the whole our whites stick to traditional rules of justice and firm government . . . and they've prevented a good many nasty tribal wars.'

'You'll probably be the first black president of Rhodesia.'

Kole laughed. 'No thanks. I'd rather be in charge of a perfect machine than an imperfect society.'

'Will you go back to Rhodesia?'

'I expect I'll visit my family, but I want to live in England.'

'Can't be fun for a black man.'

'Perhaps it depends on the man,' said Kole, with quiet confidence. 'Colour isn't the real bar. The dividing factors are education and class . . . as the British will discover sooner than any other whites.'

'Why?'

'Because the British are the most accomplished of all snobs.'

Kole and John took to working together for their examinations. Together with Andrew they went on walking holidays in France and Italy, and after a weekend at Grandmother Whitmore's cottage at Borden

67

Hill in Sussex, Kole spent every Christmas with the family. His appearance in a village, where no black man had ever been seen, created a small sensation until people rationalized that Mrs Whitmore was, of course, a Kenyan and therefore used to blacks. The village people were almost too *nice* at first, because it was the right thing, but it didn't take Kole long to make genuine friends.

After John and Kole had taken their degrees in engineering they both decided to take a course in electronics. The future lay in computers. In his last year at Winchester Andrew shopped around for a university and finally decided on becoming a doctor. He secured a place at medical school in London.

During that summer of 1968, which the brothers and Kole spent in Sussex, Terry Marsden turned up. Her parents hadn't regretted the move from Kenya to South Africa, but Terry had found little to interest her. There were horses; there was tennis; but the young farmers of the area bored her. She'd taken a secretarial course on condition that her parents would let her go to England, but she certainly didn't want to work as a secretary.

John and Andrew took her to the Four Aces restaurant in Brighton, Andrew happy to be with the girl of his childhood, John trying to gauge what kind of person she really was. In the candlelight her round face with its small nose and wide mouth still looked immature, but attractive. There was a restlessness about Terry that made John feel she needed a man. Not him. She'd cling, and he preferred women who'd sleep with him without expectations of a permanent relationship.

As Terry knocked back glass after glass of wine John remembered her fifteenth birthday party. If she'd had a hang-over afterwards it hadn't deterred her from drinking.

She'd just poured herself a glass from the third bottle when Andrew took it away from her. 'You've had enough, Terry.'

For a moment she looked rebellious, and then the curly brown head went down. 'That's right, Andy.'

He passed the glass to John. 'You have it. I'm driving.'

That night, quite openly, Andrew took Terry to his room.

She stayed with them for the rest of the summer and when Andrew started at medical school Terry began a nursing training. John distrusted her meekness, but after a year he had to concede that his first impression of her had been right. She was a girl who clung to her man with total devotion. She was one of those rare women for whom her man was the master and the centre of the universe. And she was what Andrew needed, a person all his own for whom he and no one else was responsible.

In the summer of 1969 Andrew decided to go back to Kenya without her. She didn't even question his decision. John did. Andrew assumed that John too wanted to see Lakomi and her sons again — and, perhaps, lay the ghosts of murder.

They landed in Nairobi early in the morning on 5th July. They felt sleepy after the overnight flight but the cool sunny morning was too good to waste. They took their bags to the Country Club where they'd booked a room for a couple of days. They had a swim in the pool, played tennis and wandered in the grounds. Jacarandas and flame trees splashed their brilliant purple and scarlet blossom among the banana trees; the stable block was covered with yellow, apricot and orange bougainvillaea.

Entranced by the glorious, gaudy colours Andrew said, 'Africa', like a man who'd been deprived of fresh air for years.

For lunch there was a buffet of cold meats and salads, and they took their plates to a table on the lawn. Nearby two heavy middle-aged men and a woman were talking in a language John couldn't make out. The men were dressed in black suits, white shirts and ties — looking like undertakers among the other guests in swimsuits and shorts — and the woman was wearing a black woollen dress too short and tight for her dumpy figure. They had one thing in common, apart from their unsuitable clothes; all three had visible gold inlays in their teeth.

John asked the restaurant manager who the trio were.

'They're Russians.'

'On holiday?'

'Yes and no,' said the manager in Swahili. 'Russians, they say, are not allowed to go abroad on holiday, but they can take a holiday when they're working abroad. These three are working in Tanzania, as advisers to the government. We also get Chinese from Tanzania — they're building a railway. We have some strange guests nowadays.'

Later in the afternoon John and Andrew took the Country Club's minibus to the centre of Nairobi. They'd arranged to visit Lakomi's eldest son, Naroo, who was training to be a teacher. It had been Naroo's task to keep in touch with them and he had written regularly. It had taken him a long time to achieve a place in the training college, but he'd finally succeeded after an interview. They'd have turned him down, he'd written, if his skin had been as light as Raspar's and Okot's, but thanks to a fluke of nature his skin was as black as his mother's and his Asian features had been forgiven or, perhaps, remained unnoticed. Naroo, ironically, had assumed that his admission to the college was due to a clerical error or the incompetence of the interviewers. The africanization policy had certainly not been relaxed.

Andrew was so happy to be back in Africa that he behaved like a tourist. He had to go to a market he remembered from his childhood and buy those short, fat bananas which one never saw in England. He walked into shops just for the joy of speaking Swahili again and even found a Luo newspaper seller. John noticed the changes, the neglect of good old buildings and the rash of untidy shanties with tin roofs. The European influence was waning, but what did it matter? What *did* matter was that Kenya shouldn't suffer the kind of dreadful civil war that was tearing Nigeria apart, the Biafran holocaust which was killing thousands of Ibo women and children. He hoped Kenya would be spared the confrontation of a Colonel Ojukwu and a General Gowon.

John and Andrew went into a cool little shop and bought picture postcards for their grandmother and Terry. As they stepped out into the street again the sunlight almost blinded them. Andrew said he'd have to wear sunglasses; he wasn't used to such brightness any longer.

All at once the quiet of Government Road was torn by a sharp crack, followed by several more shots. John stopped in his tracks. Shooting? It didn't make sense. The scene before him looked like a clip from a bad movie . . . a car driving off at a crazy speed, narrowly missing a boy on a bicycle; a well dressed black man lying bleeding on the pavement; the hysterical screams of a woman in a sari. As Andrew sprinted towards the gathering crowd John realized what had happened and tore after him.

He caught up with Andrew at the edge of the crowd.

'It's Tom!' Andrew was trying to push through the scrum.

John grabbed him so hard that he staggered back. 'This way.' He pulled him into the entrance of the chemist's which had disgorged Tom M'boya and the Asians. 'For Christ's sake . . . we've got to get out of it.'

'He needs help.' Andrew struggled.

'He's dead.' John pulled and pushed Andrew behind the counter. There was a half-open door. 'Andy . . . we must get out of it . . . or they'll say . . . whites or foreigners have . . . assassinated him.'

'I must . . .'

John pushed Andrew through the door. There was a yard full of packing-cases and a rusty iron fence. He managed to straddle it and pull Andrew after him. They dropped down into an alley which led to open ground and a building site. 'Andy, think!' He wouldn't slacken his grip. 'I'm taller than you. I saw Tom. I saw him. They killed him. He was dead. You couldn't have done anything for him. If we'd stayed to be questioned by the police we couldn't have told them anything. We didn't see the people in the car. You didn't, did you?'

'No . . . Let go, John. I won't go back. It's too late now . . . Mustn't have whites involved, must we?'

'Don't be stupid. Damn it, whites are not involved.'

'Someone will have seen us. Don't kid yourself.'

'No one's seen us. I'm sure. It was an Asian shop. There were only Asians around . . . they were too frightened and shocked to notice us. They weren't paying attention to anyone but Tom.'

'We can't walk away and . . .'

'We can. And we'll keep walking. Because if we don't, some innocent will pay for this . . . Do you doubt that it's a political murder? Tom was

Minister for Economic Planning and Development . . . the only Luo in the Kikuyu government. It would be a gift from the gods if papa Kenyatta could convince his people — if no one else — that Tom's assassination was a foreign plot . . . nothing to do with his Kikuyu.'

'Just another lousy political killing. It doesn't make sense, John.'

'It wasn't Kenyatta who was the leader of the Luos. Tom M'boya was their man.'

'Killing Tom won't make them accept Kenyatta . . . or,' Andrew hesitated, 'maybe you're right. Maybe I'm thinking like a European.'

'You are. This is Africa.'

Sirens were screaming, policemen racing through the alley. Confusion. Shouting.

'Run Andy . . . and keep behind them!'

By the time they reached the rooming-house at Mbotela, Naroo had already heard the news. It toned down the exuberance of their reunion, tinged it with memories of past murders and fears of the future. From the window of Naroo's spartan bed sitter they watched groups of people in serious discussion, people who looked over their shoulders every time a police car passed. A lot of police cars were around.

Naroo talked of Kisumu and his family. The town had a new, much needed hospital — built by Russia. Now the Russian medical teams who'd been working it had gone home and there was a hopeless shortage of doctors and nurses. The patients were cared for by medical assistants, mostly untrained like his brother Okot. Okot was doing his best, trying to learn by reading medical text books and journals, but such efforts couldn't replace the training he would have received under British rule.

Raspar was working at the communal plantation, formerly the Whitmores'. The administrator, who lived at the house, was inexperienced. Production had gone down, but Raspar was fighting for the survival of the estate. There was a rumour that Kenyatta was hiring white farmers to manage the plantations.

Lakomi was teaching at the primary school. The school had not recovered from the loss of the white and Asian staff and she was trying to cope with classes of fifty to sixty children. Between 1963 and '69 Naroo had seen his father only once, when the family had met and stayed at Dr McGregor's house in Rhodesia. Sarah Whitmore's sister and her husband were still trying to obtain residents' permits for the whole family. Naroo believed that they would succeed. In time. The Smith government in Rhodesia had more urgent problems than the importation of a half-Asian half-African family.

'It's the only thing in which Kenyatta's been consistent,' said Naroo. 'Once rid of an Asian Kenyan he won't let him come back. There'll never be another Luo in the cabinet either, now that Tom M'boya's gone. I

71

might have known they'd get Tom. In parliament two members — Odongo and Kariuki — spoke up and accused Kenyatta of having oathing ceremonies at Gatundu . . . his country estate. What happened? Mr Koinange, Minister of State for Foreign Affairs, said the people who were going to Gatundu by the busload just wanted to pledge their loyalty to the President before the promised election. New style oathing? No Luo believed it. Oathing's never been anything but drunkenness, sexual perversions, followed by blackmail and murder.'

'What about *harambee?*' asked Andrew.

'Kenyatta's great slogan . . . *pulling together*. Ask any tribesman . . . Kamba, Meru, Gusii, Luhya, Mijikenda, Masai, Kalnjin, Luo or any of the other sixty-two tribes . . . what *harambee* means to him. And he'll tell you *domination by the President and his accursed Kikuyu* . . . Rule by the gun and Kenyatta's GSU. In case you haven't heard . . . GSU are special para-military squads. They deal with dissidents on the spot. No need for the law; our law courts aren't overworked. Independent Kenya's a great success.'

'Give it time,' said John. 'Six years isn't long in the life of a new country.'

'Long enough for the royal family to become millionaires. I'm not speaking of the British royal family. I mean Kenyatta and his women . . . his fourth wife Mama Ngina, his daughter Margaret, his smart niece Beth Mugo. Between them the Kenyattas are raping the country . . . destroying it for ever. No white family has ever done such damage in Africa; nor any Asian family. You think I'm making a political speech?'

John shook his head. 'We know you, Naroo. Things must be bad.'

'I must give you facts . . . But first you must eat.' He opened a cupboard with a wire-net front and took out a basket of mangos, limes, paw-paws and custard apples. 'Here, you white bastards . . .' his great dark eyes were laughing. 'I remember the mountains of fruit you used to eat . . . What pigs you made of yourselves!'

John and Andrew sat on the planks of wood, propped up on bricks, that served Naroo as a bed. The room wasn't much bigger than a walk-in closet, yet Naroo had managed to get in his books on shelves made of planks and bricks, a narrow table and one chair. The box under the table probably contained his clothes. The food-cupboard hung on the wall, partly obstructing the window. It was the home of a practical man and a scholar, a poor man with a rich mind.

The Kenyan land belongs to the African Kenyans. Did John and Andrew remember Kenyatta's battle-cry for independence? *For the earth is the Lord's, and the fullness thereof.* Just so. Never had the Kenyan earth been owned by a lord such as the Kenyatta tribe . . . the royal family.

Remember the Mau Narok? asked Naroo; the greatest rain forest in East Africa, a dense forest, all-important because it brought the rain down upon the land. It had covered a thousand square miles. Not any longer. The royal family was systematically stripping it to produce charcoal for export.

Charcoal is the cooking fuel of the Middle East and many other parts of the world. It takes ten tons of wood to produce one ton of charcoal. A whole acre of scrubland would be stripped to produce these ten tons. In Nairobi a sack of charcoal would cost about 60p. In the Middle East it would cost £20. In Kenya a thousand tons would fetch $30,000, in the Middle east £900,000.

Mau Narok wasn't the only forest that was dying to enrich the royal family. There was Kakemega and there were vast tracts of scrubland in the interior, land that belonged to the Samburu and Kamba tribes. Without forests and scrubland the desert would encroach more and more, the precious soil would erode — and in the rainy season the earth which had fed the people of the country would be washed into the rivers and out into the Indian Ocean. If the criminal rape of the country continued, the people to whom Kenyatta had promised the land would inherit barren soil, malnutrition, starvation and premature death.

Another profitable business for the Kenyattas was ivory. The United African Corporation, under the chairmanship of daughter Margaret Kenyatta, was ostensibly trading in sisal, cotton and coffee; but its most lucrative export was ivory. The great bull elephants, whose tusks could weigh up to a hundred pounds, had virtually disappeared. The average tusk now weighed twenty pounds or less. A white employee of the Kenyan Game Department, reporting to the World Wildlife Fund, had worked out that the slaughter of elephants had reached fifteen thousand a year.

One of the biggest trading companies in East Africa was the Inchcape group, which had developed from the company that had opened up Kenya at the turn of the century. Kenyan citizens now owned sixty per cent of the most lucrative ventures of the company, such as the Ford franchise. Those Kenyan citizens were Udi Gecaga, Ngengi Muigai and Peter Muigai Kenyatta, the President's son-in-law, his nephew and his son.

Kenya's tourist trade was developing fast. Great hotels were being built on the coast between Mombasa and Malindi. Heading the boom in land-sales and building was a developer free of all legal restrictions — Mama Ngina, Kenyatta's fourth wife.

Of course, not all the profits went into the royal family's coffers. Raping the country on such a vast scale, accumulating such enormous wealth, required the complicity of officialdom. No one could assess the extent of money and perks filtering through, but it was known that

Kenyatta's provincial commissioners such as Eliud Mahihu and Isiah Mathenge, had become the owners of valuable building land and luxury hotels.

'Where does all this information come from?' Andrew was not questioning the truth of what Naroo had said.

'Kenya receives money from world organizations . . . World Health, World Wildlife, World Agriculture. Their officials have access to places . . . and to papers such as the Company Register. If you are interested I can give you copies of their reports.' Naroo got up and took a small newspaper from a pile on the shelves. 'This sums it up.'

Andrew read the marked paragraph and handed the paper to John. It was a Kenyan church newssheet. It stated in a few lines what was happening in the country. *A small and extremely rich élite appears to be getting ahead in everything, while the ordinary Kenyan is getting further and further behind.*

'And now Tom M'boya is gone,' said Naroo. 'Not that he was perfect. He became the owner of an important bus company . . . and he was building himself a mansion overlooking Lake Victoria . . . He was one of our better rulers . . . and he did speak for his people. Now there's only one Luo in politics.'

'Mr Odinga?' John felt that neither Naroo, nor any of his other Luo friends in Kisumu, were happy about the leader of the only opposition party to Kenyatta's KANU. Odinga had never made a secret of the fact that he was receiving financial support from the Russians.

'Yes, Odinga. Tom M'boya led the campaign for the abolition of Odinga's party . . . and now, all we're left with is Odinga and his KPU.'

'But the KPU is the opposition party in parliament.'

'With eight members . . . none of them caring about our violated land or the poverty of the people.'

John thought of his parents' funeral . . . the vicar who'd quoted Dean Swift, condemning the whole *race* of politicians. The hatred that welled up in him was a physical sensation like a fever, an ache in his limbs. He hated the demagogues who committed treachery with clichés such as *freedom, independence, equality*. He loathed the political profiteers and exploiters. He suddenly understood the passion of the anarchist — however misguided — who killed a *leader*, knowing that he too would be shot to pieces; or the Buddhist monk who'd set himself on fire in protest against the Vietnam war. But the killer of Tom M'boya had been a different animal — he didn't doubt that — a hired gun in the service of his political master.

'I'm glad you've come.' Naroo looked at Andrew and John with open affection. 'My mother and my brothers will be counting the hours . . . and I want to know what you'll be doing in Kenya . . . where you'll be going. You shouldn't have let me talk so much.'

'We wanted to hear,' Andrew told him. 'There hasn't been much in the papers in England.'

'I had to be careful what I said in my letters. If one has a family one must be careful . . . And I'm not a revolutionary. Where will you go after Kisumu?'

'To Lake Naivasha perhaps, and Nakuru . . . I want to see real animals again. And the bush.'

'Safaris? Like a tourist?'

Andrew shook his head. 'Like someone who's come home.'

Naroo listened to the siren of an approaching police car. 'I wish you'd come home at a less troubled time.'

11

They drove to Kisumu in a hired car. It was dangerous, not because the roads were poor or crowded, but because the black drivers had acquired a peculiar habit. Everyone drove in the middle of the road — that was normal and reasonble. The edges, petering out into soil or scrub, would have broken up in no time if traffic had not kept to the middle. But black drivers, trundling along happily enough, seemed to turn into maniacs the moment they met another vehicle. The two vehicles might pass each other on either side — but the decision was never made until the last moment. If two vehicles were about to pass, with a third behind, number three would invariably try to overtake at the precise point when one and two were in the process of passing one another. The narrower the road, the more likely that one would encounter the wrecks of cars and trucks.

Andrew sat unperturbed through some hazardous manoeuvres. Unlike John he stoically accepted that the blacks were comparatively recent drivers, most of them without experience of town traffic, and that — in any case — nothing in their culture had prepared them for the machine age. For him the journey was a part of the homecoming.

Much of the way he sat beside John with a notebook on his knees, writing down what he saw for Terry. He'd left her behind, thinking that it would be good for her to have to stand on her own feet for a while, but she was in his thoughts and he meant her to share his Africa.

Travelling north-west through the hilly farmlands the country was as they remembered it: fields of maize, millet and sugar-cane, coffee plantations, banana palms, mangos and baobab trees, bright green against the

75

fiery red soil. Clusters of mud-houses, usually square and tin-roofed, sometimes round and thatched in the style of Xhosa rondavels. From midday until early evening road and land were so deserted, it almost seemed that the earth brought forth its fruits without any assistance from man.

Gradually John became aware of changes. The goats and cattle of the black farmers seemed to be roaming the hills at will and unrestrained. He could see the dangers of over-grazing; there already were crumbling fissures — the early signs of soil erosion. In the bush they came across zebras and giraffe, the inevitable vultures, but few gazelles. There were a few impala, tails landscaped with the hindquarters into the elegant shape of a lyre, but no dick-dicks. Those tiny gazelles favoured areas of dense scrub, and such territory was obviously diminishing.

John believed that the acres of empty blackened land had been ruined by bush-fires, until he saw the charcoal burners. Even in the hottest hours, when no one else was working, men and women with sacks were raking in the harvest of devastation that would kill the farming people's livelihood — perhaps for ever. How long before the black farmers recognized the danger signals?

As they approached Kisumu a sudden tropical rainstorm broke. Under the steel-grey sky the town stood out in brilliant sunlight, as if lit by batteries of powerful arc-lamps. Bougainvillaea, scarlet canaas, jacarandas and flame-trees — gaudy blooms and foliage washed clean of the shimmering terracotta dust — glowed with a freshness that stirred John's memories of the day he'd first become aware of living colour. He'd never found words for what he'd felt, but the wonder of it was still in his brain — the place he regarded as the most elaborate computer of them all.

Mrs Carmichael, the owner of the hotel, was a small widow of uncertain age. Sarah had called Mrs C 'Her Imperial Legacy'. Summoned by her Luo receptionist, she appeared in the foyer, a room full of ancient African spears, shields and drums. Her hair, dyed platinum, was built into the usual high crown, her unlined face immobile. John, impressed by her unchanging, unchanged appearance, recalled that he'd seen her once only in the streets — when she'd kept out of the sun under an antique lace-trimmed parasol.

'How delightful to meet you again.' Mrs Carmichael greeted them as if they'd recently bumped into each other in Fortnum & Mason's coffee shop. 'Such a long time . . . It must be three years.'

'Six,' said John..

'My sense of time never has been good . . . It may have something to do with this town.'

The receptionist brought three glasses of orange juice and a small bucket of ice.

'On the coffee table, Vicki . . . A little refreshment.' Mrs Carmichael

76

did not invite them to sit down. 'It's the least I can do . . . You received my letter?'

'You wrote to us?' asked John.

'Yes . . . well . . . never mind. It's all very unfortunate. I do enjoy handsome young men about my place.' She turned to the girl. 'Vicki, aren't they absolutely gorgeous?'

Vicki giggled.

Mrs Carmichael took a sip from her glass. 'I'm afraid I can't put you up.'

John and Andrew looked at one another. A welcoming drink and then the refusal? The hotel looked empty.

'I'm sure you'll understand,' she said. 'These days the blacks have it all their own way. One simply can't go against . . .'

The curtains stirred; a tall, stately Luo woman came in from the garden — Lakomi, followed by Okot and Raspar. Mrs Carmichael's face moved into a near smile as the Patels embraced the Whitmores, Lakomi laughing and crying.

'You stay'n in the hotel!' Excitement had always made Lakomi's accent slip. 'Mah boys keep'n way from home! Ah never hear such crazy doin' . . . Andrew, you growd, but you won't ever be a long man like John . . . My boys . . . Ah, my boys!'

'Vicki,' called Mrs Carmichael. 'Orange juice and ice . . . plenty of ice. These people need cooling down.'

There were callers all night long, a lot of eating and a little spontaneous dancing, but on the whole the Luos were quiet, grieving for Tom M'boya. In the morning the market was packed with people trying to assess the future. The consensus of opinion was that Kenyatta would not replace Tom with another Luo. Should one then support Odinga, the leader of the opposition party and the only Luo of stature? The policy of his Kenya People's Union, a form of Communism, did not appeal to the independent farmers. It seemed at odds with the traditions of the tribal system and individual ownership of land. Yet Odinga was the Luos' only card in the political pack.

Respected Luo elders advocated support for Odinga. Kenyatta had promised the country a general election. Then let the Luo people assert their democratic rights and vote for Odinga's KPU candidates. Turn the one-party into a two-party State. But make sure that Odinga and his men truly represented the interests of the Luos in parliament.

Within the next twenty-four hours the picture of a bull appeared on walls and hoardings — the symbol of Odinga's party — or simply the word *dume*, which meant bull.

The Patels had no time for political meetings. Lakomi spent long hours at school and fitted in cooking for the family as best she could. Raspar, as estate foreman, was trying to cope with endless government

77

forms and questionnaires as well as his less than efficient workers. And Okot was at the hospital from early morning until late at night.

On Sunday, his day off, Okot took John and Andrew on a tour of his Russian hospital. The large, light buildings, with balconies running the length of each floor, looked ideal for their purpose and the climate. Trees had been planted which would, in time, make the site look less bleak, and there was an inner court with a fountain which would — eventually — be made to work.

It all looked good and modern until they entered the first ward. Some thirty small children sat in the beds or on the floor, most of them crying. Some had the pathetic faces of old men, others spidery limbs and great pot-bellies. The floor was filthy with urine and excreta, the stench almost unbearable.

Okot, apparently oblivious of his surroundings, picked up a silent little boy and cradled him in his arms. The child's head was lolling back helplessly. Okot spoke softly, stroking the boy's face. Then, very gently he put the small body back on the bed.

Okot looked at Andrew. 'He's dead.'

'When did they bring him in?'

'Yesterday . . . We get them too late. But even when they're not so sick there aren't enough of us to look after them.'

'What's the matter with them?' asked John.

'Malnutrition . . . hunger oedema. There's food enough, but the women up-country don't know how to feed their children properly. Ignorance . . . that's what they're dying of. We no longer have people who go out and teach child-care . . . the white and Asian midwives and nurses.'

John followed Okot and Andrew from ward to ward, from kitchens to dispensaries. He met a couple of other medical assistants and a few girls in nurses' uniforms. No doctors. There were some women patients about to give birth, but most of the sick were children.

He began to notice services that weren't working, an incubator not connected to the electrical supply, naked wires hanging out of walls, vacuum cleaners which weren't functioning. He asked where he might find tools and materials and Okot showed him the hospital engineer's store. The engineer, a Russian, had returned home with the medical staff.

John went through the hospital again, this time methodically listing work which never had been completed, repair and maintenance jobs. There seemed to be no end to the wards of sick children, some obviously suffering from dysentery and parasitic infestations. Nerving himself against the heat and the stench he started work on the most essential equipment. Every now and again he came across Okot or Andrew, tending the patients. He felt concerned that Andrew might catch an infection, but he knew that there was no way of pulling his brother out.

It struck him as extraordinary that he'd never heard or seen anything of the children's plight while he'd been at the plantation. He'd lived near Kisumu until he was seventeen — surely old enough to be aware of such a major problem. How could he have missed it? The answers came to him, as they usually did, while he was immersed in manual work.

The new hospital had radically changed the life-style of the up-country tribal families. They had always bred many children; they had always fed them an unbalanced diet and child mortality had always been high. The blacks, who loved and valued their young, had been totally resigned to losing most of them. They'd accepted uncomplainingly that babies were poor survivors. Long before the advent of the white man the high mortality rate had undoubtedly been nature's way of regulating the population to numbers capable of hunting or harvesting sufficient food for all.

The existence of the hospital must have become known to Luos far outside Kisumu. They were probably becoming less resigned to child-deaths and they were bringing in their sick from remote country areas. Eventually the mothers might learn how to rear their young — from the hospital staff, if ever the hospital found enough qualified staff. In that case the hospital would fulfil a valuable function; valuable, providing that black farming methods improved, that the rich and powerful stopped ruining the land, and that the land produced enough to sustain a vastly larger population.

He suddenly realized why the Luos he'd seen and known were such strong and handsome people. It had been a case of the survival of the fittest. But such laws were no longer acceptable in the latter half of the twentieth century — not even to the tribesmen up-country. The white settlers had served a purpose. Had they not arrived a hundred years ago, had it not been for the care and services of white medical people and missionaries, the Luo — and other tribes — would have died out. His contemporaries in England, if they knew such facts, were unwilling to accept them. Most of them did not know. It was easier to think in terms of politics rather than people . . . easier and deadlier.

Throughout the day John kept meeting a black, dressed in an immaculate grey suit, who appeared to be doing nothing particular around the hospital. At one point the man gave him a Coca-Cola, which he accepted gratefully. Daylight was dimming before John realized that he'd been working for twelve hours. He put away the tool-boxes and went looking for Andrew and Okot.

A door on the ground floor opened and the well-dressed Luo invited him into an office. Beside the desk sat an exceptionally good-looking Asian girl in a green sari. As John walked in she put down her cola can and rose.

'I must go,' she told the Luo. 'Thank you for the drink Mr Lambene.'

'Dr Khalid . . .' Lambene opened the door for her. 'I'm sorry . . . more sorry than I can say.'

'I believe you.'

'This is Mr Whitmore . . .'

'I know. My brother went to school with him.' She acknowledged John with a brief, forced smile and ran out of the office.

'There is nothing . . . nothing I can do about it,' complained Lambene. 'Okot must have told you; we're desperate for doctors. And Dr Khalid is a children's specialist trained in London. She works at Great Ormond Street. Do you know the hospital?'

'It's a famous one.'

'I can't give her a job.' Lambene shook his head in despair. 'One of our own Kisumu people, and I can't employ her. I tried for another Kenyan Asian doctor who wanted to come back. Went to the minister in Nairobi. Tom M'boya did everything in his power. It's hopeless. The children are dying, but we mustn't violate the cursed africanization policy.'

'What about Andrew and me?' asked John. 'Would you be able to offer us jobs?'

'Africanization doesn't apply to useful whites. We'd be thankful if you came to work for us. I don't even have to get permission from Nairobi. You can have contracts immediately, you and Dr Whitmore.'

'My brother's a medical student, not a doctor.'

'It doesn't matter. We need people like him, and you.'

'Sorry, Mr Lambene. We've got to finish our training in England.'

'I understand. Will you come back tomorrow?'

'I expect so. There are a few jobs I'd like to finish.'

Andrew and Okot were sitting on a patch of grass beside the car. They were ready to go home; they looked done in. They piled into the Ford and John opened the windows, breathing in the smell of melted tar. It was better than the stink in the wards.

He'd driven about a mile when he saw the green sari. Dr Khalid was walking slowly, head down, sandalled feet raising the red dust of the unmade road.

He stopped beside her. 'Would you like a lift?'

She wiped her eyes with the back of her hand. She'd been crying. 'I don't mind walking.'

'Straight question, straight answer.'

'Yes, I would like a lift.'

'Where are you staying?'

'At Mrs Carmichael's.'

Okot opened the door and climbed into the back seat.

'Right. I'll take you home.'

'Home . . . The hotel, at least, hasn't changed.' She got in beside him.

'Your father had the store in Victoria Street.' John drove on.

'Yes . . . You didn't recognize me.'

'You had a spotty face.'

'Puberty was hell.'

'I mended your bicycle, Leah.'

'You were always mending things. It's what I liked about you.'

'What I liked about you was your heavy black hair.'

'You noticed?'

'I notice.'

Okot and Andrew got out at Lakomi's house. John drove past the market to the other side of town. He remembered Leah in her short school skirt and white blouses, the only girl in a family of boys and the most intelligent and attractive of the Khalids.

'Why did you come back?' he asked her.

'You've come back.'

'Straight question, straight answer.'

'Very well. I read about the hospital in the *East African Standard* . . . about the shortage of doctors. I've got a British passport . . .'

'So that's why they let you in.'

'Oh, they let me in. No trouble. They just won't let me work among my own people. If only we'd never left Kenya.'

'There'd have been no future for you here.'

'Who knows? There are still Asian communities in Nyanza Province. Look at Kakamega township.'

'Aren't the Asians of Kakamega shopkeepers and businessmen?'

'What if they are?'

'Would running a shop satisfy you?'

'I can't answer that. It's Kisumu I want.'

'Won't England do?'

'Yes . . . But there's one more thing I'll try. I'm going to see Mr Gumbe . . . the Director of Social Services.'

'Did Lambene suggest it?'

'No.'

'He would have, if he'd thought it would help. He does want to employ you.'

'I'm going to see Gumbe,' insisted Leah. 'I met him at the Kisumu show last Saturday . . . and Charles Murgor, the Provincial Commissioner.'

'Their powers are limited.'

'That might change. Kenyatta might take a softer line in Luo areas. He must know how the people here feel about Tom's assassination.'

'They've taken it quietly on the whole.'

'You should have been here when the news broke.'

81

Leah described the scenes at the agricultural show on Saturday, 5th July. It had been a great festive crowd, eagerly listening to the announcements of winners for the most productive farm, the best bull, the cow with the highest milk-yield. Mrs Amayo, wife of the Kisumu show committee chairman, had been handing out awards and cups. The moment the ceremony had been completed Commissioner Murgor had taken over the microphone. 'We've heard tragic news,' he'd said in a hoarse, shaken voice. 'Because of the sad death of Mr M'boya, our beloved Minister for Economic Planning and Development, the show will be closed now.'

Men stood in shocked silence. Men and women wept openly. Those who had cars left for Nairobi. Crowds rushed to the Kisumu bus office to book tickets for Nairobi. Two shops at Anyanga Market, belonging to Kikuyus, were attacked and damaged. Fifty Kikuyu families were taken to Homa Bay Police Station for their own protection. The news had reached outlying villages fast; three miles from Kisumu, in Nyawita, bands of Luos attacked the Kikuyu villagers and the police made a number of arrests. In the tea estates around Kericho all work came to a standstill.

'The atmosphere is still tense,' said Leah.

'I know.'

Leah took a newspaper from her bag. 'It's full of interviews with people who were at the scene of the assassination.'

John kept his eyes on the road. 'What are they saying?'

Leah read out odd paragraphs. When she came to the statement the Asian owner of the chemist's shop had made to the police John asked her to read all of it. Mrs Sehmi had described how Tom M'boya had come after she'd closed the shop, how she'd unlocked the door again because Tom had been a personal friend. He'd bought some toilet articles, they'd talked for a while, and then — still talking — she'd let him out. Though she'd heard the shots she hadn't realized that Tom had been hit until he'd slumped against her and she saw the blood soaking into his shirt. 'We staggered back almost into the shop . . .'

John remembered manhandling Andrew inside and behind the counter, and then the commotion behind them as they reached the back door. According to Mrs Sehmi's statement he and Andrew must have got clear a split second before the Asians had taken Tom back into the shop.

'Is that all?' he asked Leah.

'Yes.' She glanced at him. 'Unless you want to hear how Dr Chaudhry arrived and tried mouth-to-mouth resuscitation.'

'No . . . So you think his death might make it more possible for you to stay.'

'Yes . . . a sop to the Luos of Kisumu.'

'Don't expect too much, Leah.'

'I'm going to stay for a few weeks. It might be my only chance.'

At the hotel John got out with her. 'Shall we have a drink?'

'Do ghosts drink together?'

'Straight question, straight answer.'

'Yes. John, why did you come back?'

'It was Andrew's idea, not mine.'

Mrs Carmichael herself brought their drinks to the patio, a paved circle under a big thatched umbrella. John had ordered flamingos, a mixture of gin, Campari, tonic water and slices of fresh lime; it had been his father's favourite drink.

'My family still don't touch alcohol,' said Leah, 'I do . . . on special occasions.'

When the incongruous grandfather clock in the foyer struck midnight she took his hand and led him to her room. Nothing in England had prepared him for the sensuousness of the African night. Taking possession of her graceful ivory body made him feel like a rapist. Yet he knew that the rape was mutual, and inevitable.

At dawn he wakened to find her staring at him.

'You're an African.' She stroked his long thighs.

'What does that mean?'

'Sex comes natural.'

'How would you know?'

'My first lover was an African.'

'Careful . . . Want me to rape you again?'

'Yes . . . No. Keep still. This time I'll do the raping.'

Later he asked her why she'd told him of her first lover, implying that she'd had many men.

'Not many . . . But they had to be a part of living.'

'Why tell me?' he insisted.

'Understand, John . . . My body gives and takes, but I won't be owned by any man.'

12

There was no comment, no discussion. Lakomi simply said that it was wrong to leave Dr Khalid at the hotel all on her own; she'd invite her to join her family. Leah accepted, and it was taken for granted that she'd move in with John. Every morning Okot and Andrew, John and Leah drove to the hospital and worked. Neither the Director of Social Services nor the Hospital Administrator managed to obtain permission to employ Leah, but there were no restrictions on her voluntary work.

July passed. John and Andrew talked of safaris to Nakuru or Amboseli, but there were too many emergencies at the hospital. In August Andrew made John postpone their return to England. They couldn't walk out on Okot and the hospital just yet, and they didn't have to be back at their respective colleges until September.

At the beginning of September a Kikuyu was put on trial for the assassination of Tom M'boya. Isaac Njenga Njoroge's home had been searched and a revolver found, but Njoroge denied that he'd shot Minister M'boya. 'Why pick on me, ' he kept asking the court. 'Why don't you go and get the big man?'

Later in the month there were two developments which made Andrew and John — John with great reluctance — postpone their return to England yet again. Jomo Kenyatta had announced that he would offici- ally open the hospital in Kisumu. The great man was about to show himself and allay the Luos' distrust and suspicions. Andrew was determined to be present.

The more hopeful news came from neighbouring Uganda. Two white doctors from the hospital in Kampala had written to Mr Lambene, declaring their interest in the Kisumu hospital. Lambene had offered them contracts and was awaiting their replies. John had to agree with Andrew that the doctors appeared more than anxious to leave Uganda.

Unrest in Uganda was rising. Since Prime Minister Obote had sent troops and artillery to storm the palace of King Freddie, Sir Frederick Mutesa the Kabaka of Buganda, in May 1966 there had been many tribal murders and assassinations. Several attempts on Obote's life had shown that his opposition had not been eliminated, despite the ruthless per- secution of many people loyal to the Mutese family. The Asians and Europeans of Uganda were beginning to see the writing on the wall.

'We've now got a system going at the hospital,' argued Andrew, 'We're coping with the patients . . . in a fashion. If we stay until the men from Uganda arrive we'll be able to hand over a going concern . . . on which they'll be able to build and improve.'

'You're risking your place at medical school,' said John.

'That's taken care of.' Andrew showed him a letter from his professor in London, approving his activities in Kisumu but warning Andrew that he'd have to catch up with the work.

Leah also stayed. She didn't seem to care whether or not she lost her job at Great Ormond Street. John wondered whether she was still hoping for an appointment at the Kisumu hospital. Was she staying in order to petition President Kenyatta in person? She was determined enough to try, well qualified and beautiful enough to succeed where others had failed.

In October the doctors in Kampala accepted Mr Lambene's terms. They were due to arrive, complete with wives and chattels, the week after Kenyatta's official opening of the hospital.

The night before the President's visit they sat in Lakomi's kitchen, eating the curry Leah had cooked. Raspar had come down from the plantation. Lakomi had been asked to take more than a hundred children from her school to see the President, and Raspar was to help her keep them in order. Kisumu had prepared a great reception for Kenyatta, not because the Luos had changed their attitude to him, but because they had hopes that he'd give them a sign of reconciliation, a long overdue concession that would compensate them a little for the loss of Tom M'boya. As the second largest tribe of Kenya they surely were entitled to have a say in the government of the country.

John was conscious of the long silences around the table. He guessed that he and Lakomi were sharing a sense of impending separation. Leah, perhaps because she was an Asian, had somehow made the family more complete. Unless a miracle happened, she would be leaving with Andrew and himself soon after the arrival of the doctors from Uganda. Lakomi would be left behind, waiting, waiting for the papers that would admit her and her boys into Rhodesia — into permanent exile from her tribe — for the sake of the husband from whom she'd been separated seven long years. Leah's thoughts were more difficult to read. She'd warned him more than once that no man would ever own her. Did that mean they had no meeting point outside Africa? He wanted her. He couldn't imagine days and nights without her. Yet they hadn't talked of the future. She'd evaded the subject all along.

But she touched upon it, lying in the narrow bed beside him, relaxed in the early morning of Kenyatta's arrival.

'John, I've loved you.'

'Why the past tense?'

'You'll be going back to university.'

'Hardly a monastery.'

'You'll be happy with your electronics.'

'I'm not expecting life to be all space-buggies and microchips.' Yet much of it would be. In a section of his degree thesis he'd written at some length on the building of structures for use in space. As a result he'd recently received an invitation to take part in an international symposium at Cambridge. He'd probably be the youngest graduate there; he doubted whether he'd be able to contribute anything of value, but he was looking forward to the contact with more experienced and erudite men. He hadn't discussed the symposium with Leah, but she knew that he was excited about it.

He took her in his arms. 'This has to be a part of living . . . It was you who said it, Leah.'

'It will be.'

'Is that a promise?'

'I'm afraid of promises, John. I think I'm superstitious . . . All very unscientific.'

'Straight question, straight answer.'

'I've loved you, Johnny . . . And that wasn't scientific either.'

Between town centre and hospital, all along the President's route, the lines of sightseers were thin. But the people had put on festive batik shirts and dresses in tropical-flower colours and somehow achieved a sense of occasion. The crowd at the hospital, swelled by five or six hundred school children under the supervision of Lakomi and her fellow teachers, was impressive enough for any head of state.

There was laughter when someone tested the loudspeakers which were to relay the President's speech, good-natured banter for Kisumu dignitaries who were filtering through to the improvised hall where the ceremony would take place, a stir of excitement when the people in front recognized the man in a chauffer-driven car — Mr Odinga, the leader of the opposition. Wasn't it a good sign that Odinga had been invited, people were asking one another. Did it mean that he'd be included in the next cabinet?

Leah, Andrew and John took up positions behind Lakomi and Raspar. They'd dissuaded Lambene from inviting them to the ceremony — the audience would be large enough without them — but they'd agreed to join the party at the hotel afterwards.

The combined voices of the crowd heralded Kenyatta's cavalcade long before John could see it. It was preceded by some twenty motorcycles, riders dressed in black with sunglasses so large that they looked like masks. Those faceless guards reminded him of the hell's angels he'd seen in a movie, except that the hell's angels hadn't carried machine-guns slung across their backs. Kenyatta, sitting very upright in his Rolls-Royce, wore his usual pageboy hat with the zig-zag pattern. He acknowledged the crowd by raising the fly-swatter which he'd elevated into a sceptre-like emblem of state. The bearded face smiled benevolently, but the eyes were strangely impersonal and watchful.

'He shouldn't have come,' said Lakomi. 'He is not easy in his mind.'

'No,' agreed Raspar. 'But he must want peace, or he wouldn't have invited Odinga.'

The loudspeakers crackled. Commissioner Murgor's voice came over. He talked of the hospital's conception, praised the generosity of the Russians who had given it to the town, and the builders who had constructed it. Then, using the conventional platitudes, he thanked

President Kenyatta for coming to open the hospital and invited him to address the audience.

'My friends,' began Kenyatta. 'Some of you may feel that I haven't chosen the most propitious time . . .'

He was interrupted by a rumble of hostile voices.

' . . . to visit the heart of the Luo lands . . .'

'M'boya! M'boya! M'boya!' chanted the voices.

'I share your sorrow . . . I knew Tom better than most of you . . .'

'Is that why you murdered him?' yelled a heckler.

'If it's war you want,' thundered Kenyatta, 'you can have it! What you cannot and will not have — not in my government — is your precious Odinga . . . a wealthy confidence trickster . . . A Communist . . . a traitor . . .'

For half an hour the silent crowd outside listened to the President's vituperations. He was pouring out his hatred of Odinga and his Kenya People's Union, abusing the opposition party, accusing Odinga and his henchmen of undermining the country, stirring up civil war between the Kikuyu and the Luos. When he insinuated that M'boya's murderer had been an Odinga man the uproar was such that it silenced the President.

'This is most unfortunate.' The distraught Commissioner had taken over the microphone. 'The President has decided to leave at once . . . Most distressing for us all . . . I appeal to you to behave in a restrained and orderly manner. I appeal to you . . .'

'I'm taking the children away,' said Lakomi.

Her apprehension was shared by others; some tried to push back through the crowd, some surged forward. Packed tight, the swirling milling bodies threatened a stampede.

'The children!' shouted Raspar. 'Let the children go!' He hurled himself into the mass. People trying to give way were themselves pushed on all sides.

'Children!' called another of the teachers. 'Follow me! Keep together! Close together!'

John was pitting himself against the press of bodies. The gap had to be kept open or the kids would be engulfed and trampled underfoot. Towering above the crowd, he saw Andrew and Okot with crying children in their arms, helped by a couple of struggling local policemen, their shirts in shreds. Leah had been behind him. Now they'd become separated. He caught sight of her scarlet sari; then she was gone, carried along in the stream. There was no way of reaching her.

'Dume! Dume! Dume!' chanted a demented voice.

'No!' answered the crowd. 'No! Shut him up!'

But Odinga's slogan was taken up by a large group in front. The cry rose and drowned all but the roar of the motorcycles. 'Dume! Dume! Dume!'

87

'John!' Lakomi had reached more open ground. Her children seemed safe now. 'John! Mara is missing!' She'd turned and was fighting her way back.

'Stay! Lakomi, stay where you are! I'll find her.'

She pressed on relentlessly, eyes dazed. 'Mara! Mara!'

Above the heads of the crowd someone passed him the body of a small girl. 'I've got her, Lakomi. Go back . . . go back!'

She got to him somehow, and took the child.

Behind them the roar of the motorcycles sounded much closer. He saw the roof of Kenyatta's Rolls-Royce edge slowly into the road. The motorcycles were on the move, some between fifty and a hundred yards in front, others behind the President's car. A few men had broken away from the body of the crowd and were surging towards the Rolls.

Still trying to make room for Lakomi and the child, he'd turned his back on the cavalcade when Kenyatta's guard opened fire. The sharp rattle of the machine-guns, mingled with screams of terror, exploded and died. The black figures on their machines raced ahead. The President's car slid past and vanished behind the concrete buildings up the road.

The sudden silence was broken by the desperate wails of a woman. The edges of the crowd expanded. All at once there was room, space for ambulance men and police, room for seeing the bodies on the ground.

Lakomi was fending off Raspar, who was trying to stem the bleeding from a deep wound in her right arm. Her left was still cradling the unconscious child. 'Leave it. Leave it alone!' she ordered him. 'I'm fine. Go find the family. The children . . .'

'Mother, they're safe . . . Mr Kwono's taking them back to the school.'

'So I must carry Mara to the hospital.'

'You can't . . . You're hurt . . .'

'Don't argue, man. Go find the family. John . . . you injured?'

'No. Lakomi, you go to the hospital. We'll look for Okot.'

'Andrew was with him . . . Where's Leah?'

'We'll find them. You go . . .'

'Never mind my crazy arm . . .'

'Go, Lakomi.'

'Yes.'

'Come Raspar . . . Take the other side of the road.'

John made for the place where he'd last seen Andrew and Okot. It seemed an eternity ago. Wherever he looked people were tending someone who'd been hurt. He looked at the injured and passed on, hoping against hope that the next casualty would not be Andrew or Leah or Okot.

A woman touched his arm. He recognized her as a neighbour of

Lakomi's. 'My daughter . . . Have you seen my girl?'

'She was with the children . . . helping. I think she'll be at the school.'

'Thank you. Thank you . . . Your brother and Okot have gone into the hospital.'

'Are they . . .'

'They're not hurt.'

'You're sure?'

'I saw them.'

'When?'

'Now . . . just now. They were running beside the ambulance, Bwana.'

At the edge of the road a group of people were kneeling in the dust, Raspar among them. As he approached, Raspar looked at him. He was crying.

Leah's scarlet sari. She was lying on the ground, arms flung wide, one leg bent like a dancer's. John saw his mother's body — small, neat, full of movement even in death. Not Sarah . . . Leah . . . Leah; a glistening black stain on her chest.

He crouched beside her, stroked the tumbled black hair from her face. 'An ambulance . . . Get an ambulance!'

She opened her eyes. 'No . . . Don't let them . . . touch me. It . . . doesn't hurt. Johnny . . . your hand.'

He kissed the fragile fingers, entwined them in his. 'Leah . . . love . . .'

'How many . . . dead . . . injured?'

He'd have to make her believe in tomorrow . . . or he'd lose her. 'There's work for you,' he heard himself say, 'Dr Khalid.'

'Tell me . . . How many?'

How would it affect her if he told her of the injured and dead he'd seen?

'How many?'

'Ninety,' someone answered for him. 'Perhaps a hundred . . . They shot into the crowd. At us.'

'The waste . . .'

He felt her fingers go limp. 'Leah . . .*n'gai* . . . *nyika*. Listen! Tomorrow . . .'

'Johnny . . . one promise . . . one . . .' The deep dark eyes no longer saw him, but her lips were still moving. 'Leave me . . . in Kisumu.'

Their plane was still above Kenya when Andrew handed him a page from an American journal. 'You haven't read it yet.'

'What?' John didn't want to think.

'Kole Okango sent it.'

'Kole . . .'

'The man who was at Cambridge with you. Remember? While you

were mending vacuum cleaners in Kisumu, the first man landed on the moon.'

'So what?'

'So you should read about it. It's the least you can do.'

John took the paper. It would be easier than listening . . . even to Andrew.

He got through half a page without taking in the content. He might as well have read an advertisement for burglar alarms. Then, suddenly, the meaning of the words penetrated his mind. Apollo 11 fired its service propulsion rocket and entered lunar orbit late Saturday. The following day, 20 July, the command and service modules, named Columbia, were separated from the lunar module, Eagle, and Armstrong and Aldrin began their descent to the lunar surface.

'The descent was uneventful until Eagle was near the surface: then Armstrong took control and moved the lunar module from a boulder-strewn landing-site to a smoother place nearby. Less than six hours later the hatch of the lunar module was opened and Armstrong descended to the lunar surface. As he took that first step he said, *One small step for man, one giant leap for mankind.*'

Like the precision rifle, thought John; that was a giant step for mankind too. And the bloody machine-gun was an even bigger one. But he read on. He had to read on.

'Aldrin followed Armstrong to the surface about 20 minutes later. While on the moon, they set up a camera for live television transmission, set up seismographic and laser experiments, planted a United States flag, and gathered samples of moon soil and rocks to bring back to earth. The stay on the lunar surface covered 2½ hours outside the lunar module.

'The crew ignited their ascent engine, following a 22-hour stay on the moon, then performed the necessary manoeuvres to rendezvous with Collins and Columbia in parking orbit above the moon. After the transfer to the command module was effected, the lunar module was jettisoned and the Apollo 11 crew called upon the service propulsion system to start them on their journey home.'

'Playing badminton in the universe,' said John.

Andrew looked up from his book. 'With space shuttles . . . Interesting?'

'The stuff that isn't in this article might be . . . such as the ultra-violet spectrometer or the radioisotope thermoelectric generator . . .'

Interface II
From SO2-FSS, Pretoria, South Africa
To Foreign and Commonwealth Office (African Department)
Copy to Technical Service, Hanslope

Our Ref. Rondavel 6   4th November 1969

The numbers of Russians in the under-developed African countries are increasing at the rate of 80 per cent p.a.

A chart, including locations and strength of Russian so-called advisers, as well as Moscow-trained Cuban mercenaries, will reach you under separate cover.

Within the past 3 months new KGB outfits have been set up: in TANZANIA, where KGB is monitoring the Chinese transport experts; in ZAIRE, where the German space-engineering company Otrag has set up in the business of selling satellites to commercial firms, the most likely customers being American multinational corporations; in MOZAMBIQUE, for the purpose of intensifying the training of Rhodesian guerilla forces; in two SOUTH AFRICAN areas, which are of special significance.

In the Johannesburg sector a new experimental process, code-named SASOL, which amounts to a conversion of coal into oil, could in time end South Africa's dependence on the oil-exporting countries. By far the most sensitive location is South-West Africa, generally referred to in our press as Namibia, in particular the Rössing mines and the uranium-processing plants. There the multinational corporations, detailed in my previous report, are indulging in the cut-throat free-for-all commensurate with such a mineral-rich development area.

United States policy in South Africa reflects the fragmentation of American political thinking, especially in the State Department, and the competitive pressures exerted on Congress by rival commercial corporations. As a result official American attitudes vis-à-vis South Africa are as amorphous as the devious operations of certain multinational companies. While USA Public Relations is building up world-wide antagonism against South Africa, based on the apartheid situation, USA Government's fiscal and scientific agencies are actively supporting the South African regime. Though duality of purpose in Africa has been our normal political practice – and still is in Rhodesia, as demonsrated by the latest sanction-busting operations – our American friends lack our experience of controlling such multiple policies.

I have gone into these generalities to set against the current background certain inherent dangers one can foresee. The diffuseness of America's foreign policies, presumably due to the US Government's inability to control the multinationals' exploitation of and trade in nuclear and strategic materials, is progressively increasing the political instability of the African continent.

From my vantage point it is clear that Russia is exploiting Western double-dealing in South Africa brilliantly. Moscow-trained blacks, making good use of traditional tribal rifts, are setting blacks against blacks and blacks against whites. This volatile situation on the one hand, and fast industrial growth on the other, has created the ideal conditions for civil war, industrial espionage and the establishment of new Russian strategic and naval bases.

If, as is likely, Russia succeeds in her long-held ambitions of gaining control of Afghanistan as a supply-route, and naval bases in Iraq or Iran, Eritrea or Somalia, her way into the Indian Ocean will be wide open. Her present political operations are preparing the way to a conglomerate of African Soviet states and, in turn, Soviet world domination.

We, here are convinced that the danger of a nuclear world war is escalating slowly but inexorably. The flashpoint could be A) a localized war, in which one or both parties have succeeded in illegally obtaining nuclear weapons, or B) a head-on collision between a justly confident Soviet Union and a regressing, confused United States.

FREEDOM TO KILL

America 1968 - 1969

13

By day, he said, he was a stoodent of mind-pollution psychology; at night he drove a cab. He had hair like a halo of busted bedsprings. Not a genuine Afro; it was blond so, most likely, a matter of lifestyle. He said he didn't dig freaks and maybe that was due to sensory overload.

He sure dug Greg's edoocated quiet voice right from the moment Greg had hired his cab at San Francisco airport. Some voices just freaked him. Not Greg's though. Greg's gave him the right vibes, and that was the truth. San Francisco was full of language that didn't give a guy the right vibes, language that amounted to mind-pollution.

He was climbing up Summit Road, Berkeley, throwing his cab around the sharp bends, demonstrating every reason why most San Francisco cabs were as scraped and dented as if they'd been salvaged from car cemeteries. Greg reckoned that Afro had seen too many movies that included the obligatory car-chase in a multi-storey car park. All the same, he did make it to the house at the top.

Greg tossed up with himself whether to retain the cab or let Afro go. On balance, he didn't feel like a long evening with his parents. Sure, he was fond of them; but he was in no mood to listen to his father gripe about the Tactical Squad. He'd heard enough of the Tac during the past two years, ever since the riot squads had been formed in 1967. None of the regular Bay Area Police officers liked those guys or their methods, but that was no reason why he should sit there while Detective Murphy let off steam yet again. Local politics was bad enough — what with Major Alioto aggravating civil unrest — but police politics was worse, certainly to Detective Murphy's sons.

'Can you wait ten minutes?' Greg asked Afro.

'Sure can,' he agreed.

Mary Murphy opened the door. 'I knew it was you, Greg; soon as I heard the car.'

'Wouldn't miss your birthday, Ma.'

'Come on in, boy. How about something to eat? Pastrami on rye?'

'I had a meal on the plane.'

'How did you get on in Seattle?'

He followed her into the living-room with its white painted furniture and flowered chair-covers. 'Didn't see much of the town, but the Boeing

Company place is impressive. They're doing great work on the Skylab project.'

'Will you take the job, Greg?'

'Not so fast, Ma. They haven't offered. Just interviewed me.'

'They paid your flight though.'

'That means nothing to a company the size of Boeing.'

'You'll see.'

'Ma, even if they wanted me, I'm not sure that I'm ready to leave San Francisco State. I like the college; and teaching.'

'Son, the college hasn't given you tenure. Your father says the administration could fire you any time they like.'

'No one's going to fire me. There aren't enough people who can teach physics and maths. And I wouldn't expect tenure at twenty-seven . . . after less than two years at San Francisco State.'

'Your father worries about student riots.'

'He's exaggerating. There's been no trouble from students in my faculty.'

'But the anarchy's spreading, Greg.'

'You sound like dad.'

'Well . . . he's been telling me about the riots in France . . . in Germany. You know what happened in Chicago. Young people killed on campus . . .'

'He thinks it's all one big Communist plot. Has he ever said that — maybe — some students are dissatisfied because there's something wrong with our education system? Ma, you tell him I can take care of myself.'

She looked him over, that patient affectionate smile on her ageing face. They were alike; short, slight, built for speed rather than power, devoid of aggression. All he had inherited from his father's Irish ancestors were striking blue eyes — astigmatic, in his case — red-tinged fair hair and freckles. Perhaps he could take care of himself, but she still felt protective. What would have become of him if she hadn't stood between him and his father? Dan never had understood that Greg needed privacy for reading his head off, even when it was just science fiction, that his game was tennis and not baseball, that he had more influence on the two youngest kids — Sean and Fiona — than either parent.

She said, 'Your father means well. But cops expect burglars under every bed, I guess.'

Greg took a small box from his coat pocket. 'Happy birthday, Ma.'

She kissed him. 'It's real thoughtful . . . Perfume! Estée Lauder . . . the one I like best.'

It occurred to Greg that none of his brothers and sisters was clever with presents. His four elder sisters, now married and scattered all over the States, rarely remembered birthdays. Chris, who still lived at home, usually gave candies; Sean just went to the nearest drugstore and bought bath-essence. Only Fiona, the youngest, thought of more personal gifts such as a handbag to match a pair of shoes.

'Ma, the cab's waiting. I've got to go.'

'Sure.'

She walked him out to the paved yard, oblivious of the raw October mist that was rising from San Francisco Bay, and stood until the cab had rounded the bend. She'd never asked any of her children when they'd be coming again. Only one out of eight left at home and he, like his father, a cop in the Bay Area Police. When Greg had been appointed to San Francisco State and rented the little house on Nineteenth Avenue nearby, Sean and Fiona had gone to live with him. It had left the home on Summit road, in which his parents had invested all their savings, depleted. Greg still felt guilty about it.

Perhaps it would have worked out differently if his father had been less obsessed with cop-like discipline and more tolerant of young people. The miserable rows when Sean, at twenty, had dropped out of college; the gloom when he'd taken off for Canada in order to dodge getting drafted for service in Vietnam. A son of Dan Murphy's refusing to do his duty by his country! Well, Sean had returned of his own free will. With luck he'd get back into university. His grades had been good enough. Fiona's position at home had been no easier than Sean's. When she announced that she wanted to study computer programming, father had really hit the roof. Why didn't she find herself a nicy guy, like her sisters, and get married as girls should? What was wrong with his young kids? The five older ones had given no trouble. It was those left-wing liberals and the intellectuals in universitties and state government who were inciting rebellion. They should be charged with sedition or un-American activities and put in prison.

' . . . so I went to this party . . .' Afro was throwing the cab around the corner into Nineteenth Avenue, 'and there was this guy. Jeez! was he high on acid! Brought it back from Vietnam . . . That's one fucking war we're gonna lose, not because they're lacking hardware or napalm in South East Asia . . . but on account of the mind-pollution. When I've gotten my degree I'll make millions outa treating those Vietnam veterans; there'll be that many.'

'Great . . . Pull up over there, will you.'

'Isn't this where Fiona Murphy lives?'

'Yes.'

'You her guy?'

'Her brother.'

'I get it . . . the professor.'

'Are you a friend of hers?' Greg took out his billfold and gave him a dollar over the metered fare.

'I tried to date her,' admitted Afro. 'It was no go. She's a peach, but

97

there's somethin' wrong with her I guess.'

'Because she won't go out with you?'

'That's right. I mean, usually dames are interested in mind-pollution psychology. You know, it kinda gets to them. The rest's easy. But Fiona . . . I just can't make her out.' Afro shook his big blond head. 'I mean, why wouldn't she let me date her? Unless she's a lesbian women's libber or some kinda monogamy freak.'

Greg carried in the chicken casserole, Sean followed him from the kitchen with the baked potatoes, Fiona took the beer out of the fridge. They didn't bother to take the telephone, journals and books off the table. Their father would have disapproved of such casualness at dinner. Nor would he have liked their living-room, which they'd furnished with junk from the streets.

Some householders, unwilling to pay for having their throw-out chairs, TV sets and refrigerators carted away, dumped them on the sidewalks, hoping that the hippies would take them. Sean and Greg had collected all they wanted, repaired the fridge and TV set, while Fiona had painted and re-upholstered the bentwood chairs. The work-cum-eating table was a slab of genuine marble, resting on a couple of mahogany bedside cupboards. Sean and Fiona were more than satisfied with the old-fashioned harmony they'd created.

They asked Greg about his interview in Seattle and he told them more than he'd let his mother know. They had a greater understanding of scientifically equipped satellites and sky labs. He'd expected that Fiona would like the idea of his taking the job at Boeing's, but Sean's reaction surprised him.

Sean said, 'It'll be better than your academic job. Campus riots aren't your lifestyle.'

'I've had no trouble with my students. They're sensible, hard-working people.'

'How many of them are blacks?'

'A couple.'

'Top-class guys, I guess.'

'They are, Sean. But that's neither here nor there.'

'Look here, Greg . . . Granted that science students are too occupied to think much about black power, and the system that deprives most black students of top education . . . but even they won't sit on the sidelines for ever. And when they wake up . . .'

'There are usually a few malcontents in the English and Economics Departments. Those kids haven't got enough to do, so they play around with campus politics.'

'Greg, you're not reading it right. The Black Students' Union and the Third World Liberation Front have given positive demands to the

98

governors of San Francisco State. For a start they want a Black Studies Department. And they want some say in who is to learn, what is to be learned, and who is to teach.'

'It amounts to the students controlling the colleges. You must see how absurd that is.'

'What I think doesn't matter, but . . .

'Of course it does. If you're going back to college . . .'

'Haven't made up my mind yet.'

'You know the alternative.' Greg looked at the fair boy with the lean, sensitive face. 'You're not cut out for killing Vietnamese peasants.'

'Not cut out for fighting my fellow-Americans either . . . Drop it, Greg. I'll make out somehow. The old Murphy genes will see to that. Let's put on the idiot box. After all, Apollo 7 has been launched . . . the first manned mission in space: while you were in the air above Seattle.'

Fiona put on the TV set. 'I saw the blast-off. It was great. All systems go. Next stop the moon.'

Greg laughed. 'Not yet, you nut.'

'Things are moving real fast.' She put a journal into his hand. 'You read this. Remember how we used to argue about objects in the sky that no one could explain? Well, here's news about those pulsars.'

He read, *Some radio sources have been found to emit regular, sharp, rapid pulses of radiation, with periodic times of a second or less. For a while these pulsing sources were known as LGM, Little Green Men, so sceptical were astronomers of the possibility of star-like objects emitting signals so like those a man with a good clock and a radio transmitter might send out. Now nobody is doubting that pulsars are rapidly rotating neutron stars.*

The theory is that there could be whole stars in which matter is compressed to a density comparable with that of the nucleus itself. Such a star could be very massive but very small, and so be able to rotate rapidly. If it has a magnetic field, it becomes possible for it to send a beam of radio waves out into space, which sweeps round as the star rotates, like the beam of a lighthouse. The pulses would then represent the beam sweeping rapidly across Earth.

'The sci-fi we used to read as little kids is coming true,' said Fiona. 'One day nobody will have to get coal and gasoline from inside our earth . . . that's what you said, Greg . . . one day the sun and the stars are gonna warm our homes and drive our cars.'

'Dreams.'

'So's going to the moon. But we'll make it. And you should be out there, right in front. The Boeing Company's where you belong.'

14

They walked across the campus in relaxed silence, Fiona in jeans and pea-jacket, a bundle of books under her arm, Greg — carrying a briefcase — wearing his formal dark graduation suit. President Smith had called a meeting of the teaching staff. Greg, as the youngest member, had decided to look the part. Putting on freak-gear by way of social protest seemed childish and futile — not his style, whatever he felt about the college administration.

Greg recalled yesterday's Apollo launch and Commander Walter Schirrer's almost inarticulate commentary. He'd try to get to a TV set for the next chapter of this space odyssey. If Boeing did offer him the job, for which he'd applied in a moment of scientific excitement, he'd stand a good chance of participating in the space programme, of being right there in the control-room where the action was.

Fiona wanted him to get the Boeing appointment because she was convinced he'd be doing his own thing. Sean's reaction had been more complex. Sean, like most kids between eighteen and twenty, was pre-occupied with political issues, especially the war in Vietnam. And yet Sean, aware how much politics affected the colleges and universities, wanted his academic brother right out of San Francisco State. Not tough enough for the hassle? Well, neither was Sean.

He'd be best placed in the English Department. Funny thing Sean had said after the Apollo launch programme. 'It's crazy when you consider it . . . this business of communication. There's the crew talking to us from out there in the universe. And there are educationalists in our college trying to teach students how to use their own language right . . . because they need to learn how to communicate with one another. Me, I reckon I do know my own language and yet I can't communicate with my own father. Maybe it's too early for man to go zooming into space.'

It occurred to Greg that it might be too early for him to leave the shelter of academic life. It did give him time to himself for reading and thinking — an invaluable quietude he'd probably lose if he worked for a huge commercial corporation. Then there was his relationship with his students — the brighte t in the college or they wouldn't have opted for the sciences, and not much younger than he — a bunch of people who generously returned the respect and friendship he felt for them. If Sean

100

hadn't mentioned his blacks it wouldn't have crossed his mind that they were in any way different from the rest.

Fiona asked, 'What time do you want to eat tonight?'

'Make it around eight.'

'OK. Could you buy coffee on the way home?'

'Sure.'

'See you.' Fiona walked off towards the block where she attended classes, long auburn hair swinging in the breeze. A pretty girl, as Afro had said, a young Pre-Raphaelite woman in jeans.

There was nothing beautiful about the campus. Its contemporary buildings were aggressively functional, uniformly dispirited. No redeeming curve, no cornice or balustrade. The grassy areas were dull except for a nave of redwood trees which led damply from the Business and Social Sciences block to nowhere. The great trees flanked a walk somewhat like a cathedral aisle, but there was nothing beyond except the ugly college cafeteria, the Commons, squatting glass-eyed on the slope below.

The students, standing around in tight scrums, looked no less dispirited. Greg had the impression that they were hanging around under the cold sky trying to generate enough energy to fill the grey corridors or go and smash up the town instead. He'd seen apes like that in the zoo — still and aimless one moment, frantically shaking the bars of their cage the next. The frustration of the kids was palpable — like an odour. Not one of his students was among them. His students had minds. They were different.

At the main entrance of the Administration Building Greg met Dr Bierman of the Philosophy Department and they went up to President Smith's office together.

'Full house,' said Arthur Bierman, surveying the large staff gathering, the improvised platform already occupied by President Smith and the Vice-President for Academic Affairs.

'There's been a student riot at Berkeley,' Smith began bleakly. 'A great deal of damage was done to college and private property . . .'

'Damage to private property,' murmured Bierman. 'That hurts.'

Smith's voice rose. ' . . . and I will not tolerate vandalism on my campus. I wish to inform you of the preventative measures I propose to take. But first I'll update you on the demands — not suggestions, mind you — which the Black Students' Union has submitted to me and the governors of our college . . .'

Similar demands had been made before. There was nothing new in the request for an integrated Department of Black Studies empowered to grant a degree in Black Studies: the chairman, faculty and staff were to have sole power of hiring faculty, controlling and determining the destiny of the department — the admittance of all black students wishing to attend college — and the allocation of twenty full-time teaching positions to the new department.

The demands were reasonable from the students' viewpoint, but unreasonable in the eyes of a white society which had made inferior citizens of its blacks and was terrified of relinquishing any of its wealth and power.

'Would you like to live next door to a black?' asked Bierman, under his breath. 'You wouldn't mind, except that the value of your house would drop if blacks moved into your suburb. Too bad, but you've got to keep them out.'

Greg stopped listening. If the student unrest wasn't about Black Power it would be about something else. He'd read somewhere that students had fought on the twin stairways of Vienna University 250 years ago. And if one went into the subject in depth, one would almost certainly discover that students had made demands and trouble ever since universities were established. It was normal that students should want to create their own world to live in. It was no more unreasonable than his own break-away from his father or Sean's and Fiona's rebellion against the Murphy stranglehold.

Greg got up and made for the door. Now he didn't give a damn whether President Smith noted his exit or not, interpreted it as rebellion or not. His job was teaching, not listening to a load of political bullshit.

All through October there was a great deal of conferring among the staff. Some of Greg's colleagues were siding with President Smith's hard line on the students' demands, others with the increasingly frustrated and angry students. Greg kept out of faculty meetings. His students presented no problem; and he'd been hired to teach them, not to get involved in internecine quarrels.

The cold November mists rising from San Francisco Bay enhanced the forlorn, unreal atmosphere on the campus. The students, males and females in jeans, African shirts and beads, long hair drooping clammily over their shoulders, looked like doomed El Greco saints.

They had occupied two buildings and were picketing the entrances of others. Here and there placard-carrying groups were shouting, *on strike, on strike, education not regimentation.* They meant to shut down San Francisco State until the governors and President Smith gave in to their demands. They no longer lacked purpose. There were moments when President Smith, urged by members of the staff, seemed willing to negotiate, but in the end he reverted to threats.

On 5th November even some of Greg's students went missing. He taught a couple of depleted classes, dismissing the last one twenty minutes early. No use working with kids unable to concentrate. When they trooped out, apologetic and embarrassed, he went to watch them from the window. They were leaving the campus. Would the pickets out there deter them from completing their course?

The Science Building was as silent as a deserted ship. Even the chanting seemed a long way off, distant but urgent. He walked across to the faculty secretary's office. She wasn't there but the purring of the telephone was comforting. He picked up the receiver.

'They're occupying the buildings,' an anonymous voice told him. 'Are you Dr Goodlett?'

'No, Murphy.'

'President Smith's instructions are: no member of faculty's to enter into discussions with the students. Stay where you are until I call you.'

'Who are you?'

The line went dead. Outside, groups of twenty or thirty students, some carrying placards, were marching towards the Administration Building. Nearer his Science block, a few students in twos and threes were quietly walking away in the direction of Holloway Avenue.

He was debating with himself whether he shouldn't disregard the instructions conveyed by the unknown caller, when he saw a long line of patrol wagons drive up the campus. What had possessed Smith to call in reinforcements? Why wasn't he talking to the students? Why didn't he let the campus police talk to them?

The line of black wagons split, the greater number making straight across the grass towards the marchers, the last two racing at the students below the Science Building. Doors flew open and out spilled dark-uniformed figures in helmets, clear plastic visors down, truncheons in gloved fists. The Tactical Squads.

Suddenly the watching students moved. 'Don't run!' Greg yelled. 'Don't run!'

They ran, and the squad-men in their improbable space-gear rounded them up like sheep, truncheons cracking down on unresisting bodies. When one boy, obviously unconscious, was thrown brutally into a wagon the students began to fight. Greg, paralyzed with horror, saw a boot smash into a young face, blood spread like a voracious flame. A girl, on the ground, was defending herself with legs and arms; a boot in the groin made her double like an embryo and lie still.

Students and squad-men were locked in one mass of flailing limbs and batons when Greg saw the girl on the ground, a slight black girl lying motionless, while frantic boots were trampling her. In seconds he was out of the office, out of the building, running across the soggy grass. Hurling his weight against the one man who was still close to the girl, he picked her up and charged to the side of the block.

As he walked along the lines of parked cars, the girl in his arms moaned. Despite the ugly gash across her forehead the coffee-coloured face with the small, straight nose and the great dark eyes was very

103

beautiful. As she looked at him the expression of an animal at bay changed to resignation or indifference.

Greg found an old Chevrolet with the key in the ignition. He lifted the girl into the passenger seat. He'd think about the owner of the car later. The kid needed medical attention. The battering she'd suffered could have caused internal injuries; she was certainly in a state of shock.

He started the car and drove between buildings to the exit that would take him into Holloway Avenue.

'How are you feeling?' he asked. A stupid question but he was hoping for some response.

The girl touched her forehead, then stared at the blood on her hand — bewildered, confused. 'I hurt him? Did I hurt somebody?'

Greg was half-way home before he realized that he'd got his priorities wrong. He should have made for Fiona's building the moment he'd set eyes on the Tactical Squad vans. Instead he'd watched like a hypnotized chicken and acted on impulse. He rationalized that Fiona's building was at the far end of the campus, a considerable distance from the battle-ground; but it didn't relieve his anxiety.

What now? Should he take the girl to the nearest hospital? Better not. There'd be an influx of casualties delivered by ambulance. She might be kept waiting. He glanced at his watch. If he took her home he'd be able to get Dr Chandler fairly quickly. Chandler, who'd looked after the Murphy tribe ever since he could remember, was one of the few doctors still prepared to make house-calls.

He drove on. No use hesitating now. His passenger had turned a disturbing grey colour. Her eyes were closed. He hoped to God she was still breathing.

The family Ford was parked at the house; Sean was at home. Greg put the Chev in behind the Ford and ran up the porch steps. When Fiona came out of the living-room he could have cried with relief.

Sean, behind her, said, 'OK, we've seen her. We'll take her in. You call Chandler.'

Greg almost told him to be careful, but he stopped himself. Sean was no longer a moody schoolboy. He'd matured since he'd taken off on that long hitch-hike to Canada. He hadn't said much about it, except that the Canadians had turned him back at the frontier because he hadn't had enough money on him. So Sean had gone back to Detroit, worked as a navvy, and got into Canada second time round. He could have stayed there and escaped from Hobson's choice of going to college or Vietnam, but he'd returned home of his own free will. Yes, Sean had become a responsible adult, and he'd better remember that.

Greg saw Sean and Fiona ease the girl out of the passenger seat, and went to phone. The nurse said the Dr Chandler had finished morning

104

surgery and would be right along.

Sean came in and sat down at the table. 'We've put her in Fiona's room. Who is she?'

'I don't know.' Greg told him what had happened.

'I heard the sirens,' said Sean. 'I was at the library. I got in the car and went to fetch Fiona. I've been expecting this. Smith was bound to call in the Tac Squad; it's what father would have done. Think the girl's bad?'

'Well . . . She spoke.'

'She's unconscious now.'

Dr Chandler had diagnosed concussion, a broken bone in the girl's right foot, otherwise no damage apart from the gash on the forehead — which he'd stitched — and some painful bruises. He'd advised that the girl was not a hospital case and could be looked after at home. The injection he'd given her had put her into a deep sleep.

Fiona went through the pockets of her jacket. She found a couple of keys, five dollars, and an envelope addressed to Stella Ossip at a downtown address. Greg called his father at the office; his father located the name and address of the Chevrolet's owner, a janitor at the college. When Greg told the man what had happened he was quite sympathetic. What with the trouble on campus he hadn't noticed that his car had gone. He'd stayed indoors. It would be safe for Mr Murphy to return the car. The Tac Squad had gone; they'd arrested some fifty students. Thirty-three had been injured, one killed. All was quiet now. There was a rumour that President Smith had resigned and that Dr Hayakawa was taking over, though there'd be no teaching at San Francisco State in the foreseeable future.

Later that afternoon Greg drove to the address Fiona had given him. It was a run-down rooming-house where the tenants appeared to keep to themselves. He knocked on door after door; no one seemed to have heard of a Stella Ossip. He was about to give up when an elderly black woman came puffing upstairs. Stella Ossip? A student? Oh yes, she'd be the girl in number ten. Nice, quiet kid; worked in the supermarket part time; did her shopping when she was sick last fall.

Greg thanked her and went to the floor below. Stella's key opened the door of number ten. He felt like a thief in that tidy little room. It contained nothing but a divan, with a bright blue cotton cover, a table and a couple of wooden kitchen chairs. In the closet was a shelf of books, all on business and accounting apart from the poems of Dylan Thomas, and a shelf of toilet articles and neatly folded clothes. The whole lot would have gone into a medium-sized suitcase. He wondered whether there was anything he should take for her, but decided that it might embarrass her to know that he'd walked into this room, which seemed curiously private and forbidding.

On Dr Chandler's advice Greg didn't see Stella for several days. She was to be kept in bed, and quiet. Fiona told him that she slept a good deal, ate what she was given and had little to say. But one evening she appeared in the living-room in one of Fiona's dressing-gowns. She stood at the door, shyly, until Fiona went to help her into a chair.

'I want to thank you for taking me in, Mr Murphy,' she said, stiffly. 'I can go home now.'

'We should let Dr Chandler decide, Miss Ossip.'

'My foot's much better and . . .'

Fiona said, 'Cool it, Stella. We don't want to get rid of you. We'll let you go when the doctor says so and not before. OK?'

'OK.'

Greg thought he'd never seen a more attractive smile. He'd never considered ugliness or beauty in blacks. He saw Stella as a black and suddenly remembered the Song of Solomon: *I am black, but comely, O ye daughters of Jerusalem, as the tents of Kedar, as the curtains of Solomon. Look not upon me, because I am black, because the sun hath looked upon me . . .*

He said, 'We have time on our hands. The College is closed.'

'You're blaming the black students,' said Stella bitterly.

'No.' Her aggression had taken him by surprise. 'I'm not blaming anyone.'

'That's great. Whatever you touch, keep your hands clean.' As she turned away she saw the expression on Fiona's face. 'I'm sorry, I shouldn't have said that. I had no right.'

'You have every right to speak your mind,' said Fiona, 'in this house. But Greg's a scientist, not a politician.'

'How can you divorce science from politics? In the end even the great Professor Einstein made a political commitment.'

A political commitment? Greg, who'd been three or four years old at the time, had second-hand memories of the letter Einstein — with some distinguished colleagues — had written to the President of the United States. It must have been shortly after the Second World War and the dropping of the first atom bomb on Japan. Einstein had appealed publicly to President Truman to stop all production of nuclear weapons, because such power in the hands of politicians would terminate all life on earth.

That document must have had a great impact if people his age and younger knew of it. Would America have heeded the warning if Russia hadn't striven so hard to crack the nuclear nut — and succeeded? But such speculation was fruitless. Greg reckoned that the Second World War had never stopped; it had fragmented in an explosion that had split and changed the structure of societies throughout the world. There'd been no intervals between violent revolutions and *little* wars. How long before one of these flashpoints sparked off the ultimate nuclear holocaust? The war in Vietnam, which was dragging on year after year? Or an even smaller war by world standards . . . a stolen rocket with a nuclear warhead fired on a college campus?

Greg said, 'You're right, Miss Ossip. One can't divorce science from politics . . . Even the transparent visor that protects the faces of the Tactical Squad men was designed by a scientist.'

She looked at him, clear dark eyes childishly hopeful. 'What will you do about it?'

'You don't expect an instant decision, do you?'

'I guess not. But nobody will ever make me believe that man is totally helpless against man.'

Within three weeks Dr Chandler told Stella that she was fit for work. Fiona somehow persuaded her to stay, at least until the fracture in her foot had mended. With the aid of a stick, Stella went back to her cashier's job at the supermarket, but she always returned in the evening.

Gradually Fiona pieced together Stella's history. She'd been the only child of an engineer in the Los Angeles Water Department. The family had lived in the respectable black suburb of Watts, and Stella had attended a racially mixed school. In 1962, almost seven years ago, a patrolman in downtown Los Angeles had stopped a black suspected of drug-peddling. The boy had made a run for it and the policeman had shot him dead. That incident had sparked off a riot which had devastated whole areas of the city, claimed victims on both sides, and filled the prisons.

Stella's mother, who'd been caught up in the violence, had died of injuries. Her father had become an alcoholic. Three years later his car had caused a serious accident and he'd been charged with manslaughter. He had died in prison. His legal defence had swallowed most of his savings. Stella had spent the rest on moving to San Francisco.

Just another bleak all-American story, Stella had said. Yet, after that first confrontation with Greg, she'd shown no bitterness or aggression. She seemed to have recovered from her mental injury.

In December Dr Nagel of the Boeing Company called Greg back to Seattle. His security clearance had come through, he'd be offered an appointment, and Alan Nagel wanted to discuss with him the areas best suited to his qualifications.

Greg, still uncertain whether or not to give up academic life, went to see acting President Hayakawa at the college. His decision to resign was clinched finally by the dead silence of the deserted campus. One day San Francisco State would function again; but he would remember the line of black vans, the blood of vulnerable young students, every time he looked out of a window. And that image would always be bound up with the revulsion and horror he'd felt when he'd seen Stella trampled on the ground like some discarded piece of junk.

107

15

Alan Nagel was the kind of person with whom Greg could be frank about his reasons for resigning from San Francisco State. He had a quality of warmth which anyone who didn't know what his profession was might have interpreted as naïvety. It struck Greg that the most erudite and intelligent teachers he'd known had been similar characters — transparently sincere and humane.

After a morning in the workshops and laboratories, Nagel took Greg for lunch in the executives' dining room. Tables, chairs and light-fittings were functional, original in design and surprisingly comfortable.

Nagel ran his palms over the polished rosewood table. 'Simulated wood . . . all of it. Here we're guinea-pigs for the space-furniture research boys. Our reactions to different materials and fabrics — our states of euphoria or depression — are scientifically monitored and recorded. If there's one thing we've learned from our astronauts it's that they are as human in space as they are on earth. For peak-performance they should be surrounded by objects that look and feel good. For instance, they've been found to react differently to woods and plastics; they've shown a positive preference for wood — if it's well simulated — and other natural materials. Research of this nature will become increasingly relevant.'

'If people go to live in space for any length of time?'

'Precisely. According to the latest medical data, physical problems will be overcome. Man will be able to stay in space for considerable periods without permanent damage to health. It opens up staggering prospects.'

'We've already had benefits from space research . . . that's if we make proper use of them,' said Greg. 'Remote sensing techniques — such as multispectral scanning and high resolution photography — could gather valuable information on crop-diseases . . . on water resources, or fault zones prone to earthquakes.'

'There might even be fewer wars when countries can watch one another from space.'

'Science controlling man for his own good.'

'If we have more luck than sense.' Alan Nagel smiled. 'I read your article in the *New Scientist*. You visualize a transfer of industry from earth to space.'

'Theoretical ideas.' Greg felt embarrassed. That article had been meant as an entertainment — a thing of imagination rather than science.

'Your ideas didn't seem far-fetched to me.' Nagel helped himself from a dish of salads. 'Take the manufacture of glasses . . . essential components of telescopes, microscopes, lasers and mirrors . . . crystals made from indium antimonide and gallium arsenide. These crystals are the very heart of electronic devices; they'll become more and more essential in the near future. The case for manufacturing them in space is very strong indeed. On earth their production's beset by gravitational damage, which creates different temperature zones in liquids. In space we'd be able to make crystals, which transmit electrons in a controlled manner, without the impurities which contaminate them on earth. Wasn't that the kind of thing you had in mind when you wrote your article?'

'Sure. My article just missed out on details . . . how to get the men and materials for building factories out into space, and who'd pay for it all.'

'That'll be someone else's concern.' Nagel was being perfectly serious. 'There's been an assessment from . . . intelligence sources, that political upheavals — such as the Nigerian civil war — could play havoc with our economy. Our enormous energy requirements make us vulnerable. America's too dependent on imported raw materials, especially oil. On the basis of these reports there's been a high-level government decision . . . to explore the feasibility of placing a satellite in space which could relay energy from the sun to earth. We, at Boeing, have received government funds for this research. I guess it's a job that will appeal to you.'

'It's hard to believe . . .'

'I know.' There was understanding and amusement in Nagel's pleasant, lined face. 'That's how I felt when the chief told me I'd be co-opted to the Space Programme. We'll put you to work on the problems of photo-voltaic cells. You seem to have a special interest in cells and glasses.'

Alan Nagel had arranged one more interview. He took Greg to the office of the Co-ordinator, introduced him to Mat Scobie, and left. Scobie remained seated behind his desk. The top part of him looked too heavy for the long, narrow head, the face so featureless that Greg wondered whether he'd recognize Scobie next time they met.

'You've been teaching in San Francisco State.' Scobie opened a folder and studied it. 'Been having some nasty riots there.' He made it sound as if Greg had been responsible for the troubles. 'I assume you're feeling sorry for the students.'

Greg didn't care for the tone. 'That's your assumption.'

'Well . . . you academics tend to be liberal.'

109

'What's your definition of *liberal*?'

'The current one . . . where the students are always right, where their stupidities and excesses are excused as a valid part of the drug-culture. The fact that the words *drug* and *culture* have been combined — by intellectuals, of course — speaks for itself.'

'If you want to know, I hold no brief for drug-takers.'

'But you feel sorry for them, I guess.'

'If you're looking for a scapegoat, blame our elders.'

'Sure . . . Your father's a police officer?'

'As you can see.'

'That's right.' Mat Scobie ignored Greg's stiffness. 'So you should understand the meaning of security . . . national security. You'll be involved in work which is graded Top Secret; not to be written up in learned journals or books . . . not to be discussed with your family, friends, or even colleagues who're working on other projects . . .'

'Mr Scobie, I've read the security clause in my contract.'

'I believe in personally drawing attention to it. The modern intelligence agent is an industrial spy. Keep that in mind, Mr Murphy. A careless word in a bar . . .'

'I do most of my drinking at home.'

Scobie laughed, a mirthless bark that reverberated around his wide chest. 'How about a bourbon right now?'

'No thanks. I don't drink in the middle of the day; it makes me sleepy.' Greg got up. 'Any other point you want to raise?'

'I think we've covered the ground.' He picked up the telephone. 'Brenda, I want you to take Mr Murphy over to Personnel. OK? Personnel have their uses,' he told Greg. 'They found me the right kind of apartment. They might do the same for you.'

Despite his undoubted dislike of Mat Scobie, Greg left the Boeing complex in a state of euphoria. What could be better than earning a good living by working at what one enjoyed? The contract he'd signed was more generous than his academic one by five thousand dollars.

On the flight home he estimated costs. He'd be able to pay the college fees for Sean as well as Fiona. Sean had refused financial help from father — saying he'd work his way through college — but he wouldn't have qualms about accepting Greg's support. Sean would prefer to take his degree sooner rather than later.

No problems. The move to Seattle would suit all three of them. No problem? What would become of Stella? Not that she was helpless; just a lot more solitary than she'd ever admit, even to herself.

Fiona had prepared a typical Murphy celebration, the kind of meal that had been rare and special when her mother had raised eight children on a police officer's salary; clam chowder, roast duck and cheesecake. Sean

110

had bought a quart of the best Californian burgundy, Stella a bottle of French brandy.

Greg talked, and the more he talked the more details he remembered; the equipment in a new electronics pilot-plant, the diffusers on light-fittings, the secretary's apology for Mat Scobie's unpleasantness, the commercial success of the latest laser range-finders.

'For guns?' asked Stella.

'That's right.'

Stella put down her fork beside the half-eaten cheesecake. 'Whatever would America do without the war in Vietnam? What would happen to big companies like Douglas and Boeing if they didn't get big fat government contracts for war machines?'

'You tell us,' Sean said acidly. 'Not stopping you.'

'Why can't you see it!' Stella sounded exasperated with Sean, as if they'd argued before on the same subject. 'If this country wasn't manufacturing endless military hardware our industries would go bankrupt, and unemployment would go so high no government would be able to cope with it.'

Greg looked at the beautiful, dark face across the table, disturbed by the bitterness it didn't show. 'Stella, are you saying that our government's dragging out the war in Vietnam deliberately?'

'Sure. Either our armies are too incompetent to finish it — and that I can't believe — or the government's dead scared of a peace that would dump us into a recession. Wars are profitable . . . for industries. And industries can exert a lot of pressure on governments. That's how the cookie crumbles.'

'Haven't you forgotten something?'

'Our casualties? Our boys who're getting killed in Vietnam? Nobody can say that we don't care about them. You can see what we're doing for them . . . All that's necessary, if you want to reassure yourself, is to take a short drive to the other side of the bay. Go to the Golden Gate Cemetery. The scenery's just beautiful . . . a great expanse of roses, carnations, gladioli, spring flowers under acres of white headstones; a scenic masterpiece between barren hills and the sparkling Pacific Ocean . . .'

'Stella . . . not tonight,' murmured Fiona.

Stella ignored the appeal. 'From the cemetery go on to Valencia. It's not far away either. There you can watch the Navy trucks arrive from Travis Air Force Base. Each truck has tiers, like a sleeping car, on which lie long aluminium containers. On each container is a stamped warning DO NOT TIP. It's because the contents have been packed in ice at the Tan Son Nhut Air Base in Saigon; and one doesn't want a water-spillage. Mind you, these containers are shifted pretty fast. They travel from South East Asia by C-141-A jets — Starlifters the boys call them — and they touch down at Travis at the rate of thirty or forty every twenty-four hours. At the undertaker's in Valencia the containers are emptied and then taken back — for re-use — to the Air Force Base. If you hang around a while you'll see the arrival of Naval limousines fitted with clothes-racks. They deliver fine new uniforms to the mortuary. Trouble is . . . often there's not enough left of the young serviceman to go into the uniform the Services provide . . . There's another couple of places you should take in while you're about it; not far away either. The Naval Weapons Station and . . . within ten minutes walk — Port Chicago. Nine per cent of all the explosives sent to Vietnam — including napalm bombs — leave from Port Chicago.'

Greg felt numbed. Though he understood Stella's feelings he resented the way she'd spelled them out. 'There's a lot you have to learn about big industrial corporations,' he said. 'Boeing, for one, aren't just churning out war-aircraft for profit. They're deep into scientific projects that'll create good standards of life for people in peacetime . . . I certainly won't be working on military hardware.'

If she had heard, she was paying no attention to him. She was looking at Sean, who was sitting slumped over the dinner debris. 'Have you ever spared a thought for the Asians in Vietnam? Do you realize that there are two generations in South East Asia who've never known peace? who've never been free from the fear of guns and bombs? And you — you nice, white, American boy — you have the freedom to kill them. How does it feel?'

Greg was reading in bed, trying to concentrate and not doing too well, when Stella walked into his room. She took off her short red nightdress and lay down beside him.

'You gone crazy!' His heart was beating up to his neck.

She put a finger on his lips, as light and fragrant as a blade of summer grass. 'I'm sane, lover . . . You want me, don't you?'

'Yes . . . Not like this . . .'

'Jesus, I'm not attacking you. What's wrong with you?'

He had to laugh. 'So you're not attacking.' Unthinkingly he ran his hand along her slender flanks, caressed a full round breast. 'Stella . . . I don't want you to spoil your stay with us. Go back to your room . . . please.'

'Know somethin'? You're in danger of becoming a fucking saint. You're already half-way there.'

'Why pretend that you're a tough third-world hooker?'

'Maybe I am.'

'You're not fooling me.'

She took his hand and put it between her legs. He felt the dense hair, surprisingly soft, the warm moisture.

'There was another man,' she said. 'He gave me a child . . . She was still-born. He was a no-good black . . .'

'I don't want to know, Stella.'

'There is nothing more to know . . . Greg, I want you like you want me. You're gentle.'

He was gentle, and slow, giving himself up to every second of her sunlike heat, waiting for her to reach the climax before letting himself go. She held him inside her, face buried in his neck, murmuring love.

They talked of the good times they'd spent together in the little house on Nineteenth Avenue and he realized how attached Stella had become to Fiona and Sean. He called her *O thou fairest among women*, and told her how the Song of Solomon had come into his mind the evening she'd hobbled into the living-room for the first time. *Look not upon me, because I am black, because the sun hath looked upon me*, he quoted for her.

In the middle of the night, between sleeping and waking, he became aware of her standing over him, her red nightdress bright as a flame in the lights of a passing car. It seemed he'd heard her say, 'I've paid what I owed you.' But that couldn't be — surely. A nightmare. The nightmare had stopped; he turned over and went back to sleep.

He was up early, before the others. He took a shower, dressed and went to the kitchen. Swedish pastries for breakfast. He put them in the oven and switched on the coffee-pot. The leafless sycamore in the yard was gleaming in the winter sun, dark and vital like the body of his girl. On the top branch a couple of starlings were quarrelling over a crust of bread.

Sean came in, fair head tousled. 'Letter for you, Greg. Coffee ready?'

'Help yourself.'

There was no postmark on the envelope. Greg slit it open with a kitchen knife. Stella's handwriting. *Dear Greg, I don't know how to say this, but it's goodbye. Give my love to Sean and Fiona. I'm moving right away from California. It's best for you and me. Don't waste time on trying to find me. I've given up my room downtown and I've left no forwarding address anywhere. My thanks to the three of you for everything.*

Greg kept reading and rereading the note. It hadn't been a nightmare after all; she had said *I've paid what I owed you.* And yet he couldn't believe that she was capable of such cruelty. He could see her in the Chevrolet beside him, battered and sick, and all she'd said had been, *I hurt him? Did I hurt somebody?* She'd been in a terrible state, yet what had worried her most had been the thought that she might have been defending herself and hurt someone in the process. That was the thing to hold on to; she was capable of aggression, but not cruelty. In any case, why should he be thinking of his finer feelings? It was Stella he should be thinking about. What would become of her, without anyone of her own, without a job, without a college that would give her the chance to claw herself out of the Third World pit?

'Hey,' Sean was looking at him. 'You OK?'

'Sure.'

'Stella's late. There's something wrong with her time-switch.'

'What do you mean?'

'The way she mistimed her spiel about Vietnam last night. We meant to celebrate your new job.'

'We did.'

'What she said stuck in my gullet.'

'She was too cynical about industrial companies profiteering from military hardware. But she was right about Vietnam. It's a tragic, futile war; and it won't stop Communism in South East Asia.'

'Greg, you'd better be wrong about that. I didn't want to spoil our evening but . . . you see, I've opted for Vietnam.'

'We've worked out . . .'

'Yes. But we didn't take into account the kinda thing that's happened at San Francisco State, did we? Seems I'm my father's son, Greg. I have no use for anarchy, neither do I like the idea of fighting my own friends on campus.'

'You're making too much of it.'

'I don't think so. As I've got a choice of . . . enemies, Communists will make a more justifiable target.'

'It's not a matter of targets. It's people who . . .'

'Who are innocent? Greg, I've seen a film . . . fifty seconds of on-location camera-reporting. A small boat full of American marines sailing along the Meekong Delta, close inshore. Little Vietnamese kids on the banks, cheering and waving their arms. A marine throwing them candies. A child throwing something back . . . a hand-grenade that obliterates or mutilates half the marines on board . . . Maybe if Stella had seen that clip she'd quit using emotive phrases like *freedom to kill*. Innocent people? In Vietnam innocence is dead, and it's Communism that killed it.'

'What's happening at San Francisco State's hitting all of us. But when we move to Seattle . . .'

'That's not the answer. You know it, don't you? Stella meant well last night. She guessed what was on my mind. Trouble is, she's got a lousy time-switch.'

Greg folded her letter and put it in his pocket. He suddenly felt ice-cold. That self-conscious grin on Sean's face . . . like eight years ago, when he'd thrown a ball for the dog and broken mother's kitchen window.

He said, 'You're in the army. You've gone and done it.'

'Yeah . . . I should have told Stella before dinner. It would have stopped her freaking on us.'

114

ACADEMIC FREEDOM

England 1970

16

Greg watched a flurry of snow drift over the quadrangle of Churchill College. The buildings he could see from the speakers' platform were modern enough for Cambridge, Massachusetts. A pity. Having landed in Cambridge, England, on his first ever trip out of America he would have preferred a vista of the beautiful ancient buildings of King's College. But he was not ungrateful to the abominable Mat Scobie for sending him to the symposium, an international gathering of engineers and scientists interested in space technology.

Mat had told him that he'd be meeting a catholic mixture of chemists, physicists, mathematicians, astronomers and specialists in unlikely subjects. It's what he himself would have expected; in space studies all the sciences seemed to connect or overlap. Greg didn't flatter himself that he had been sent to Cambridge as an academic prodigy. As a former university lecturer he'd been chosen for his ability to give a well-structured talk — not so much a learned dissertation but a plug for United States achievements, a bit of flag-waving in the unfortunate climate of the Vietnam war.

Greg reined in his thoughts. The chairman — must remember not to call him Mr Convener — had almost finished his introduction. The people in the lecture hall, between three and four hundred of them, looked a good audience — a mixture of teenagers in the obligatory jeans, a sprinkling of women, and a number of gentlemen with distinguished white hair and with-it whiskers.

'Since the first man landed on the moon,' continued the chairman,' on 20 July 1969 — a brief seven months ago — we've had the privilege of welcoming distinguished Americans who were actively involved in extending the frontiers of science . . . and who shared with us the excitements of their new worlds.

'As the data, gathered during the Apollo 11 Mission, are being analysed by the experts of the National Aeronautics and Space Administration new questions arise . . . In fact, the new knowledge is already suggesting new lines of investigation.

'Future missions to the moon will be asked to carry out experiments such as . . . measuring the make-up of the ambient lunar atmosphere including gases as thin as one billion billionth of Earth atmosphere. They will study the gravity waves, predicted in Einstein's theory of relativity.

'Medical tests and experiments are likely to include determining biological effects of exposure to high-energy heavy ions in cosmic radiation . . . and the phenomenon of light-flashes penetrating closed eyelids.

'Many of the space achievements and future plans – conveyed to us via the media – have become part of our everyday lives. Yet I, for one, must confess to abysmal ignorance about the organization and administration – which must be vast and incredibly complex – that sent men to the moon and brought them back to a pre-arranged point on our globe, south-west of Hawaii, to rendezvous with a ship of the American navy.

'I have no doubt that our speaker, Dr Gregory Murphy, will disabuse us of any idea that space missions come about by spontaneous combustion.'

Greg picked up the chairman's point. There had, in fact, been an element of spontaneous combustion in the development of space programmes – the ambition of President Kennedy who, on 25 May 1961, had proposed to Congress that the United States accelerate the space programme, land a man on the moon and return him safely to earth by 1970. No doubt it would be left to future historians to assess the importance of that appeal in the light of subsequent events, the assassination of John F. Kennedy in Dallas and the accession to the presidency of Lyndon B. Johnson.

Johnson certainly maintained the impetus created by Kennedy, earning the distinction of having a key complex of the space project named after him – the Lyndon B. Johnson Space Center, JSC, twenty-five miles south-east of downtown Houston, Texas. The headquarters of NASA were in Washington DC; but Greg suggested that he could best demonstrate the scope of the whole undertaking by telling the audience something of JSC's tasks and commitments.

JSC covered an area of 1620 acres where previously there'd been small towns and pastures. Its one hundred buildings had opened for business in September 1963. The building most familiar to television viewers of the moon-landing would be Mission Control, where flight controllers at rows of consoles had been studying the data that helped them make mission decisions.

JSC was responsible for the design, development, and testing of the spacecraft and associated systems for manned flight; the selection and training of the astronauts; planning and conducting the manned missions; and participation in medical, engineering and scientific experiments designed to help man understand and improve his earthly condition.

Greg outlined some of JSC's facilities designed to help determine that spacecraft systems and materials can stand up to the rigours of space-flight: Building 32, for example, Environment Simulation Laboratory, containing two vacuum chambers — one of them 120 feet high and 65 feet in diameter — where a complete spacecraft could be subjected to a space-like vacuum as well as temperature extremes of 280 degrees F. below to 260 degrees F. above zero. In nearby Building 49 — Vibration and Acoustic Test Facility — space hardware was buffeted by equipment simulating the shakes and sounds the spacecraft would experience in flight. Mission Simulation and Training Facility, one of the most sophisticated installations, could be tied in with the Mission Control communications system so that crews and flight controllers could practise the entire mission many times over before the actual flight.

On the management side JSC was responsible — to mention one specific area — for co-ordinating the work of hundreds of contractor companies who were helping to build the space programme. These companies were located throughout the States and ranged in size from small workshops with just a few employees to corporations employing tens of thousands of people.

John Whitmore, sitting with Kole Okango, in the third row, surrendered to the fascination of the facts and figures bombarding him from the platform. The task of bringing together the products of hundreds of companies, hundreds or thousands of miles apart, assembling them in the proper place at the right time and making the whole work as planned, was truly monumental.

'Some cricket team,' murmured Kole. He was making notes which he'd later share with John. Dr Murphy's talk didn't exactly contribute to their new electronics course or postgraduate studies, but it was somehow relevant.

Greg told the audience that the space programme had so far involved 20,000 contractors from American industry and 420,000 employees, 35,700 of them working for NASA, and federal funds of $40 billion. Up to the first moon-landing they had spent less than $20 billions of the funds — which was cheap at the price when one considered that the Americans had spent four times as much on liquor, twice as much on cigarettes and more on betting and foreign travel during the same period.

As Greg talked of the Life Sciences Directorate at JSC, and the advances in the work of that department, John wished that Andrew had had time to attend the symposium. But at medical school a student's nose was kept to the grindstone.

He took a notebook from his pocket and began to jot down headings. *Blood pressure or heart-monitoring sensors so small that they can be inserted by a hypodermic needle rather than surgery . . . Contamination control procedures to keep operating and recovery-rooms infection-free . . . Remote monitoring equipment that lets one nurse keep a continual check on 64 patients at once . . .*

119

A health-care system for the 4400-square-mile Papago Indian reservation in Arizona using telemetry and other space electronic techniques . . . An adaptation of space food as a means of ensuring that senior citizens have easy-to-prepare nutritious meals . . . Transducers used to measure spacecraft splash-down-impact incorporated into a device for precision fitting of artificial limbs.

It occurred to John that the speaker might help him obtain more material on these medical advances. If only he could persuade Andrew to continue his studies in the United States, eventually. Postgraduate work after qualifying in 1974. Anything to keep him out of Africa. Andrew hadn't talked of the future. After the massacre of Kisumu neither of them had spoken of Africa. Yet John suspected that even Kisumu hadn't turned Andrew against the continent he loved. He was keeping in close touch with Aunt Helen McGregor and Uncle Angus in Rhodesia.

What John feared was that Andrew might eventually go off to work in Angus's practice. For the moment Ian Smith, going it alone, was holding Rhodesia together . . . with some help from the South Africans and certain commercial companies who were defying the sanctions imposed by Britain, America and others. But how long would the Smith regime last? Kole Okango, his black Rhodesian friend, received sufficient private information to make him stay out of his country. It wasn't only a matter of guerilla attacks on white farms but feuds between the Ndebele and Shona tribes. Kole predicted that the whites would suffer while black killed black. Kole, with his fastidious, scientific mind, wanted no part in it. He meant to stay in England.

John was aware that Gregory Murphy was looking at him and forced his thoughts back to that excellent talk.

Greg was winding up with a short list of companies which were taking part in the space program, illustrating the immense distances involved and the formidable range in industrial effort. Manned Space Flight Support Operations, Department of Defense, Air Force Eastern Test Range, Florida; The Boeing Aircraft Company, Seattle, Washington State; H-Alpha Telescopes, Harvard College Observatory, Cambridge, Massachusetts; Chrysler Corporation, New Orleans, Louisiana; Martin Marietta Corporation, Denver, Colorado; McDonnell Douglas Corporation, St Louis, Montana; Rockwell International, Downey, California . . .

'If such diverse companies can work together,' said Greg, 'if companies that have at times been in cut-throat competition with one another, can be co-ordinated in one great achievement, then surely there is hope that − one day − the widely diverse countries on our planet will weld into one united, peaceful world.'

'Or split up,' said Kole, 'into even more vicious . . . better equipped war-machines.'

John had been programmed to give the final talk of the day. After listening to Greg Murphy's polished performance — the man hadn't referred to his notes once — he'd reduced his own paper to a half dozen headings on a card smaller than his palm.

He'd been thinking about the presentation of his paper on and off for months, even at Kisumu. The only audience he'd ever faced had been fellow-students in a debate at the Union — and that had been a political debate on the African situation. One could fluff about politics and situations, not science and engineering. When he'd prepared his lecture he'd been satisfied that it was all good solid meat; now he was acutely conscious of its small scope and theoretical nature.

Professor Carey, the man responsible for putting him on this platform, was briefly and elegantly introducing him by referring to his graduation work, mentioning that he was now studying electronics and predicting a brilliant future for him. Dear old Carey. He might as well have said, 'The lad's been one of my brighter students. He's keen on his subject and I want to encourage him. He's young and earnest — only twenty-four — so kindly put up with him. We've all got to learn, haven't we?'

As John rose he felt weak in the knees, dry in the throat. And then he saw Kole's black, anxious face. It hadn't occurred to him that his cool, ironical friend might be suffering on his behalf. Suddenly calm, he began to speak.

It was as if some unknown force, a quirk in his personality of which he'd been ignorant to this moment, had taken possession of him.

He talked easily, lucidly, of the structures, soldered components, and joints welded by laser, which he'd subjected to a range of stresses, weights and compression processes. It came to him as a revelation that he was speaking to individuals who were interested in what he had to say. Their eyes met his, and he became aware of the connections building up between him and them.

There was the swarthy athletic-looking man — possibly a Spaniard in his thirties — sitting with an attractive fair woman who reminded John of his mother. Or perhaps they were older than they looked; the boy beside the woman — not far off twenty — was obviously their son. He'd inherited his mother's honey colouring and his father's square chin and aquiline nose. A family whose attention didn't stray for one moment.

There was the bulky man in his fifties, with the uncompromisingly short haircut and luminous grey eyes, who was making notes. And Gregory Murphy, wiry, with an Irish face which might have appeared sharp-featured but for the peculiar gentleness John had observed in other intelligent and highly educated Americans. Gregory Murphy, John assessed, was no more than three or four years older than he. But the small age-gap was perhaps the most vital of one's life at this stage, making all the difference — professionally — between a floundering fledgling and an adult travelling with assurance in his chosen direction.

John made himself blot out the individual faces and took in the whole of the audience. Now . . . to convince these people that his work hadn't been a waste of time — and arid academic exercise; that there was one area at least in which it could be applied practically. What he had in mind was the Deep Space Network, which was open to improvements to its system of large antennas arranged at stations around the world.

As the earth turned on its axis, he concluded, the antennas helped provide constant communication with distant spacecraft. The antennas in Australia, Spain and California passed information back and forth between spacecraft and the control centre at the Jet Propulsion Laboratory, Pasadena, California. Each of the three Deep Space Network stations had a sixty-four metre antenna and a system of smaller antennas. The Network, still in the early stages of communications development, provided a large and exciting field for study and experimentation.

John sat down to applause which sounded genuine. He felt as drained as if he'd taken his aged stallion over the jumps at Hickstead. But it had been worth it. He'd learned something about mastering his nervousness, and Kole appeared satisfied with his talk. Professor Carey was inviting questions from the floor. It would have been a moment of happiness if the woman who'd raised her hand had been the girl in a sari.

The tag on the bulky man's lapel identified him as Dr Igor Balatov, Byurakan Astrophysical Observatory, USSR. He cut a runway through the cocktail party, lumbering at John's group as stolidly as an Aeroflot Ilyushin. 'Now ve have reached our true purpose.' The luminous grey eyes twinkled at Kole, John and Greg. 'You know what a symposium is? No? I tell you it is a drinking party.'

'Is that right?' Greg smiled at the Russian who was so obviously enjoying himself. 'I looked it up too. Symposium is the title of one of Plato's dialogues. In twentieth-century usage it's a convivial meeting for drinking, conversation and intellectual entertainment.'

'For me it is entertainment.' Balatov took a sip from his tiny liqueur glass — he was drinking crème de menthe — and had some difficulty peeling the glass off his full lower lip. 'Who cares about the *intellectual*? In England, I have learned, it is not good manners to name a man an intellectual . . . It is a big rudeness. For sure I am not one. I am only a humble star-gazer.'

'A practical one, I reckon,' said Greg. 'I read about your work on radiometers when I was a student.'

Balatov shrugged. 'A gadget for measuring heat radiation from a planet.'

'Or a satellite,' suggested John.

'I am here to compliment you,' Balatov changed the subject. 'Mr Whitmore, you gave a very good paper. Have another drink.' He took John's glass and cut across to the bar.

Greg watched him shoulder into the crowd. 'He's quite a guy. Did some real pioneer work on the radio frequency spectrum. It was his plan that led to the international agreement on allocating the S-band and the X-band to space communication.'

'He did his masters a service,' said Kole. 'Here we are, with the S-band between 2290 and 2300 megahertz and the X-band from 8400 to 8500 MHz. And that made an end of space privacy.'

'Not for long,' said Greg.

'Privacy will operate for shorter and shorter periods as we go along . . . on both sides of the Iron Curtain,' agreed Kole. 'But when Balatov's scheme was adopted it gave Russia an advantage.'

Balatov came back and handed John a very large whisky. 'Your good health, young man.' He raised a wine-glassful of crème de menthe. 'I favour sweet drinks. Why not? Think of the energy I derive from the sugar. When it snows one needs much energy. I come from Russia with snow on my boots; I come to Cambridge . . . more snow. At school, a hundred years ago, I learn that palm trees grow iń England in the open. Where are they?'

'In Torquay or Brighton,' John told him.

'You have seen them?'

'I have.'

'They must be as vigorous as my rose trees. But every winter I have to bend the heads of my rose trees to the ground and cover them with straw and sacks. Ah!' He'd caught sight of a tall, fair man at the far end of the reception hall. 'My nanny is looking for me. The Soviet Union is looking after her sons, my friends. Abroad they always give me a nanny to say "Igor, you have had enough liqueur" . . . to take me to my hotel . . . to get me to the airport on time . . . to vipe my bum. Adieu my friends: I vill hasten to my nanny.'

'First Russian I've met,' Greg was puzzled, 'outside Americans of Russian extraction. What do you make of him?'

John said, 'He's just giving himself a good time.'

'Have you met other Soviet Russians?'

'I saw a party of them in Africa.'

'Where?' asked Kole.

'At the Country Club in Nairobi. And they were not enjoying themselves.'

'It's hard to think of a man like Professor Balatov as an enemy.' Greg shook his head. 'Even the word *enemy* is outdated. We're supposed to be fighting Russianism or Communism in Vietnam. Where will it get us? What if the Communists did capture the whole world? What would they do with it? They couldn't possibly control it.'

'They'd have a good try,' said Kole. 'Power isn't something that people like us find easy to understand. A politician's desire to dominate must be a form of disease . . . though a lot of people who're not politicians enjoy a milder version of the same disease; professors, who build their departments into little empires . . . businessmen, who build up industrial and commercial conglomerates . . .'

'The pontiffs at the Pentagon,' said Greg. 'Some general whose signature on a piece of paper sent my brother to Vietnam.'

David Volatian stood alone, with an almost empty glass in his hand.

'What are you drinking?' John asked him.

'Orange juice, but I've had enough . . . This symposium isn't good for me.'

'Why's that?'

'It's proving to me that I'm ignorant.'

'That's what a lot of us are learning. What do you do?'

'I'm going to study geology. But first I'll do my army service . . . two years.'

'It's compulsory in Israel?'

'Of course. We are a small country surrounded by Arab nations who're pledged to destroy us. We're not going to let it happen.'

'Your English is excellent.'

'My mother is an American . . . an Israeli of American extraction.' David told John the history of his parents — his father's fantastic walk across Russia, his mother's survival in a German concentration camp — with an uninhibited pride John found admirable. There was no false modesty or reticence; David knew that his parents were exceptional people and took it for granted that John would be interested in them. He talked of Israel with equally strong affection.

'You see this?' David took a stone from his pocket, a polished pebble in brilliant colours of emerald green and navy blue. 'Eilat stone . . . you won't find such malachite anywhere else in the world; only in the Sinai Desert, in the old workings of King Solomon's copper mine.'

'It's a beautiful stone.'

'Sinai and the Negev are full of wonderful minerals. People have the wrong idea about deserts; they're not desolate or barren. I can look at our deserts all day and not be bored . . . just watching the changes; early in the morning the sky and the rocks are asbestos grey and you can feel their age. Then, as the sun rises and travels through the day, the colours change all the time . . . from a misty rose-colour to burning red, from deep gold to purple. Just by looking at the rocks at different times you can tell what they are and what lies beneath them.'

'You'll make a good geologist.'

'Perhaps. I might work with my father. His firm will be building an improved body-scanner. It's a machine for taking pictures of people's bodies in transverse sections: it shows up more than ordinary X-rays. The firm's going to make its own semi-conductors soon.'

'What are semi-conductors?' John tested him.

'Oh, it's a sweeping term for all transistors,' said David grandly and accurately. 'Geology — minerals — comes into their manufacture. One uses quite a variety for growing crystals in the laboratory . . . germanium, silicon, gallium arsenide, indium antimonide. Why should we import microchips from America or Japan if we can make them ourselves? Israel must become self-sufficient. In time we'll even grow enough food.'

'I've read about your farms in the desert.'

'Sure. We've followed the agricultural advice in the Bible. It's all there. And it's beginning to work for us . . . My mother's signalling. She wants me to change for dinner. Black tie. Is it necessary?'

'You won't be thrown out if you don't change.'

'What's the point of black tie?'

'A tradition, I suppose.'

'Maybe it makes everyone at the tables feel that nothing more important than the dinner's happening anywhere in the world . . . not even revolutions and wars. All's nice and safe until after the Queen's been toasted.'

'You've got something there. My grandmother still changes into a long dress in the evening, even when the dinner's baked beans on toast. She says it's the sort of custom that made the British Empire great.'

David laughed. 'An innocent arrogance . . . *Now, you savages; put away your bows and arrows this instant. Can't you see? We're dressed for dinner.'*

The evening took off in an unexpected way — after dinner. John and Greg had walked to their hall of residence together and were strolling along a corridor to their rooms when they heard the sounds of a guitar-like instrument and a magnificiently rich baritone voice. They stopped and listened at the door.

'Could it be live?' asked Greg.

'I think it is,' said John.

'What's he singing?'

'A Scottish folksong. Only, he's making it sound Russian.'

'Professor Balatov?'

'Don't think so. Balatov's got a higher voice.'

'He's great, whoever he is.'

Suddenly the door opened and they were face to face with David Volatian and his mother.

125

'I'm sorry,' said Greg, 'I guess we were eavesdropping.'

Shmuel, mandoline in his arms, joined them and all at once they were laughing.

'Come in, come in,' Shmuel invited. 'Do either of you know "The wee Cooper of Fife"?'

'I do,' said John. 'An aunt of mine's married to a Scot.'

'What does *nickety nackety roo roo roo* mean?'

'Nothing . . . they're just nonsense words that sound Scottish.'

'There was a wee cooper who lived in Fife,' sang Shmuel, 'Nickety nackety roo roo roo . . . and he did have a pretty wife.' He looked up at John. 'Does that sound right?'

'Try it a bit faster.'

'Don't try it,' said David's mother. 'Not now. You'll waken everyone in the building.'

'Esther, I'm singing quietly.'

'Man, you don't know the carrying power of your voice.'

'I'll run through . . . just once.'

Esther suppressed a smile. 'Sit down everyone, if you want to listen to him. I'll make tea . . . Shmuel, keep it below radio noise-level.'

Shmuel did, yet even his quiet tones were full of rich music. He sang on between cups of tea — Israeli songs with echos of older countries, English and French songs, American railroad ballads.

As spontaneously as the party had started it changed moods. They talked of the places that meant most to them in Israel and Kenya, America and England. They talked of themselves, discovering points of shared experiences and concerns. None of them felt complacent about the future.

The Second World War had formed the lives of Shmuel and Esther. Their son David, unlike his parents, accepted the probability of violence as a fact of normal life. He had a country of his own; he'd fight anyone mad enough to dispute his rights as an Israeli, and he would — naturally — win. John and Greg, born years after the World War in a period when negotiations between the superpowers still seemed a solution to conflicts, had lost their illusions in the little wars which had hit them personally; they dreaded, above all, those *minor* incidents throughout the world, deeply aware that any one of them might spark off all-out nuclear war — the destruction of life on this planet.

John asked Greg about the medical advances in space research, making no secret of the fact that he wanted to keep Andrew out of Kenyatta's Kenya or guerilla-ridden Rhodesia. By the time Andrew qualified the world-pattern might have changed considerably, but he still considered the States a safer place than Africa. Greg promised to send John details of space-medicine research projects. John didn't doubt that he would.

126

Greg handed round colour pictures of Sean and Fiona. John knew that it wasn't unusual for Americans to travel with family photographs, yet he was touched when Greg produced his. It seemed Greg's way of saying, 'I know how you feel about Andrew.' Sean, in uniform, looked as immature and self-conscious as a schoolboy; Fiona, with her gleaming auburn hair and inquisitive blue eyes, was beautiful even in the amateurish snapshot.

Esther showed pictures of her house and garden at Ramat Hasharon, bright tropical photographs protectively shrouded in a plastic folder.

In case they missed an opportunity of meeting again during the symposium, they exchanged adresses. John and Greg left the Volatians with the sense that the evening had been a beginning. As Esther closed the door John heard the aggressive buzz of her telephone.

He looked at his watch. One in the morning. Who'd be calling at this time? He said good night to Greg and went to his room. While he undressed he worked out the time-difference between Israel and England. Though why shouldn't the Volatians get a phone-call in the middle of the night? None of his business, in any case. Yet his anxiety persisted until he fell asleep.

By morning it had stopped snowing and the sun was lighting up the windows of Churchill College. John looked up his programme. There was no major lecture until the afternoon. He'd find Greg and the Volatians and suggest taking them on a tour of the old colleges.

Down in the dining-hall he saw the Israelis sitting at a table by themselves. John, noticing their grave faces, remembered the late-night telephone-call. He was tossing up whether or not to join them when Shmuel caught sight of him and called him over.

He said, 'Bad news I'm afraid.'

'I wondered . . . I heard your telephone.'

'That was nothing, John. It's Greg.' Shmuel gave him a scribbled note.

Greg had written that he was taking the first plane back to the States. Sean was being flown home from Vietnam, badly wounded.

17

'You selected an odd time for making this appointment,' said Shmuel.

Kirov sat down in the carved pew beside him. 'Yes. I had to cope with the great Professor Balatov, who got drunk but wouldn't lie down.'

Shmuel didn't let wariness interfere with his enjoyment of the King's College chapel — those soaring pillars, the miraculous lace-work in stone. Fifteenth century craftsmanship that had survived the lunacy of civil and world wars. No matter what part of the symposium he missed, he'd take Esther and David to the choir practice, hear voices filling this magnificient building.

He said, 'I should have thought you're too senior for playing nanny to Balatov, Alexei. Not even a GRU job, is it?'

'I made out a good case for joining him. Balatov's work has military . . . significance. He's important.'

'That important?'

'We're not keen on another defection like Medvedev's.'

'Balatov's suspect?'

'Not yet. By the time a comrade's aroused suspicion it's usually too late.'

'I take it our meeting in Cambridge is not accidental.'

'No, Shmuel. I've gone to a lot of trouble over it.'

'What for?'

'I owe you for saving my life in Eritrea.'

'Touching, but I don't know what you're talking about.'

'There's no tape-recorder. The chapel isn't bugged.'

'I have nothing to say to you. It's you who wants to talk.'

'Very well. I want to talk about our last encounter. My party was ambushed by the Eritrean Liberation Front. Our transports were blown up, my men killed. I was flung clear . . . as you well know. With that severed artery I'd have bled to death if you hadn't dealt with me.'

'So you say.'

'I regained consciousness when you dumped me — considerately, where I'd receive medical attention. Why deny it?'

'You certainly did your duty as a Soviet officer,' said Shmuel, 'sending your men to hunt me down. If they'd suceeded, what would you have done with me?'

'Let's stop pretending, Samuel. You weren't sent to Eritrea by anyone in the Presidium. I checked you out.'

'So?'

'I know that Misha Borodin no longer exists. But Samuel Volatian is not unknown in Israel.'

'Smug bastard, aren't you . . . Count Krasnykov.' Shmuel studied the troubled face — younger-looking since the Colonel had lost weight. What was Alexei driving at? admitting that he'd *checked* him out; saying, in fact, that he might have stirred up a hornets' nest in Soviet intelligence. If Alexei was so grateful for the rescue in Eritrea, why risk exposing him? And why, having drawn Soviet attention to him, make a confession of it now? Warning him? Yet such behaviour was not uncharacteristic of a Russian; do the damage first, then wallow in remorse and show your gratitude. 'All right, Alexei. You've relieved your conscience — if you have one — so go back to Balatov. He might be recovering from his hangover.'

'Don't go.' Kirov put a hand on Shmuel's arm. 'I know what you're thinking; but it wasn't quite like that. When we met in Eritrea, I believed your story that someone in the Presidium had sent you . . . you were convincing. All the more reason why I couldn't afford to be wrong. Yes, I did send my men after you; but my orders were that you should be treated as a VIP. Don't you see? I had to be sure. I gave you the benefit of the doubt even after you'd disappeared . . . Back in Moscow I didn't report our meeting. I made my enquiries privately. You must believe me.'

'Why should I? Have you forgotten Marayevo?'

'Is it likely? If you hadn't taken care of me the typhoid would have finished me off.'

'So? I scraped you off the floor and you stuck a knife in me.'

'You believe I was doing much the same when I sent my men after you in Eritrea?'

'Yes.'

'And again, checking on you in Moscow.'

'Looks like it.'

'Samuel, what can I say?'

'Don't torment your Russian soul, Alexei. Let me be. I'm an electronics engineer, the director of a commercial company making medical diagnostic machines. My interest in Eritrea was scientific . . . not military and not political. Is that clear?'

'Yes, I accept that you do something beside *obtaining* shiploads of uranium for Israel. The point is . . . I need you.'

Shmuel laughed. 'That's better. Now you're making sense. How can I be of assistance to you, Count Krasnykov?'

'Your people must have arrived at *some* conclusion.' Kirov stared into the distance, at the priest silently reading at the lectern.

'What were your final conclusions?' asked Shmuel.

'We got nowhere; and we lost our geological specimen. You might have been more successful. I'm sure you didn't walk out of the camp without taking samples.'

'So that's what's bothering you.'

'I want to know — personally — what caused that sickening holocaust in Eritrea. Those faces . . . they still give me nightmares.'

Shmuel had visions of Alexei in his tent, smug and overfed. The face before him now was tormented — the face of the boy who'd seen his mother killed by starving marauders, the flotsam of a savage war; the boy who'd been on the verge of death. Was Kirov to blame for what he'd become? It must have taken great courage to survive the aristocratic upbringing — to live an irrevocable lie — and hold one's own as an officer in Soviet Army Intelligence. He said, 'I know no more than you. What happened to the Eritrean village is still a mystery to me.'

'No radiation?'

'None.'

Kirov nodded. 'I have negative confirmation of that. We had a nuclear disaster . . .'

'In Russia?'

'Yes. In the Urals. A device was being tested. Several hundred people were killed by accident. I myself didn't see the aftermath, but I saw reliable reports and pictures of the bodies. They weren't husks like the Eritreans. What you and I saw in Eritrea is completely unrelated to any known killer. Do you agree?'

'I'm no expert. But, yes, you're probably right. Where does it get us?'

'We now know that someone's designed a weapon more terrifying than anything in the atomic arsenals.'

'Nothing I can do about it. You said you want help.'

'I don't know what to do, Samuel.' Kirov put a hand to his forehead. 'I don't know. You can tell your people about the nuclear accident in the Urals.'

'You're volunteering information?'

'For what it's worth. At the moment I can't think what more can be done to help identify the new killer.'

'Are you planning to defect, Alexei?'

'Is America more humane or high-principled than Russia?'

'The American people have more power than the Russian people.'

'Yet they can't control their politicians any better than we can. Vietnam proves it.'

'It doesn't. Nixon's going to run down the war in Vietnam. I talked with an American yesterday; he told me that the President's pulling out fifty thousand troops, and that these reductions will continue. The sad

130

thing was that his brother — who'd just been sent to Vietnam — has been shot. Greg Murphy believes that popular pressure in the States will force Nixon to finish the war, whatever the result.'

'The result will be a Communist victory and the ruin of the American economy. In the States wars create prosperity. The continuing demand for military goods keeps unemployment down and profits up.'

'You haven't answered my question. Are you going to defect to the west?'

'I'm trapped.'

'What's that supposed to mean?'

'Nothing would make me leave my wife and my sons behind. They're all I care about. Even the holocaust in Eritrea wouldn't affect me as it does if it weren't relevant to my family. I'm like a blind man, straining to see into the future . . . and I'd give my life if I could stop desecrations such as we've seen in Eritrea. The nightmare is that it could happen to my own family. How is it going to end?'

'If it's the world you're talking about . . . Russia believes that the western empires are encircling her. It's what Russia's believed for a long time . . . when she fought for a sea-exit in the Crimean War a hundred and seventeen years ago, and now, in 1970, when she's instigating little wars such as the Eritrean conflict . . . yet again trying for a sea-exit, this time past the Horn of Africa into the Indian ocean. In case the Eritrean adventure fails, Russia's now working on an alternate strategy . . . political subversion in Iran. It's beginning to show results. The Shah is being driven into maintaining his position by police-state methods. Given an unstable Iran, there's nothing between Russia and the sea-exit except Afghanistan . . . a relatively primitive country.'

'But not a country the west is unaware of, Samuel. The British fought no less than three wars between 1838 and 1919 to keep Russia out of Afghanistan. At least, that was Britain's excuse.'

'No mere excuse, as it turned out. In the end Afghanistan did conclude an alliance with Soviet Russia.'

'My point is that the British — now the American — *empire* isn't blind to Afghanistan's strategic importance. You over-simplify Russia's options.'

'Yes, and her ambitions. Your people want the oil of the Middle East, uranium from South-West Africa, etcetera. Yet greed is not Russia's driving force. The aquisition of raw materials would be a bonus rather than the objective. What keeps Russia on collision course is her traditional fear of encirclement and invasion . . . her old-fashioned claustrophobia and paranoia.'

'And the West?'

'To the West, Russia inevitably looks like an aggressor, hell-bent on expanding politically and territorially.'

'A world at cross-purposes . . . Yes, it is the underlying problem. If it isn't solved — soon, very soon — human life on this planet will have ended by the turn of the century.'

'Alexei, this is getting us nowhere. You're unhappy about the future of your family. So are parents throughout the world, I imagine. We've had a friendly belly-ache about the unfriendly world. What's the point?'

'Information, for a start.'

'On the new mystery weapon? You think both sides should have it.'

'Yes . . . unless it can be destroyed.'

'There's nothing you or I can do about that.'

'Between my organization and yours . . .'

Shmuel shook his head. 'Can you see exchanges of information between your GRU and Mossad?'

'Hardly. But you and I are well placed for . . . comparing notes.'

'To what purpose?'

'If one can identify the danger one can protect one's own . . . perhaps. I want a means of contacting you; that's all for the moment.'

'You contacted me.'

'It wasn't easy.'

'Who was your Israeli informant?'

'A man inside Mossad . . . Lipski.'

Shmuel hadn't expected the brutally direct answer. Was it supposed to prove Kirov's good faith? *I give you the traitor in your organization; you trust me forthwith.* Naïve? No, sheer desperation. Kirov's proposition was not uninteresting. If the Rav Aluf agreed, a contact venue might be arranged. He said, 'I can't give you an answer now. There's someone I must consult.'

'One person?'

'Yes. How often do you go abroad?'

'Three or four times a year. It depends . . . I'm free to travel.'

'Your freedom, Alexei, is academic.'

'I'm not denying it. But I have ways and means.'

'Let's keep it simple. Give me your private address.'

'Very well. One has to begin somewhere. Samuel, I trust you.'

'Count Krasnykov trusting an Armenian Jew? How have the mighty fallen!'

There was affection in Kirov's smile. 'How will we fall — all of us — if we don't even understand what's about to hit us.'

'I've got the message, Alexei. Go back to your hung-over professor. I expect we'll be in touch.'

'You'll let me know if anything emerges?'

'That won't be my decision.'

'Your chief will take your advice.'

'Perhaps. I'm less hopeful than you. We haven't much to go on, have we? A holocaust in Eritrea, accomplished by means unknown, except that radiation was not involved . . . unless it was short-lived radiation. A nuclear accident in Russia, which resulted in deaths of a dissimilar nature. The rest is ignorance.'

Someone had begun to play the organ — a quiet passage from a Bach fugue. Kirov sat slumped, too drained to make a move, delaying his return across the divide.

'Balatov was drunk,' he said, at last.

Bulky Balatov, a little glass of green liqueur stuck to his bottom lip . . . not amenable to supervision by his *nanny*.

'Drunk, Samuel . . . though not too paralytic to kick me in the teeth. He positively relished telling me who perpetrated the Eritrean slaughter. Not the Americans — as I had been led to believe. It was a Russian experiment. It went wrong, but Balatov finds the results . . . encouraging.'

18

Greg Murphy stood facing the machines in the intensive care ward. The machines appeared to have claimed the frail body on the bed, made him a mere component of the life-support systems. As Greg saw it, the current purpose of Sean's body was to keep the monitor screens going, supplying them with a continuous record of his blood-pressure and pulse-rate.

Impulses conveyed along the wires at his chest and ankles were activating the electro-cardiograph; the tube emerging from his mouth connected with the monitor showing his respiration-rate; the tubes in his arms and his nose maintained the functions of machines dispensing proteins, fluids, blood, drugs, electrolytes, etcetera. Nothing was inviolately Sean's. Even the eyes, as impersonal as the buttons on an electronic console, expressed nothing. Greg no longer believed that he'd seen recognition in those eyes; it had been a trick of light or his imagination.

The scientific young doctor had given Greg a run-down — on the machines. Even the floors in intensive care were made of a space-age thermosetting polyurethane plastic, the articulated drip-feed dispensers of a new tungsten fibre-reinforced nickel super alloy four times as strong as previous nickel-base alloys. And the fasteners on the doctor's gown were of the latest pressure-sensitive type, designed for use in spacecraft.

Sean Murphy? The doctor had made a visible effort in trying to relate to the *component* on the bed. Oh yes, the patient. Multiple injuries.

Chances of recovery? Well . . . he'd survived the flight from Vietnam for no good reason. The odds now? Ten per cent in his favour. Wouldn't put it higher than that.

'It's a vicious circle,' the doctor told Greg. 'The billions that go into war should be spent on medical research and equipment; but without the war we — in the veterans' hospitals — wouldn't get the wide range of injuries necessary for testing equipment-performance.'

The bleeper in his breast-pocket sounded off. He nodded distractedly, crossed the thermosetting polyurethane plastic floor and disappeared through the electronically operated doors.

Greg touched his brother's sunken face. 'You can make it, Sean. Show them, for God's sake.'

He walked out into the wide empty corridor and stopped at a window. Was the frame made of the new tungsten fibre-reinforced nickel super alloy? If so, what for? to make the garbage of the ultimate war more durable? Dusk was paring away the concrete and steel walls of the high-rise company offices until they seemed disembodied columns of light suspended in mid-air.

Sleek high-technology structures erected upon the rubble of obsolete redstone family houses which had been built by obsolete people, craftsmen whose skills were now out of date. Some obsolete people were in the back-alley down below, hanging around in a litter of cola cans and wind-shredded newspapers; derelict drunks, too, who'd probably die of exposure during the night. Sean shot to pieces. What for? And he? A man of the progress-process. That's how the doctor had seen him; that's why he'd spent so much of his precious time explaining the machines served by Sean's body.

Someone had come to stand beside him. He knew it was Stella. Unsurprised, he turned and looked into the alien black face that was so familiar. In his curious state of fatigue and clairvoyance he understood her dread of the racial divide which had made her escape from him in San Francisco. She'd fled because of her fears — fear of her own people as much as his, fear of the lacerations that would be inflicted upon them both if they ignored the divide.

'Sean . . .' she murmured. 'I had to come . . .'

'I know.' *Whitey*, she'd once called him — fighting the love in her. Smug whitey in his safe white world. Now no longer untouched by grief. No safer in his white world than she in her black; there was Sean, wired up to the machines. Greg took her hand. 'Let's go home, Stella.'

They took the elevator down to street level. Fiona was waiting in the foyer. 'There's been a call for you. Mat Scobie wants you.'

'How does he know I'm back?'

'He telephoned England. There's been a break-in at your laboratories.'

Reply to Overkill 2000 Pol-Strat.   16 December 1970

Dear Bob,

As you have anticipated it will take my Committee several months to process the information and estimates you have sent us. Obviously, your request for additional funding cannot be considered in isolation. We cannot cut back on the war in Vietnam at this stage, nor can we contemplate further reductions in the Space Program without wasting NASA's impressive schedules. The President, rightly in my opinion, is totally opposed to raising extra funds in the normal way; there is a limit to the burden the tax-payers can tolerate. Take away the profit-incentive and you lose vital private investment in industry and research.

This brings me to the points you raise concerning the technical problems with a re-usable spacecraft. I agree, for once, with the guys in FBI that it would be bad for public morale to release news of the prototype's crash. Any report of failure in the Space Program, at this sensitive time in the Vietnam war, would be counter-productive.

I cannot see how my Committee can be blamed for the crash. The project was more than adequately funded. It is Rockwell's consistent overspending which has made nonsense of the budget. I can accept that something might go wrong with a heat-shield consisting of 30,000 plus tiles, no two alike, which have to fit within two- or three-thousandth of an inch. But why have such a hell of a lot of other things gone wrong? blown valves, faulty welds, cracked turbine blades, broken ball-bearings, split fuel feeds. You cannot blame the whole lot on lack of funds. I reckon NASA engineers and scientists are not yet ready to build a craft that can stand up to temperatures of 2700 F. In my opinion, no amount of money will make them more ready.

I also question the CIA report included in your package. I've heard the same CIA song since the Berlin Airlift. Russia is overtaking us with bigger and better guns, bombs, missiles, sputniks. This part of the report is, in my experience, blatant CIA empire-building. CIA's latest story that the

Russians have developed — or are developing - a killer worse than any nuclear missile lacks credibility, based as it is on a speculative report on a poorly defined satellite picture. Besides, the report admits that the disturbance might have been caused by a freak weather-pattern.

According to my information there is nothing wrong with our American equipment. It is still second to none. My colleagues in the Senate should know, exposed as they are to the pressures of lobbying armaments manufacturers who present genuinely impressive cases in their quests for Government contracts.

The geopolitical side of the CIA report is another matter. It is most disturbing. Believe me, Bob, none of us here is underrating the shortcomings of NATO. Our European Allies are still divided among themselves on their budget-contributions. None is prepared to spend the realistic rate on defense. And France's isolationist attitude constitutes a positive danger to the coherence of the European Alliance. The vital factor, that Europe is permanently in the Russian firing-line, seems to have become submerged in the interminable financial and tactical squabbles.

I agree with you; the latest CIA report makes one fully aware that one will wake up one morning to find that the Russians have smashed through western Europe, that 150 million Europeans including the NATO Forces are dead and that the rest of the Continent is dying from radiation. I am unhappily convinced that the holocaust is not far off. Therefore your request for additional NATO funds must take priority over all your other defense needs, including the Vietnam requirements.

As you say, the bulk of Europe cannot be saved. The wasting of the NATO Forces can achieve no more than save us precious time for carrying out the First Strike policy.

I am glad that Montana has made it into the Pentagon, but should he too fail in stopping the infighting among the Generals, even the First Strike policy will misfire. I cannot bear contemplating the resulting carnage among our people. I assure you I am under no illusion that we are facing the gravest ever threat to our survival.

I regret that I am in no position to go along with all the issues you have raised, but I assure you that the whole package will be exposed to careful consideration at the next full meeting of my Committee.

With all best wishes for Christmas and 1971,

yours,

Edward

FREE ENTERPRISE

America, Rhodesia, Israel 1973

19

The thief who'd broken into Greg's laboratory had found nothing of scientific or industrial value. The theft of a typewriter and a visual display unit deceived no one; the burglars had been searching through the files, and the break-in was treated as an attempt at industrial espionage.

While Sean, in hospital, was slowly but successfully fighting for his life, Greg was beset by the security men called in by Mat Scobie. The Co-ordinator's attitude puzzled him. If he had been in Scobie's position he'd have contented himself with the fact that the intruders had done no real harm and stiffened his security arrangements against future attempts. He certainly wouldn't have blown up the incident into a full-scale investigation resulting in a five-hundred-page report that travelled all the way to the White House.

Alan Nagel, who'd known Scobie for some five years, believed that the whole exercise was designed to draw attention to Scobie's thoroughness and dedication. It was Alan, determined that he wouldn't assist Scobie's ego-trip, who suggested that Greg should withhold the information where he kept his research-notes on *Project Glass Mountain* , his work on new types of photo-voltaic cells.

Nine months after the burglary Greg had a final interview with Scobie. He paid little attention to the Co-ordinator; he had more important people on his mind. Stella and he were about to get married. His parents were coming to Seattle for the wedding. Soon afterwards, Sean, now fully recovered, would be returning to his base in California. Greg had hoped that he'd leave the army, but Sean had made up his mind to train at Military College and go for a commission. It pleased their father if no one else. Sean's friend, Fergie, who'd also been injured in Vietnam, was optimistic; by the time the two of them got through college the war in South-East Asia would be over. President Nixon was keeping his promise; the troop withdrawals were continuing.

' . . . no exception to the rule,' Mat Scobie was saying, 'that all files must be locked up in thirty-two B.'

Greg returned his attention to the incongruously long, narrow head — not unlike a snake's and equally expressionless. 'I've read the instructions, and initialled the file copy.'

'There's still a lack of written information concerning your department which I find surprising.'

'I've had no complaints from Dr Nagel.'

'I know, we've been into the subject more than once; but I still don't understand how you store the data you gather in the course of your research work.'

'In my head . . . as I've said before, Mr Scobie. When the experiments are completed — successfully or not — I'll write them up and give my report to Dr Nagel.'

'It should be quite soon.' Scobie got out from behind his desk and accompanied Greg to the door. 'You must have some observations on the silicons. You introduced some impurities, didn't you?'

'Yes.' The question had jolted Greg. One of the lab-technicians might have mentioned the *impurities* . . . without giving away a secret. What wasn't known to anyone but himself was the nature of the impurity. But why should Scobie take an interest in this particular area of his research when — by his own admission — he was just a security man who knew nothing about electronics? He replied, 'One doesn't get results overnight.'

'Well, science is advancing fast these days,' said Scobie, in one of his rare attempts at cordiality. 'I guess the stuff you're putting into the silicon's meant to act as a catalyst.'

'What would be point of a catalyst?' asked Greg blandly.

'I don't understand crystals and silicon chips but wouldn't an impurity — deliberately introduced — loosen the electrons . . . make them more mobile?'

'Where did you get this idea?'

Scobie managed to look embarrassed. 'I've had a stab at reading science journals . . . not that it's getting me any place. Reckon I've got it wrong.'

'Reckon you have.' Greg didn't care whether the dislike he felt for the man showed or not. 'I'll give you some literature — including an article I've written — that'll explain to you why it would be a good thing to manufacture crystals in space. Up there they'd grow clean and big. The trouble we have growing them on earth is that they get contaminated with impurities! However, the articles won't be news to you, will they?'

Scobie's face tightened in anger. 'As I said,' he spoke slowly, 'I do not understand silicon chips.'

After the final mission to the moon, by Apollo 17 on 6 December 1972, there were signs of depression in firms which had been contractors to the programme. The projected Skylab, the plan for sending scientific satellites into space, was still in a state of flux.

Alan Nagel, anticipating contraction and unemployment in the large space-industry firms, decided to leave Boeing for a comparatively small but highly specialised firm, Lake Erie Electronics Corporation of Detroit, LEEC had a second opening, at newly built laboratories in Ann Arbor, for a technical director. Alan persuaded Greg to apply. There were more than thirty candidates but Greg got the job. It meant more responsibility and additional administrative work. It also meant a move across country to a university town, into a community which would accept more readily than most Greg's black wife and their year-old son Steve. Fiona agreed to move with them. In Ann Arbor there was no shortage of work for computer programmers.

As LEEC had been under contract to the National Aeronautics and Space Administration throughout the Apollo project Greg succeeded in steering his firm into the Skylab programme.

He was at the Kennedy Space Center in Florida when the first un-manned Saturn workshop was launched on 14 May, 1973, at 17.30 Greenwich Mean Time, atop a Saturn V launch vehicle from Pad A of Launch Complex 39.

The workshop's initial orbit was 269 miles circular with an inclination of fifty degrees to the equator. The blast-off went according to schedule, but within an hour of the launch ground controllers became aware that something had gone wrong with one of the two solar array wings which provided about half the electrical power in the Skylab. Then the meteoroid shield failed, with the result that Skylab was unprotected against solar heating and the inside temperature rose to 126 degrees Fahrenheit.

Troubles mounted. The break-up of the meteoroid shield broke the tie-downs that secured one of the solar array systems. Complete loss of this array system occurred when the exhaust plume of the S-II stage retro-rockets impacted the partially deployed solar array system.

Eleven days later, a number of Skylab's problems still unsolved, a Saturn 1B lifted off with a repair crew. After five revolutions and ninety minutes of station-keeping the Saturn docked with Skylab.

Greg was too absorbed in the bedevilled space mission to think about food or sleep. He fed on the nearest available thing — usually hamburgers — and snatched two or three hours' rest after the more acute problems had been solved and the astronauts were taking a break.

Astronauts Kerwin, Conrad and Weitz succeeded in fixing a parasol type and two sail shields of reflective cloth which protected Skylab's exposed areas from direct sunlight and brought down the inside tempera-ture to seventy-five degrees. They coped with yet another power pro-blem when four of eighteen battery packs in the telescope-mount power supply system showed that they were taking less than half the charge from the solar arrays — a result of overheating earlier. Conrad and Kerwin spent more than four hours in extravehicular activity — floating in zero gravity — and freed the jammed solar wing and the array.

By 8 June it became clear that the mission would succeed in carrying out its research programmes, such as the monitoring of solar flare and the gathering of data on man's adaptation to zero gravity.

Greg left the Kennedy Space Center as relaxed as if he'd been on holiday rather than spending twenty-hour working days. The Skylab Programme would go ahead until the third was functioning in its orbit, and the third Skylab would be designed to stay up for at least ten years. The amount of information it would yield was incalculable.

On the flight home he was joined by a man with a deeply tanned face and thick white hair, someone he'd noticed among the Skylab controllers at the consoles.

Harry B. Resnick was an engineer at Rockwell International Corporation. He'd been in space research from the beginning and he'd lost none of his enthusiasm.

'I don't know where the years have gone,' he said to Greg. 'When I was a boy my father told me that I'd be flying in airplanes that would cross the States between lunch and dinner. Look at us now. I sure hope I'll live to see those factories in space . . . and power satellites that'll provide the world with all the energy it needs. Imported oil's getting expensive and it won't last for ever. I'd like to see us independent of foreign countries, especially the Middle East.'

Greg thought of the Israelis he'd met in Cambridge — David Volatian, with his unspoken but uncompromising devotion to the single idea of his people's sacred right to its homeland. A new breed of zealot, combining an ancient sense of direction with scientific ingenuity and modern knowledge. 'How well do you know the Middle East?' he asked Resnick.

'I've made a study of it, Mr Murphy.' The engines were droning evenly through the white skies, the jet moving north as unspectacularly as a subway train. 'The oil-sheiks' money can buy them Manhattan, but not the minds of their own people. The minds of the poor — the underprivileged as we call them when we're running scared — are not for sale. That's one thing the Soviets understand better than us. You should read a book by one of the earliest Communist defectors, a man called Jan Valtin. I'll send it to you . . . No need to give me your card; I know where to find you.'

'You've been in touch with my firm?'

'No . . . With a certain investigation at Boeing.'

'I see.'

'A curious business, that burglary.'

Greg suddenly remembered where he'd come across Resnick's name before; in an article on Nixon's space policies. Harry B. Resnick was a scientific adviser to the President. 'What did you make of the report?'

Resnick shrugged. 'A minor Federal Bureau of Investigation exercise.'

'Mat Scobie, an FBI agent?'

'Yes. I reckon he figured he'd earn himself promotion. It was a trivial affair . . . yet there was something about it that didn't smell right.'

20

It was at breakfast that John felt most aware of his grandmother's absence. She'd always begun the day in pleasant silence, reading her newspaper and mail but passing the toast and pouring the coffee. She'd worn long housecoats in brilliant colours which had looked good with her dark eyes and immaculate white hair.

There'd been no obvious reason why he should have become increasingly reluctant to let her live on her own, but one of his reasons for taking the job at Seespeed Engineering had undoubtedly been the firm's proximity to Gran Whitmore's village.

One evening after dinner she'd shown him a report in *The Times* of a massacre in Rhodesia, the savage killing of a white farmer and his family. 'I can't tolerate it any more,' she'd told him imperiously. 'How our British government dare call those murderers *freedom fighters* is something I'll never understand. It's nothing less than treason against our own people . . . who made Rhodesia . . . who turned the wilderness into fertile land. I've written to your aunt, John. Helen and Angus must come home. As to Andrew and Terry, you should put your foot down. You really shouldn't allow them to settle in Rhodesia.'

'They have settled in Rhodesia.' He'd tried to dissuade his brother. Greg Murphy had unfailingly kept him informed of the advances in space-medicine and of job opportunities for newly qualified doctors. Andrew had been interested in the American idea, yet in the end Africa had pulled him back. Terry had encouraged him. She'd go wherever Andrew went, but her African roots were as strong as his. 'Gran, I have no control over Andy.'

'You're not without influence,' she'd insisted. 'You've always been close, the two of you.'

'What do you want me to do?'

'Andrew and Terry have been in Rhodesia for almost a year. Their rose-tinted spectacles will be off by now.'

'They weren't on in the first place.'

'Be that as it may . . . I think you should go to Salisbury and deal with

143

the situation on the spot.'

He'd laughed. 'Perhaps you should go.'

'And arrive for my own funeral? I think not.'

'Gran . . . aren't you well?'

'Perfectly. But I'm not inclined to witness the destruction of Africa — and this country — by cheapjack Communists and wealthy Socialists.'

'You're looking tired.'

'At my age I'm entitled to. John, worry about Andrew and Terry, not me. I've never had a day's illness in my life.'

'Lakomi told me you almost died of pneumonia.'

'Now that's a strange thing . . . I've never accepted pain or sickness. Whenever something was wrong with me I had the curious sensation that it wasn't me who was ill, but someone else . . . some outsider I didn't know. It'll be that outsider who'll die, much to my surprise, not me . . . John, there's a cheque on my desk, made out to Inland Revenue. Send it off to my accountant, would you. I've considered withholding my income tax until the government changes its Rhodesia policy, but I've discovered that I dislike such . . . demonstrations even more than the government. . . . And to see to it, please, that my obituary goes into *The Times*. Challoner does this sort of thing admirably, but check the dates; he's not always accurate. He's not to mention my age.'

'Gran, hadn't I better call the doctor?'

'Certainly not. As you said, I'm a little tired. That's all. Don't worry, dear boy; I'm as durable as a dead butterfly.'

In the morning he'd found her dead in the armchair at her open window, facing the Sussex Downs.

She'd been gone from the old flint cottage for more than three months and he still missed her. He'd carried out all but one of her instructions; he still hadn't gone to Rhodesia.

John cleared the breakfast table and put Greg Murphy's letter in his pocket. Vincent Squire, grand old man of Seespeed, would be interested in Greg's description of Skylab's engineering problems. Between them they might even come up with a constructive suggestion. And with something like a thousand contractor firms working on Skylab, wasn't it possible that an English firm might be cut into the project?'

Seespeed Engineering was not working to full capacity. In the past Squire had been famous for his advanced boat and car designs. His firm had been in the forefront of the race for land and waterspeed records. Now there were few sportsmen left who could afford those expensive individually built machines. Though Squire had used genius and inventiveness in incorporating advanced electronics into his machines, the firm was building for reducing numbers of customers — chiefly foreigners.

144

Squire had decided that he was too old for the rat-race and that the firm needed new blood. He'd engaged John as his successor and he was handing over more and more of his responsibilities. From their first meeting Squire had been clear about his requirements; he wanted a well-qualified young man who'd stay at Seespeed and take the firm into the twenty-first century, allowing him to forget about business and enjoy himself in old age as he'd enjoyed himself as a youngster — in the workshops. At seventy he had the right to slip into low gear.

John locked the cottage and went across the yard to the old barn he used as his garage. He drove out his Saäb and opened the door for Billy. The King Charles spaniel, now a fit ten-year-old, hopped into the passenger seat.

Driving through the village to Burrow Hill John noticed the signs of an early autumn, the gold and brown of the trees, the last roses flowering on leafless stems. As a tropical man he wasn't looking forward to the English winter, mild as it was in the south. He'd be prolonging the summer if he went to Rhodesia now. He hadn't taken a holiday since he'd been at Seespeed Engineering. He'd suggest to Squire that he could combine the business trip they'd discussed with a visit to his family.

He might save the firm money if he took a round trip — London, Johannesburg, Salisbury, Tel Aviv, London. The political segregation of Rhodesia precluded a direct flight to Salisbury. Grandmother had been right. What was the point of imposing sanctions against Ian Smith's Rhodesia if Andrew could go to work there, if one could fly in via South Africa, if — according to Kole Okango — multinational companies were managing to trade with the outlawed country as profitably as ever.

John parked his car beside a familiar red MG and went into the office block, Billy at his heels.

'Miss Squire's waiting in your office,' his secretary told him.

Why couldn't she phone? or better still, wait until he called her? John didn't like Debbie's morning disruptions. Squire was aware of his daughter's relationship with him, but John doubted that the old man understood how casual it was — certainly on his part.

'I'm in two minds about it, John.' Vincent Squire gazed across his workshop at the new lathe. He didn't like interruptions in the middle of a job. 'What you're proposing is business rather than engineering, isn't it?'

'We'd be the sole British agent for the Karmel Company; that's the business side of it. On the other hand we'd be the only firm responsible for the maintenance and repair work on the body-scanner . . . the only firm with a stock of spares.'

'We haven't handled this kind of thing before . . . which doesn't mean that I'm against it, in principle. It seems to me our men would need training before we could let them loose on a million-pound machine.'

145

'The Israelis would let us have one of their engineers for a whole year. Two, if necessary. It would depend on how many body-scanners we, and they, can sell in this country.'

'At a million a time?'

'There have been a number of enquiries from teaching hospitals already. Some of the early scanners are out of date. The Israeli model's the most advanced.'

'No competition?'

'Some . . . from Germany.'

'Yes, I looked at the specifications from Siemens. A sophisticated machine. But I agree with you; I prefer the Israeli job . . . on paper. Obviously you'll have to go out there and see what goes on at shop-floor level. What I like about Karmel is that they produce their own computers.'

'But you still have reservations, Mr Squire?'

'We'll be letting ourselves in for a lot of administration and office work . . . meaning extra staff.'

'We should be able to afford it. The Israelis are offering generous terms.'

'An agency . . .' Squire wandered across to his bench and picked up the fractured piece of metal from a component he was rebuilding. 'Recognize it?'

'Looks like a fitting for a cathode. From an X-ray machine?'

'That's right.' The creases at Squire's eyes deepened. 'Dr Taylor's old machine . . . a good one that's been overtaken by new models. He can't get parts any longer.'

John sympathized. The old man was anxious to preserve the individuality of Seespeed, the flexibility that enabled them to produce components and whole machines which a large, more automated firm couldn't take on for economic and technical reasons. His attitude was not unjustified. According to Greg's letter, some of the most effective contractors working on Skylab employed as few as five to ten men. At Seespeed there were thirty-five engineers and specialist workers — a number small enough to operate as a team and large enough to build complex prototypes.

'I'm probably biased,' admitted John, 'in favour of the Karmel Company. Samuel Volatian's a personal friend.'

'You have a good case, all the same. It isn't as if we haven't handled computerized medical equipment before. Nothing as large as the body-scanner; but we're not inexperienced. John, put my hesitations down to old age . . . a certain reluctance to deviate from the beaten track. When do you want to go to Israel?'

'It'll have to be in October, after Yom Kippur. That's an important religious holiday for the Israelis. I thought of going to Rhodesia first.'

146

'Not the safest place in the world. I met a young journalist at the golf club who's just back from Rhodesia. He was required to carry a gun . . . and shown how to use it.'

'Outside Salisbury I suppose.'

'Yes. You don't seem to mind.'

'I'd rather face an ambush armed. Andrew and I learned to shoot when we were kids.'

'Ah yes . . . Kenya.' Squire shook his head. 'What a world. I've seen a film on TV; ten-year-old Arab children, drilled like soldiers, being trained to kill . . . Very well, John; make your arrangements for the trip. These days one can't turn down new work.'

John put out the bedside light. Debbie, stretching across his chest, switched it on again.

He resigned himself. How long before she'd let him sleep? 'What are you staring at, girl.'

'You, of course.' She ran a hand over him, tracing the bones. 'You have a beautiful body . . . long . . . lean . . . hard. Someone once painted men like you.' The fingers wandered to his face. 'Your eyebrows . . . so dark and silky; like a blackbird's wings.'

'All very poetic.'

'You're laughing at me.'

'Right. Debbie, don't light another cigarette.' He disliked the stink of stale tobacco in his bedroom. 'You don't need it.'

'I do.'

'I prefer the smell of your skin undiluted.'

'My chain-smoking's a cry for help.'

'OK, I'm listening. What's the trouble?'

'You. If only I could find you!'

'In case you haven't noticed . . . it's me you're holding down with your legs.'

'I'm serious. You know what I mean, John. We go out to dinner . . . show-jumping . . . parties, but you're with nobody, or anybody. I don't *feel* you with me. You're a stranger — always dressed in clothes which are so impersonal, so indifferent. There's something arrogant in the way you don't care a damn what you look like. You're making no effort to please me.'

'Haven't I pleased you tonight?'

'Sure. When we're alone your eyes sort of . . . heat up. It's the signal that you want to screw. Not me in particular. You're super in bed, but I think any woman would do you.'

He didn't care for her analytical moods. 'I'm a cold fish.'

'That you are not. You're not fooling me. You're passionate. I wish I knew what you're feeling passionate about.'

'Seespeed Engineering Ltd.'

'You're laughing again.'

'Why not? People laugh when they're happy.'

'Are you, John?'

'Sleeping with a pretty girl's no hardship.'

'Well, I suppose you've given me an answer.'

'Debbie, what is it you want?'

'To make you love me.'

'There are different kinds of love.'

'Oh, very profound.' She ground her cigarette into the ashtray. 'Every time I'm near to touching you . . . really touching you deep down . . . you slide out sideways.'

'Accept that I'm an unsatisfactory person.'

'But you aren't. That's my trouble. Hold me, John.'

The touch of her skin aroused him automatically. What he liked about her was her physical responsiveness. They were alike in their sexual voraciousness, if in nothing else. He played her body until he felt the impatient thrust of her pubic bone, then pulled her on top. She knelt across him, head thrown back, eyes closed. He watched the throbbing pulse in her neck. Her sensuality was a good substitute for love — the love he'd known with Leah. He was grateful to her, and in his gratitude he fondled her with the affection he felt for the old mare in his paddock or his dog.

He was still inside her when the telephone rang.

'Johnny, don't answer.'

He took her hips in his hands and lifted her off. 'People don't normally phone me at one a.m.'

'You bastard.'

'John?' The caller's voice was quiet but wide awake. 'Have you heard the news?'

'No, Mr Squire.'

'I've been listening to the BBC World Service. Better not book your trip just yet. Egypt's attacked Israel. Sounds like a full-scale war.'

148

21

The deep yellow light on the flowering hibiscus reminded Shmuel of Odessa — walking to the temple, hand in hand with his father, feeling the warmth of the cobbles through the soles of his shoes. A quality of ancient sunlight. He'd discovered it that day and worshipped it ever since. Worshipping in the synagogue had little meaning for him. In formal prayer he was addressing himself to tradition, not to God. Over the years he'd reduced his attendances until he went to the temple once a year only — at Yom Kippur. For the sake of his parents, who were entitled to one regular conscious act of remembrance, he did keep that sacred day together with the majority of Israelis.

Shmuel listened to the Cantor's performance — Jacob had a fine voice — but the ritual of prayer passed over his head, allowing him to contemplate the sundrenched flowers outside the austere temple. There was a commotion at the back. It wasn't unusual for someone to faint from hunger. Not everyone found fasting as easy as he did. He turned and looked for his son.

There seemed to be an exodus of young men. David motioned that he too was leaving. Shmuel waited to the end of the prayer, then made his way out.

People weren't supposed to use cars at Yom Kippur but many, who'd come into Tel Aviv from a distance such as Ramat Hasharon, did. David had been with a couple of fellow students; their Ford had gone. So had many other cars. Shmuel, as conscious of the quiet and the depth of sunlight as if he were feeling it for the first time, went along the border of scarlet and yellow canaas to his Toyota.

The usual Sabbath emptiness of the city reassured him, but beyond the centre he came upon a convoy of army trucks, lorries and cars packed with young men in uniform. No doubt now. They wouldn't be on the road at Yom Kippur unless a major alert was on. What had happened to the Arab-Israeli gentlemen's agreement that there was to be no act of aggression at Yom Kippur and at Ramadan, the Muslim holy day? Whichever country attacked on such a day would have the advantage of surprise.

Like other motorists Shmuel ignored the speed-limits and made fast time into Ramat Hasharon. He'd change into uniform and report to his unit. So would David. Normal procedure for reservists. David had been too young for army service when Israel had fought the six-day war in 1967. This time he was not. There'd be no one left to support Esther except her pupils, who would themselves fear for their fathers and elder brothers.

Shmuel left the car in the road and walked through his garden, oblivious of the orange and avocado trees which normally gave him pleasure. In the living-room the blinds were down, deadening the brilliant colours of Esther's Kelim rugs. She was in the kitchen, making sandwiches.

Without looking at him she switched off the radio. 'The Egyptians. They've started with an air attack. Their planes were picked up on radar, and they've been driven off. But there's a big army on the move. At Yom Kippur, Shmuel . . .'

'I know, love. Where's David?'

'Taking a shower.'

'He had one this morning, the boy.'

'He says . . . he doesn't know where his next wash is coming from.'

David appeared at the door, fair hair brushed flat, khaki trousers and shirt newly pressed — as immaculately turned out as if he were taking his girlfriend to a dance.

Esther wrapped an applestrudel in foil and put it in a plastic box.

'For me?' David lifted her off her feet. 'Mama, where am I going to put all this food?'

'In your stomach, son . . . where bigger strudels than this have gone.'

'I've got no room in my kit. *Ma-yesh*, the Egyptians will be dead scared when they see me come with an applestrudel under my arm.'

As Shmuel walked into the lecture-room at Strategic Command the briefing for the regular electronic technology officers was about to begin. Joram, his second-in-command at the Karmel Company, handed him a printout giving the geographical and tactical details which had been collated since the '67 war. The map screened on the wall would have been sufficient to remind Shmuel of the terrain, but he read what the computer had produced.

The Sinai Peninsula has three principal axes. One is the coastal axis, from Rafiah to the Canal; the other one is Ketziot — Abu Ageila; the third one is Quntyileh-A'Temed-E'Nahl-Port — Fuad-Suez. In addition to these three there are other axes which are marked on the map on your screen. Other than that, the approaches to Sharm el Sheikh are principally by air or sea along the western coast of the Peninsula. The aims of the campaign are to secure our borders, to halt the massive forces of our enemies and to drive every Egyptian out of Sinai. The 4th Armoured Division is moving from Bir temedeh . . .

The thirty officers in the room fell silent, eyes on the screen. The Rav

Aluf came in from a side door, his face pale and tight.

'This war,' he addressed the men, 'at Yom Kippur has caught us napping . . . almost. The result: our forces regularly stationed in Sinai are bearing the brunt of the Egyptian attack. They are outnumbered twenty to one. Reports are coming in of heavy casualties. Every one of our men is precious. None shall be wasted.' There were tears in the eyes of the man whose own exploits and courage were legendary. He made no attempt to hide them. 'Reinforcements are on the way. The first will be landing . . . about now. Before giving you your orders let me remind you — though most of you know — that you should not rely on the experience of past desert battles. No two have been the same.

'Though the Egyptians vastly outnumber us their professionalism and their — mostly Russian — equipment is inferior to ours. I see this as a war that will be won — by us — on the technological front. Laser will give us faster and more accurate communications than any system the Egyptians can deploy . . . which means that our forces will be better co-ordinated than ever before. Our progress in electronics — as you well know — is such that our bombs and rockets will hit their targets with unprecedented accuracy.'

'Rockets with nuclear warheads?' asked the major beside Shmuel.

'No. The brakes on nuclear war are still on, thank God. In any case we'll never be the first to use nuclear weapons . . . According to our intelligence reports the Soviets have supplied Egypt with their giant SS-9 missile. Our American Minuteman-III is more sophisticated and up-to-date. The warheads for Minuteman III are our own non-nuclear adaptation.'

The Rav Aluf was not telling Shmuel anything that he didn't know, but the dispassionate tactical discussion that followed brought a bitter taste into his mouth. Minuteman-III, with its multiple independently targetable warheads, was the most precise destroyer he knew. Oh yes, a technological war. Perhaps the first of its kind. Long-distance slaughter — without the aftermath of nightmares — by both sides. But on his side — hopefully not on the other — the new computer-based equipment he had developed since 1967.

Active service, such as his European travels in search of a shipload of uranium or the interlude in Ethiopia and Eritrea, had held back his work on medical and military computers. But his team at Karmel, made up of graduates from Harvard and Moscow, Cambridge and Heidelberg, had made up for lost time.

Shmuel would have liked to test his new computer systems in peace rather than war, but the Egyptians were forcing his hand. His fifteen miniaturized systems were going into operation now. Out there in the desert, four-ton trucks and armoured personnel carriers would keep the computers on the move; officers would be able to call up the enemy's order of battle on a screen and advise each other of their own positions from considerable distances. He caught himself speculating with excitement how well his systems would perform; then, almost immediately, the horror of lives lost overshadowed all other thought.

He saw hygienic, air-conditioned man at a console selecting the long-range target of a crowded city. It was possible now; it would become increasingly simple. And he? He was helping mankind build obsolescence into itself. If he wanted to be a true humanitarian he should encourage his medical and pharmaceutical colleagues to complete his work and abolish love. It shouldn't be too much of a problem; there already were drugs in existence that could change a person's feelings and responses.

The aircraft droning overhead hurt him as a physical pain. David was somewhere up there. Soon he'd be landing among the baking desert rocks, climbing into his tank and looking for a space for Esther's plastic boxful of applestrudel.

It was not one of Israel's short, sharp wars. The ten or fourteen days Shmuel had anticipated lengthened into weeks of savage fighting for the land east of Suez, for the Mitla Pass and the nomads' desert beyond. Shmuel, staring into the face of death yet again, went into a state of suspended animation. It was a time to be lived through, a time to shut out all thought of music, of cultivating one's garden and of the future.

He saw David once, shortly after the Israeli forces had gained control of the Mitla Pass and reopened the road to Sharm-el-Sheikh. The Egyptians had lost the initiative, the tide was turning, yet David's self-confidence troubled Shmuel. While he admired the young soldiers' convictions that they'd already won the war, he knew that he wouldn't be satisfied until the last gun had returned to the arsenals. David showed him specimen of rocks he'd been collecting. He said the mineral wealth of Sinai had yet to be tapped and he would specialize in exploring it . . . for oil, copper, even uranium. Sinai had lain dormant too long.

The end of the war seemed as sudden as its beginning. Shmuel, driving north along the coast road to Elat, found it hard to bend his thoughts to the work awaiting him at the Karmel Company, to life with his family in their orderly little house. He was still attuned to the disciplines and dimensions of the desert.

The sides of the road were littered with damaged tanks and trucks, cans and rags. He was about to pass a derelict tank when he saw something move. He stopped the scout car. His companions asked no questions, assuming he'd got out to relieve himself. The fluttering yellow object turned out to be a scarf, one end still attached to an Egyptian soldier. The man was sprawled over the side of the tank like a maggot hanging out of a rotten apple.

152

Shmuel lifted the dangling head. A boy not much older than a child. An unforgivable, stupid, ugly waste; but the tank had been knocked out with commendable precision

Shmuel received the message at Elat airport. He was about to board a troop-transport when one of his men handed him a flimsy envelope addressed to Major Volatian. Inside was a photostat copy of a page from *The Case of Sergeant Grischa*.

'Where did you get it?' Shmuel asked him.

'It was pinned up on the information board.'

For a moment his thoughts veered to Russia, the vandalized ballroom of Marayevo, the precious book in his hand. Alexei, as he'd discovered over the past couple of years, took calculated risks, but he'd cured himself of the Russian-roulette mentality and panache of his youth. He'd always put the safety of his wife and sons first.

As the plane trundled through the air, Shmuel studied the page. Having devised the code himself he had no trouble extracting Kirov's message. The war must have provided Alexei with a near perfect cover. The Egyptians had been fighting with Russian equipment, and Russian military advisers normally went with the hardware. Nor was it surprising that Russia had injected an experienced GRU officer into Israeli-Egyptian negotiations. One aftermath problem was the great number of Egyptian prisoners-of-war, many of them injured, who would be handed over to the Egyptian Red Cross — though not before agreement was reached on how many Egyptians were to be exchanged for one Israeli.

In Jerusalem Shmuel located Kirov at the hotel where the Red Cross personnel had been accommodated, and led him out into the steep narrow streets of the old city. The two of them attracted no attention in the crowds along the Stations of the Cross. At the temple where Christ had ejected the money-lenders, local Arabs were peddling souvenirs among sightseeing parties — as if the war had been no more than a rumour.

They leaned on the rails, looking down into the ruins of the ancient temple, ignored by tourists and traders. Jerusalem was full of uniformed men, many in far from conventional khaki.

'Your son?' Kirov's concern was genuine.

'Fine, last time I saw him. I haven't been home yet.'

'My Mikhail's managed to get into medical school.'

'That's good.'

'I think so. A doctor can make a living anywhere in the world.'

'Thinking ahead, Alexei?'

'Far ahead . . . very far.'

'Anything new on the Eritrean . . . experiment?'

'Nothing, except that Professor Balatov's been transferred to Semi-palatinsk . . . the back of beyond, where they're building new installations. I don't know what . . . yet. The African stew's simmering on . . . '

Kirov gave Shmuel a run-down of the Russian advances on the African continent. Within the year the number of Cubans training in Russia had doubled. Some had already gone to Angola. Frelimo, the guerillas fighting the Portugese in Mozambique, had been equipped with Russian SKS 7,62mm self-loading rifles and were forcing Rhodesia to redeploy her troops in the north-eastern sector. The Rhodesian guerilla forces of Mugabe and Nkomo were being equipped and trained by the East Germans. Political warfare against South Africa was succeeding beyond expectations, driving a wedge between the South African government and its British and American friends. Russian funds were going to dissidents inside South Africa. Money and arms were still being pumped into Communist groups in Ethiopia, Eritrea and Somalia.

'What I find most disturbing,' said Kirov, 'is the amount of plant and technology American firms are selling *us*. It's insane. There are peaceful uses for laser, but hasn't it occurred to our suppliers in the west what *more* the laser can accomplish? . . . such as separating uranium 235, for manufacturing nuclear bombs out of uranium 238. Your leaders in the west should put embargoes on the sale of electronics . . . but, above all, on nuclear reactors for so-called peaceful uses. Your western commercialism . . . the crazy scramble for big profits . . . is putting nuclear power into the hands of all and sundry. None of you can stop my people from producing new weapon-systems . . . but by not selling us the means of production you could slow us down. And you could slow down the rest of the world as well by stopping such sales . . . to 800 million Indians, 1000 million Chinese; oh yes, and your Arab neighbours. God protect us from your western *free enterprise*.'

'And your Soviet expansionism.'

'You don't have to rub it in.' Kirov helped himself to a cigarette and passed the packet to Shmuel. 'For you, old friend. It won't be my fault if your people waste what I'm giving them.' He turned and gazed into the deepening shadows of the crowded lanes. 'Adieu. I'll find my own way back . . . Thanks to my orthodox Christian upbringing, I recognized the Stations of the Cross as if I'd been here before.'

'Take care of yourself.'

'*Bien sûr*. I'm a family man.'

The rain had washed the dust off trees and shrubs; the garden smelled of clean air and wild flowers . . . like the Russian meadows, when he'd walked with his mother in high summer. His mother had bribed him to keep his mouth shut; ten minutes' quiet — one walnut biscuit, an hour's stillness — a slice of honey-cake.

Shmuel opened his front door. He'd ask Esther about that. What would a modern educationalist think of such bribery? He looked for

154

traces of his son. When David was at home he always left something on the hall-table . . . his keys, books, a comb or a newspaper. Nothing; except a bowl of shrivelled hothouse roses. Esther must have been uncommonly busy to leave dead flowers around.

He followed the sound of voices to the back of the house. A familiar sight on the verandah — Esther in her rocking-chair, surrounded by David's young friends and her own students — sitting on the floor.

As he walked in they stood up, all of them. He couldn't make it out. The *sabras* weren't renowned for showing respect to their elders — not that kind of respect. He became conscious of their silence, and in the silence the screech of a night-bird sounded like the voice of a lost child.

Esther came to him. No expression on her face; nothing at all. The smooth face of a sleeping girl. It was how she'd looked that day on the beach in Cyprus when she'd talked of the years in Buchenwald concentration camp. She held out her hand; opened it. On her palm lay the small star of David on a thin gold chain which their son had worn round his neck ever since she'd given it to him on the day of his bar mitzvah.

22

John's purpose in going to Rhodesia had been to see for himself how the country was making out under external political pressures and internal guerilla attacks but — above all — to persuade his family to leave.

A couple of days in Salisbury were enough to change his perspectives. On site, the outpourings of the British press seemed almost hysterical, the attitudes of the Rhodesians he met calm and purposeful. Andrew and Terry were working at the hospital — Terry as a theatre-sister — and neither was prepared to consider a move.

Aunt Helen, who'd married Angus McGregor in Kenya almost thirty years ago, told John that she sympathized with white farmers up-country who were leaving Rhodesia. They were the people under attack. But no one would go out of his way to murder a general practitioner — especially not in the middle of Salisbury — who cared as much for the blacks as the whites. Even if Prime Minister Ian Smith gave up and handed over to a black government nothing would change for doctors. The fact that marauders had killed teaching and medical missionaries in outlying districts was dreadful but probably unavoidable in a guerilla war.

155

Lakomi was happier than John had seen her since the separation from her husband. Helen and Angus had succeeded in getting Patel to Salisbury. He was teaching at a school for black children and living with Lakomi in a bungalow in the McGregors' garden. Their eldest son, Raspar, was still working on the Whitmores' former estate at Kisumu, Naroo teaching in Nairobi. Yes, the family was split up again, but the separations were such as normal life would bring about. It was natural for children to grow up and go their own way. If the Patels were worried about their youngest son, they didn't show it. Though far away, Okot was in Rhodesia and able to visit them every few months. Okot was now a qualified medical assistant running a children's clinic in an isolated country district. The Patels were proud of him.

In Lakomi's living-room John came face to face with the past, recent and yet so distant. Framed snapshots on the wall; Charles and Sarah Whitmore on the terrace with Andrew and Okot, Gran Whitmore holding John on her lap, the little fawn with Billy the pup — no doubt photographed by Andrew, John and the three Patel boys on horseback. And a picture of Leah Khalid outside the Kisumu hospital.

Lakomi had put a hand on his arm. 'She was like a daughter to me, John. It's right we live with her beautiful face and her spirit . . . with the joy, not the grief.'

Seeing the country from the air gave John a strange sensation of homecoming. How could he pretend not to understand Andrew's affinity with Africa when he himself felt moved at the sight of those imposing mountain ridges, the unique contours of the high veld. Whoever had called Africa the cradle of mankind had expressed no less than the quality of virile antiquity which the machine-age world had lost for ever.

As the plane turned south-east the country changed to savanna woodland and he could pick out the shapes of Australian wattle, thorn trees and mohoboho with their large spadelike leaves. Then the read earth faded into a sand-coloured distance, the arid Karoo of shale and grit between the Sabi River and the Mozambique frontier.

Andrew gave John the seatbelt buckle. 'Landing in five or ten minutes.' He'd made the flight from Salisbury to Fort Victoria before, accompanying medical supplies for Okot's Mission. 'You don't want to stop at Victoria, do you? Jeremiah — that's Okot's driver — will want to push on to Sibatanda. Best to get there before nightfall.'

'Unsafe to travel after dark?'

'One's got to be sensible, that's all . . . avoid making a target of oneself.'

'Can it be avoided?'

'I think so.'

'Andy, is it necessary for you to go within a few miles of the border?'

'It's not obligatory, but they're glad of surgical help. Okot's doing a fantastic job out in the wilds — with very little back-up — and I'm probably more use to him than some stranger who doesn't appreciate conditions in such an area . . . I had my doubts whether I should take you for the ride.'

'In case of a guerilla attack?'

'It can't be ruled out. Reckoned you haven't forgotten how to handle a gun. Okot will be happy to see you. It's an isolated existence at Sibatanda. He hasn't even got a woman.' Andrew smiled. 'Quite a while since we've been on safari together. Zimbabwe National Park's not a game reserve like Tsavo . . . but we'll be going through early enough to see a few baboons and impala. You didn't bring a camera? Never mind; you can use mine.'

The plane landed smoothly and emptied quickly. Jeremiah and the Mission's Mercedes truck were waiting for them. The old Shona tribesman was shaking his head at the sun. Too hot for November. The monsoon, which usually swept in from the Indian Ocean and Mozambique, had given Sibatanda very little rain in October. Now the drought was killing off the vegetables. There wasn't even enough grazing for the goats.

In the Zimbabwe reservation the waterholes had almost dried out. The long leaves of the gumtrees looked brittle with dryness, the tough Karoo grass as brown as if a bushfire had swept the land. Families of baboons were migrating towards the high veld, where they'd attack crops on the farms. The deer, in groups of ten or twelve, were also travelling west, away from the arid Mozambique frontier.

John watched the golden impala, their lyre-shaped black and white tail-markings aflash in the sun, with the spontaneous pleasure of rediscovery. The gazelles, moving more languidly than usual, were ethereally elegant and graceful.

Beyond the reservation the road deteriorated into twin tracks of tarmacadam, cracked or broken in many places. Eventually it petered out altogether; the Mercedes bucked through the bush kicking up a great plume of red dust.

Andrew unwrapped a package in the rear of the truck and took out a gun. He gave it to John. 'Routine. But keep your eyes open.'

Sibatanda Mission was a group of eight wattle and mud houses behind a stockade. Okot's staff consisted of four boys, untrained medical assistants, and three elderly women who did the cooking and cleaning, with Jeremiah — driver and man of all works. Conditions were primitive, yet the twenty children in the hospital looked clean and well cared for. Okot's work was his life. Most of the children were suffering from nutritional diseases, such as kwashiorkor, due to lack of protein, from gastroenteritis and bronchopneumonia. Okot had a couple of surgical patients for Andrew, a boy with appendicitis and a girl with a knee injury which required the removal of a torn cartilege.

Okot had arranged a special meal for Andrew and John — a young goat, roasted on an open fire out of doors, followed by paw-paws which Andrew had brought from Salisbury. For a while they talked about the family, the McGregors and Terry, Okot's parents and brothers, but Okot soon returned to the subject of his patients.

The bulk of his work was done in clinics for outpatients, mothers bringing their children — sometimes considerable distances — for treatment and advice. The majority had come from the poor Karoo country on the borders of Mozambique. Suddenly the flow of patients from the area had stopped — some three weeks ago. Okot was puzzled and deeply concerned. He was thinking of going there himself. After Andrew had operated on the children he should be able to spend a couple of days away from the Mission.

'You aren't thinking of going on your own?' asked Andrew.

'Jeremiah's the only one I could spare, and he's frightened of the guerillas. We've had one visit from them.'

'What happened?'

'We were lucky. I'd been treating the child of the leader. They took some food and left us in peace.'

'Okot, you mustn't go on your own. You can't drive and shoot.'

'Shooting mightn't be necessary.'

'Too much of a gamble.'

'I've got to know what's stopping those mothers. They meant to come back to the clinic . . . their babies were getting better.'

Andrew looked at John. 'Well?'

'All right.'

'We'll go with you,' Andrew told Okot.

'Good.' It was no more than he'd expected. 'When will you operate?'

'Tonight.'

'Then we can leave first thing in the morning. I'll put Kwendu in charge. The children like him. He'll manage.'

They'd been driving for a couple of hours before the sun soaked up the heat-haze and made the Land-Rover as hot as a furnace. The country was dull semi-desert, outcrops of rock, grit and stunted thorn. They saw the odd pole and dugga hut, but apart from a skinny goat the land looked deserted.

It was afternoon before they reached the village of mudhouses with a petrol pump and a shop advertising Coca-Cola. They stopped under a gumtree. Okot walked down the empty road, John and Andrew went over to the shop. It was wide open but unattended.

When Okot returned to the car he looked worried. 'There's not a soul in this village. At this time of day people should be indoors.'

'Guerillas?' asked John.

'No.' Okot wiped the sweat out of his eyes. 'There's no food in the houses, but it doesn't look like they've been looted . . . The place is abandoned.'

'People leaving their possessions behind?'

'Nothing they couldn't carry . . . Let's go on.'

Andrew asked, 'Isn't this where your patients came from?'

'Some. But most of them live on the other side of these hills. In the valley they grow enough to keep them going . . . there's some water draining down from the Sabi. Come on; we'll make it in half an hour.'

Andrew took the wheel. John and Okot, guns at hand, watched for movements among the bleached rocks. They were close to the Mozambique frontier but there was no sign of guard-posts or patrols. John thought how easy it would be for bands of guerillas to infiltrate Rhodesia at this point. But what for? Precious little to live on, no one to terrorize, nothing worth stealing.

'That's it.' Okot was pointing to a curved boundary ahead. It looked like the scorch-line of a bushfire. 'What have they been doing?'

'Sure it's the right place?' asked Andrew.

'Yes. But this . . .'

They stopped at the edge of a black crater, at least a mile in diameter, and got out. Okot stared into the deep, empty hole. 'What's happened? I don't understand it.'

John picked up a grey lump and examined it. 'Concrete?'

'There used to be an army post,' said Okot, 'a military training area. Then the farmers moved into the concrete blocks. Cooler than their dugga huts.'

'Could someone have dropped a bomb?' asked Andrew, 'to spoil it for the guerillas?'

It was a theory they soon abandoned. Driving along the edge of the crater they were struck by the comparative absence of debris. The piece of wall John had picked up was the only one of its kind. Had the place been dynamited or bombed the periphery of the crater would surely have been littered. Another curious feature was that thorn trees within a few feet of the scorched edges were green and undamaged — not a branch, not a twig marked or broken.

'They should have told me,' muttered Okot. 'Why didn't they tell me?'

John loosened his grip on the gun. His palms were wet, his body stiff with tension. There was something weird and menacing about the great black hole under the white-hot sky and the thick total silence.

They had almost completed their circuit of the crater when Andrew suddenly jammed on the brakes. 'Someone . . .'

159

Before them lay the body of a woman, a baby beside her. John had never seen faces so contorted with terror and pain. The bodies were naked and almost transparent — like cocoons which had disgorged the life within them. They stared at the gruesome husks, locked in the nightmare of the creatures' suffering. At last Andrew stirred and picked up his camera.

He trained it on the bodies. 'We must find out how it happened . . . If it was a nuclear accident . . .'

'No.' There was no doubt in John's mind. 'It was no explosion . . . of any kind.'

'We'll have tests for radio-activity.'

'They'll be negative. Are you taking pictures of the crater?'

'The whole area.'

As Andrew panned into the distance something beside the bodies stirred. A black-necked cobra came sliding forward between the stones, making for the woman's hip. It lifted its head, darted nearer, retreated, hesitated, then struck. As it touched the fragile husk a barely perceptible tremor passed over the body. Caving in on itself it crumbled and disintegrated, leaving a human silhouette on the ground.

Back in Salisbury Andrew and John went to see Colonel Hobart, a personal friend of the McGregors. In his office at the barracks a whole wall was covered with a detailed map of Rhodesia and the neighbouring countries. Red studs indicated war areas and guerilla bases.

Andrew's photographs obviously shocked the Colonel. Grim-faced, he studied them with a magnifying glass. 'Never seen anything like it. As you know, we did run a training base down there, but we gave it up more than three years ago. Too awkward for supplies.'

'You left the buildings intact?' asked John.

'We did. Let the Shonas have them. Harmless farming people. Would like to know what happened to them . . . Tell you what. Man called Nambusere . . . comes from that district. Member of Parliament. Lawyer educated in England. Suggest you have a word with him. Might know something. Want me to organize it?'

John told him that he was leaving the day after tomorrow.

'See what I can do.'

That evening Mr Nambusere called Andrew and suggested a meeting at his office in the morning.

Nambusere's partnership occupied a suite in a prestige block in the centre of Salisbury. The black lawyer — middle-aged, corpulent and dressed in a cream shuntung silk suit — received them in a room panelled in fine African oak, furnished with an antique desk and expensive leather armchairs.

If Andrew's pictures distressed him he didn't show it. 'Some accident,

160

obviously. It's an area where there are bad thunderstorms during the rainy season. I imagine the woman was struck by lightning.'

'If she had been,' said Andrew, 'the body wouldn't have been . . . gutted like this.'

'Ah yes,' Nambusere smiled, 'you're a doctor. There is, of course, another possibility. An accident caused by something in the air.'

'We think bombing can be ruled out,' said John. 'There was no debris. The whole area was pulverized and driven deep into the ground . . . including the people.'

'You have proof that . . . more people were killed?'

'The whole population's disappeared . . . What did you mean by *an accident caused by something in the air?*'

Nambusere shrugged. 'Just a thought. Have you heard of Otrag?'

'No.'

'It's a German commercial company which is said to be making modules that assemble into satellites . . . communication satellites . . . spy satellites, whatever their customers require. They'll be selling to anyone, anyone who wants this kind of thing. Otrag has bought 250,000 square miles in Zaire . . . about 200 miles from Angola. No one really knows what's going on there.'

'A company permitted to build satellites commercially?' The implications made John feel uneasy.

'There are international air-space agreements, I believe. But Zaire's an independent country. If President Mabuto's government has sold certain concessions to these Germans, no one can intervene. There's been trouble of course . . . the revolt in Katanga for one. America's been protesting. So has Russia. In fact the Russians have put up a Cosmo satellite which is keeping a twenty-four hour watch on Zaire. None of it seems to worry Lutz Kaiser . . . he's the president of Otrag . . . or his technical director, Kurt Debus. Herr Debus used to work with Wernher von Braun at Peenemünde, making the first unmanned rockets for Hitler. One Otrag man — Wolfgang Pilz — has been physically attacked by Russian agents. Nothing happened to him, but his wife was blinded. So, you see, the German venture in Africa is generally unpopular. It's my opinion that Otrag's responsible for whatever happened in the Karoo.' Mr Nambusere fingered the pictures. 'Are these the only photographs you have, doctor?'

'They are.'

'You have the film?'

'Yes.'

'May I keep your prints?' Nambusere heaved himself up from behind his desk, trying to end the interview. 'The accident will be investigated, I assure you. But I must admit, I'm not optimistic about the result of our enquiries. I personally accept your opinion that those people were taken by surprise and that they perished. The difficulty is, how can it be proved?'

'Our friend at Sibatanda is convinced that the people of Watemi could help,' said Andrew.

'They deserted their village, didn't they?'

'Some of them must have seen the holocaust and got scared — not surprisingly. Okot Patel knows them well. He thinks they'll be returning. For one thing, they've nowhere else to go. The area — apart from the destroyed settlement and Watemi — is too arid to sustain them. When the food they've taken with them runs out they'll have to go home. You *could* start by questioning the people of Watemi.'

'Yes . . . yes.' It was obvious that Mr Nambusere had already dismissed that line of enquiry. 'Thank you for coming to see me.' He walked John and Andrew to the door. 'Take my advice; forget the whole business . . . Leave it with me.'

His last evening in Rhodesia. John sat on the edge of the McGregors' swimming-pool letting the sun dry him off. Terry, still ploughing through the water, made a wake worthy of a dolphin. Under the palm trees, at the far end of the pool, Lakomi and Helen were setting the table, Angus and Mr Patel preparing a barbecue. Andrew would be coming straight from the hospital, late as usual.

Something to be grateful for; Andrew, Okot and he had not been exposed to radio-activity. The tests *had* proved negative. The happening in the Karoo — whatever it was — had not been a nuclear accident. Take Nambusere's advice and forget the whole business? Easier said than done. John couldn't imagine Andrew putting the thing out of his mind. Andrew wouldn't dwell upon it — too sensible to give himself nightmares — but he'd keep a watch on medical and scientific events that might be relevant.

He'd shown John a photograph in one of his books, the shadow of a man imprinted on a wall. It had been the atom bomb dropped on Hiroshima which had produced it . . . the permanent silhouette of a ladder and a soldier two miles from the explosion. Twenty-eight years later no one had found an entirely convincing scientific explanation for that phenomenon. Unlikely there'd be a quick answer to the accident in the Karoo.

Terry came climbing out of the pool and sat down beside John. She shook the water out of her auburn curls; an attractive woman now with her round face, delicate little nose and wide smiling mouth.

She said, 'Andrew will miss you. Must you live so far away?'

'It can't be helped. I'm in the right job.'

'You could find the right job in South Africa. They need engineers and electronics people.'

John laughed. 'Something wrong somewhere. I meant to persuade you to return to England.'

'It's no good. Look around you, John.' Terry gazed into the shimmering light that kindled palms and flowers into a blaze of bright jewel-colours. 'Here one lives with all one's senses wide awake. We love it, Andrew and I. We're Africans. I can see us now — old, leathery and full of rheumatics — the last whites on an all-black continent, buying powdered monkey-shit medicine from an Umtali witch-doctor.'

They had a happy, intimate family evening. When John left with Andrew and Terry, at two in the morning, his imminent flight to Johannesburg and Israel seemed totally unreal. Back at his brother's bungalow Terry went to bed, he and Andrew had a lager before turning in. John went to sleep to a concert of cicadas, syncopated with the croak of a fire-bellied toad.

He wakened in near-silence. It was still dark outside but the African night-sounds had stopped. Instead there were halting footsteps passing his door . . . not going to the bathroom but making for Andrew's study and photo-laboratory on the west side of the bungalow. Suddenly there was a crash followed by noises that sounded like someone shifting furniture.

John swung out of bed. In the limited light of Andrew's desk-lamp he saw his brother and a stranger on the floor, Andrew struggling to break the man's grip on his throat.

As John grabbed the burglar's shirt collar, jerking his head back, he caught sight of a pale blur. The intruder was a white man. He choked and let go of Andrew, then twisted free and dived through the open window.

John, aware that Andrew was about to go after him, vaulted out and followed. The man was heavily built but agile on his feet. There was enough moonlight to help him past trees and shrubs to the gate. John had shortened the distance between them when he heard a shot. His brief hesitation was enough to take the man over the gate. By the time John reached it a car had come screeching to a stop and the burglar was flinging himself inside.

In the split second before the car took off John saw the intruder's open mouth. His mind raced. Nairobi. The stolid guests at the Country Club. Gold teeth and gold inlays . . . the one and only time he'd seen such teeth. Russians. The intruder's mouth had been full of gold.

23

The session had been organized with the competence and attention to detail John had come to expect of the Israelis. In the three days he'd spent at the Karmel factory outside Haifa they'd shown him the manufacture of a complete body-scanner from the smallest microchip and the 52 Bismuth Germanate detectors to the gantry and the body trolley. Shmuel had helped him study the drawings and given him a crash course in the assembly of the machine. John hadn't admitted to Squire that he shared his reservations about acting as a service company for Karmel, but now he felt certain in his own mind that the association of Seespeed and Karmel would be of great benefit to both companies. He'd enjoy handling the machine, as would Vincent Squire.

Some thirty doctors of all ages were taking their seats in the demonstration room. On display were the latest body-scanner, the linked computing system and the independent viewing system — a million pounds' worth of sleek, highly sophisticated electronic machinery.

The session began with a talk by a radiologist, too specialized for John. He let his thoughts stray to Shmuel who sat by a window that looked out on an olive grove and the sun-drenched hill beyond. Shmuel was staring into space, his dark intelligent face devoid of expression, the pain of David's death held in check with extraordinary self-control. John had meant to stay at an hotel but Shmuel had insisted on taking him home. It would do Esther good to have a houseguest. And Esther had welcomed him with the assurance that his visit would take Shmuel's mind off their loss. They'd survive, the two of them, because Israel had been David's country and because Israel needed people like them.

At Karmel they called Shmuel the *balabos*, the chief, but in fact John had never seen a team quite like those highly trained scientists and engineers. They understood one another like the members of a family, yet they'd come from countries all over the world — Joram Mendoza, Shmuel's second-in-command, a Puerto Rican who'd left behind his people's ghetto in New York, Guy Pokorny — trained at Moscow university, yet an outcast by virtue of being a Jew, and Peppi Goldmann — a Bavarian trained at Heidelberg. With their varied backgrounds it wasn't surprising that they'd become a team of uncommon talent and ingenuity. 'We're the result of historical accidents,' chubby Goldmann had told John, 'so we fit together ferry gut.'

A surgeon had taken over from the radiologist and caught John's attention. He explained the purpose of the body-scanner with a gruesome smile. The patient on the trolley was — not literally of course — sliced up like a sausage and each slice or picture showed an in-depth section of his body. The machine made cumbersome and often uncomfortable investigations unnecessary by producing clear pictures of small blood vessels, details of the spinal column, of diseases such as a tumor of the atrium or cancer of the pancreas.

The surgeon had brought a couple of patients and gave practical demonstrations of the machines in action. He finished by saying that he hoped the Yom Kippur war would be the last and that the Israeli government would in future have money to spare for equipping his hospital with diagnostic machines from the Karmel Company.

When Shmuel offered to answer questions a little man with a big head of white hair held up his hand like a schoolboy. 'Please, I am forlorn,' he declared in a heavy German accent. 'I am a family doctor. Yes? So what do I know about electronic things? This microchip is the same thing as a semi-conductor?'

'It is,' said Shmuel.

'So what is it?'

'A computer.'

'And the computer? What is it? Am I to become an engineer at my age?'

'Doctor, you don't have to be an engineer to understand the principle of computers.'

'So, you vill tell me in simple words?'

Shmuel smiled. 'You know what an idea is?'

'Noo . . . I have ideas in my head. You going to talk philosophy now?'

'No doctor; but you asked for a simple explanation.'

'Philosophy is simple?'

'Let me put it this way . . . You have knowledge . . .'

'Yes, yes. I'm seventy-five. Have I wasted all these years?'

'I'm sure you haven't. Let's say you have an idea, derived from knowledge. What size is an idea, Doctor?'

'Dear God!' groaned the old man. 'Do *you* know what size an idea is? Or knowledge?'

'I know what size it can be. You can translate an idea, which is a result of your knowledge, into a code which is a visible and palpable object. You take a sliver of crystal and etch your code on it . . . in lines, angles, curves, dots, *circuits*.' Shmuel took a microchip from the table and gave it to the old doctor. 'Here it is . . . knowledge, the logical development of an idea, with instructions to convert the idea into action. This is a big microchip. We can now make one no larger than a pinhead and we can

165

put a thousand circuits on it. Does that make sense, doctor?'

'It does and it doesn't. Now I know that you're a clever man. So you make a medical machine. But will the machine tell me why Mrs Cohen has become fat again? Is it the machine that can tell me that Mrs Cohen is eating like a pig because she's unhappy . . . because her husband has a girlfriend again?'

'Doctor, it's people — people like you — who have to tell the machine what you want it to do. It's people who have to feed in the information.'

'So what do I want a machine for? I say to Mrs Cohen, you tell me everything so that I can feed the machine?'

When he'd persuaded Andrew to let him take the film of the holocaust John hadn't known what he would do with it — not consciously. It was Shmuel's gentle, sympathetic handling of the querulous old doctor that decided John to consult him. Clearly the loss of his son hadn't damaged the essential nature of the man. Shmuel, the Jew — more than anyone John had ever met — lived by Christ's precept of loving his neighbour no less than himself. His warmth and compassion seemed to encompass everyone with whom he associated. He was one man who wouldn't dismiss the holocaust as an unfortunate accident of unknown origin; he'd see it as a human tragedy and it would engage his fine, analytical mind.

That evening, after dinner, Esther went to a meeting at her school; Shmuel and John stayed on the verandah where a light breeze was carrying the scents of the garden. They discussed the contract between Seespeed Engineering and the Karmel Company. Then Shmuel asked John how the sanctions against Rhodesia were affecting life in the country. John told him as much as he knew, which led him into an account of his visit to Okot's Mission and the devastation in the Karoo.

Shmuel's reaction surpassed anything John had expected. He was impatient to see the pictures and afterwards suggested putting the slides through his projector. He wanted to study the details. They spent an hour doing just that.

Back on the verandah, Shmuel said, 'It's not the first time I've seen a massacre of this kind. Much the same thing happened in Eritrea four years ago. There were thirty-four husks of bodies on the periphery of the crater. The sheer terror on the faces is something one can't forget.'

'Do you know what happened to these people?'

'No. But I believe we'll find the answer eventually.'

'We?'

'Some of my . . . military friends are interested. If there's a new kind of killer we want to know what it is before it can hit us. We're a small vulnerable country . . . All I can tell you now is that the holocaust in Eritrea was the result of an experiment . . . a Russian experiment.'

'Hideous.'

'If we don't get to the bottom of these . . . events, it won't be for want of trying.'

'I believe the Russians were responsible for the *experiment* in Rhodesia too. My brother and I showed the pictures to a Rhodesian officer. He put us on to a black politician who's concerned with defence matters . . . a lawyer called Nambusere.'

'What was his reaction?'

'He muttered something about an official enquiry, but my impression was that he'll do damn all about it. He suggested that the thing was an accident caused by a German commercial company who're building satellites in Zaire.'

'Otrag,' Shmuel nodded. 'We know about that firm. We hold no brief for Germans — which won't surprise you — but so far Otrag have kept their hands clean. They're just interested in the future. Right now America has about 300 satellites in space, Russia nearer 350. The whole lot belong to one or other state. Otrag reckons, the time isn't far off when large business empires — anywhere in the world — will want to own private satellites . . . first, communication satellites, later — when manufacturing in space becomes economical — laboratory and supply satellites. Otrag's anticipating the demand; gambling, if you like. They might fall flat on their faces. On the other hand, if they become the first company capable of supplying commercial satellites, they could make a staggering fortune. So . . . I think your Mr Nambusere's barking up the wrong tree.'

'He probably intended to mislead us. I don't trust him. It wouldn't surprise me if the Russians paid him . . . for finding them a suitable site and for scotching rumours, if any.'

'Why do you think the Russians are involved?'

'After we'd given the photos to Nambusere, a man broke into my brother's bungalow. From the mess he made it was obvious to us that he was after the film.'

'You actually gave Nambusere the pictures?'

'He asked for them. He also asked my brother whether he had the film. It didn't seem significant until the break-in.'

'Was the burglar picked up?'

'We chased him, but he got away. I'm almost certain he was a Russian. I didn't see him properly but I noticed his teeth. They were heavily mended with gold.'

'What age was Goldteeth?'

'I have a vague impression that he was . . . not young.'

'If you're right, John, the man needn't have been Russian. German dentists used gold a good deal, in such a way that it showed. I don't think they do it now, but a man of my age — I'm forty-four — with gold crowns could be either Russian or German. All the same, I'm inclined to agree

167

with you that Goldteeth was a Russian. Who knows about the accident apart from Okot and your brother, and the two men you saw in Salisbury?'

'No one.'

'Except me. Thanks for telling me. There are two men only with whom I've discussed the Eritrean experiment. Both are trustworthy. Both are in a good position . . . provided there's *any* chance of finding out what the new killer is. It surely must be a device operated from space.'

'That's what I think. In a way Nambusere — trying to sell us the Otrag story — confirmed it.'

'John, may I pass on your information to my people?'

'Yes.' No need to ask Andrew. He'd be sure to agree. 'But I don't want my brother involved.'

'We aren't going to involve your brother. The chances are that the Russians are keeping an eye on him now. I suggest you have the film copied and get the original back to him. He'd better send the film to Mr Nambusere with a note saying that it's of no further interest to him but that it might help Nambusere in his enquiries.

'That would get the Russians off Andrew's back?'

'I don't doubt it.'

'Surely it would occur to them that the film's been copied or printed . . . or both.'

'No. They won't credit your brother or you with strong enough motivations for pursuing the matter. You've been conscientious enough in reporting the accident. That's how they'll see it. The last thing the Russian intelligence services would understand is why people like you or Andrew — or I — should keep concerning ourselves.'

'Shmuel, why do we concern ourselves?'

'Because we have to live with the grief and consciousness of wasted lives . . . the lives of our families. We hate the politics that cause the waste of precious lives. Above all we want to stop such waste. You and I . . . we're a kind of fanatic.'

'True.'

'We're committed. Such commitments — in this mindless, dangerous age — are generally considered outdated and ridiculous. Ideals have become sentimental academics' toys. Can an idealist change the course on which our world is travelling? Can anyone prevent Russia and America from annihilating one another? and from destroying every country in their path?'

'Does any one Russian or American *want* a third world war?'

'No. That's one of the tragedies. Nor has any one politician the power nowadays to make or stop a world war. The Russian and American governments have become conglomerates of little men with conflicting interests . . . financial and industrial interests, academic, military and political interests, all exerting their pressures on the so-called heads of state. And those that have no clout, no money and power — the great majority in Russia and America — have never been less in control of their own lives. The kings of the dungheaps rule.'

'A third world war caused by the selfishness and ambitions of a clutch of individuals . . . all bent on attaining their own ends, no matter at whose expense.'

'Plus those individuals' lack of compassion and imagination. Most people can't imagine their own death until it's actually upon them, let alone the suffering of strangers.'

'A world run by monsters.'

'Worse; by appallingly ordinary men and women . . . like any one of Hitler's minions, who went to work in the morning, murdered five thousand people a day in the gas chambers . . . came home . . . bathed his baby . . . enjoyed his wife's cooking . . . made love to his wife and slept his untroubled sleep . . . got up and decorated the Christmas tree for the kiddies. With angel-hair. If the world were run by monsters one might capture them and put them on a desert island . . . but not whole brigades of respectable generals and experts in every field, all absorbed in their personal relationships and careers, all playing their own games.'

'What's your game, Shmuel? what's mine?'

'Peace on earth.'

'What an impossible dream.'

'You know better, John. Nothing is impossible until it's been proved to be so.'

'Christ has proved it.'

'I don't think so. It's too soon to judge. Nineteen hundred and seventy-three years are a short moment in the history of our planet. No one's yet proved — to my satisfaction — that peace on earth is unattainable, even if I won't live to see it.' Shmuel poured fresh orange juice into John's glass. 'Now . . . let's get down to specifics. We're both convinced that a new destruction technique is being evolved, are we not?'

'Certainly.'

'I would like Greg to know the facts we have.'

'Because he's into the space programme?'

'That in itself wouldn't be a good enough reason. It's important that we should have confidence in him as a person. I have. If ever Greg was complacent about the world he lives in — which I doubt — he's learned better . . . from the campus riots and from his brother's involvement in the Vietnam war. Greg too wants peace on earth above all. He detests all forms of violence . . .'

'Shmuel, you're preaching to the converted.'

*　　*　　*

John found Andrew's letter in the stack of unopened mail which his charlady had put on the desk. It had been delivered by hand.

'We've had a visit from an American engineer,' Andrew had written, 'a Mr Van Larski, who'd heard from Nambusere that we saw the site of the accident in the Karoo. Mr Van Larski has explained to me that it was caused by the failure of an American communications satellite. I suppose the thing just plunged down. All very unfortunate.'

All very unfortunate was a phrase Andrew never used except when expressing doubt or scepticism. John, who'd been feeling sleepy after his flight from Israel, suddenly felt alert.

'Van Larski', Andrew had continued, 'is keen to have the film I took, so that his firm can conduct a full investigation. I can't find it anywhere. Assume you must have packed it with your photographic stuff by mistake. Van's going to England before returning to the States. He'll be in touch with you. Let him have the film. It's no use to us but might help his people. How was the latter part of your holiday? Good safari in the Kruger Park?'

John re-read the note. So, Andrew hadn't swallowed Van Larski's story of a satellite failure; nor had he mentioned the business trip to Israel. Caution throughout. Well, he'd play it Andrew's way. If Van Larski turned up he'd give him the film. Why not? Shmuel had a perfect copy of it.

The telephone rang. He knew it was Debbie before he lifted the receiver.

'John?'

'Hello there.'

'Darling! Why didn't you let me know? I could have fetched you from the airport.'

'Kole did.'

'Black chauffeur . . . more impressive,' she bitched.

'How about dinner at the Spotted Dog?'

'Oh . . .'

'You've got a date.'

'Nothing important. I'll ditch him.'

'No. Debbie. I'll take you out tomorrow.'

'Is that all?'

'Sorry. I'm brown with jealousy.'

'Bastard. The man's an American . . . Van Larski. I met him at the works. It's you he wants to see. He's staying in Brighton. Why don't you come along . . .'

'No. Tell him to call me tomorrow. Enjoy yourself.'

'I don't know why I bother with you.'

'Neither do I.'

John unpacked, took a shower and poured himself a dry Martini. He

170

put the drink and his mail on the table beside the couch. Billy, who'd been staying with Kole, leaped up beside him and put his paws possessively across his knees. Not a lapdog, his dignified King Charles, but for a homecoming an exception was in order. The telephone disrupted the dog-man communion.

'Something's happened . . .' Debbie sounded breathless. 'John . . . I don't know what to do. John . . .'

'Debbie, where are you?'

'In Brighton . . . at the Old Ship. I can't . . . ' She was weeping.

'Want me to come?'

'Yes . . . yes. John, I . . . I . . .'

'Get yourself a scotch. I'll see you in the bar.'

He made the Old Ship hotel within the half hour. The car park was full but he found a space for the Saab on the sea front. Judging by the numbers of people in evening dress in the foyer and the bar a special function was about to begin. He was wondering whether Debbie had left when he saw her come out of the cloakroom, her fur jacket over her arm.

'Let's get out.' She seemed calmer now. 'Please John . . .'

He got her through the crowd, into the cold wind from the sea. 'Where's your car?'

'Haven't got it . . . He fetched me, in his hired car.'

'All right. Let's get inside the Saab. You're shivering . . . What happened?'

'Van took me into the bar . . . got drinks. Then he said he had something for me . . . in his room, and went. I waited . . . He didn't come back . . . I waited for an hour. Then I went up . . . His door was open. John . . . he's dead . . . I think.'

No good asking her questions. She was still in a state of shock. No good wishing she'd alerted the manager of the hotel instead of calling him. He'd better see what it was all about. 'What's his room number?'

'Fifty.'

Easy to remember. She must have got it right. 'Debbie, he may need a doctor. I'd better go up. You'll be all right in the car?'

'Yes.'

He lifted the King Charles on to her lap. 'Billy will keep you warm. Won't be long.'

John crossed the road, walked back into the hotel and made for the stairs. The door of room fifty was not locked. On the bed lay a man in his forties, dressed in the American idea of an English suit. The right shirt and jacket sleeves were pushed up to the elbow. At the man's left hand lay a hypodermic syringe and a brown bottle. The man was dead, undoubtedly. To all appearances he'd been injecting himself, probably with heroin.

John began to take in other aspects of the room, the open briefcase on

171

the dressing-table, the silk scarf that matched Debbie's dress. He picked up the scarf from the floor and put it into his pocket. Then he examined the passport he'd found in the briefcase. An American passport in the name of Vanya Larski. Well, Americans of Russian origin were not uncommon. According to Larski's business cards he worked for Rockwell International Corporation in California; or rather, he had worked for Rockwell until something had gone very wrong.

What was he to do about a junkie who'd been mainlining once too often? Yet . . . a junkie that age, working for Rockwell? It didn't fit. John made himself turn the bare arm of the body. One needle mark; that was all. No marks on the other arm. He was still examining the skin when he noticed something black under the nail of the middle finger. What he pulled out was a wisp of short hair — negro hair.

So that *was* it; Americans experimenting on the same lines as the Russians in Eritrea. As America had joined the sanctions-club against Rhodesia and wasn't supposed to have dealings there the location should have been nice and discreet. But there had been dealings, no doubt highly profitable for Mr Nambusere. So, after Andrew and he had seen Nambusere that gentleman had alerted Larski. With the idea of getting more money out of him? Nambusere must have had second thoughts. What if Larski mishandled the affair so badly that his connivance became known? That would be the end of Nambusere's promising political career. Better get rid of the American who'd organized the project.

Not a bad theory. John decided to make himself scarce. Take Debbie home. Tell her there was no reason why they should get involved with a dead junkie. She'd be thankful to be out of it. In the morning he'd follow Shmuel's advice; airmail the film inside a parcel of books to South Africa. Terry's father could be relied upon to forward it to Andrew, as he'd sent on previous gifts.

John bent over the body on the bed and forced back Larski's upper lip. Four of the man's teeth were encased in gold. That didn't tell him the whole story. Who was Larski? A Russian or an American of Russian origin? There had to be an answer.

FREE FROM ATTACK

America, South Africa 1974 - 1975

24

Greg's natural source of information was the man he'd met at the unforgettably complicated Skylab launch. Harry B. Resnick had kept his promise of sending him Jan Valtin's book on the workings of international Communism and they'd kept in touch since. Resnick was due to leave Rockwell International for a full-time advisory post at the White House, but he was still at his Californian office when Greg telephoned him from his parents' home a couple of days before Christmas.

Resnick called him back on Christmas eve. The Rockwell personnel computer had produced the information that Van Larski had worked for the company, that he'd changed jobs six months ago and joined the Alpha Corporation of Boston. His speciality had been translating technical material from Russian into English. Van Larski had defected from a Soviet delegation during trade talks in England.

'Greg, how come you're interested in the guy?' asked Resnick.

'A friend of mine wants to know whether he's Soviet or American. They met in Rhodesia.'

'In Africa? That's strange. According to Alpha Corporation he went to England in November. Guess he took a holiday while he was in Europe.'

'If he's a defector, why does he travel under his own name?'

'He didn't. His name was changed from Polyanov to Larski. I reckon they had to provide him with a name that matched his Slavonic accent. You can reassure your friend on one score; Larski held a position of trust at Rockwell. He was certainly not Soviet-polluted. According to Mat Scobie, it's here Larski got polluted . . . Oh yes, Scobie's been moved on from your old firm to a top security job. After the Boeing enquiry, it was to be expected; that's how the FBI works. He's now co-ordinator to a choice little group of contractors to the Air Force. Alpha's one of them.'

'You've taken a lot of trouble,' said Greg.

'Not at all. It's your old thorn-in-the-flesh who took the trouble. I called Alpha, just to check that Larski could be contacted at their Boston complex . . . Half an hour later Scobie was on my line. Wanted to know my business with Larski.'

'What did you tell him?'

'Nothing. I recalled that he gave you a hard time over that break-in. Didn't think you'd want Mat Scobie round your neck again. I told him I wanted to query a point in an article Larski had translated for Rockwell.'

'Thanks, Harry.'

'My answer must have satisfied him. He was quite forthcoming. Apparently Larski'd been one of the best, as defectors go; until he got polluted . . . Scobie's words. Nobody got wise to his weakness until it was too late. Greg, the man was found dead in an English hotel. Afterwards his apartment in Boston was searched. Scobie says there was enough heroin to kill an elephant.'

Christmas at the old family home on Summit Road, Berkeley, with everything going right for once. Greg's parents in their element because there were his small children making Christmas what it was meant to be, and because the old cop was happy with Sean making it in the army. A lieutenant. A regular guy. What if Stella was a black? Got to move with the times; black was beautiful nowadays. And little Steve and Greg junior weren't all that dark. Just a nice suntan colour. In any case the Murphys' youngest grandchildren were special, cute, more like their father than their mother.

After the roast goose dinner they moved out on to the patio. The mist had lifted. Beyond the still waters of the Bay, San Francisco spread shimmering tentacles deep into the green hills.

Sean said, 'I'd forgotten how good it looks.'

Fiona was watching her mother coax the children indoors for a belated afternoon sleep. 'I'd forgotten how much we liked our parents.'

'Until we got into the generation gap,' said Sean.

'It was more of an occupation gap.' Greg saw his father collect the coffee cups, lining them up on the wooden tray like soldiers. A neat man. A man who never doubted that there was a proper place for everything and everyone. Fiona and he, with their tales and dreams of outer space, must have worried the old cop; especially Fiona. Girls were supposed to be interested in boys, not computers. And Sean, a drop-out in his first year at college; a disaster.

'He's learned a lot,' said Fiona. 'Let's go walk off the dinner . . . before Inspector Murphy starts on his wartime stories.'

Sean laughed. 'He sure wants to teach me to run the army.'

The three of them strolled down the garden and left by the private exit of their childhood, a gap between the fence and a eucalyptus tree.

They scrambled through the undergrowth of the hillside up to the science museum. Greg thought they'd been lucky to live so close to such a playground — those futuristic halls and wide sweeping passages where children could play electronic games on a great range of computerized machines.

They sat down at the edge of the plateau, facing the Bay and the long arm of the Golden Gate Bridge.

Sean looked back at the clean sharp lines of the science complex. 'A funny place to grow up in. Not for you . . . Sure was for me. It's only now I realize that the machines in there didn't leave me unaffected. Just that I got to them late in life.'

Fiona smiled. 'Poor old man. He's all of twenty-six. And what are the machines you've got to?'

'Military hardware. Warfare's changed since I was in Vietnam . . . changed out of all recognition.'

'There's no war now,' said Greg.

'No, but there would be if we weren't turning ourselves into the ultimate scientific deterrent force. I'm including the navy and the airforce. Think what would happen if the Soviets launched a ballistic missile.'

Greg didn't want to think, but he had to listen because it was his own brother who was speaking with such cool authority. Fire a ballistic missile, Sean was saying, and the heat of the engines will be found by infra-red sensors inside early-warning satellites within minutes. In peacetime those satellites, stationed over many parts of the world, monitored individual missile tests. In war they would certainly spot an attack whether from land-based or submarine-launched rockets. The warning would be taken up by radars, who'd detect the missiles in flight, at Clear in Alaska, at Thule in Greenland, on Fylingdales Moor in northern England.

As the missiles approached their multiple warheads would begin to fall on different targets. Missiles approaching the United States over the Arctic would be picked up on a special radar at Concrete, North Dakota, capable of predicting where the warheads would hit.

Imagine one attack on one of many typical airforce bases — say the Whiteman Base in Missouri. Around this base are some 150 missiles housed in silos. In the course of destroying Whiteman Base ten million people would be killed by blast, heat and direct radiation. Depending on the prevailing winds many more would die from nuclear fallout. So much for American Minuteman rockets or Soviet SS missiles with multiple independently targetable warheads. A single modern high-yield bomb, delivered by air, had the explosive force of one megaton and would be a hundred times more destructive than the Hiroshima bomb of 1945. It would leave a burn-out area of sixty square miles.

Greg was not ignorant of the ever more sophisticated nuclear weapons and delivery systems devised by Russia and America, but he had subconsciously shied away from a total image of future wars. Sean, with his strangely single-minded faith in the vital balance of military power between Russia and America, induced a vision he could not escape. NORAD, the North American Air Defence Command, and its hundred computers was situated 1400 feet inside the granite of the Cheyenne

Mountains in Colorado. A thousand people inside the mountain behind twenty-five-ton doors. The United States studded like a hedgehog with rockets in silos. A plan to put the rockets underground in twenty thousand deep holes throughout the country. Plans for special roads and carriers to keep the missiles continuously on the move. Nuclear submarines in the seas. Nuclear bombers in the air. All the time. No protection for populations except mutual deterrence; *in war Russians and Americans alike will be slaughtered.* The pawns on the political chessboard — whole populations. In a nuclear war five hundred millions would die in the northern hemisphere alone — a conservative estimate.

However, according to Sean there was one really dirty trick which neither Russia nor America wanted to play. ASATS, anti-satellite weapons capable of destroying either Russian or American space hardware, were frowned upon as foul play, not to be contemplated by either side. On this there was full agreement between America and Russia and so far it had not been violated.

'Oh my God!' Fiona laughed. 'I can see thousands of Charlie Chaplins go up and down elevators inside mountains . . . polish missiles and commune with computers. I can see guys load rockets on to carriers, drive them for little walks, unload them, put them to bed . . . And guys who make dummy missiles to put in dummy carriers, to be driven around on dummy roads, to fool the spy satellites.'

'It isn't funny,' said Sean.

'Sure isn't. But if I weren't laughing I'd be crying. Does anyone really believe that bigger and better arsenals of nuclear missiles in Russia and in the States is going to prevent another world war?'

'I do.' Sean stared into the distance where nose-to-tail traffic was etching long snakes of light into the gathering darkness. 'Can you think of anything more effective?'

Greg sensed that this was a moment he'd never forget, the feeling of total unity and total despair. Looking down on San Francisco there was something very beautiful and savage about those glowing traffic streaks hurtling like missile trails into the distance — converging, crossing, curving, falling apart and finally dying in the luminous mist; an unending Calvary of vehicles casting streams of bodies across the land. 'Insanity.'

'Insanity . . . perhaps,' said Sean. 'But it's kept this country free from attack. One's got to be rational about keeping war in check.'

'How?' asked Fiona. 'By computing what percentage of the population the Soviets and we can do without? By computing how radio-active we can make this planet without killing off the entire human race? Or do we hope for the best and keep financing little wars in Asia . . . the Middle East . . . Africa? But that's something the Russians do better than us.'

'Our technology's ahead of theirs.'

'Amen.'

*   *   *

Snow in April. From his study window Greg could see into the trees of his back yard as if he were in the middle of a forest. Squirrels, as large as well-fed cats, were chasing one another from pine to maple to hornbeam and birch, wrecking the white quilts and sending showers of flakes down on the children below.

They were building a snowman — Stella, her wiry plaits arranged in a tight intricate pattern all over her head, Steve and Greg junior in red anoraks that made them look like small eskimos. Fiona came out of her apartment on the south side of the house, carrying charcoal and a paper hat.

Greg resisted the temptation of joining his family. Better finish the costing of his new photo-voltaic cells. If he didn't convince the Energy Research and Development Agency that his cells were a sound commercial propostion he wouldn't get the government contract on which his firm depended and Lake Erie Electronics Corporation would have to lay off half its workforce.

When Harry B. Resnick had visited his factory and laboratories in the new year he'd given him a frank and disturbing run-down on the situation; a squeeze in government spending, severe cut-backs in the space programmes, ever increasing numbers of *obsolete* people — men and women who'd never again find employment, many of the smaller firms — like LEEC — going bust. Competition between the large multinational companies such as General Electric, Westinghouse, Babcock and Wilcox, and Combustion Engineering had become a force to be reckoned with politically.

Though Greg had faith in what he was doing at LEEC, he considered himself lucky to have caught Resnick's scientific imagination. Their personal friendship wouldn't have been enough for the President's adviser to support him in a committee whose very existence was classified — virtually unknown to Congress and the Pentagon. Apart from Harry B. Resnick, the committee — the National Reconnaissance Office — consisted of the Assistant Secretary of Defense for Intelligence, the Director of Central Intelligence and the Assistant to the President for National Security Affairs — Dr Kissinger.

Resnick had made Greg no promises, but the very fact that he'd urged him to prepare a commercially viable project for his photo-voltaic cells, and mentioned that high-powered secret committee, surely meant that his firm was in the running for a government contract of considerable importance.

It was getting dark when Greg looked down at the snowman again. He now had charcoal eyes and buttons and was wearing the hat. Fiona was taking the children to her apartment, Stella had already gone indoors. A moment later she looked into his study.

'Someone to see you, Greg . . . a Major Cordell.'

'Don't know him,' he suddenly felt uneasy. 'Anything to do with Sean?'

'A friend of Sean's, I think.'

'Why not offer him a drink? I'll be right down.'

'He wants to see you . . . alone.'

Major Cordell said it had been a routine army exercise, a routine assault on a routine military installation. The regrettable fact that three soldiers, including Lieutenant Sean Murphy, had gotten themselves shot and killed had not been routine.

What Major Cordell — a suitably mournful middle-aged man — wanted of Greg was his agreement to the army-routine disposal of Sean's body: all nice and reverent, military honours to the nearest crematorium — in this case in Albuquerque, New Mexico, the coffin draped in the Stars and Stripes, a guard of honour, etcetera. As Lieutenant Murphy had cited Greg as his next of kin, he could give instructions where the ashes should be sent, and if he so desired the army would arrange a memorial service in a church chosen by the family.

Greg, feeling as icy and remote as if he had a high temperature, heard himself say, 'I'll be going to Albuquerque.'

'You are, of course, entitled to go to your brother's funeral,' Cordell hesitated, 'but we don't advise it.'

'Why not?'

'His injuries were such . . . You wouldn't be able to see him.'

'I see . . . I want to see where my brother was killed.'

'That won't be possible, Mr Murphy. It's a high security area.'

'I have high security rating, major.'

'Sorry, it makes no difference. The procedure laid down . . .'

'Procedure? Is it so normal for one army unit to kill another?'

Cordell ignored that. 'The regulations cover all eventualities. But we don't want you to think . . .'

'No, you don't want me to think. When's the funeral?'

'On Thursday, sir. I'm not empowered to organize a flight for you, but . . .'

'Thank you, I'll make my own arrangements. I assume your people are holding an enquiry.'

'Certainly. It should be concluded by Wednesday. You'll be informed of the result.'

Late that night Greg had a call from New Mexico. He'd forgotten Fergie, the friend who'd been in Vietnam with Sean, who'd been injured and sent home with him. Sean's partner.

'Greg?'

'Yes, Fergie. We know. I'll be in Albuquerque tomorrow. I want to see for myself . . .'

'Reckoned you would.'

'Can we meet?'

'Movement's restricted out here. Know what I mean?'

'Yes.'

'Greg, hire a car to meet you at the airport . . . from Wagner Cabs. Take a note of the number . . .'

25

The sense of remoteness had persisted throughout the flight. In the blinding light outside Albuquerque airport, Greg felt he'd arrived in an alien world where no one would speak his language, where people would look upon him as a maverick. His detachment was like a sickness, yet he was functioning normally. He took in travellers, porters, luggage trolleys and coaches and easily located the parking lot.

He cut across the road and walked along a line of dusty sub-tropical shrubs until he saw the Cadillac with the notice *Wagner Cabs & Car Hire* on its hood. As he approached a man in his early twenties — a big swarthy fellow with a short haircut — got out of a truck.

'Mr Murphy?'

'Yes.'

'I'm from the Santa Fé Hotel. Major Cordell's reserved a room for you. I'll take you over right now.'

'There's a misunderstanding. I told Major Cordell I'd make my own arrangements.'

'Sir . . .' The man kept pace with Greg. 'Colonel Piper will be calling you. He's going to make an appointment.'

'Ask him to leave a message at the Santa Fé.'

The man didn't argue, but he watched Greg all the way to the Cadillac. He watched him get in and go, driven by Paul Wagner.

Greg gathered that Wagner had a son in the airforce, stationed at Roswell Base. It figured; Fergie, anticipating that the army would want to *look after* Sean's brother, had arranged the hired car through this airforce connection.

At Wagner's down-town garage they went into the office. Greg signed the standard form and Wagner gave him a hand-drawn map.

'You've got a two-hundred-mile drive ahead of you, Mr Murphy . . . to the Coon Motel . . . down here. Roads ain't good, ain't as bad as some.

The Ford I got ready for you ain't no luxury limousine, but what counts is the engine inside her. Best there is for desert country.' He studied Greg's spectacles. 'You OK for night-driving?'

'Sure. I'm short-sighted, that's all.'

'Ain't too dark this time of year . . . I put water and pastrami sand-wiches in the trunk.'

'Good of you. Thanks.'

'I'm sorry about your brother.' Wagner looked embarrassed. 'Real sorry . . . Take care, boy; New Mexico ain't as healthy as it used to be.'

Some twenty miles out of Albuquerque Greg noticed the Chevrolet behind him. For the next fifty miles the distance between them remained about the same and Greg assumed – with indifference – that the driver was following him.

The area he passed through was an intermittent string of no-man's-lands; the usual gasoline station with a cat's cradle of coloured plastic pennants, a supermarket with a big parking lot. If there were any inhabitants who made use of these facilities their dwellings weren't visible.

Around three o'clock in the morning it occurred to Greg that Fergie would be none too happy if he allowed his shadow — no doubt an army-nanny — to follow him all the way. When he came to a Y-junction he made a sharp turn right, drove off the road into the scrub and switched off his lights. The Chevrolet soon passed him. He ate a couple of Wagner's pastrami sandwiches, slept for half an hour, and returned to the road. For the next fifty miles he kept looking into his mirror. There was no sign of the Chevrolet and he was satisfied that he'd shaken it off — not because his evasive tactics had been brilliant; more likely his shadow had dreamed up a good excuse for dropping the pursuit.

The Coon Motel was a sprawling ranch-style building backed by a range of mountains. Greg walked all round the silent place until he found the dimly lit coffee-shop with a child curled up on a bench. The girl, an eleven- or twelve-year-old, said if he was the guy Lieutenant Ferguson had booked in, his room was ready; and he was to put his car in the garage.

Greg went to sleep as soon as he hit the pillow. When he came to, the sun was streaming into the room and Fergie was putting a breakfast tray on the table.

He said, 'Sorry about your long drive.'

Greg realized gratefully that Fergie would cut out any conventional condolences. 'That's OK. You got things organized pretty well . . . So had the army. Guy met me at the airport. Said he was from the Santa Fé Hotel. Later, outside Albuquerque, they put a tail on me. I lost him.'

'There's one of them sitting in the coffee-shop right now.'

'What's it all about, Fergie?'

'Place is studded with missile silos, operational bomber and support bases. Guess they don't want anyone like you asking questions.'

'Then they're going the wrong way about it.'

'They don't know you. If intimidation doesn't work they'll put on the Sean's-buddies-act . . . and play you the Stars and Stripes.'

Fergie's anger took Greg by surprise. 'As bad as that?'

'Yeah. I reckon that even our Commander — that's Colonel Piper — didn't know what he was letting us in for. When he briefed us for the assault exercise he said that Sean's location was close to a top security complex . . . a place even more heavily defended than a base where nuclear-armed bombers are on stand-by. He admitted he didn't know exactly what went on at Los Alamos . . .'

'Los Alamos?'

'Right . . . the historic place where they exploded the first nuclear bomb that proved that fusion was possible; at 5.30 am on 16 July 1945. We learned it at school, as something to be proud of.'

'What makes you think Colonel Piper's in the dark about Los Alamos?'

'Just my impression. The guys asked questions. Piper said he guessed Los Alamos was used for testing anti-missile missiles. I reckon he *was* guessing. Greg, I'm making no excuses for him, but I figure he'd have put the east side of Los Alamos out of bounds to the assault parties if he'd known that the defence would shoot without warning.'

'Is that what happened to Sean?'

'Yeah.' Fergie shook his head. 'It doesn't make sense. My own party was supposed to sabotage an airfield with fully-loaded bombers. But we were told there'd be red lines across the runways . . . and that we'd be shot if we crossed the lines. These security tests against thieves or saboteurs are going on all the time.'

'Maybe Sean and the other two haven't been the only casualties.'

'I don't know, Greg. But I want to know what Los Alamos is all about. Reckon you do. There's guys in the airforce who're going to help us. The party's tonight.'

The jet cut through the star-studded night on its routine reconnaissance of the vast New Mexico defence area. The airforce jet was equipped with sensors capable of distinguishing minute gradations of heat, new devices for measuring radiation-levels and identifying sound-waves.

Greg, studying the sectioned overfly map, noted that the flightpath was rigidly charted and that the computer-print instructions warned against any lowering of permitted heights. Such deviations, even in cases of instrument failure, were liable to provoke *defensive action* from ground installations.

Ted Wagner, the pilot, told Greg that a jet like theirs had crashed a couple of months earlier. The crew had been killed. The subsequent enquiry had not satisfied Ted or his fellow pilots who were sharing reconnaissance and air-police duties over Los Alamos. The verdict of human error had been an insult to men with their highly sophisticated training and ability. They'd suspected a cover-up. Ever since, they'd been determined to discover exactly what had been covered up. The accident involving Sean and the two other men had found them ready — with unauthorized infra-red cameras, normally used in satellites and spacecraft, installed in their jet.

The fact that Ted and his crew had succeeded in carrying out such modifications undetected indicated that the hidden mutiny had spread beyond the aircrews. Now Ted was taking serious risks in allowing unauthorized passengers aboard — Fergie for his familiarity with missile and back-up installations, Greg for his wide scientific knowledge and his relationship with Sean.

Sean. Greg's mind suddenly dredged up a scene that blotted out all sense of place and time. He was crossing a sunny road in San Francisco, a child of five, his hand in his father's. They were about to visit his mother and her new-born baby in hospital. They were on the steps of the maternity wing when his father stopped and stared at his feet. 'Greg, we're in trouble. You're wearing your slippers. Your mother will say I should have told you to put your shoes on. Guess she'll be shooting me down in flames.' Incapable of looking after the children properly. But she didn't say it. The parents were watching him . . . laughing at the way he was exploring Sean's minute hands and feet, touching the fine light hair . . . all warm and alive.

Another small white room when Fiona was born. He was eight then, not bothered about infants any more. Same gentian blue eyes as Sean's but brown hair. Poor Fiona . . . in the house on Summit Road now. No way of healing the parents' grief. Not even the small comfort of a heroic action. No war. No enemy.

The monitor was flickering. New shapes were forming. Greg wrenched himself out into the present. He was in the air as an Observer. Observe, damn you! Concentrate! He became aware of the engine-sounds. They were changing. He felt the jet plummet like a becalmed kite. A sickening dive, though Ted had warned him.

He forced himself to keep his eyes on the monitor. This was his one and only chance of getting a look at the complex where Sean had been killed. He saw curious sets of twin towers, great ball-shaped radars and a battery of arrays on which thousands of bowl-like mirrors were mounted. Then flashing lights took over. Anti-aircraft fire. The warning on the overfly map was no exaggeration. Down there they appeared to have no compunction in shooting down anything that broke the invisible height barrier.

184

The jet climbed and hurtled forward on a steep trajectory. In seconds, which had seemed like hours, it was clear of the area, on course for the run to base.

'We've made it!' shouted Ted Wagner. He handed over to his co-pilot and joined Greg. 'See anything you didn't expect?'

'Yes . . . though I don't know what it is.'

'It'll come. Maybe the pictures will help you. We'll have them ready by tomorrow.'

Chalk it up to experience, Fergie had told him; put it in the memory-bank. You never know; may be next month or next year you'll find an article in the *New Yorker* or the Greenwich *Village Cuckoo* that'll tell you all about how a Mexican chihuahua breeder got lost in Los Alamos . . . and how she saw computers that were just like her little doggies. And, wham! suddenly it'll jell . . . you'll link up our air pictures with the chihuahua woman and you'll know exactly what they're playing at in that benighted complex. Isn't that how scientists find the answers to problems?'

Something in Fergie's theory. Better give Los Alamos a rest. Greg got out of the bath and dried himself. He'd thought about the hardware he'd seen from the jet all the way back to Albuquerque. It still didn't make sense. Now there were other things to attend to. Down below, in the foyer of the Santa Fé Hotel, the guy who'd tried to pick him up at the airport was waiting to take him to Colonel Piper's office. Having seen Fergie, and a lot more besides, he was ready for the interview.

He put on the grey suit he'd be wearing at Sean's funeral in the morning, pocketed his room-key, and took the elevator down.

Pont, now in sergeant's uniform, got up. 'I'll call a cab.'

'We'll go in the Ford,' Greg told him.

'You still got the hired car?'

'Sure.'

They picked up the car in the underground park and drove out into the rush-hour traffic, Pont giving directions.

'Why didn't you tell us where you wanted to go?' he asked.

'You knew. Why did you have me followed?'

'Security.'

'Some security!'

'We located you, didn't we? We had orders not to harass you . . . not so you'd feel we minded you meeting your brother's friends.'

'Real handsome of you.'

'You could have met Lieutenant Ferguson tomorrow. He and your brother's men will be at the ceremony.'

'I'm sure you've thought of everything, sergeant.'

Pont glanced at Greg suspiciously but decided to drop the subject.

'Take the second intersection on the right, sir. The office is three blocks up.'

The building was indistinguishable from the banks and business houses in other streets — concrete, steel and glass cubes in the typically bleak and utilitarian style of the 'seventies. Pont marched Greg through the tiled hall and sent the elevator to the sixth floor. Either the army had moved in recently or it wasn't advertizing its presence. There were no names, no numbers on any of the doors.

Pont showed Greg into an office with a bare desk and a couple of chairs, the kind of room that could belong to anyone or no one. 'I'll tell the Colonel you're here, sir.'

Colonel Piper didn't keep him waiting. He was a tall, grey man in his fifties with a thin-lipped dyspeptic's mouth. He made an uneasy little condolence speech, subsided into the uncomfortable fibreglass chair and waited.

Greg said, 'I found your letter at the hotel. You seem to have done everything necessary.'

'The memorial service?'

'That's something my parents will decide.'

Piper straightened his shoulders. He appeared to have come to a decision. 'Mr Murphy . . . None of us like serving in the New Mexico desert. Your brother volunteered.'

Greg refrained from asking the expected question.

Piper stared past him at a lightswitch that was hanging off the wall by its wires. 'An army is meant to operate through its chain of command. That's how it functioned when I fought in World War Two, in Korea, in Vietnam. No civilian had the power to issue orders to the military. Ain't so any more . . . not in New Mexico. The armed forces are supposed to be employing civilian companies or corporations to update our hardware. In the past few years those civilians have built themselves complexes which look like cities out of science-fiction — with taxpayers' money — and they tell *us* what *they* want us to do. The chain of command's been short-circuited. All that's needed nowadays is a person-to-person call from Los Alamos to Washington . . . to General Montana. Next thing, the General — who's never set foot in New Mexico — passes on the order for assault exercises on installations we here know nothing about.'

'You should press for information,' Greg goaded.

'Oh sure. The feedback is, *The installations are still at the research stage . . . security can't be relaxed for the moment. By order of the President,* just to remind us that he is the Supreme Commander. For crying out loud! What do they take me for? I'm an old dog to learn new tricks, but I've half killed myself mastering the new technologies . . . of nuclear missiles on the ground, in submarines and aircraft, of satellites, antiballistic missiles, computer-junk, laser-junk . . .'

'It can't be easy.'

'Keeping up-to-date at my age is not easy. If I could I'd retire tomorrow. But where would a professional soldier like me fit in at fifty-five? OK, I have nothing against military progress. I can accept that the enhanced radiation warhead — the neutron bomb — may be a more attractive weapon than the C4 missile . . .'

Greg couldn't see the attraction of killing a million people with an enhanced radiation warhead rather than a C4. 'Attractive?'

'Sure. It'll be more cost-effective and . . .'

'Cheaper, Colonel?'

'So we're told. It seems like a promising development . . .'

'Promising mass murder.'

'Beg pardon?'

'Nothing, Colonel. I'm learning a lot.'

'As I was saying . . . I accept that we must have more advanced nuclear defence systems. In the forces, we all do; but the penetration of the military by civilian empires makes our task impossibly complicated.'

'Why not send this message up your chain of command?'

'That'll have to be attempted — sooner or later — by a younger man than me . . . a guy who'll be serving in the army long after I am gone. In any case, right now I'd achieve nothing . . . not while big business is in power. Take the case of NUMEC . . . the Nuclear Materials and Equipment Corporation of Pennsylvania.

'An inspector of the Atomic Energy Commission discovered that 382 pounds of enriched uranium belonging to NUMEC couldn't be accounted for. It had just . . . gone missing. The inspector, who was going to report the scandal, resigned from the Atomic Energy Commission . . . and accepted a job at NUMEC. End of story? Not at all. Another 190 pounds of enriched uranium went missing and another inspector tried to get the Justice Department to treat the *loss* as theft, and investigate. A very serious case, Mr Murphy . . . a theft of material that could unbalance the nuclear arms situation in the world. Know what the upshot was? Our government found the smuggling of nuclear material on such a large scale politically embarrassing. End of investigation. The whole thing was swept under the carpet . . . except that the owner of NUMEC had to pay the Atomic Energy Commission $1.1 million in penalties for the *lost* uranium. Then he sold his company. According to the newspaper stories he didn't make a loss. No, I can't stop the misuse of the military by multinational commercial empires . . . nor their buying of senators or of our political parties.'

'You seem to see corruption just about everywhere, Colonel.'

'You think I'm paranoiac? Well, you're young. I'm thankful I'm not. Maybe I won't have to witness the nuclear holocaust . . . brought about by Russian politicians and American big business.' Piper heaved himself out of his chair. He was looking tired. 'I'm glad we had this talk, Mr Murphy. Reckoned you're entitled to know the circumstances of your brother's death.'

'Sure. The responsibility wasn't yours, but some faceless commercial corporation's . . . if I understood you correctly.'

'Precisely.' The Colonel appeared unaware of Greg's accusation.

'You said my brother volunteered for that assault exercise.'

'Yes. In cases of this nature I send out volunteers only. I make a point of it.'

'Why did Sean volunteer?'

'Haven't I made myself clear? The army is a career.' There was something like affection in Piper's passing smile. 'It used to be a fine, rewarding career. Your brother was genuine officer-material. He opted for leading one of the assault parties because he wanted promotion. He knew I'd be recommending him for a captaincy. Yes Mr Murphy . . . above all, the army's a career.'

Greg walked out. The man in the stifling, characterless room had become intolerable. Ignoring the elevators he made for the fire exit and went running down the stairs. As if to confirm Piper's views the doors on each floor bore the name of some commercial company or corporation.

On the second floor he came up against a name that stopped him. He was back in the co-ordinator's room at the Boeing Company, with Mat Scobie asking questions about the deliberate impurity he had introduced into his silicon crystals . . . wanting to know where he was keeping his research notes. Mat Scobie using an abortive break-in at his laboratory for advancing his status. In the FBI?

Greg recalled Harry B. Resnick's voice on the telephone; Scobie had told him that the Russian who'd died in an English hotel had been a drug addict. Not John Whitmore's version of the Brighton affair. How had Resnick put it? *Scobie's now co-ordinator to a choice little group of contractors to the airforce. Alpha's one of them.*

The name on the door below Colonel Piper's office was *The Alpha Corporation of Boston.*

26

Shmuel heard of Sean Murphy's death in South Africa. Greg had written to John as a matter of course, John had passed on the full story to his brother. And Andrew, aware that the loss of the American lieutenant deeply concerned his wider *family*, had told the Volatians — who appeared to belong to this family.

They were sitting on the terrace of Andrew's bungalow in a quiet residential road in Pretoria. It was so cool under the high cloistered ceiling that the garden, seen through the stone arches, looked like the mirage of a tropical landscape. The house was a hundred years old, antique by South African standards, solidly built with the Boers' faith in permanence.

Shmuel recognized that it was faith in South Africa's viability as a country that had induced Andrew and Terry to move to Pretoria. From what Andrew had told him of the guerilla war in Rhodesia a move had become unavoidable. Terry was pregnant. Andrew had felt that he couldn't risk her and the child.

'You didn't consider going to England?' asked Shmuel.

'We're Africans,' said Andrew. 'Even John's accepted it.'

'Doesn't apartheid worry you?'

'The misrepresentations of South Africa's policies worry us. To understand apartheid you must know something of this country's history. When the first white settlers arrived some three hundred years ago this land was empty. There were no more than five or six thousand blacks; dying tribes. Unlike the white settlers of America, who killed vast numbers of Red Indians and took their lands, the settlers here broke and farmed virgin ground and looked after the blacks. Surely the population figures speak for themselves. There are about four and a half million whites, seventeen million blacks, and over three million people of mixed or Asian descent.

'The aim of the white governments has always been separate development . . . a federation of black and white states. The blacks have their own culture, too . . . which they want to keep as much as the whites want to keep theirs. Evolution is slow, inevitably . . . if you keep in mind the figures I've given you and the enormous differences between white and black cultures. At the moment the choice is between control by the whites or tribal wars. What most whites abroad have never understood is that you can't impose European-style democracy on any African country and make it work. Europeans don't appreciate the strength of tribal traditions. If certain tribes were left to their own devices they'd slaughter one another. It's happened often enough in the past. And if the tribes got at each other's throats nowadays Russia would step in.'

'You make it sound simple,' said Shmuel.

'Fundamentally it's the anti-apartheid lot who over-simplify. The man who made me see the real problems is Lakomi's husband. Mr Patel — he was born and bred in Kenya, exiled in South Africa when Kenyatta kicked out the Asians — advised us to move to this country. He's suffered independence and africanization in Kenya. He believes that Rhodesia will become another independent black state. And he's tired of running. South Africa let us come in together. Patel is teaching again — in a school for Asians. His son, Okot, has a job that satisfies him — in child welfare. And Lakomi . . . Andrew smiled at the stately black woman who was setting the table for tea, 'She's ruled two generations of Whitmores and she's all ready to rule the third.'

'They'll let her?'

'*They* don't trouble those that don't trouble them . . . whatever the foreign papers say.'

Shmuel told Andrew and Terry of the American woman who had sat next to him and Esther in the jet. She'd complained that the journey to South Africa had been forced upon her because her daughter had married a Johannesburg businessman. It had been a terrible blow to her. She loathed South Africa and all it stood for. She guessed she knew the country real well; some ten years ago she'd done a forty-two day safari. Had he and Esther heard about apartheid? Blacks weren't allowed to speak to whites in the street. But she'd shown them! She'd stopped a black in Cape Town, not a stone's throw from a cop. She'd asked the black guy where he lived. He'd acted scared. He'd told her to let him go. So she'd said to him. 'I'm an American citizen and I'll speak to anyone I wanna speak to. And if that cop says one word to me I'll call the American ambassador. The cop had come real close to her. And she? She'd looked him up and down, down and up — hard — like he was dirt. The cop hadn't dared address her or the black. He'd passed by as though he'd seen nothing.

Terry laughed. 'I'd have been tempted to say a thing or two to the old idiot.'

'Such as?' asked Andrew.

'If apartheid had been what she thought it was, her ego-trip would have got the black into trouble. Not her . . . the black.'

'You'd have wasted your time,' said Andrew. 'Americans like her don't listen. Shmuel's story shows why America does herself so much damage

190

abroad. Even her altruism turns sour . . . not that most American intentions are free from self-interest.'

'Andy's becoming cynical,' said Terry.

'Let's say sceptical. My brother's been a good teacher of politics.' Andrew watched the flight of a brilliant blue starling. 'In the letter John wrote about Sean's death he asked . . . what kind of a country is it where a soldier can be killed by his own people — on a military exercise — deliberately killed.'

'It's been known to happen elsewhere.' Shmuel thought of a moment in 1967 — the Six-Day War. He had known the pilot of the Mirage III who had gone astray in the Negev near the Dimona nuclear complex. They'd shot him down — his own Israeli comrades. An accident? The Rav Aluf never had answered his questions.

Esther, who'd been listening quietly, turned to Shmuel — a haunted look in her eyes. 'It wouldn't happen in Israel.'

'No,' he took her hand, 'not in Israel. We are few. Every man counts.' How often had the Rav Aluf counted him *out* . . . out of Mossad, out of the inexorable intelligence network? a regrettable but unavoidable casualty for whom a replacement would be hard to find.

He gazed into the golden wilderness of palm trees, scarlet canaas and bird-of-paradise flowers — so like his idea of the Garden of Eden — and suddenly felt tired. He was forty-six, for God's sake! What more did they want of him? Why couldn't they let him go on with the manufacture of his medical computers, the sale of the body-scanner abroad — world-wide but harmless trade?

He should have known that the Rav Aluf's offer of the plum job in the Karmel Company wouldn't be a simple reward for services rendered but another kick up the backside into the ubiquitous labyrinth of Mossad. He'd known from the beginning — the Rav Aluf had been straight about it — that his Karmel Company was part of Koor Industries, the most important armaments producer in Israel. But the Rav Aluf had lied when he'd assured him that Karmel would remain independent from Koor.

Independent? Now he was supposed to sell South Africa the Kfir, the tactical aircraft produced by the group of companies, and his Karmel body-scanner would come a poor second. Governments were more ready to spend money on armaments than on medical equipment. He could have refused the sales trip to South Africa. The Rav Aluf wouldn't have been stupid enough to force him.

He *would* have refused if his advertisement in the *Jerusalem Post* had remained unanswered.

The visit to Cape Town's botanical gardens had helped Shmuel to sort out his impressions of the past week. The South African Airforce had flown him thousands of miles. He'd seen a staggering variety of settlements, industries and terrains; conifer-clad mountains that might have been part of Switzerland, deserts as arid as Sinai, neat little towns of Dutch-style houses and churches, round African mudhouses on lands where primitive farming had caused irreversible soil erosion. The Europeans had consistently planted imported pines, gumtrees, stinkwoods, oak, and trees native to the Continent; they were growing crops from wheat and sugar cane to olives and vines. The black Africans had not yet learned how to prevent their cattle from causing permanent damage to their lands. They *were* learning, Captain Joost had assured him, but agricultural evolution was making slow progress among the Bantu.

Captain Joost had taken him up the Atlantic coast to Namibia, or — as he'd called it — South-West Africa, flown him over the Rössing mines in the Namib Desert and the uranium mine-workings of Swakopmund. He'd shown him Walvis Bay, Namibia's only deep-water port and harbour for the uranium-transporting ships. They'd landed on the gravel airstrip at Arandis and visited mining camps and plants. The purpose of the long trek — to give Shmuel an idea of the security problems in areas where Russian-trained Swapo guerillas had launched a number of attacks and were intimidating the black native tribes. On paper the United Nations had ended South Africa's administration of Namibia in 1966; in fact, the people of Namibia were dependent on the food and money South Africa provided.

Shmuel picked up his hired Renault and drove out into Government Avenue. He'd enjoyed taking a close look at the trees and palms he'd been seeing from the air. Most of his horticultural ideas were impractical for his little garden in Ramat Hasharon, but he might find room for one or two proteas and frangipani. There were similarities in climate. Other similarities, too, between South Africa and Israel, each was beset by neighbours bent on destroying the advanced, modern state in their midst, each had become increasingly aware of the growing Russian shadow.

Stopped at traffic-lights — *robots*, as they so aptly called the things in Cape Town — Shmuel promised himself that he'd take Esther to the botanical gardens. Though the Ambassador Hotel was providing a good swimming-pool and excellent food she'd been alone too much. The varieties of protea in the gardens would interest her. Afterwards they'd visit the synagogue and the Jewish museum, sights which appealed to her more than to him. He'd make time for her somehow.

One more meeting would tie up the contract for the Kfir aircraft. Then there was the discussion, which might turn out to be lengthy, on the South Africans' request for Israeli instructors in anti-terrorist techniques.

Shmuel slid into the traffic lane for Sea Point. The prospect of his rendezvous with 'Mr Arnold' sent his thoughts scuttling into another time-dimension, from the rustling palm trees to silver birches dipped in cool northern sunlight, to the abandoned manor house and the defiant boy with the maize-coloured hair. Did anyone nowadays read Arnold Zweig's *Case of Sergeant Grisha*? Except him, when he wanted to convey a coded message, and 'Mr Arnold'.

Shmuel left the Renault in the forecourt of the Ritz Plaza Hotel, nose facing the exit. It would get uncomfortably hot, but in the covered car park he might get boxed in — a position he'd always avoided.

The Ritz Plaza was a high-rise building capped with a revolving restaurant. There'd be a spectacular view of Cape Town, the harbour and Table Mountain. He'd take Esther there for dinner. The food — judging by most meals they'd been served in South Africa — would be excellent, and it was the kind of place where there might be music.

The spacious foyer was surprisingly empty; one man on duty, another — clearly a holiday-maker — striding up to the reception desk. He was an old man in a striped towelling-robe, which covered him as effectively as a monk's habit; only his wrists and ankles stuck out like clusters of razor-sharp barnacles. Shmuel, remembering his first contacts with the British army in Berlin at the end of the war, promptly dubbed him the Colonel.

'You the manager?' demanded the Colonel.

'The under-manager, sir,' said the man behind the desk.

'Been turfed out of my room, y'know.'

'Sorry, sir.'

'Like a rest before my sundowner, y'know . . . What's all this non-sense?'

'It's a bomb-alert and . . .'

'Yes, yes. I heard what the chambermaid said. Bomb-alert!' snorted the Colonel. 'Rubbish. War's been over for years. Nothing to worry about except civilians. Should be able to control your bloody civilians. Better explain.'

'It was a telephone call, sir. The man said that a bomb's been planted in the hotel. We think it's a hoax — it usually is — but we're taking no chances. We've got the police in . . . with dogs. It'll take them about an hour to check all the rooms.'

'An hour? That's too slow. Get hold of the officer-in-charge and tell him I'll give him a hand. Know all about explosives. Bloody nuisance. Got to work fast, y'know.'

'Thank you, sir.' The young manager glanced at Shmuel, suppressing a smile. 'I'm sure the police are doing their utmost. Of course, sir, I'll let them know that you've volunteered.'

'Good man.' The Colonel seemed satisfied.

'Would you mind joining the other guests, sir? On the badminton courts beside the swimming-pool.'

'Got a bar set up out there?'

'There was no time, sir.'

'Organize it for you in a jiffy.'

'Better not upset police routine, sir. They've asked us to clear the building.'

'Oh well . . . fair enough. This sort of thing happen often?'

'No, sir.'

'Blacks rioting . . . Soweto . . . Jo'burg. Read all about it. Shouldn't allow black terrorists into your cities, y'know. Bad show.'

'We think it's a hoax. It usually is.'

'Soon deal with that. Damned impudence . . . interfering with the tourist industry.'

'I agree, sir. Now, if you wouldn't mind joining the other guests . . . through the door over there.'

'Fair enough. Did you say *dogs*?'

'That's right.'

'What breed?'

'Alsatians.'

'Temperamental. Tricky. Will have a word with the officer-in-charge; should get labradors from England.'

'Can I help you?' the under-manager asked Shmuel.

'I'm meeting a friend. I expect he'll be outside with the others. Coming, Colonel?'

The old man turned smartly and fell into step with him. 'Do I know you?'

'I don't think so.'

'South African, are you.' It was a flat statement. 'French descent, I shouldn't wonder. Dark chaps, the frogs. Had a quartermaster in my outfit. Efficient man. Something foreign about him though.'

Alexei Kirov did not look foreign among the sunbathers on the badminton courts. Tall and light-haired he easily melted into the tanned crowd of English and South Africans. Seeing Shmuel, he put a pair of shorts over his swimming trunks and slipped on a T-shirt. He picked up his book and towel and wandered over to the low building that housed the swimming-pool machinery.

The two of them sat on the ornamental wall facing the hotel.

'Better than usual,' said Kirov.

'No one to worry about except policemen with tracker dogs.'

Kirov smiled. 'You're over the worst. You're playing your mandoline again?'

'Yes, at Esther's request. It began at Kol-nidri; she wanted me to play something David used to sing.'

194

Kirov touched Shmuel's shoulder. 'I'm glad . . . I remember the first time I heard you. You were singing "A oomru ya". It sounded good.'

'Because you were sick.'

'The one I liked best was "The red sarafan". Did I ever tell you? it was one of my mother's songs. When I hear it Mareyevo comes alive — even now. I can see myself walk through a bed of phlox; I must have been about three . . . the flowers were above my head. Big clusters . . . pink, white and purple. All the scents of summer. What peace!'

'Alexei, get out while you can.'

'Not without my family.'

'I don't think you *want* to leave Russia.'

'Perhaps not. Most of us make unhappy exiles.'

'Anything new?'

'Yes. PVO Strany are stepping up research in Kazakhstan. Apart from Semipalatinsk they've built a new complex — top secret — at Sary-Shagan. I'm still trying to find out what's happening there. Work on particle beam technology says Professor Balatov. But even he doesn't know what it amounts to. I know he means to find out. Balatov's an angry man. Semipalatinsk isn't enough for him; he expected to be put in charge of Sary-Shagan as well. They've appointed a younger man. I'm beginning to think that Balatov will befriend me at last . . . given time.'

'Could be useful.'

'Undoubtedly.'

'You had no trouble getting to South Africa.'

'Not much. We have a team here training blacks as political activists and saboteurs.'

'It's becoming obvious.'

'I know.'

'You put it to your masters that you should go and check your men on the ground.'

'Yes . . . and take a look at the nuclear trade. South Africa's becoming a market-place for the world. It's terrifying.'

'You mean, uranium-mining and sales.'

'That . . . and the whole picture. The multinational companies have moved in with a vengeance. They want the uranium which South Africa can supply to any country of the western world, and South Africa — in return — is buying all the technology she needs . . . nuclear power plants, uranium equipment, computers; from Britain, Germany, France and America.'

Shmuel shrugged. 'What do you expect? It's trade; it's business.'

'With one difference. When South Africa exports diamonds to America and imports microwave cookers from the States — that's plain trade. But when South Africa sells her nuclear raw materials in order to acquire up-to-date nuclear arms it becomes a strategic and political matter. You understand?'

'I do, Alexei, I do. But South Africa has no choice between extermination as a modern state and membership of the nuclear club.'

'True.' Kirov surveyed the building before them. At such close quarters it looked like a towering honeycomb, uniform windows and curtains adding to its surrealist perspective. 'But we're not concerned with South Africa alone, are we? It's naïve to look upon any technologically up-to-date state in isolation. Any one of them − directly or indirectly − could turn into the root cause of the ultimate nuclear holocaust. South Africa's merely a microcosm of your western democracies − God help us.'

Kirov's story complemented everything Shmuel had seen in South Africa, but the Russian's information was more specific. The list of multinational companies, which were at once developing and exploiting South Africa's political and defence needs, seemed endless. Interspace Inc., Arther G. McKee, Anglo-American, Union Carbide; *American*. Rio Tinto Zinc, Davy Ashmore Engineering; *British*. Falconbridge Nickel Mines and Rio Algom; *Canadian*. Aquitaine and Minatome; *French*. Urangesellschaft and Uranerzbau; *West Germany*. Foxboro Corporation, *American;* and all round the democratic world again and again.

If Shmuel had doubted that the multinational companies of the countries which had signed the Nuclear Non-Proliferation Treaty had become the most dangerous empires in the world, Kirov's list would have convinced him. Their sole purpose was high profits − hardly a criminal aim in companies not connected with nuclear industry, yet a menace where the multinationals were creating another and yet another country with the capacity of selling nuclear materials and technology in politically volatile areas of the world.

There was appalling poverty and political instability in South America, yet German firms had sold Brazil equipment for the complete nuclear fuel cycle − from which weapon-grade materials could be manufactured. French companies were selling nuclear equipment to Pakistan and building reactors for Iraq − which worried Israel, Iran and Iraq's other neighbours around the Gulf. American companies had traded so profitably in Asia that India had recently been able to blast off her first nuclear bomb.

'Not to mention my own country,' said Kirov. 'My colleagues in the GRU and in the KGB's Science and Technology Directorate are made more than welcome in the States − by the big companies. Top corporations invite − actually invite − our teams to inspect their technology. They even provide training programmes for our scientists and engineers. Our team that visited Boeing returned with masses of documents and useful photographs − kindly provided by Boeing.'

'It's always America you blame,' said Shmuel.

'Yes . . . because America's leading the rush of the Gadarene swine. Look at the latest report from COCOM. There *is* this international committee which is trying to limit the export of strategic goods. But it does agree to exceptions. What stands out is that the greatest number of exceptions has been made in order to allow America to sell embargoed goods to Russia. If so-called democracy's to survive, America will have to control this situation. Government by the big corporations must end.'

'Who's to end it?'

'An American President strong enough to mend the splits in his administration . . . and the inter-agency rivalries. He'd have to give teeth to the State Department, and the people in the Defence Department, who oppose the uncontrolled spread of nuclear technology. And he'd have to alter — or even outlaw — organizations like the Energy Research and Development Agency who work hand in glove with the corporations . . . and who want nuclear proliferation accepted as an unavoidable fact of life.'

'How can one find such a man, Alexei?'

'One can't . . . not under the current American system of electing the President.'

'And America — unless it becomes a Soviet satellite like East Germany — won't adopt a Communist system of producing leaders.'

'Well . . . I just don't want Lenin's prediction to come true; that the capitalists will sell the rope with which Communism will hang them.'

'I'm a practical man, Alexei. I keep asking myself what I can do to stop the rot. The answer's *nothing* . . . at the moment.'

'*At the moment.*' Kirov raised his eyes to the honeycombed hotel-tower. '*There* is our hope.'

Shmuel had never spoken of John and Greg to Kirov. Now he felt that he had to, if he wasn't to lose his precious contact from inside the Soviet Union sooner or later. He gave Alexei an outline of the two young men's lives and qualifications.

'You have the nucleus of an organization.' Kirov was excited.

'You can put it like that, I suppose.'

'We'll need money.'

'We need the latest technical information. We still don't know enough about the holocausts in Eritrea and Rhodesia.'

'What if we get it? Without money it'll be wasted. All right, the information's essential but so's the money.'

'Once a capitalist, always a capitalist . . . Count Krasnykov.'

Kirov smiled. 'We're realists, both of us . . . when we're not dreaming of peace on earth.'

'Dreams grow from the imagination, Alexei. Without imagination man would still be trying — unsuccessfully — to invent the wheel.'

'How are we to teach all those inventive businessmen and technocrats in 1975 to imagine the feelings of the Eritreans . . . in the moment before their guts were vaporized from outer space? It's a matter of *God save us from powerful men who lack this kind of imagination*. Can't you see the average western corporation-man? He's just heard that COCOM has given his firm the go-ahead for selling his latest computer — much wanted by Russia or Iraq for making a bigger and better missile. He's a happy man.

'On his way home, he stops at the shopping precinct and buys his wife a box of candies. He's planning a baby-sitter — his niece always wants the money — to take his wife out to dinner. Poor girl; it's hard on her that he's so busy. He lets himself into his apartment . . .'

'And his little boy', continued Shmuel, 'Aims the latest death-ray gun at him and shouts, "Bang, you're dead," Papa says. "Isn't he cute?" Mama agrees. But she's tired; she's been dealing with a human problem that really got to her. Bobby's been threatening to leave Tricia on account of her drinking . . . unless she finds herself the right kind of analyst. Over dinner, at their celebration restaurant where everything's served in flames, the pair discuss their less well-adjusted friends. Bobby didn't exactly want to walk out on Tricia; so it would be a tragedy if they split up. Our pair get real close to one another — like before Papa became an executive too busy to talk through human problems. They decide they'll give Bobby and Tricia moral support. What are friends for?

'Home and to bed. While they're performing the usual conclusion to a good evening out, the radio — which is on at all times — mumbles news on a million made homeless by some little war, somewhere in the third world. Unless aid arrives fast many of them will starve to death. The pair achieve one of their better climaxes; it always goes well when Papa's pulled off an uncertain foreign business deal. He feels real good, and he goes to sleep trying to work out the best timing for speaking to his chairman about a raise and promotion.'

Shmuel saw the Colonel stalk into the hotel. 'Salt of the earth . . . as he would say if he met Papa.'

'Oh yes, salt of the earth . . . the worst kind of killer because he can't see beyond his private mini-world. And the big world is populated by the likes of him.' Kirov was staring at a window on the thirteenth or fourteenth floor. 'I have to leave you.'

Shmuel became aware that the small muscles of Alexei's face had tightened. 'Anything wrong?'

'Nothing drastic. Inter-departmental snooping's not too unusual.'

The hotel guests were leaving their temporary bomb-refuge, some diving into the pool, others making for the nearest bar. The alert appeared to be over. Shmuel went through the foyer, out to his car. The interior was burning hot. He remembered the beach-towel Esther had left in the boot, took it out and spread it on his seat.

He eased the car out of the forecourt and stopped at the end of the drive, giving way to passing traffic. The road before him had been narrowed by parked police cars, but they were beginning to move off. Shmuel crossed over and joined the line. Ten minutes to get to the Ambassador, ten minutes for a shower and change. Not too bad. Esther would be ready. She didn't like eating late in the evening. They should get to the fish restaurant in the harbour by eight-thirty.

His thoughts were on lobster thermidor when he heard a noise that made him flinch. It wasn't loud — he'd heard something like it when David had once dropped a jar of honey. A muted sound, yet it had risen above the throb of traffic in the main road ahead like an explosion.

The car in front of him stopped with a judder. A couple of policemen went running towards the hotel. He became conscious of a sudden silence. Not just robots holding up the flow of traffic. Something else. Voices stilled; like after a shell had exploded near him in the Yom Kippur war, temporarily deafening him. There were two figures on the forecourt he'd just vacated.

A uniformed porter was staring at a window high up the towering hotel. A curtain was hanging out, fluttering in the breeze. In the seconds before the police blocked his view Shmuel saw the man on the ground. He was lying spread-eagled, a blood-red lump between his legs. He must have fallen on his head, spilled his brains, and overturned.

He called Kirov from a pay-telephone in the fish restaurant, confirming Esther's assumption that he didn't feel like eating because he was preoccupied with business.

He heard the click of the receiver. 'Arnold?'

'Yes.'

'Anything I can do?'

'No . . . The matter solved itself.' Kirov's voice was unsteady.

'Not quite what you'd expected?'

'You know.'

'Yes, Arnold.' Unthinkable that a double agent like Alexei should have been unaware of being followed or less than suspicious of the bomb-alert which had emptied the hotel-rooms. That fool of a shadow would be alive now if he hadn't launched a physical attack. Instead he'd left Kirov a legacy of torment. The sequence of actions that had led to the accident were as clear to Shmuel as if he'd witnessed them, and his sympathy was with the man on the line. The silence between them said all there was to say.

'Thank you,' Kirov's voice sounded more controlled. 'Thanks for calling. Travelling as far as we do one's got to be prepared for . . . a dislocation.'

199

FREEDOM OF MOVEMENT

America 1976 — 1977

27

John Whitmore had been reading his way across the Atlantic, catching up on research reports in publications he'd been too busy to read at home. Then the bearded passenger beside him — a student, he supposed — had offered him a glossy business journal which he'd accepted from politeness rather than interest.

Unexpectedly he became fascinated with a survey of multinational companies that were *opening up* the South African market. The majority were directly or indirectly in the nuclear business. As South Africa was one of the world's largest producers of uranium this wasn't surprising. In peacetime the two-way traffic would have passed for normal trade. Not in a politically unstable era in which any little country, never heard of before, might acquire the means of unleashing a large-scale nuclear war.

John glanced at the student. Had such thoughts crossed his mind? 'Have you read this article?'

'Yes. It sure gives you an insight into practical economics.'

'Well . . . obviously American companies are making high profits in South Africa. Isn't there a contradiction? I thought your government objects to apartheid in South Africa.'

'That's right. We don't support the race policies of the South African government.'

'But you don't let that interfere with trade.'

'My subject's business studies,' the bearded man frowned. 'I guess I don't know too much about politics.'

'You're against apartheid though?'

'Sure . . . but that's a human-rights issue.'

Not his subject. Therefore — clearly — nothing for him to worry about. John left it at that. On the cover of the student's journal was a picture of Andrew Young — American ambassador to the United Nations — surrounded by obviously enthusiastic blacks, fist raised in the gesture typical of Communist agitators. Hypocrisy or schizophrenia or both? In any case, divorce between big business and politics. Apparently neither the publishers nor the owner of the journal had seen any connection between the cover and the contents. It had been an American who'd exhorted his countrymen, *only connect*. John doubted that the student was capable of connecting, except perhaps in bed.

Connecting all right, he thought wryly. On his return from the States his bed would be empty. The sudden death of Debbie's father had made their relationship somewhat less casual. Vincent Squire's will had left him in undisputed charge of Seespeed Engineering, Debbie free to spend her father's money.

She'd bought an expensive apartment in London — without consulting him — and put pressure on him to sell his cottage and move to her country house. She hadn't mentioned marriage. Her plans had been based on the predictable reactions of their neighbours and the work-force at Seespeed, mostly country-bred people. While they were tolerant of extra-marital relationships among the young without social responsibilities, they'd expect the head of Seespeed to be either a bachelor or legally married. Debbie understood these tenets of private and professional stability and she'd known that he would conform. There was just one thing she'd miscalculated; he'd never wanted to be tied to her.

At the end of a gruelling night of tears and soul-baring Debbie had finally accepted that she didn't own him and that blackmail would deprive her of any concern he felt for her. She'd cut her losses — which would have seemed impossible to her before she'd become financially independent — and taken heself to London.

Not until he'd seen the FOR SALE board at the gates of Vincent Squire's house had he allowed himself to believe in the end of a relationship which had turned into a trap of compassion. Not Debbie's fault. Had he been older and more experienced he wouldn't have involved himself with her in the first place. Not true. Andrew had been younger than he — and less experienced — when he'd seen beyond Terry's drinking and aimlessness and taken her aboard. Andrew had made no mistake.

Andrew . . . South Africa, probably safer than he'd imagined — under the umbrella of the multinational companies. On the one hand the dangerous spread of nuclear technology, on the other — short-term security for the whites in South Africa. And he? feeling free . . . his own master . . . travelling, for the first time in his life, in pursuit of a purely personal interest — neither on business nor because he was worried about his brother.

Ths trip to the States had been easier to organize than he'd expected. Greg Murphy's letter on the imminent unveiling of the futuristic Space Shuttle, had revived the excitement he'd felt when the first astronaut had made it to the moon. Then Kole Okango — established in a science post at National Research and Development — telling him, 'I can get you observer status for the show if that's all you want. But don't expect HM Government to pay for your trip. HM Government's got to pay out enough for globetrotting Members of Parliament without subsidising useful chaps like you or me.'

John stretched and banged his knees on the seat in front. No room in this jet for long-legged people. Fast-rising fuel costs were making the airlines economize on space. Never mind; he was heading for Rockwell International Space Division at Palmdale, California — surely his first step into space.

The tarmac, glistening like the skin of a giant whale, stretched into the flat distance fusing with a watery sky. The aircraft on the runway was a great deal larger than John had anticipated — about the size of a DC-9 commercial transporter. It dwarfed the people, some two thousand of them, who were milling around the Space Shuttle Orbiter 101 *Enterprise*.

Rockwell International's guests at the unveiling, Greg had told him, were representatives of the armed forces, Congress and industry plus a select number of foreigners from ESA — the European Space Agency. The scientific laboratory, which the Space Shuttle was scheduled to carry into earth orbit, had been a joint production by Belgium, Denmark, France, Italy, Holland, Spain, Switzerland, Great Britain, Austria and West Germany. The laboratory was an example of scientific interest in space-exploration and the sharing of costs.

The crowd on the tarmac was splitting into small groups — dividing, John guessed, into professional clubs of men who'd worked together or met in the course of earlier space programmes. There were very few women, none as attractive as Greg's sister. He'd seen a snapshot of Fiona in Cambridge, but it hadn't done justice to the girl with the shining auburn hair and eyes as blue as scilla siberica.

As Greg was joined by acquaintances — a white-haired man Greg introduced as Harry B. Resnick, and a couple of airforce officers — John took an opportunity to withdraw. He didn't want to be in the way of business discussions. He strolled to the hatch-backed tail of the Space Shuttle, then waited for Fiona to catch him up.

She said, 'I wish they'd show us the laboratory this bird's going to carry into orbit. Greg says it's much the same as an earthbound one, but it's been adapted to operate in zero gravity. The people living and working in it will be able to wear ordinary clothes . . . no cumbersome spacesuits. During the launch the gravity load will be only 3g, at re-entry less than 1.5g. The flights will be so smooth that they'll let women go up.'

'Is that what you want?' asked John.

'It's what I've been working for,' she said simply. 'I'm now qualified in systems analysis.'

'From computer programmer to systems analyst. Quite an achievement.'

'I didn't want to be left behind.'

'On earth.'

Fiona laughed. 'Confined to one small planet.' She looked at the scudding clouds. 'We're going to get wet. Do you mind?'

'No . . . But your hair . . .'

'It can't get any straighter. It'll soon dry in this warmth.'

A loudspeaker on the platform above them crackled. 'Ladies and gentlemen . . .' Rain as fine as mist swept across the runway. 'We apologize for this . . . unscheduled landing. You're welcome indoors but our information via weather satellite is that this shower will be followed by a long sunny interval . . . For those of you who wish to stay we're relaying a short talk by our chief engineer who'll give you on-site information about the Space Shuttle flight system prior to the demonstration.'

Another voice took over. '17 December 1903 Orville and Wilbur Wright successfully achieved flight in a power-driven aircraft. That first flight lasted twelve seconds over a distance of thirty-seven metres. Sixty-six years later, a man stepped on the moon for the first time and was watched by approximately five hundred million people round the world. On this historic day, 17 September 1976, we're on the threshhold of a new era in aviation. The beginning of regular runs of NASA's Space Shuttle to and from earth orbit in the 1980s marks the coming of age in space. The Shuttle will turn formidable and expensive space missions into economical routine operations that will benefit people throughout the world . . .'

'I hope to God they will,' said Fiona.

Her vehemence surprised John. Was she thinking of the top-secret research complex where Sean had been killed? 'We've had *some* benefits from space exploration, especially in medicine.'

'And in communications . . . perhaps; though I don't know to whose advantage it is when we show the world — via satellite — the pathetic circus of our presidential election.'

'What about the gold and the minerals on the moon?'

'A brand new reason for future wars I guess.'

Greg was listening to the talk aware that the man beside him had been the originator of the visionary machine. He wondered why Harry B. Resnick had left his sphere of achievement at Rockwell International at a time when his drawing-board ideas were turning into reality. What had been the attraction of taking on the job of special adviser to the President? surely a move into the political arena. Greg acknowledged that there was a great deal he didn't understand about this remarkable man, yet he felt totally convinced of his integrity as a person.

'Space Shuttle is a true aerospace vehicle,' the voice from above droned on. 'It takes off like a rocket, manoeuvres in earth orbit like a spacecraft and lands like an airplane. It's designed to carry heavy loads into earth orbit. Unlike other launch vehicles which were used once only, each Space Shuttle Orbiter may be used again and again . . .'

A versatile machine indeed. Its crew could repair unmanned satellites in orbit, or return the satellites to earth for repairs that couldn't be done in space. It could therefore maintain satellites that served energy, weather forecasting, navigation, farming, oceanography and communications in general. The Shuttle could also be used for placing interplanetary spacecraft into orbit, together with a rocket stage that was being developed by the Department of Defense. The rocket, called Interim Upper Stage, would be ignited to accelerate the spacecraft to higher orbits than the Shuttle's maximum altitude of six hundred miles.

The Space Shuttle was undoubtedly opening up new worlds, making possible projects which had been no more than wishful thinking at the beginning of the 'seventies. It could carry into orbit the building blocks for large solar power-stations that would convert the solar heat and sunlight of space into unlimited supplies of electricity for an energy-hungry world. The building blocks would be assembled by specialists, transported and maintained by Space Shuttle.

Eventually the Shuttle would carry up the materials for human settlements in earth orbit. The inhabitants of the settlements would build and maintain solar power-stations, manufacture drugs, metals, glass for lenses and electronic crystals. The quality of those products would be much higher than the quality of similar earth-produced materials. Production would begin as soon as the space laboratory was in orbit, long before the establishment of the settlements.

The speaker concluded with a brief explanation of the Space Shuttle flight system. It was composed of the Orbiter, an external tank − ET − that contained the ascent propellant to be used by the Orbiter main engines, and two solid rocket boosters − SRBs. Each booster rocket had a sea level thrust of 2.6 million pounds. The Orbiter and SRBs were reusable; the external tank was jettisoned on each launch.

The Orbiter was the crew − and payload − carrying unit of the Shuttle system. It was 122 feet long and 57 feet high, with a wingspan of 78 feet, and weighed 150,000 pounds without fuel. The Orbiter could carry a payload of 65,000 pounds into orbit. It carried its cargo in a bay 60 feet long and 15 feet in diameter. The bay was flexible enough to accommodate unmanned spacecraft of various shapes and fully equipped scientific laboratories.

Each of Orbiter's three main liquid fuel rocket engines had a thrust of 470,000 pounds. They were fed propellants from the external tank which was 154 feet long and 28.6 feet in diameter. At lift-off the tank held 1,550,000 pounds of propellants, consisting of liquid hydrogen (fuel) and liquid oxygen (oxidizer). The hydrogen and oxygen were in separate pressurized compartments of the tank. The external tank was the only part of the Shuttle system that was not re-usable.

In orbit, the Orbiter used its manoeuvering sub-system (OMS) to adjust its path, for rendezvous operations, and at the end of a mission for slowing down on the way back to earth. OMS propellants were mono-methyl hydrazine as the fuel and nitrogen tetroxide as the oxidizer. They ignited on contact eliminating the need for ignition devices.

In the light of the chief engineer's information the shape of the shuttle made sense. The machine, not yet commissioned for space-flight, re-minded Greg of a lizard pursued by a snake which had escaped the enemy by casting off its expendable tail-section. He hadn't expected to see Space Shuttle launched into orbit, yet he felt unreasonably disappointed that the bird was about to perform like any ordinary form of air transport.

Resnick said, 'It's a modest preview. It'll be years before Enterprise reaches the all-systems-go stage . . . in the early 'eighties, at best.'

'What's the interim programme?'

'The Russians will blast up another hundred spy satellites. We will send up as many as we can afford. Presidential elections slow down cash allocations and progress. There'll be no firm policy until the new man's in the White House. The Russians have no such problem.'

'Harry, why have you gone into politics?'

Resnick kept his eyes on the Shuttle, which was rolling along the runway. 'I'm an old man. This craft should be developed by the young who'll provide the necessary continuity. The only useful function I can perform now is to try and hold off some of the military in the Pentagon . . . those who have already rejected the peaceful potential of the Space Shuttle . . . the Montana faction.'

Greg recalled the bleak office in Albuquerque, Colonel Piper's di-spirited apologies. *The civilians have built themselves complexes which look like cities out of science-fiction — with taxpayers' money . . . They tell us what they want us to do . . . The chain of command's been short-circuited. All that's needed nowadays is a person-to-person call from Los Alamos to Washington.* 'General Montana?'

'Yes, General Montana . . . a young Vietnam veteran . . . clever, ambitious, a menace in a peacetime army. But you probably know him.'

'I don't. My brother's commander mentioned him.'

'General Piper.'

'He was a colonel.'

'He's been promoted.'

'For getting his men killed on army exercises?'

'I understand your feelings.' Resnick put a hand on Greg's shoulder. 'But you should have another talk with Piper before you judge him. Don't reject this idea . . . it's relevant to your brother's death. Let me arrange a meeting.'

When Sean's friend, Fergie, had said, 'I'm making no excuses for Piper,' he had in fact been defending the Colonel.

'What do you say?' asked Resnick.

'I'll see him.'

'That's good.' Resnick watched the Shuttle soar into the air. 'You asked why I've gone into politics . . . It's got a great deal to do with your work at Boeing and LEEC and it's future application . . . which I consider crucial. If all goes well, the Space Shuttle will advance your project by years. But make no mistake . . . the bird up there's started a period of kill or cure.'

John had never seen a restaurant more perfectly geared to the Anglo-Saxon gourmet than the Wells Fargo; a huge cavern with solid pine tables and chairs; in the centre a battery of spits turning and roasting piglets and sides of beef. White-capped chefs were serving customers cuts of their choice, while girls in early-settler dresses were offering salads from a forty-foot counter.

'It's a romantic version of Wild West life,' said Fiona, 'one of our American dreams. Don't worry John, you can eat as little or as much as you like.'

A waiter in Red Indian head-dress showed them to a table for two and offered a choice of cocktails — Lone Ranger whisky sour, Minihaha highball, Buffalo Bill vodka, Chapaquiddic firewater. They ordered tomato juice.

'Greg's been looking forward to this evening,' said Fiona. 'He wouldn't have missed it for anyone but Harry Resnick . . . and if all goes well, a government contract for LEEC.'

'Hope it does go well.'

'We won't know for months . . . probably not until after the presidential election. You'll be staying the weekend with us?'

'Yes. Greg's changed my flight. We'll be leaving together.'

'After his meeting in the morning. Sorry about the tight schedule, but there'll be time to talk at Ann Arbor.'

It surprised John that she saw herself as her brother's locum, second best company for him. She seemed to be naïvely unaware of her effect on the men at adjacent tables, and on him. She was that rare thing — an unselfconscious beauty. 'Fiona, what made you go into computers?'

'I guess it was the new language part of it . . . a language my parents didn't know. Naughts or ones, the yes or no information . . . *Bits* . . . eight bits to a byte, bytes that represent a letter or numerals. When I was a kid it was a game Greg played with me. One evening he took me to a science for children lecture at the university. Afterwards he showed me a room where two new computers had been installed. He unlocked the door . . . it was dark inside. We just stood and listened. There were sounds . . . whispering. It was like the computers chattering with one another . . . weird . . . exciting.'

'You didn't know about static electricity.'

'No. I imagined the computers gossiping about the people who worked with them by day. Later on . . . Well, when you get to designing systems your ideas keep stretching. You come to realize that computers have only just begun to change the way we're living . . . and the ideas keep coming, and the whole universe opens up. You know what I mean, John.'

'The most beautiful and most profound emotion we can experience is the sensation of the mystical. It is the sower of all true science. He to whom this emotion is a stranger, who can no longer wonder and stand rapt in awe, is as good as dead.'

'That's marvellous!'

'Einstein's words, not mine. Come on, let's get some of that old-fashioned beef.'

Fiona smiled, 'Cooked on an electronically programmed spit.'

As John followed her past the crowded tables a shockwave passed through his body, a moment of pain and panic. Before him a girl in a scarlet sari, hair like the sunlit wings of an African starling. Kisumu. The girl's blood seeping into the red earth. 'Leah . . . don't go.'

She turned, her eyes understanding and concerned.

He took her hand, Leah's small, slender hand. Suddenly the journey through time and space was over. The people around him were American, not Luo. He was within a few miles of Palmdale, California. The girl was wearing a scarlet dress, not a sari.

The Wells Fargo had emptied, the spits stopped turning.

'What made you think of it?' John put the last of their wine into Fiona's glass.

'The common denominators.'

The common denominator was violence . . . the slaughter of his parents in Kenya, the campus riot in which Greg's wife had been injured, the destruction of Shmuel's parents and his long trek across war-devastated Russia. The terrible waste of lives . . . Leah killed in the massacre of Kisumu, Shmuel's son in the Sinai desert, Fiona's brother in the course of a questionable military exercise. 'Isolated events, repeated in God knows how many families throughout the world.'

'A pattern's been emerging, and that's no accident. You and Greg and Shmuel have been influenced by personal losses. Your losses have made you exceptionally aware of the world beyond your own back yards . . . because you're exceptional people. The three of you share professional interests which — naturally enough — brought you together at the Cambridge conference.'

'We happened to meet.'

'At some point all friends happen to meet. Friendship has to have a beginning. Each of you allowed the others to know him; each gave his trust.'

'You make it sound like a contract.'

'That's how I see it.'

'You're a party to it, Fiona.'

'Just an extension to Greg.'

'Not the impression he gave me. I gathered he'd be putting you in the picture.'

Fiona nodded. 'Let's look at the pattern . . . or picture. Seven years ago the Israelis became aware of an unexplained event in Eritrea. So did Russian Army Intelligence. Russia's had a long-standing interest in the coast stretching to the Gulf and the Strait of Hormuz. The Russian army sent a fact-finding party to Eritrea, the Israelis your friend Shmuel . . .'

'The Russians tried to hunt him down, yet later . . .'

'Yes,' Fiona interrupted, 'but what matters, from the point of view of my computer analysis, is the strange manner in which the Eritreans of the area died. Neither Russians nor Israelis found the answer. The sight of those bodies . . .'

'Husks.'

'I saw the pictures you sent Greg . . . The holocaust made Shmuel realize that he, personally, was still at war.'

John said, 'He touched one of the bodies; it disintegrated into dust before his eyes. He told me it was his flashpoint.' A moment that ignites and activates a driving force in one's life, a moment that dictates its future direction; the single moment that rules how one will spend one's self. He'd been too young when Mau Mau had murdered his parents, too full of hate for finding his direction. His flashpoint had happened at the massacre at Kisumu.

Fiona put her hand on John's. 'I know what Shmuel meant. Greg's flashpoint came when he realized how easily we might lose Sean . . . Sean back from Vietnam, in hospital, wired up to life-support machines.'

'He'd flown back from England, half-way through the Cambridge symposium.'

'Six years ago. From then on the three of you exchanged information. No explanation required.'

'The pattern building up, as you've said.'

'Then, about three years ago, you went to Africa again. On the frontier between Rhodesia and Mozambique you found people who'd been killed like the Eritreans. Your brother took the photographs you sent us. On your return to Salisbury you reported what you'd seen to a black Member of Parliament, and you gave him pictures. Afterwards a man burgled Andrew's house.'

'He certainly wanted the film.'

'But you surprised him and he didn't get it. You believed the man was a Russian because of the gold inlays in his teeth. From Rhodesia you went to Israel, on business. Am I right?'

'Yes . . . you've put together a pretty accurate dossier. It was when I showed Andrew's photos to Shmuel that he told me about the Eritrean holocaust. He's since found out that it had been caused by Russian experiments in space . . . experiments which were kept so secret that even Army Intelligence had no knowledge of them.'

The connections between the three of them had become more conscious and deliberate, the incidents that concerned them increasingly complex and world-wide.

Goldtooth had gone to England, almost certainly to negotiate with him about the roll of film he'd failed to secure in Rhodesia. He'd tried to approach him through Debbie. But he'd yet again missed the target; someone, staging a suicide, had killed him in a Brighton hotel room. The one man who might have known who was responsible for the holocaust, and how it had been *accomplished*, was dead.

There was, of course, OTRAG — the West German rocket firm building satellites for commercial use in Zaire. Shmuel had assured him that OTRAG was harmless — as far as any rocket producer could be. Yet now, in the autumn of 1976, Russia and East Germany were exerting such political pressure on the African state of Zaire that its government was ready to lose the large OTRAG revenue and break the contract with the company. According to a newspaper report OTRAG had been given notice to quit. Why should Russia and East Germany worry about OTRAG? Was it because commercial companies by their very nature worked for the highest bidder? who — in this case — was more likely to belong to the American than the Russian camp.

When the information, gathered in Eritrea and Israel, Rhodesia and England, had reached Greg in the States, the emerging pattern had begun to make sense to Fiona. Through Harry Resnick, who'd worked for Rockwell International, Greg had discovered that Goldtooth had been a Russian deserter who'd left Rockwell for the Alpha Corporation of Boston. The chances were, therefore, that the Rhodesian holocaust had been due to an American operation; the logical conclusion — that Russia and America were engaged in similar death-dealing research on an entirely new weapon.

If that was the case — and neither John nor Fiona doubted it — a good many minor incidents and observations, which Greg had collected over the past few years, fitted into Fiona's computer analysis.

'The computer can't solve mysteries,' she said, 'but it can and did come up with possible permutations and relevant questions. There's Mat Scobie; Greg first met him at Boeing, as the co-ordinator with a special interest in security. While Greg was at the Cambridge symposium his laboratory was broken into. There were no indications of industrial espionage, no reason to suppose that there was more to it than ordinary thieving . . .'

'Then why did Scobie make a song and dance about it?' asked John.

'We still don't know. Harry Resnick believes that Scobie was an FBI agent . . . and that he wanted to attract attention to himself as a punctilious investigator. Now Greg's established that Scobie left the FBI before he took the job at Boeing . . . which knocks down the theory that he was after promotion. So why did Scobie make a major case out of the break-in? Then there's the connection between the Russian defector — Larski — and Scobie; both working for the Alpha Corporation. What was Larski doing in Rhodesia? Why was he so anxious to get hold of the holocaust film?'

'Because someone didn't want those pictures to travel any farther. A film is a lasting record.'

'Exactly. But by the time Larski had reached England, and was about to contact you, he'd lost his bosses' confidence. They'd decided he was safer dead. According to Mat Scobie the death was an accident; Larski was a drug-addict. Heroin — sufficient to kill an elephant — was found in his Boston apartment. You don't agree with that, do you John?'

'I don't. There was no sign that Larski had been injecting himself in the past. It was confirmed at the inquest and reported in the *Mid-Sussex Times*.'

'So, Scobie told Harry Resnick deliberate lies. And then . . . Sean.'

'Fiona, I understand. Afterwards, Greg's interview with Sean's commander . . .'

'Piper was extremely bitter about his men being used for testing security at plants owned by commercial companies. He implied that certain corporations had corrupted high-ranking officers in the Pentagon. That the Alpha Corporation of Boston has offices in the same building as the army in Albuquerque doesn't look accidental to me. Did you know that Scobie quizzed Greg about his experiments of introducing impurities into silicon crystals?'

'Controlled impurities?'

'That's right.'

'A new one on me.'

'I guess Greg forgot to mention it because it happened so long ago . . . way back at Boeing. At the time it didn't figure. Scobie told Greg he was just a layman; he was no scientist, simply an administrator. Greg is convinced he was lying — that he knows a lot about semiconductors. If so, why did he deny it? Maybe Piper will be able to answer a few questions. Harry Resnick's asked Greg to see him. They'll be meeting tomorrow morning.'

'What's the point?'

'Perhaps he wants to explain his promotion to general,' said Fiona bitterly. 'Oh . . . sorry, John. Greg and I don't feel . . . rational about Sean's commander.'

'What was the connection between Resnick and Piper?'

'They met this morning, at the Space Shuttle demonstration.'

'Piper must have done some fast talking.'

'Well, he seems to have impressed Harry Resnick. Harry told Greg that whatever Piper has to say is relevant to Sean's death.'

'Why approach Greg through an intermediary?'

'Their talk in Albuquerque wasn't exactly cordial. John, no matter what Piper tells Greg, I intend to concentrate on Scobie.'

'You, Fiona?'

'I've made certain enquiries. There's a firm in Washington DC that functions as Corporation Agency Inc. It's a rent-a-professional or rent-an-executive business . . . the only one of its kind in the country, perhaps in the world. The firm supplies highly specialized managers and executives to big corporations − mainly multinationals.'

'Surely such people are bred within their own companies.'

'That was my first reaction,' agreed Fiona. 'But Corporation Agency exists and − in principle − it sounds like a good idea. There must be room for outside troubleshooters in a company keen on introducing drastic changes; that is, when no one on the inside wants to act as hatchet-man.'

'How to kill without firing your own gun. I can imagine other purposes for appointing a top outsider. You think that Scobie's one of them?'

'I know he is.'

The candle on their table was spluttering, the red wax dripping on the gingham tablecloth. John moistened his fingers and put out the flame. 'Keep away from Corporation Agency.' He hadn't felt such anxiety since Andrew had accepted the job in Rhodesia. 'Fiona,' he took her hands, 'don't you get involved − please. If nothing else, one thing's clear to me . . . the Agency must be supplying very clever and ruthless men − and probably women − to the kind of firm I wouldn't trust.'

She leaned over and kissed his lips − a light spontaneous touch. 'Johnny, trust me . . . When you've been raised like me, in the States, you get so you pick up the vibes of violence like a geiger-counter.'

Greg put on the light above his bed and sat up. Past midnight, and he was still awake. No use tossing from side to side; he'd read himself to sleep. He picked up the file Harry Resnick had given him, a set of plans and notes dating back to 1971 when a team at Boeing had worked on the industrial potentials in outer space. Visionary ideas which couldn't have been carried out at the time. Now a vastly improved technology was making such plans feasible. Not as they stood, of course.

Harry Resnick had been right; in the light of up-to-date knowledge most of the Boeing plans would have to be discarded or re-designed. Greg tried to assess how long that would take him. Certainly several months of hard grind, on top of his work at LEEC. Worthwhile, though he'd be neglecting Stella and the boys. Stella would be understanding. She'd come to feel secure in the Ann Arbor university environment where mixed marriages were not uncommon. He'd been sensitive to the chip on her shoulder in the early days of their marriage, but it hadn't been apparent for the past couple of years or more. Yes, she'd be able to cope.

He'd be glad to get home. The Palmdale Motel was OK but the rooms — grouped around the swimming-pool — were poorly sound-proofed. He could hear the fast gabble of a familiar TV voice, the muted whines and screams of a piped pop-group. Greg put down the file. No use trying to concentrate. He got up and changed from his pyjama trousers into trunks. A few lengths in the pool might relax him.

The day's drizzle had blown out to the Pacific. The night was mild and starlit. In the garden between pool and parking-lot a bullfrog's bass was arousing the cicadas. Their high-pitched shrills were answered by the dismal, repetitive calls of a mocking-bird.

Greg swam the length of the pool and turned under water. As he surfaced he heard the slam of car doors. He changed from a crawl to a silent breast stroke. If it was Fiona and John returning he didn't want them to think that he'd been waiting for them.

The people who came walking across the paved area towards the rooms were strangers, a couple of large men in dark trousers and shirts. Greg kept still at the side of the pool until they had passed.

In a window near his own room a light went on. The curtains were drawn but he saw an agitated silhouette. There was something inevitable about the scream that followed the shadowy movements. What shocked Greg was that the desperate cry was a man's. It rose, weird and drawn-out, above the natural night-sounds and then stopped abruptly.

Greg heaved out of the water and ran to the square of light. The curtains fitted too well for him to see more than moving shadows, but it seemed to him that the intruders were ransacking the room.

He was about to make for his telephone when the floodlights flashed on. Running footsteps were pounding along the pool area, armed guards closing in. Someone else must have heard the scream and alerted the motel's security men.

The door of the room suddenly swung open. One intruder came racing out, followed by the other. The second man was carrying a limp body across his shoulder. Greg recognized the unconscious man's face. The guards had spotted the escapers and were doubling back, trying to cut off their retreat to the parking-lot.

Greg made a decision which filled him with distaste. He'd leave the criminals and their victim to the guards. And he would search the room before anyone else thought of it. He didn't know what he should be looking for — only that the man who'd just been attacked would probably not have gone to Palmdale without a good reason, without a case he could prove.

For a career-soldier, who regarded civilians as a lower form of life, the very thought of approaching Sean's brother must have hurt General Piper.

28

The police handled the abduction of General Piper promptly and quietly. No wailing sirens. The officers who checked staff and guests at the motel wore plain clothes. The man who came to interview Greg in the early hours of the morning suggested that a kidnapping of this nature might have security implications, but he didn't labour the point.

The officer exuded quiet confidence. The kidnappers would not escape. As the Space Shuttle demonstration at Rockwell International had brought many prominent people to Palmdale and district, extra police had been drafted into the area. Contingency plans had gone into operation. Nevertheless, it would be unwise to omit the normal routine of looking for witnesses. Greg's information — even a relatively insignificant detail — might be helpful.

Greg, listening to the courteous cop, felt he'd got stuck in a nightmare. If he made an effort and held out a hand he'd be touching Stella's body and find the way back into his own identity. How could it be? a man screaming with pain on an ordinary night? Such things happened in movies, not in real life.

'What did you do after you heard the . . . commotion, sir?' asked the officer.

'I wasn't sure what I should do. I went to the steps . . .'

'You got out of the water.'

'Not right away.'

'You listened?'

'I guess so.' Greg took off his spectacles. A brief diversion. Better not let the cop take charge. 'I heard nothing, but I thought I should find out whether anyone needed help. As I got out of the pool I saw some men running past . . .'

'Did you notice how many?'

'Two or three. I'm not sure. The lights came on. It was confusing . . .

216

someone was obviously chasing these people . . . I went into the room; the door was open.' The police were bound to have noticed the wet marks on the carpet.

'You assumed the occupant had been injured?'

'Yes.'

'What did you do next, sir?'

'I realized that someone had given the alert and went back to my room.'

'The man who called the guards is an airfore officer . . . General Jabotinsky. Do you know him, sir?'

'No.'

'But you knew General Piper?'

'We met, once.'

'He mentioned you to General Jabotinsky. Seems he was planning on meeting you in the morning. Do you know why?'

'I don't.'

'Neither does Jabotinsky. He reckons Piper was interested in your work on semiconductors.'

'Yes, it figures.'

'This is a hypothetical question, sir . . . but have you any idea who'd want to kidnap General Piper?'

'I haven't.'

'Or why?'

'Sorry, I can't help you.' It happened to be true. After a cursory examination of the envelope Greg had found under Piper's mattress he'd hidden it, forcing himself to put the contents out of his mind. Those pictures hadn't made sense. He'd have to examine them with a magnifying-glass.

When the police officer had gone Greg locked his door and collapsed on the bed. Should he have concealed his find? Was he obstructing the search for Piper and his kidnappers? Too late for doubts. Piper would have given him the envelope; he was convinced of it. Yet the recollection of carrying it from Piper's room to his own made him shake with delayed nervousness and shock.

Greg wakened at sunrise. He'd slept less than three hours but he felt restored. John was here. John would help him analyze Piper's photographs, which appeared to pose an engineering rather than an electronic puzzle.

Like most good motels the Palmdale had provided a kettle and an assortment of small packages. Greg made coffee and drank it while he collected the Space Shuttle hand-outs and the Boeing file and put them into his briefcase. He stuck Piper's envelope into one of the glossy brochures. As an afterthought he changed the combination of the lock.

When his doorbell chimed he expected Fiona, John or both of them.

But the caller was a man in his fifties who gave an immediate impression of physical strength — narrow hips, wide shoulders, thick black hair streaked with grey and a strong face with high cheekbones. A Slavonic face, which reminded Greg of the best athlete in his year at school. They'd called Mietek *the Polack*, not a flattering name for people of Polish extraction, but it hadn't bothered that one. Mietek had taken it for granted that everyone liked and admired him; he'd been blessed with a superiority complex which had made him a tolerant and surprisingly gentle person.

Greg's visitor walked into the room, obviously assured of a welcome. 'I'm Martin Jabotinsky.'

'General.'

'Right. Glad to know you, Murphy. Greg, isn't it?'

'Yes. Sit down.'

'You making coffee?'

'Be my guest.'

'Sure appreciate it. Black with plenty of sugar. Dick Piper told me a lot about you.'

'He hardly knew me.'

'Not that hard to collate information on a guy's professional standing . . . in your speciality. Your rating's high . . . very high. He hoped you'd be able to help us. There are special reasons why you should.'

'Are you referring to my brother, Sean . . . the carelessness and stupidity that killed him?'

If the General resented the attack he didn't show it. 'I'm referring to the fact that the official explanation of the . . . accident didn't satisfy you. For what other reason would you have taken the risk of overflying the Los Alamos complex?'

'A pilot took the risk.'

'Ted Wagner, his crew and your brother's friend — Lieutenant Ferguson. You're surprised that I know? Then you'd better realize that my men — and Dick Piper's — are disciplined professionals, not anarchists. They did use — let's say, their own initiative — in organizing the reconnaissance over Los Alamos. But once they felt sure that they had a valid case, they presented it to their commanding officers. Besides . . .' Jabotinsky smiled, 'if the enquiry into the Los Alamos complex is to be pursued, fairly large resources have to be made available. And it takes the top of a command to provide them.'

'Piper went to a lot of trouble to explain to me that the chain of command has been broken . . . by commercial corporations and corrupt officers at the Pentagon.'

'He was right about the disproportionate power of the companies — especially the multinationals — and corruption, in government agencies, in Congress and — least of all — in the armed forces. Don't take what he told you too literally. Whether you believe it or not he was deeply distressed about your brother's death. It made him feel overly pessimistic. The truth about the chain of command is that it had been circumvented on several occasions, but not broken . . . My men, who were killed when their airplane was shot down over Los Alamos, and your brother's death have had a profound effect on us.'

'Ah yes. Colonel Piper was promoted to general.'

'It was one effect,' said Martin Jabotinsky evenly. 'Those of us who've served with Dick Piper in World War Two . . . in Korea and Vietnam, succeeded — at long last — in getting him the promotion he should have had years ago.'

'You're saying he'd been passed over?'

'I am. I can think of no other commander of his distinction who's been treated more shabbily. He's always been a bad politician and rat-racer. Too honest and outspoken. Putting the welfare of his men above his own career.'

'Your picture of him doesn't tally with mine.'

'First impressions aren't always reliable. You'd change your mind about Dick if you met him again . . . He wanted your advice on the Los Alamos complex. The pictures taken on your flight with Ted Wagner are puzzling. Our scientists don't know what to make of them.'

'Neither do I.'

'Dick had additional information for you. We didn't have a chance to discuss it yesterday. I was tied down with some guys from Rockwell. But Dick and I would have got together after he'd seen you. Now . . . Gawd knows when that'll be . . . I've called the police. There's no news. I've persuaded the cops to accept airforce help as of now.'

'Why do you expect your men to be more successful than the police?'

'My helicopters might make a difference.' Jabotinski put down his cup. 'We're treating the abduction as an inside operation.'

Greg wondered what to make of that outrageous statement. Was this fit war-veteran unhinged? 'Are you suggesting that one of your fellow-officers is responsible for the kidnapping? General Montana?'

'So Dick told you about him.' The luminous grey eyes looked unperturbed.

'He told me nothing, except that a certain General Montana is of some assistance to commercial corporations.'

'To the Alpha Corporation of Boston, in particular. I'm not accusing Montana in particular . . . I'm telling you that there's a caucus in the armed forces — as there is in Congress and in the administration — which is convinced that America's prosperity and future depends on our becoming the nuclear arms dealer to the world. The members of these factions believe that there should be no control of nuclear technology . . . that nuclear missiles should be sold commercially to any country that can pay for them, not excluding Russia. What do you make of such a policy?'

'It would be suicidal . . . obviously.'

'Glad you agree with me.'

'Yes. But a policy is one thing, abducting an army general another.'

'Not in my book. If the opposition suspected that Dick Piper came to know too much of the research — or whatever — that's going on at Los Alamos they'd remove him without hesitation. The only hope I have is that he'll be able to stall his kidnappers — keep them guessing — until we find him.'

'It's a poor prospect.'

'Perhaps not. Dick's been in tight spots before, and got out. We'd appreciate any help you can give us. You might hear of technological advances that could throw a new light on the Los Alamos photos.'

'It's possible,' Greg admitted.

Martin Jabotinsky took a card from his wallet. 'Here's my private address. Call me if anything turns up . . . any time. If I'm not there leave your number.' He got up and held out his hand to Greg. 'We should work together, Greg.'

'I'll do what I can.'

'In a wider sense. Before long this country will have a new President. It's scientists like you who should persuade the new administration that there must be tight control on the export of . . . electronic and nuclear technology. If you people make out an irrefutable case against irresponsible commercial interests, and we make war on corruption, the nuclear holocaust might yet be prevented.'

'You make it sound too easy.'

'It isn't. You know it as well as I do. But peace or war never has been in the hands of the masses. All through history it has been a handful of individuals who caused or prevented wars. That's something one shouldn't forget. We must learn to control the politicians. They're supposed to serve not to run us.'

'I have friends who'd agree with you.'

'Then tell them that they have allies in the armed forces . . . even in Russia.'

'Is that a fact?'

'It is, I assure you.'

California and Michigan, startling in their contrasts, gave John some idea of America's sheer size and scope. In California — almost tropical heat and thunder, luxurious residential developments a long way from hypermarkets and gasoline stations, in between vast no-man's-lands of savannah, and industrial complexes which looked as if a modern set of gods had dropped them from the sky. In Michigan, the well-planned and still growing university town of Ann Arbor in a gracious setting of gold and russet autumn trees.

John would have liked to walk around the town and the campus, but time was short and distances too great. Fiona drove him to the law school, built in a mellow Victorian style, a spacious quadrangle donated by William C. Cook in 1859. She showed him the Carl Milles fountain, 'Sunday Morning in Deep Waters', which fronted the Michigan League of the same period. They circled the enormous University Hospital and medical school complex, which had been founded in 1869, yet looked functionally up-to-date. But it was the Earl V. Moore building, the music school, on a grassy hill above the Huron River, which most impressed John. Designed by the world-famous architect Saarinen, it possessed the massive magnificence of Beethoven's symphonies. John saw it as a confident forerunner of the twenty-first century.

That evening he and Fiona returned to Saarinen's masterpiece for a brilliant performance of the *Missa Solemnis*. John listened sporadically, unable to concentrate, his thoughts darting from one American achievement to another, from the genius that had built the Space Shuttle to the talent and energy which had created this superb university town.

So much scientific and artistic culture, yet forty-eight hours ago a senior army officer had been savagely attacked and abducted. Unfortunately it figured that the American crime-scale should be commensurate with America's vastness and vitality. Greg was surely right in his assessment of the kidnapping, of Piper's importance to people who were gambling for high stakes.

They'd spent hours analyzing every dot in Piper's photographs. The pictures taken from Ted Wagner's aircraft and Piper's showed certain connections, such as a link between the arrays of mirror-reflectors seen from the air and the equipment in a computer control room. Yet the details photographed in laboratories and engineering shops looked far from familiar. Lasers figured in what appeared to be experimental work, but their operational use was a mystery. It could have been anything from measuring the distance between earth and a satellite, or transmitting light through glass-fibres to the production of gun target-designators or aircraft sensors for tracking missiles.

Greg had speculated that Los Alamos was working on the new science of photonics — still largely in the theoretical stage — which had been hailed already as a possible successor to electronics.

There were, however, a couple of photographs that wrecked all the neat theories which Greg, Fiona and he had put together; a picture of machine-parts — out of focus — that didn't fit into any of their ideas, and a scene of some twenty men and women — seen through a gate of steel bars. They might have been part of the work-force had they not been bunched together like a herd of frightened animals. The figures and faces were blurred, yet they conveyed unmistakable tension and terror.

Whoever had done the camera work inside those buildings must have defeated the most sophisticated electronic and human security systems and penetrated at the risk of his life. Greg, despite his personal reservations, believed it had been General Piper himself.

John felt angry with himself for letting his attention wander. Too late. He'd missed a singular experience. The voices of the singers stormed the hall in a final burst of music, a great choral paeon resolving into a single triumphant note.

'You weren't bored?' Fiona studied his face anxiously.

He took her hand, leading her out through the crowds. 'What do you think?'

'Preoccupied.'

'Yes . . . and regretting it.'

'I know.' She looked up at him, a rueful smile in her eyes. '*I've* done this kind of thing . . . niggling away at some idea at the back of my mind, and missing out on something beautiful that'll never happen again.'

As she unlocked the car he gazed at the Saarinen building, at the reflection of lights in the river. 'We'll make it happen . . . in England.'

She turned and came into his arms. He held her, cursing his body for inflicting on him a desire he hadn't felt since he'd made love with Leah in Kisumu. Damnable; but a cold night and a damp grass verge were hardly the time and place for laying Greg's sister.

'Get in,' he said. 'I'll drive.'

Fiona handed him the keys and slipped into the passenger seat. She made no comment when he took the wrong road.

He used his sense of direction and eventually found himself on the north side of the medical school. He stopped her Chevrolet and sat leaning over the steering-wheel, trying to dredge from his subconscious the ghost of an idea which had plagued him all evening. Staring at the sprawling medical buildings, it suddenly came to him.

He put his arm around Fiona's shoulders. 'You drive us home . . . I'm sorry.'

'Don't apologize, Johnny. What have you figured out?'

'You know the picture that's out of focus? The one of the machine parts.'

'Yes.'

'The whole machine must be similar to the one that Shmuel's firm is making. Seespeed's got the British agency for it; we do the sales back-up and maintenance.'

'Greg mentioned it. Isn't it an electronic system for diagnosing certain diseases?'

'Yes . . . a body-scanner.'

'You must be right. But how does a body-scanner fit in with the equipment in the other photos? the mirrors, the lasers and all the rest.'

'It doesn't fit . . . unless it's got something to do with those scared people behind bars.'

'Prisoners? Human guinea-pigs? Where's the connection?'

'I don't know . . . yet.'

29

On the way to the White House Harry Resnick had told Greg that the President would receive them in the famous oval office — the one room his predecessor, Gerald Ford, had vacated with the greatest reluctance. In fact President Carter met them in an unassuming panelled room with a teak table and straight-backed chairs.

The President shook hands with Greg and introduced him to Bob, the Undersecretary for Defense, and — unaware that they'd met before — to General Jabotinsky . . . Martin. 'I've kept this group down to five, gentlemen.' He waved them to the chairs, and sat down at the head of the table. 'The reason is that I'm hoping to learn more from you than from any large committee. You'll please treat the proceedings as strictly confidential. You agree?'

They muttered assent.

'Right . . . I'd better fill you in. Or . . . would you, Bob?'

'Better do it your way, Jimmy,' said the Undersecretary.

Greg studied the man who'd won the election a few months back. He still wasn't responding to the toothy TV smile; but then he hadn't liked Nixon's nutcracker grin either, nor the arid solemnity of Gerald Ford. Why was the choice of American heads of state so limited? Stella, incurably cynical about politics, had said that no man could make the White House without financial backing and — maybe — the backers didn't like candidates with unbendable characters. Well, for better or worse, sunny Jim had arrived and it would be churlish to deny him *any* chance of developing into an effective head of state.

'Well, now . . .' the President dithered, 'You know the energy situation as well as I do.' His eyes flickered towards the Undersecretary, who had become absorbed in defacing the blotter before him with doodles of matchstick men. 'Well . . . I guess I'd better start. When I was elected

223

President, I was aware that I'd inherited problems. But I had no conception of the size of them. The Vietnam war was a period of relative prosperity. The end of it — inevitably — caused a lot of unemployment in the military production and ancillary industries. Things have been kinda tough on firms that relied on government contracts.

'In addition, technology's been advancing so fast that there are increasing numbers of obsolete people . . . guys who're not retrainable and who'll never find another job. It means more and more public spending on social benefits. To save money, we've had to cut down on space programmes . . . with the result that the Russians have almost caught up with us in the satellite stakes. I don't like it. Nor do I like the state of our economy. The steel industry's on the verge of a major recession. So is our great automobile industry . . . due to Japaness imports. It's my opinion that the economy would be in better shape now if we'd been less dependent on imported gasoline. Since the increases in the cost of imported energy — beginning with the OPEC price rise of November 1973 — the oil-producing countries have had us by the throat. Though my predecessors have held down the price of energy to our public artificially, it's become expensive . . . and that's hit industry so hard that a lot of firms are going bust. Our adverse trade balance is running at around $30 billion a year.

'My energy committee's been looking at every likely alternative . . . extracting oil from sand in Alberta . . . getting oil down from Alaska, which requires enormous pipeline systems . . . Mexican offshore oil . . . even oil from coal, a process the South Africans have been developing. Sure, the raw materials are around, but we can't exploit any of them without vast capital expenditure . . . which government and industry can ill afford. We'll come out on top, gentlemen. I just know we'll make it. Things will get a lot worse before they get better, but I have faith in God and in the ingenuity of our scientists. I've asked you here to meet Greg Murphy. Harry Resnick says he's a man of the future, and Harry — as you know — isn't given to exaggerations . . .'

The Undersecretary looked up from his doodles. 'I wonder if Greg's aware of our atomic energy problems.'

The President's face loosened, its boyishness suddenly transformed into the mask of a tired elderly man. 'Yeah . . . well, the reactors aren't popular nowadays. The conservationist lobby's getting powerful. It's one more reason why we've got to become self-sufficient.'

'Depends on the cost.' The Undersecretary wiped out the marching matchstick men with one stroke of his felt-tipped pen. 'The Defense Department is looking to the government for a considerable budget increase. According to the latest CIA report, PVO Strany — the Russian counterpart of our High Command NORAD — is testing the new multiple warhead SS-missile a whole year in advance, and . . .'

'Bob, could we stay with the energy subject?'

'It's all connected, Mr President — everything *is* . . . the Soviets training more Cubans for raising hell in Africa . . . the Communist gains in the Ethiopia-Eritrea-Somalia wars . . . the money Russia's handing out to rebels inside Afghanistan, Iran and certain South American states . . .'

'Bob, what counts is that Brezhnev and I are negotiating. And I assure you, I'm taking a firm stand on human rights issues.'

'That's dandy, provided you see to it that you have the military back-up to make your ideas stick . . . And provided you stop the multi-national companies from selling the Soviets our know-how for missile-guidance systems, for coupling space capsules, etcetera . . . and provided you stop the multinationals from selling their technology to little, and not so little, countries that could easily become flashpoints for World War Three . . . And provided you get control of your Federal bureaucracy and stop your Congressmen from working for special interests . . . like the multinationals . . . instead of for the United States.'

'Sure, Bob . . . sure. But you want to remember that Rome wasn't built in a day.'

'Mr President,' Martin Jabotinsky cut in, 'Rome had more time for getting itself built. In those days there were no nuclear missiles.'

The President's lips parted, displaying his fine array of teeth, but the smile didn't reach his eyes. 'Enough's been said, gentlemen. I guess Greg's got the picture. I move, we listen to what he's got to tell us about . . . a breakthrough in his work, which is of vital importance. The impact on the world could be even greater than the splitting of the atom.'

Greg took the drawings from his briefcase and put them on the table. 'The idea of turning the sun's energy into electricity — and of beaming it to earth — is not new. Scientists throughout the world have been considering it . . . an unlimited, cheap power-supply.'

The President nodded. 'Gentlemen, think what it would mean to industries throughout the world, including agriculture . . . to poor and underdeveloped countries. Sorry, Greg. Please continue.'

'Theoretically it should have been possible, years ago, to put up a space power station. In practice the cost in resources and money would have been prohibitive. Now it would be possible and reasonable to build the first power satellite within three or four years.'

Greg handed round copies of a drawing. 'This satellite would measure some fifteen miles by three. It would be placed in an orbit 22,152 miles above the earth, so that it would circle the earth once a day . . . appearing to hover without moving. It would be covered with a grid of photovoltaic cells which would convert the energy of sunlight into electricity.

This would require 45 square miles of photo-voltaic cells. Until fairly recently these cells cost about twelve thousand dollars per square yard . . . I have been working on semi-conducting glasses which can reduce the cost to about ten dollars per square yard.'

'That *is* a breakthrough.' The Undersecretary, who'd so far ignored Greg, looked at him with interest. 'The structure on this drawing looks rather fragile for such a large . . . island.'

'It's a comparatively delicate structure, but it'll be more than adequate for the weightless conditions in space. If we built it on earth it would collapse under its own weight.'

'You're planning on building it in space?' asked the President.

'Yes, sir. The same goes for the manufacture of the photo-voltaic cells. The glasses for the power satellite will pay for themselves if we sell the surplus commercially, on earth. Such crystals — which transmit electrons in a controlled manner — are essential components of computers, telescopes, microscopes . . . cameras, lasers. Up there we'll produce better crystals . . . without the impurities that contaminate them on earth. It means that the only impurities will be those that I've deliberately introduced into the silicon chips . . .'

'You've lost me,' said the President. 'I guess I don't really understand what the chips are.'

'Basically . . . we grow the crystals in the laboratory, then cut them into slices. That's your silicon chip. You can use minerals other than silicon, such as indium antimonide or gallium arsenide. There are a number. The circuits are put on the chip by various processes — photographic, for instance. Nowadays a chip the size of a pinhead can accommodate over a thousand circuits.'

'You require pure crystals . . . that's why you want to make them in space,' the President was puzzled, 'then you introduce impurities deliberately . . .'

'Yes, I put in boron.'

'Why?'

'I discovered that it loosens the electrons. It acts as a catalyst.'

Harry smiled. 'I think Greg's well on the way to revolutionizing the whole science of semi-conducting glasses.'

'You're convinced, Harry, aren't you?'

'It's a viable proposition, Jimmy. Of course, you must realize that the whole power station project depends on getting the Space Shuttle into full operation. It'll provide the freedom of movement essential for ferrying building materials and workers between earth and space.'

'Won't you have problems with the work-force?'

'No, a lot of technicians are keen to go up. The long-term space trips — ours and the Russians' — have proved that people can live and function perfectly well in space.'

The Undersecretary pushed the drawings aside. 'The Shuttle's unlikely to be operational before 1981. Rockwell haven't yet overcome stupid little problems like insulating tiles dropping off.'

'That's no minor problem,' Harry told him. 'The existing epoxy resins haven't passed the tests. What's needed is a bonding material strong enough to withstand the fantastic stresses and strains on the body of the Shuttle in flight. I'm sure someone will come up with the right bonding.'

'What's so important about these tiles?'

'They'll enable people to live and work in space in ordinary clothes. Space suits are cumbersome.'

'So it'll be four years or more before the power station will be built. Greg, I've noticed you're proposing to experiment with an existing satellite. How will you beam down the energy?'

'A system of aerials will be incorporated in the structure.'

'They'll direct the beams where you want them?' asked the President.

'No. The direction will be controlled by magnetic mirrors . . . which will be able to bend the beams through an angle of up to forty-five degrees.'

'A whole lot of other things come to mind,' said General Jabotinsky. 'How are you going to protect the . . . power station from enemy attack? We've got to face such a possibility.'

'I've thought of a couple of systems. One: The satellite could be screened off — or hidden — in a natural magnetism background based on the built-in magnetic coils in warships. Two: I've worked out a system of confusing an attacker with groups of devices which will be picked up by the enemy's sensors — missile-sensors, for instance — and deflect the attack. When the missile hits a deflector — which will not be an expensive piece of hardware — both will blow up.'

'You seem to have considered all aspects,' said the President. 'What size of crew do you envisage for manning the satellite?'

'It won't have to be permanently manned in space. It'll be a matter of periodic visits by small maintenance parties. The rest of the time the power station will be controlled from earth by remote manipulators — a system of computers and terminals.'

'A formidable plan,' said the President.

'On paper,' murmured the Undersecretary.

'Greg's gone beyond the theoretical work,' Harry Resnick reminded him. 'The cheap photo-voltaic cells are a reality now. Greg's shown me the first draft of a feasibility study he's worked out with colleagues in the engineering and computer-manufacturing fields which convinces me. . .'

Greg wondered what the President and his advisers would think of his team — John Whitmore of Seespeed in England and Shmuel Volatian of the Karmel Company in Israel. He didn't doubt that he'd encounter some opposition to foreign sub-contractors.

*   *   *

The discussion, in which Greg did not take part, was tilting in favour of his project. He wanted the contract. It would save LEEC from the worst effects of the recession, from having to make workers redundant who were too good for the scrapheap of obsolete men. LEEC, because it was not a mammoth conglomerate, was adaptable, a firm ideally equipped for making largely experimental prototypes. Work on the energy satellite would save the company going to the wall like so many other smallish all-American manufacturers.

Greater than his concern for the future of LEEC was his hatred of the organization — Shmuel had called it a state within a state — which was even now usurping the powers of America's democratic system. Democracy was far from perfect, but he believed that the alternative would lead to destruction unequalled in the turbulent history of the planet Earth.

Studying the President at close quarters, Greg didn't think he *would do*. Jimmy had been tough-minded enough to get himself into the White House, but he was not the man to stop the criminal misuse of space technology. His carefully worded promise of legislation to deal with exports of sensitive technology convinced Greg that he, John and Shmuel would not find an ally in this President of the United States.

Greg had been working on the power station plans when a pattern had emerged which terrified him. He'd called John and Shmuel, and the three of them had met in London. They'd discussed and sifted past events and information and arrived at positive conclusions.

It now struck them that the holocaust, which Shmuel had seen in Eritrea in 1969, and the husks of bodies John had found on the Rhodesia-Mozambique border, were the results of experiments that fitted in with the space principles of the space power station. A Russian group, and someone in America, had succeeded in harnessing the sun's energy — not to produce electricity for a power-hungry world, but to obliterate rocks, concrete buildings and people.

The aerial pictures of Los Alamos and General Piper's photographs fitted in, though not as yet the pictures of the prisoners and the body-scanner. They had no doubt that Piper had been kidnapped, vanishing without a trace, because he'd taken too keen an interest in the Los Alamos complex. The death of the Russian defector in England made sense. Larski's connection with the Alpha Corporation and Mat Scobie made sense; and the location of Alpha Corporation offices in the building of Sean's army command made sense.

For the first time Greg even saw a glimmer of reason behind the break-in at his laboratories at Boeing and Mat Scobie's subsequent investigations. Wasn't it likely that Scobie had *borrowed* the original

228

Boeing plans for a space power station and staged the break-in to confuse someone who might have become aware that the plans had gone missing?

Greg, John and Shmuel agreed to co-operate on the power station project — if LEEC succeeded in landing the contract — primarily because it would give them the means of discovering the murder-technique and of exposing it. Shmuel warned that such work might bring them uncomfortably close to the killers. He said that any schoolboy, who put a mirror in the sun, angled it at a piece of paper and set it alight, might have conceived the idea of the heat-ray from a satellite. It was the acceleration of the beam that must have given it the force for instant destruction by heat, the acceleration which still defied speculation.

Greg believed they'd find the answer in the course of building the space power station. He didn't expect a quick solution. *If* the President's enthusiasm for the project was genuine, *if* he succeeded in convincing the exchequer that money should be spent on a space power station, *if* the contract went to his firm, he would still have to make out a good case for sub-contracting the engineering work to John in England and the production of the remote-manipulator system to Shmuel in Israel.

At this stage nothing was certain except that the SRB — the killer they'd come to call a Selective Reflector Beam — was available to Americans as well as Russians and that it would take the ingenuity of all three to discover how it functioned and who controlled it.

'It went better than I'd expected,' said Harry Resnick. He turned his Buick east, avoiding the rush-hour traffic of downtown Washington. 'Bob's a genius at giving the wrong impression. Listening to him you'd think he'd fight any scheme that might cut Defense Department spending. In fact he's got a realistic appreciation of the country's industrial and social problems . . . energy being the most crucial. He'll advocate your project.'

'And General Jabotinsky?' asked Greg.

'A soldier with a vested interested in peace and prosperity. He's a catholic with seven children. The President? Well, he's still an unknown quantity.'

'He didn't strike me as a decisive man.'

'I can see him respond to pressures . . . when they happen to coincide with his personal views. He genuinely wants the scaling down of nuclear arms by us and the Soviets.'

'How do you rate his chances?'

'Marginally better than Nixon's and Ford's. Not because he's stronger or brighter. He isn't. But the pressures are increasing; the anti-nuclear lobby's gaining in strength . . . even in the armed forces. As you know, Greg, scientists all over the world are publishing warnings against nuclear power . . .,

'They've done it ever since the first bomb dropped on Japan.'

'Sure, but now they've reached the popular press and the media. There have been accidents in the past. No one heard of them. Suppression's become almost impossible. Here and there — in New Mexico, Arkansas and Kansas — nuclear missiles have deteriorated and leaked radio-activity, and the whole country knows about it. People object to missiles in their neighbourhood. They object to nuclear power stations. The medical people have proved that there's a higher incidence of cancers in areas close to nuclear plants . . . even in locations where the old atom bombs were tested in the 'forties and 'fifties. There's new information on the long-term effects of fall-out; it doesn't deteriorate as fast as we believed twenty years ago, and the dose of radiation people can tolerate without getting sick is much smaller than we used to think.'

'What difference does it make to the politicians or to the companies that make nuclear hardware?'

'Greg, a lot of politicians are getting scared.'

'Russian politicians?'

'That I don't know. But the thinking of some very courageous Russian scientists is in line with ours. They've strongly denounced the nuclear arms race; some of them have been locked up in mental hospitals, a few have managed to escape. The revulsion against nuclear hardware is fiercer . . . more widespread than most of us realize. The climate's changing, Greg.'

'Among politicians?'

'I think so, and I've known quite a few in my time. If young scientists like you gave the political leaders cheap energy from the sun and a new concept of an industrial revolution in space you'd change the whole character of political leadership.'

'What's needed is a new breed of presidents and prime ministers.'

'Given genuine means of peaceful progress, genuine statesmen — as distinct from politicians — will emerge.'

'Optimist.'

Harry laughed. 'At my age one's seen the unthinkable become possible. I reckon I'll live to see Einstein's theory of relativity disproved. And the speed of light will be superseded as surely as the sound-barrier was broken. Greg, lock your door, will you.'

Greg looked out on the scabrous slums; tall, crumbling warehouses, which had been turned into living-quarters for blacks and Puerto Ricans. It was a typical badland, which might have been anywhere in the States — in New York or Los Angeles, Chicago or Detroit. In the streets of the dispossessed it was not uncommon for the *obsolete* people to hang around traffic lights, pull drivers and passengers out of their car and mug them. Would the new industrial revolution, of which Harry Resnick was dreaming, make any difference to places such as this?

230

A couple of miles on they turned into Jefferson, a well-lit avenue of individually designed family houses. General Jabotinsky's place, at the end of a tree-lined drive, was built in Regency style with a fine pillared entrance.

The invitation to dinner had been in the nature of a command. Greg, remembering with affection the Polish boy at his school, had accepted it with some amusement. Martin Jabotinsky was running true to Polish form. If he'd had initial reservations about Greg, he'd decisively disposed of them. And once he approved of a person, with whom he might be collaborating professionally, he'd reveal himself unreservedly. Back in Poland, the Jabotinskys would have boasted of their victories over Russian invaders and exhibited their hospitality and their superior horsemanship. The American Jabotinsky would not, presumably, demonstrate his prowess at shooting clay pigeons from a galloping stallion; but he'd take as much pride in showing off his wife, his seven children and his elegant home.

Harry Resnick stopped his Buick behind a stationary car. In the light of the brass coach-lamps the petals of a flowering cherry on the gravel looked like a dusting of late snow.

Greg was about to mount the stairs when he noticed a dark bundle propped against one of the four pillars. He bent down, expecting a meths drinker who'd strayed from the slums. No smell of alcohol, but the man was filthy. On the sides of his head dark stains showed through the matted hair. The ears had been cut off, the face disfigured with vicious wounds. Yet the corpse had not been mutilated beyond recognition.

The sickening travesty of a man, on Martin Jabotinsky's doorstep, was his friend General Piper.

FREE FOR ALL

Europe 1978 - 1981

30

'Still working?'

John Whitmore looked up from his drawing-board. 'Come in.' Kole Okango's head, above a stiff white collar, looked aggressively black — an image Kole cultivated for his own amusement. 'I've finished.'

'Worst of being the boss,' said Kole, 'working on a Saturday afternoon . . . while civil servants like me play at being country gentlemen.'

'Is that what you've been doing?'

'With a vengeance.' Kole wandered to the open window. 'What are the flowering shrubs over there?'

'Forsythia.'

'The Easter bush. It's good to be home, John. Nothing like Sussex in the spring . . . and a garden party at the vicarage.'

'You went?'

'Sure. Wouldn't have missed a jamboree with the friendly natives for anything. The vicar calling me *hrrm, our friend from Rhodesia* . . . Mrs Chandler and her cronies calling me Mr Cole-Cole . . . And I had fun with the new librarian. We were strolling on the impeccable lawn, discussing the works of Graham Greene. I asked her, apropos of nothing, "Do you realize that I'm black?" '

'Bastard.'

'Don't worry; she won. Looked at me, blinked her blue eyes, and said, "I'm so sorry. Should I have noticed?" ' Kole laughed, 'It all goes to show . . . England's my village.'

'And Sussex is *home*. So why not come and work at Seespeed? I could do with you.'

'Man, I'm worth more to you at Research and Development. Before long you'll need government support for your project. I'm well placed for getting you a direct line to the Minister. Wheels within wheels and all that.'

'Thanks, Kole.'

'No skin off my nose. I like my ten-to-five job. Besides, it leaves me time for playing with your toys. What's the new body-scanner all about?'

'A revolutionary diagnostic machine. The NMR . . .'

'Translate.'

'Nuclear Magnetic Resonance. It makes transverse-section pictures of the body — like Shmuel's original scanner — but these are infinitely sharper and more reliable. Look,' John took a colour picture from his desk. 'Even I can recognize the cancer-mass.'

'How does it work?'

'Well, I still have a lot to learn about the machine. The basic principle is that the cancer shows up because the abnormal tissues have a higher water-content. The clear definition's brought about by the effect of the radio-waves on the protons of the body.'

'Protons . . . particles. The message is getting loud and clear.'

John collected the NMR pictures and put them in a drawer of his steel filing cabinet. 'Which message?'

'That the manufacturer of the universe has been consistent all the way. He produced x number of particles — protons, electrons, neutrons, mesons, etcetera — and then made them into building-blocks, like the pieces of a meccano set. The kiddies can stick the bits together into dogs or supermen, stars or garages. Doesn't matter what they build, all the components fit in somewhere and they're all made of much the same particles.'

'What about the particles we haven't yet been able to identify? Quarks, hadrons, neutrinos, gravitons . . .'

'Patience, man. It's only a few months since the Americans launched the Voyager spacecraft. By the time that pair have travelled 2.8 billion miles along their interplanetary trajectories we'll know more about many more particles. Have you noticed? the Voyager journeys read like a railway timetable; depart Earth 8 August 1977, arrive Jupiter 7 September 1979, charting all stations in between — Callisto, Ganymede, Europa, Amalthea. Depart Earth 20 August 1977, arrive Saturn 27 August 1981, all stations in between — Titan, Rhea, Tethys, Enceladus, Mimas, Dione. You bet, by the time the Voyagers are through travelling we'll be wise to enigmatic particles.'

'Kole, 1990 will be too late.'

'You think the human protons will have smashed each other into particle combinations that'll be useless for anything, except cosmic dust . . . John, you depress me.'

'You're depressing yourself. Sure, the Voyagers will teach us more physics. Meanwhile . . . we know *something* about charged particles and magnetic fields. We'll have to work on what we have.'

'If that space power station's to become a reality, we'll need to discover how to generate the high velocity that's required for accelerating the charged particles. The electrons . . . '

John thought of Cambridge; Kole and he arguing and debating; long hours that passed like minutes. Their common creed, perfectly expressed by William Blake, a genius of the past with a vision of the future — always provided that mankind didn't convert itself into cosmic dust.

To see a World in a Grain of Sand

And a Heaven in a Wild Flower,
Hold Infinity in the palm of your hand
And Eternity in an hour.

John wished he'd kept his mouth shut. In telling Kole of the holocaust experiments he had drawn him into the dangers he shared with Shmuel, Greg — and now, with Fiona. By what right had he involved Kole? A Shona tribesman whose people were totally innocent of the whites' technological abuses and crimes.

Yet Greg, himself involved with outsiders such as General Jabotinsky, had been in favour of including Kole. And Shmuel — the sensible, compassionate Jew — had put into words the unease in his mind. 'We've become an organization with an urgent purpose. We'd better acknowledge it. We can no longer function in isolation. We've got to accept that our numbers must grow.'

' . . . the behaviour of the same particles,' Kole was saying. 'You consist chiefly of water. I'm water . . . the rain's water. Plants and pussycats, stars and oceans . . . water, like us. The manufacturer of the universe didn't have as much imagination as he's been given credit for.'

'That's blasphemy.'

'Shit. Who says I'm not a proper God-fearin' blackie? Man, ah sure like the manufacturer. Ah know he's a white gen'leman, but all mah best frien's is white gen'lemen too.'

'Bloody fool.' John jabbed a fist at Kole's stomach. 'Come on. Let's find Fiona.'

'Hey, you're worried about her.' Suddenly Kole was serious. 'What's on your mind?'

'I've been back-tracking,' admitted John.

'That's no good,' Kole stopped in the middle of the path between offices and workshops. He gazed across the industrial estate amid the flowering gardens, and touched the forsythia. He took a knife from his hip-pocket, cut a twig, and put it in his button-hole. The yellow blooms flared a small flame against the dark cloth.

'Larski,' said John, 'Goldtooth, who died at the Brighton hotel, was murdered . . .'

'Because he bungled his job in Rhodesia.'

'Yes. But part of the bungling implicated Andrew and me. Andrew sending the film to the black MP seemed to end the matter . . . as far as he and I are concerned. Did it end there? Remember, Greg made enquiries about Larski . . .'

'Through Resnick, who got the information from Mat Scobie, and who did not mention Greg's name.'

'Scobie may be aware of the connection between Greg and Resnick . . . between the President's scientific adviser and the boss of LEEC, which has just landed an important government contract.'

'How public are such contracts in the States?'

'In the States everything seems to be public . . . even the specifications of the Space Shuttle.'

'Well, well. Democracy's where man makes the other guy responsible for his disasters; dictatorship's where the other guy causes disasters that nobody's responsible for. I suppose your American friends confuse democracy and indiscretion.'

'Just about. A couple of days ago I heard on the radio — in BBC news — that America's about to spend real money on research for the space power station. Even if Scobie hadn't found the connection between Greg and Resnick until now, he won't overlook it after this announcement. There aren't all that many pioneers of photo-voltaic cells in the States; and Greg's the top man.'

'OK, John. So Mat Scobie — who sure sounds like a monster — connects Resnick with Greg. Say, he even knows that Goldtooth *might* have contacted you and connects you with Greg . . . But I can see no reason why Scobie should associate you with Fiona . . . or Fiona with the unknown person who took an interest in the Corporation Agency.'

'An interest! She asks a lot of questions about Scobie. She finds out about the rent-an-executive firm. She changes jobs for the sake of living around the corner from Corporation Agency. She makes friends with the old hag who runs the office . . . finds out where she keeps the keys . . . knocks the woman out with a spiked whisky-sour . . . gets inside the Corporation Agency offices . . . takes Xerox copies of the personnel file, which gives her every detail of the three men who control the set-up . . . and gets caught by one of them. Scobie.'

'Take it easy, John. Let's look at it again . . . Yes, Fiona's done all you say. But she changed her appearance; black hair, outsized tinted spectacles. Girls are good at this sort of thing. She took the Washington job on a freelance basis, under an assumed name . . .'

'What about that office manager? She wakes up . . .'

'After Fiona's put the keys back.'

'Scobie must have been on to the old woman quite fast.'

'Right. It's unlikely that she was in a state to answer the phone. Let's say he went to her apartment and managed to rouse her. Would she admit — the set-up being what it is — that she was fast asleep while she had a visitor who might have made off with the keys? I shouldn't think so. John, you're making too much of Scobie running into Fiona at the offices. Firstly, he was out of breath because he'd had to climb the stairs. Fiona had stopped the elevator on her floor. Secondly . . . He sees a small figure in jeans at the outer office door; he grabs hold of it and gets a hard kick in the crotch. He lets go, of course, and while he's doubled up Fiona makes it down in the elevator. She's gone. By the time Scobie gets to his office manager, Fiona's on the highway, clear of Washington . . . Well? Anything I've left out?'

'No, Kole . . . except that Scobie's clever and ruthless, not a man who'd forget that an outsider probably searched the offices thoroughly.'

'*Probably*. But he's got no proof. Three months have passed and there haven't been any repercussions. By now Scobie's almost certainly decided that the person who kicked him was a run-of-the-mill junkie, after money for the next fix.' Kole lifted his head and listened. 'Hear it? that's where she is.'

The door of Vincent Squire's old workshop stood open. Fiona, hair shining like polished copper, was bending over a makeshift soldering hearth, directing the flame of a blow-torch on a small iron crucible.

'What are you doing?'

'Melting down my charm bracelet.' She dipped her left hand into a jar of black flux and scattered granules into the crucible. 'I never wear it. Here . . .' She gave John a gold ring with the texture of wave-like ripples.

'Beautiful.' He passed it to Kole.

'You *made* it?'

'Yes.'

'How's it done?' asked Kole.

'Cast in cuttle-fish.'

'This stuff?' Kole picked up a sandwich of white ovals, some five inches long, two dried fish wired together, with a hole cut into the blunt end. 'Isn't it what you give budgerigars?'

'Right. Hey! put it back . . . propped up against the asbestos, like it was.'

John watched the metal in the crucible move, the edges glinting like quicksilver. 'You're going to pour the molten metal into this cuttle-fish?'

'Yes, darling.'

'It's so fragile and brittle. Won't it burst?'

'No . . . though I don't know why. The liquid metal's got a very high temperature.' Fiona shifted the blow-torch to her left hand, gripping the stem of the crucible with her right. Still playing the flame on the crucible, she lifted it and tipped the fluid gold into the hole at the top of the cuttle-fish. 'There . . . that's my wedding ring. It won't be the same as yours, John . . . not the same texture. Cuttle-fish vary like fingers . . . no two give the same imprint.'

The fish-mould crackled like a fire of damp wood. The workshop had filled with the distinctive smell of singed hair. Had the 'manufacturer' made human hair and cuttle-fish from the same particles?

Kole spoke, but John wasn't listening. He was watching — fascinated; Fiona dipping the mould into a bucket of water, undoing the wire which had sandwiched the two cuttle-fish together, parting the pieces of the mould.

The inside of each was charred black. Yet the molten gold had not destroyed those fragile ovals. They'd stood up to the fantastic heat, their husks unmarked and undamaged . . . like the husks of men, women and children on the borders of Rhodesia and Mozambique. A thought was forming in John's mind, nothing more than the shadow of an idea. Yet he recognized that he'd just learned something about the holocausts in Africa which would lead him into essential new knowledge . . . about particles.

'Man,' Kole put a hand on his shoulder, 'You dreaming?'

'Sorry.'

'I was saying . . . Fiona's safe with you . . . '

She was easing the circle of gold from the burnt-out husk. 'Darling, I think Kole's right . . .'

Yes, Kole *was* right. Fiona wouldn't be in danger . . . not while Greg was safe. But how safe was Greg? One man along the line — a senior army officer — abducted, mutilated, murdered. A warning to Greg? Another warning from Greg's associates; *carry a gun.*

31

Konrad was twenty minutes late.

Shmuel sat facing the doors of Munich's Café Feldherrnhalle. A heavy April shower was driving the shoppers inside.

A young couple approached his table. '*Erlauben Sie?*'

'*Ja.*'

As they dumped their parcels on the floor a determined manageress bore down on the table. Would they mind if she took their coats and bags to the cloakroom? The man agreed, reluctantly.

'*Dafür wirst zahlen müssen.*' The wife let the manageress know that she found the cloakroom charges objectionable.

The couple sat down and lit cigarettes. A family at the next table looked disapproving.

Such a tidy, *proper* place — Munich. Shmuel expected to see the effects of Germany's economic miracle on the city, but not such numbers of luxury cars and diamond-studded housewives. Did any of these people, earnestly stuffing themselves with cream cakes, remember Marshall Aid? Did they have any conception of how they would be living if America and Britain had not given them those vast amounts of money to rebuild their war-devastated country?

Konrad was half an hour late.

Shmuel could still see the ruins of Munich; broken stairways open to the sky, an iron bedstead — sheets flapping in the wind — hanging crazily from what was left of a top floor, skeletal cats and ragged women scavenging among the weeds in the parks. Over all the acrid stink of dead fires.

There'd been enough to eat at his Displaced Persons' Camp. It had been a rest-cure after that nightmare journey across Russia . . . in retrospect. It hadn't been so good at the time. He'd wished away the days and the weeks, always watching for the wiry figure of the British army sergeant who'd given him the half-promise of a future.

The Rav Aluf, his Major General, creator of the most efficient intelligence network in the world; in his sixties now but still a controlling influence. Had the Rav Aluf told him after the Yom Kippur war that he'd be serving Mossad at the age of forty-nine, he'd have told him in no uncertain terms that he was through with escapades such as sailing the high seas with a shipload of nuclear raw materials. Wasn't it enough that he'd made the Karmel Company one of the most advanced and profitable in Israel? No, not enough.

Konrad was fifty minutes late.

Not the Rav Aluf's fault that the Gadarene swine of this world were once again rushing to destruction. Not a little irony in the fact that he had been the one to put atomic power into his fellow-Israelis' hands, and that he was now expected to find a way out of the nuclear jungle.

Konrad was an hour late. Yet he trusted the punctilious German. Without his help there would have been no uranium cargo for Israel, no Scheersberg. That Konrad worked for money and nothing else was unimportant. So did most of his compatriots, judging by the typically lush crowd at the Café Feldherrnhalle. Who was he to quarrel with German materialism. It had served Israel well enough.

The hands of the gold-plated clock above the counter were moving to lunch time. There was no way he could contact Konrad. Had he underestimated the volume of files which the Ludwigsburg Justice Department had agreed to open to him? One hundred and sixty thousand dossiers on Nazis, all proven murderers still at large. Were there even more? Or was there no such dossier after all on the man he was hoping to find?

'*Darf ich noch etwas bringen?*' A neat waitress put the menu on his table. She looked anxious. If seats were wasted on customers who refused lunch the management wouldn't be happy.

Shmuel told her to bring him another lemon tea. He'd wait for his friend. A muted loudspeaker summoned *Herr Samuel* to the telephone. The waitress directed him through the velvet drapes at the back.

He lifted the receiver. 'Yes?'

'Sorry I'm late,' Konrad answered in English. 'Our appointment is at three-thirty. You know where to go.'

'I do. What kept you?'

'Car trouble. Nothing drastic . . . slashed tyres. My own fault.'

'How?'

'Certain people object to those who visit Ludwigsburg. I should have remembered that.'

'A wasted trip?'

'Certainly not. I've dug out a lot of information on our man. Your guess was correct.'

'Konrad, where are you?'

'At home.'

Shmuel looked at his watch. 'Stay where you are. I'll contact you.'

'You can come to my place. I haven't been followed.'

'Sure?'

'Yes. The tyres . . . a warning to lay off. That's all. It's not un-common. I should have left my car at the hotel . . . taken a taxi.'

'All right. I'll be round in half an hour. No need for you to go to Nymphenburg with me.'

'I'm not worried.'

'I'd rather keep the appointment on my own.'

On the outside the Otrag offices gave the appearance of an elegant private residence built in an appropriate district, close to the baroque Nymphenburg Palace where former Bavarian kings had recreated the splendours and toys of Versailles. The inside of the Otrag villa had been treated with respect; in place of the usual strip-lights there were standard- and wall-lamps, the furniture — though functional — was nineteenth-century.

Herr Franzer, manager of Otrag, received Shmuel in a library of leather-bound books, velvet-covered armchairs and professionally arranged spring flowers. Shmuel made an initial judgement; Franzer was in his thirties, young enough not to have been involved in Nazi crimes. His English, with a faint American accent, was fluent.

He talked openly of his firm's achievements and future plans. Otrag had made rockets capable of launching commercial satellites. Though there was work to be done on perfecting their rockets, the tests in Zaire had been successful. Unfortunately politics had reared its ugly head. Russia and East Germany had exerted a great deal of pressure on the Zaire government, with the result that Otrag's African site would have to be abandoned. There was, however, one alternative on the African continent . . . a move to Libya. Negotiations were well advanced. All going well, the tests in Libya would be sub-orbital. By 1982 Otrag should not be experiencing any problems in putting satellites into orbit for its customers.

'Where are you looking for your customers?'

'Chiefly in the Third World.'

'You're not concerned that your . . . services could lead to wars likely to endanger — among others — your country?'

'How our customers use their satellites isn't our responsibility, Mr Samuel. If we didn't provide this service for them, someone else would . . . a firm in France, most likely. Our shareholders, who do not include a single government, are entitled to sound returns on their investments. We're a purely commercial firm. Politics are of no interest to us.'

'My information confirms that,' said Shmuel. 'You launched a satellite as early as 1969 for an East German company.'

'You have investigated us.' Franzer seemed unperturbed. 'But the 1969 satellite wasn't the only one we launched.'

'I know. You also sold your services to an American corporation . . . Alpha.'

This time Franzer looked uneasy. 'The names of our customers are strictly confidential, Mr Samuel. I can't understand how . . .'

'Israeli firms won't do business with any company they haven't checked very thoroughly.'

Franzer sat back in his armchair, relaxed. 'And is Karmel satisfied with our record?'

'We're interested in the services you have to offer . . . very much so. But I'd like to know what your current commitments are . . . how much effort you could devote to any contract of ours.'

'We're not fully stretched, Mr Samuel . . . which isn't entirely our fault.'

'Are you involved with any firm in eastern Europe?'

'We're not . . . as you probably know. Our East German assignment was a one-off job.'

'Who's on your books now?'

'Libya . . . which is no secret. A commercial firm in Libya,' Franzer corrected himself, 'and a company in Iran, owned by the Shah's family. Both contracts have been mentioned in the press.'

'What are your commitments to the Alpha Corporation?'

'We've fulfilled *our* obligations.'

Shmuel sensed the man's hostility. 'Alpha still owes you money?'

'They paid up . . . eventually. But they've failed to honour an unwritten agreement . . . the most important part of the contract. We made a special price for our services to Alpha on the understanding that their president would assist us in . . . obtaining a concession for building an industry in space.'

'Surely Alpha are in no position to grant such concessions.'

'The American govenment is. An astonishing number of concessions have already been granted to firms in West Germany, Belgium, France,

Japan and — naturally — in the United States. Mr . . . the Alpha representative who dealt with us promised that he'd have no difficulty in obtaining a concession for Otrag.'

'That was . . . let me see . . . about five years ago.'

'Exactly. In 1973. Since then our letters have remained unanswered. It's clear that Alpha never intended to keep their promises.'

'You dealt with a man by the name of Mat Scobie.'

'You have done your homework, Mr Samuel. I hope you will offer us a contract. We'd work well together.'

'I think so too. Therefore I'll put my cards on the table. I need all the information you can give me about Scobie.' Shmuel opened his briefcase and took out a photograph. 'Is this the man you dealt with, Mr Franzer?'

'Yes.'

'How and where did you meet?'

'Scobie came here . . . That was the first time we met. Then he spent a week with us in Africa, shortly before we launched the Alpha satellite.'

'Did he understand the mechanics of the operation?'

'Certainly.' Franzer looked surprised. 'I understood he was the corporation's scientific director . . . he was very knowledgeable. After the launch he visited the offices here twice . . . or three times, at most. I was still in Zaire, so I didn't see him.'

'Does Scobie speak German?'

'Fluently. To hear him you'd think he comes from Berlin.'

'He did come from Berlin . . . originally.' Shmuel gave the manager a Xeroxed document. 'Take a look. Your tricky business associate — Mat Scobie — is former Sturmbandführer, Manfred Schober . . .'

'A war criminal!'

'A deserved title, when a man's known to have murdered over a thousand Jews and Frenchmen.'

'This is . . .' Franzer was lost for words. 'How could he travel in and out of Germany? I don't understand.'

'That he hasn't been caught? People like Schober still have many friends in Germany.'

'But he's a scientist, Mr Samuel.'

'The doctors who injected air into prisoners . . . who subjected them to agonizing deaths . . . were scientists too. If you want to see a more modern way . . .' Shmuel gave Franzer a folder of photographs, 'these people — Eritreans — were killed by a beam from one of your satellites. I'm not blaming you for it. You produced — what you considered — innocent hardware for an East German firm. You weren't to know that it passed into the control of a Russian group . . . who used it for these appalling experiments.'

'*Du lieber Gott!*' The colour had drained from Franzer's face. '*Du lieber Gott!*' he repeated, sick and bewildered.

'The same kind of experiment was carried out by Scobie and his friends . . . except that they were equally interested in pulverizing concrete buildings. They chose a more comprehensive site — an abandoned military training base — on the Rhodesia Mozambique frontier.'

'It's the end . . . the end of Otrag.'

'There will be work for your company . . . work which won't have lethal results. I promise you.'

'Das darf nie wieder passieren . . . it must never happen again. Never.'

'Not if we can help it, Franzer . . . Is there any more you can tell me about Scobie-Schober . . . anything at all?'

Franzer nodded. He looked at his hands, which were shaking, and clamped them together. He was in a state of shock, realized it, and made a courageous effort to control himself. Shmuel sat still, listening to the distant hum of traffic, the ringing tones of a church clock.

At last Franzer got up and fetched a book from a drawer in his desk. He wandered back and forth between desk and windows, the book — unopened — in his right hand.

Shmuel waited. He was so close to what he had come for. Was it safe to let Franzer make his own decision or should he speak? The man was a German of the honourable kind, a man of his word. Even now he'd rather go to prison than betray a confidence.

'I have information from America,' said Shmuel quietly, 'that Schober, alias Scobie, visited Germany regularly . . . about every eight weeks.'

'You're . . . Israeli intelligence?'

'Yes. But I'm also in a position to provide work for your company.'

Franzer opened his address book. 'I have an unlisted telephone number . . .'

'Given to you confidentially.'

'Yes.'

'By a man who committed murder during the war and long after the war . . . a man liable to cause further mass murders unless he's stopped without delay.'

'I'll give you the number.'

'Thank you. I know this hasn't been easy for you.'

'No. Mr Samuel . . . we must treat each other's information as confidential. Now, and in the future.'

'I agree.' Shmuel suppressed a smile. Germans; they seemed to have a special need for crossing the t and dotting the i. At best, it made them the most meticulous associates.

'Schober owns a house about twenty kilometres from Munich.'

Shmuel sat at the window of his hotel room, reading the Munich newspaper which had been delivered with his morning coffee. The world on Friday, 28 April 1978, was as cheerless as the rains outside. The single page of foreign news contained just about every menace he feared.

NUCLEAR RACE OUT OF CONTROL. *Dr Barnaby of the International Peace Research Institute, introducing the Institute's 1978 Yearbook, said that the nuclear arsenals of the nuclear powers add up to an explosive power one million times that of the bomb which destroyed Hiroshima in 1945. The Yearbook takes the view that after 10 years of relative restraint by the superpowers, a new arms race is under way . . .'*

LUNS WARNS OF SOVIET BUILD-UP. *Russia has built the biggest military machine the world has ever seen in peace time, Dr Luns, Nato General Secretary said in London yesterday . . .*

RUSSIA SEEKS FALKLAND ISLAND FISHING BASE.

GET USED TO OUR THREATS. U.S. WARNED. *This blunt statement was made to members of the House Armed Services Committee during a recent meeting in the Kremlin by Marshal of the Soviet Union N.V. Ogarkov, First Deputy Defense Minister . . .*

U.S. MARINES SEEK MORE HARRIERS. *Concerted efforts are being made in Washington to reverse Pentagon Budget cuts and give the British Harrier jump-jet a more important role in American military aviation . . .*

INCREASED MARXIST GUERILLA ACTIVITY IN SOUTH-WEST AFRICA.

ETHIOPIAN CHILDREN OFF TO 'REVOLUTION' SCHOOLS IN CUBA. *Cuba's role as the crucible of Moscow-orientated revolution in Africa was taken an important stage further yesterday when it was disclosed that Ethiopian schoolchildren were being sent to Cuba for 'revolutionary' education . . .*

SAUDI F-15 JETS DEAL. *Saudi Arabia has promised the United States that American engineers and ground crews would maintain the F-15 fighter jets which President Carter proposes selling the Arab State despite opposition from Israel and many Congressmen . . .*

At the sound of the telephone Shmuel dropped the paper thankfully. '*Ein Anruf aus America,*' said the operator. 'You have a call from America,' she repeated in English. The uninterested announcement conveyed that she was accustomed to hotel-guests who made and received international calls.

'How're you doing, Sam?' The line was clear, Greg's voice unmistakable.

'Well,' Shmuel answered the all-American question. 'I'll be contacting your friend today.'

'He's over there?'

'Yes, on one of his regular visits.'

'Wish you success.'

'Thanks. How's your end?'

'It's a bigger enterprise than we'd envisaged, but we're making progress. The place where Sean used to stay's under new management. The former . . . co-ordinator made a lot of money.'

It was no more than Shmuel had expected. General Montana wouldn't have provided protection for nothing. The Alpha Corporation under Scobie was bound to have paid a high price for the use of the army at Los

Alamos. 'Is the former co-ordinator out of the running?'

'Sure. He's given up business and is on the way to a holiday resort.'

On his way to a small uninhabited island in the Pacific, where his provisions would be dropped by Japanese with a special reason for hating men in the nuclear racket. Montana's former colleagues at the Pentagon would make very sure that the bent general faded into obscurity. Montana would be *travelling on active service*, on the move as perpetually as Sisyphus. There'd be no mention of him in the *Gazette*. There'd be no Pentagon scandal.

'I've been consulting with the two experts on our list,' said Greg. 'Now I'm through with them.'

'Good.' Scobie's associates at Corporation Agency Inc. would be joining General Montana on the Pacifica Ocean island. 'Is there no one else?'

'One. He's being contacted. No problem on that score.'

'See you next week.'

'The meeting will have to take urgent decisions, Sam.'

'What is it?'

'Martin was right, I'm afraid. The guy who's gone into retirement . . . He pared down maintenance. The equipment's below standard.'

Jabotinsky had feared the worst. Now his suspicions had been confirmed. If there'd been any doubt Greg wouldn't have mentioned Martin. The terse message was that General Montana had misused Defense Department funds for the lucrative private space project at the expense of missile maintenance.

The implications were appalling. Greg's statement that the equipment was below standard meant that America's nuclear weapons, stored in silos from New Mexico to North Dakota, had been allowed to deteriorate to a danger point where accidental explosions were liable to threaten the lives of large populations throughout the United States.

32

Konrad had been right. The woman was predictable. At three o'clock sharp she came out at the back of her house, a basket of daffodils over her arm. She was one of the village residents who regularly arranged flowers in the church. She was a tall, heavy woman in her late thirties with a tranquil face and straight, pale hair.

Shmuel, watching her through Mike's service binoculars, thought that Hitler would have approved of this German specimen of womanhood.

But she'd be too young to have been tainted by the Nazi race ideas. According to Konrad she'd been married to Scobie ten years. The name Schober would mean nothing to her. She strode along the cart-track — the original road to the village — passing within a few yards of him.

He went into the copse where Mike was waiting. Mike, dressed in jeans and anorak, looked the part — not an airforce sergeant from the American base; just any young man out on a TV repair job. The van was almost hidden among beeches and hazelnut bushes; the camouflage was good without appearing too deliberate.

'I'm going in now.' Shmuel opened the back of the van and put on the dun golf jacket with the deep pockets. He handed Mike a plastic box. 'Your sandwiches.'

'Right, sir.'

Anyone seeing Mike in the van, eating in such a quiet spot, would assume that he was waiting for his mate or just taking a break in his firm's time.

'If you're not back . . . '

'Take it easy.' Shmuel put a hand on his shoulder. 'Two hours . . . Don't move before.'

'No, sir.'

It took exactly ten minutes to walk down the cart-track into the garden of the house, a typical Bavarian chalet with a wooden balcony encircling the whole of the first floor. A restful place, far removed from urban American life.

Shmuel had moved silently half-way across the orchard when the Alsatian began to bark. The big dog came hurtling out of the back door, straight at him. Shmuel, gun in hand, veered out of his path and aimed at his haunches. The Alsatian, his speed checked, rolled over. He got up, gave a deep growl, stalked Shmuel slowly and angrily and then suddenly toppled over on his side. Shmuel went to the dog and pulled out the dart. He'd done no damage. In a few hours the animal would come to, none the worse for the drug-induced sleep.

He swiftly covered the ground to the door and walked into a lobby with a washing-machine and a work-bench. It led to a hall with a highly polished parquet floor and several natural pine doors. Scobie was standing framed in one of them.

'Who are you?' His pale eyes were alert and cold.

'A friend of Greg Murphy's.'

Scobie relaxed. 'Why didn't you ring the bell? Didn't you see the dog?'

'There are times when I don't ring bells. And, yes, I did deal with your dog . . . Don't worry, I haven't hurt him.' Shmuel pushed past Scobie into the room, which was furnished as an office.

Scobie followed him. 'I knew Greg would . . . make an approach sooner or later, but I didn't expect it quite like this. Where is he?'

'At home, I imagine.'

'What? not in Germany?' Scobie sat down behind his desk and motioned Shmuel to a chair. 'I see . . . He's sent you to talk terms.'

'So there *are* . . . terms?'

'Of course. I don't understand why Greg's playing games. I suppose it was Greg who hired some woman to sniff around my Washington office . . . '

'Corporation Agency Inc.'

'Yes; he's briefed you. It's all very childish . . . this cloak and dagger stuff. Why didn't he phone me at Alpha . . . make an appointment like any normal applicant?'

'So you'd consider him for a job? At Los Alamos perhaps?'

'Sure. He's a funny guy; there's a lot I don't understand about him. But he's a brilliant scientist, and we need electronics men like him.'

'You didn't tell him.'

Scobie shifted in his seat. 'We don't work that way.' In profile the long, narrow head with the flat skull did — as Greg had said — look strangely snakelike.

'How do you recruit your scientific staff?' Shmuel asked him.

'We get to know the guys personally . . . at Boeing, Rockwell, McDonnell Douglas, wherever they happen to be working. One meets on the golf course . . . at parties. When the time's right one has a discussion. The trouble with Greg is that he's unsociable . . . could be because his wife's a nigger.'

'Perhaps he doesn't like you.'

'That's something one can overcome, if one pays enough. You can tell Greg that I'm prepared to double the salary he gets at LEEC.'

'He doesn't have to do work he'd find uninteresting.'

'What do you know about it?'

Shmuel decided to use the brush-off, though it was something of a gamble. 'What do we know, Greg and I? That Otrag launched a satellite for you, and that you've been experimenting with particle beams ever since. What isn't clear to us is your purpose.'

Scobie stared at Shmuel. 'You've told me you're a friend of Greg's. Who are you?'

'My name's Samuel. I'm an electronics engineer, and I work with Greg.'

'It'll do. The two of you seem to have taken a lot of trouble . . . finding out about Alpha, Corporation Agency, and about me —personally. You can't expect me to be pleased about it. My security arrangements will have to be changed drastically. On the other hand, I appreciate your thoroughness. Greg and you are the kind of men my organisations need.'

'For what?'

'I'm coming to that. You want to know the purpose of our experiments? *Peace*, Mr Samuel . . . the one thing all sane people want.'

*   *   *

'Change of government by revolution is a twentieth-century phenomenon,' Scobie was saying. 'There's no reason whatever why it should
happen in Cuba and not in England, in Pakistan but not in the United
States. If the world's to survive into the twenty-first century we must
accept the trend and develop it in the right way.'

'Hitler talked of *bloodless revolution*', said Shmuel, 'when he sent his
armies into Austria, Czechoslovakia, Poland . . .'

'I *am* speaking of bloodless revolution. Hitler failed because he was
bent on territorial conquest. There are better ways of using the military,
mostly for the removal of obsolete systems of government. Democratic
governments have become corrupt and weak. We must get rid of them.
Dictatorships are corrupt and vicious. They too will have to go. If we let
the present-day styles of government continue, the ultimate nuclear war
will become inevitable. Russia, America and their allies have had more
than thirty years to stop the nuclear arms race. What have they done? All
their governments have allowed the nuclear menace to spread to
politically unstable countries. They've built up nuclear arsenals which
they themselves can no longer control. Samuel, whether you know it or
not, there's an ever increasing number of nuclear accidents . . . such as
the explosion in Palomares, Spain, in Thule, Greenland, in many
locations in Russia and America where information has been suppressed . . .'

Shmuel found it hard to believe that this man, this superannuated war
criminal, could be as bitterly opposed to nuclear hardware as he was
himself. Yet the message was clear. 'You seem to think that there's a way
out.'

'There is. All nuclear weapons — and power — must be made illegal.'

'God! Nothing can be made illegal — a punishable crime — unless you
have a government, an authority capable of enforcing the law.'

'There will be an authority, Samuel; the most effective ever. World-
control by practical businessmen and scientists . . . backed by a
judiciously deployed clean weapon, a non-nuclear weapon.'

'The science-fiction deathray?'

'As Greg's associate you must know better. The *deathray* has become
hard fact. We're still having problems with DEW — Directed Energy
Weapons — but we're ahead of the Russians in this technology. By 1981
we'll have a Beam which we'll be able to direct from space on any chosen
target — instantly, on command. We'll be in the position to wipe out any
trouble-spot, anywhere on earth. A few days ago President Carter announced that America will *not* develop the neutron bomb. Instead the
money will be spent on a power station in space. It's precisely what my
organization needs. We already know how to harness the sun's
energy . . . which, unlike oil, is inexhaustible. We know how to direct it
on Moscow or Washington, Bonn or London, in the form of a beam so
powerful — yet so controlled — that it can wipe out such cities in minutes.

250

Yet there will be no backlash, no after-effects . . . no fall-out, no radiation sickness . . . '

'No escape, no survivors.'

'Not inside the burn-out area. But we'll keep destruction to a minimum — naturally. Once we've scorched a city or two, the odd installation or trouble-maker, off the face of the earth, opposition will collapse. We envisage a managerial revolution . . . not government, but governance, by the heads of the major multinational companies. Believe me, Samuel, there are no more efficient men anywhere on this planet.'

'What are your plans for . . . backward populations?'

'We'll train the trainable . . . develop agriculture . . . set them to make the deserts flower. Of course, the size of populations will have to be rationalized. There'll be some wastage.'

'Back to concentration camps and gas ovens?'

'Not at all. Too unpleasant. We've outgrown such primitive methods.'

'You'd rather use the SRB.'

'What?'

'Greg and his associates call it the Selective Reflector Beam.'

'DEW or SRB . . . much the same thing no doubt, though I like the term *selective*. We'll certainly select the people we need for the efficient running of the Corporation States. I reckon you and Greg will be included. If you're working with Greg you must be pretty good. You can tell Greg that I'm still interested in his photo-voltaic cells. I guess he'll have ironed out his early problems by now. The fact that you're here proves that Greg's developed semiconductors worth having . . . and that he considers he's now in a bargaining position. You can tell him I'm ready to talk.'

'*He* won't be ready until he's seen the specifications of your Beam.'

Scobie laughed. 'Then he's over-estimating his position. I can have him picked up any time . . . and make him see reason.'

'Why haven't you done it before?'

'Isn't it obvious? Duress isn't the best method of making a brilliant man give of his best.'

'I want to see the Beam specifications . . . now.'

'You must be out of your mind! Do you think . . .'

Shmuel glanced at his watch. He had nine minutes to press the button that would open the electronically controlled gates to Mike's van. He hoped the woman wouldn't get in the way. He felt sure that he had nothing more to learn from Scobie himself. The rest would be in the papers.

'Where's your safe?'

Scobie's head moved — an involuntary glance towards the filing cabinet, which he immediately tried to mask by looking at other objects in the room. As his hand crept to the desk drawer on his right, Shmuel took the Smith & Wesson .38 from his pocket and fired. The shot ripped into the flesh of Scobie's left upper arm and smacked into a stack of journals. Scobie, stunned into silence, put his right hand over the bleeding wound.

'Get up,' Shmuel ordered. 'Out from behind the desk . . . Schober.'

The name sent the blood rushing into Scobie's face. He obeyed, sidling towards the door.

'Stop.' Shmuel raised the gun. 'Either you do as I say or I drill you full of holes. We could manage without your specifications, but they might save us time. Over to the safe.'

Scobie went to the filing cabinet.

'Open it.'

'Listen . . . I can explain . . .'

Shmuel fired again. The bullet hit close to the first wound. 'The next one goes into your guts.'

Scobie didn't hesitate. He opened a drawer, which came out less than an inch, and activated a mechanism underneath. The false cabinet swung out, revealing a safe behind. Scobie turned, looked at the gun, and dialled the combination.

Shmuel motioned with his gun. 'Sit down. Over there, where I can see you.' The contents of the safe were arranged in neat bundles. It would be easy to find what he wanted.

'You won't get away with it.' Scobie was recovering some of his nerve. 'An attack on an American national . . . The German police will . . .'

'Shut your mouth, Schober.'

'Listen to me. You've got it wrong. I . . .'

Shmuel went to the wall-telephone beside the door and pressed a button. A red light flicked on, indicating that the gates into the drive were opening. Scobie's blood was splashing on to the yellow carpet. A pity to leave such traces of violence, but the shooting had been unavoidable. By the time the police arrived Mike and he would be in another van. Within the hour they'd be comfortably ensconced in Munich's rush-hour traffic. Shmuel felt safe.

'Are you going to kill me?' Schober's voice broke in hysteria. 'You're going to . . .'

'No,' Shmuel stopped him. 'I don't believe in killing, not even a mass murderer like you. We'll fly you to a place where you can't do any more damage, except to your own kind . . . crooks like General Montana. The police will be looking for you, for a while. I expect the American authorities will take an interest in your case. Your past will be raked up. And then your name — Scobie alias Schober — will disappear in some non-urgent *Missing Persons* file. You will be forgotten, even in Israel.'

'Israel!' Sweat broke out on Schober's forehead. The sweat was running into his eyes. His body tensed. He was listening. Footsteps.

Not a woman's footsteps.

33

John put *Le Monde* on top of Fiona's suitcase and wandered out on to the balcony. It was no use; his French was too limited for the detailed accounts in the newspaper. He leaned on the iron railing, scanning the rooftops of old Marseilles — a jumble of wavy terracotta tiles. On the hill below, a woman was hanging out her washing. A couple of scrawny, long-legged cats were squaring up for a fight. The fishermen, their boats tied up in the harbour, were selling their catch to crowds of housewives with large shopping bags. Sea and sky were an opaque blur. No dividing line.

No dividing lines in space either. After his trip to the Alpha satellite he'd suddenly understood why past cosmonauts had found no adequate words for the sense of limitlessness up there, nor for the awesome magnifications of light and colour. Yet there'd been little time for idle observation. He and Greg had worked as if they'd rehearsed every move, every operation, yet — in converting the satellite to their purposes — they'd had to make unforeseen changes. They'd returned to earth satisfied that SRB 1 would function as planned. Greg's photo-voltaic cells had passed the early tests; *his* system of aerials and magnetic mirrors had performed consistently.

From beginning to end the run-up to the rebuilding of the Otrag-Alpha satellite had progressed as Shmuel had predicted. The secrecy Scobie and General Montana had enforced on the Los Alamos site had served them in changing the civilian and military organization. Three men only, one of them a radiologist, had understood that the body-scanner was used to establish the physical fitness of prisoners for spare-parts surgery. Alpha Corporation had supplemented its Defense Department grant by meeting the constant demand for healthy hearts, kidneys and eyes. The prisoners in Piper's photographs had been the reserve, missing persons who'd guessed that they were destined for a place of no return, who'd dreaded removal from their hygienic cages. The prisoners had been released without learning the truth about those that had disappeared. Their keepers had been taken to the island in the Pacific, fit company for Scobie and General Montana.

John wondered whether the change-over had been as troublefree as Greg had reported. And yet equally difficult plans had succeeded, such as NUMECs' theft and sale of 572 pounds of enriched uranium from under the noses of the Atomic Energy Commission. The apparent smoothness of the Los Alamos take-over hadn't worried John for almost a year. Now, suddenly, he had misgivings. Too easy? Or was he suffering from a Kenyan childhood hangover. The Luo people, not excepting Lakomi, had been suspicious of bonanzas. When the harvests had been outstandingly good they'd taken some of the produce out in boats and dumped it in Lake Victoria. John brushed off the thoughts of sacrifice. Yet the unease stayed in his mind. He shouldn't have allowed Fiona to become involved in this French . . . adventure. Now there was nothing he could do about it . . . except stare into the opaque distance and wait, and wait.

His trouble was that he hadn't yet come to terms with the fact that he, Shmuel and Greg were no longer on their own. What had begun with searing personal experiences — the murder of his parents, the holocausts in Eritrea and Rhodesia, the criminal waste of Sean's life — had led to the inexorable building up of evidence and knowledge. Their passive anger at death-dealing politicians and irresponsible corporation men had turned them into active fighters. Now — inevitably — their *club* had grown larger and even more world-wide . . . Kole Okango and a British cabinet minister, Harry Resnick — adviser to American presidents, General Jabotinsky and an untold number of his airforce personnel, the Israeli commander Shmuel called the Rav Aluf and his intelligence agents in the Middle East, in Germany, France and wherever needed. Kirov, the Russian GRU officer, had been something of an adjunct to Shmuel. John had become used to the idea of his involvement. Yet, after two years with Fiona, it still worried him that she had worked herself into the *team*. It had become a free-for-all.

Madame Pascal had come into the room and John went back indoors. He looked at his watch. 'It's time.'

'In five minutes, Monsieur. You are . . . *prêt?*'

'Yes, I'm ready.' The plump woman, looking younger than her sixty years, had been in the French Resistance during the war. She'd been tortured by the Gestapo and imprisoned in a German concentration camp. Now her only son was fighting on a new front. Yet she stood there, calm and smiling, looking at the machine in his compact suitcase. 'Madame, what will you do if the line is engaged.'

'But it has been discussed.'

'Yes . . . of course.'

'It is your wife. You are so *craintif*. You must have faith, Monsieur.' She checked her watch. 'I will ring the bell.'

John went to stand beside the terminal in its case. All systems go . . . all systems go; the space-age phrase was hammering his brain. The link had been tested and tested again . . . Satellite SRB 1, computer, terminal or remote manipulator . . . SRB 1 computer, terminal. The terminal in the suitcase would instruct the computer in Toulon which would activate SRB 1. And SRB 1 would release a beam which would travel earthward at the rate of 186,000 miles per second. The Selective Reflector Beam in operation, for the first time, on a genuine target. And if there had been a mistake in the calculations, if the Beam failed in selecting, it would kill.

'I am a businessman, Mr Murphy, not a politician,' Monsieur Jerome told Greg. His office certainly looked businesslike; progress charts on the walls, a long table full of papers and files, worn but comfortable bentwood chairs. 'Politics is an aggravation, *n'est ce pas*?'

'The Middle East's been an aggravation for a long time.' Greg watched the railway yard outside. A goods train was being shunted to another line, buffers clanging. *Companie* Mondial's workshops and warehouses were well placed for transport, with those handy trains taking its products to Marseilles where they could be transferred to ships — all within the harbour.

Jerome turned his hands palm up. 'What can people like us do? We make our contracts and try to meet the delivery dates. One hopes that there will be no local war to intervene.'

Mondial had almost completed building two nuclear reactors for Iraq. The plan, Greg assumed, was to send them by ship through the Mediterranean, the Suez Canal and the Red Sea. 'There have been reports in the States that you've been supplying weapon-grade uranium to Iraq. Is that right?'

The expression on Jerome's face made it obvious that he considered the question somewhat naïve — the kind of question one would expect from an American. 'When we supply a reactor to a customer we must be prepared to supply the necessary nuclear fuel. How the customer uses the uranium afterwards, *c'est une autre chose* — not our responsibility. My *Companie* is buying your *Companie's* double-diode-triode valve. You will not worry what we do with it,eh?'

'No.' Greg refrained from pointing out that there was a slight difference between his harmless valve and M. Jerome's nuclear reactors.

'*Voilà*. Sometimes I don't understand American thinking, Mr Murphy. You are against South Africa because of her racial politicies, *n'est ce pas*? You want independence for Namibia which is administered by South Africa. You are angry because South Africa doesn't abandon the richness of Namibian uranium to a regime of Communist guerillas. You are so much against South Africa, and what do you do? You — how do you say it? — you fiddle the gold market so that South Africa's gold goes up and up . . . and your enemy South Africa becomes very rich, and suddenly she has plenty of money to buy your American technology. What kind of diplomacy is that?'

'I don't understand it any more than you do.' Greg glanced at his watch. It was almost time for Pascal to bring Fiona back into the office. Shmuel had assured him that Ostermann — alias Pascal — was totally reliable. He'd have to be, if their timing was to work.

There was a knock on the door. Jerome went to open it. 'Come in, Madame.' His eyes took in Fiona's elegant figure with genuine pleasure. 'You found the reactors interesting?'

'Very much so,' she assured him. She turned to the man in white overalls. 'Monsieur Pascal had to explain them, of course. I don't know much outside computers.'

'But that is *fantastique*. In France we do not think of beautiful ladies as computer experts.'

Fiona smiled at Greg. 'I just wanted to be able to talk with my brother . . . Monsieur Jerome, it was kind of you to let us come here on a Saturday. I didn't think I'd get the chance . . .'

The telephone buzzed and Jerome picked up the receiver. As he listened his hand began to shake. He flung the receiver down and spoke to Pascal in incomprehensible French. Pascal pressed a button at the side of the desk and a siren began to wail.

'Please!' Jerome was yelling above the banshee howls. 'You must go *immédiatement*. It is a bomb alert . . . The telephone . . . She said the reactors will blow up. Go!'

'Anything we can do?' asked Fiona. It sounded ludicrously bland.

'No . . . no. I will write. Yes? Now go! It is perhaps somebody mad . . .'

'A hoax?'

'Yes. But who can tell? Quick!'

'OK.'

'*Au revoir. Écoute* Pascal . . .'

Greg took Fiona's elbow. No reason why they shouldn't run — like Jerome, Pascal and a few men who came rushing out of the warehouse.

Their hired Citroen was facing the exit at the end of the goods-yard. They were out of the complex and within a hundred yards of the Marseilles road when the warehouse behind them exploded with a roar.

Greg pulled into the curb and looked back. Tall flames were spurting into the pale spring sky; a pall of smoke began drifting out to sea. It was like the fires the students had raised on Berkeley campus a decade ago. Ugly fires. But this time nobody was going to get hurt; not in Toulon. 'Israel will be safe from nuclear neighbours for a couple of years.'

'Or more.'

'I doubt it. *Companie* Mondial will collect the insurance money . . . turn round, and build Iraq a new set of Tamuz reactors.'

'Which won't reach Iraq. Pascal's done a great job.'

'So have you, Fiona.'

'Let's find a telephone.'

Greg was reading *Aviation Week* in the back of the Citroen. Fiona, sitting beside John with a French map on her knees, was working out the distance to Monte Carlo. They'd decided to relax in Monaco for a couple of days before returning to England.

'Listen to this,' said Greg. 'It's in an article on war in space: *Senator Malcolm Wallop, a Republican, warned recently that if the Russians became the first to place a single high-energy laser weapon in space, they would acquire the capacity to destroy United States satellite systems without warning. The potential of particle beam weapons in space is still more awesome . . .*

John looked at him in the driving mirror. 'Nothing new in that.'

'Wait . . . There are some speculations on the pulsed-iodine laser and electron beam weapons. The article ends, *These weapons could be a tremendous force for peace, ending the long reign of thermonuclear terror — provided they are in the right hands.*'

Fiona said, 'It's still the old idea that — at best — future wars will amount to both sides shooting down satellites. No destruction on earth.'

'That's it. As far as I know no one's mentioned the Reflector Beam. Our satellite's still years ahead.'

'Unless the Russians have developed theirs on similar lines.' John made a right turn, taking the car south towards the coast. 'That's Shmuel's department. Meanwhile we've got to carry on as if Russia didn't know a musket from a precision rifle.'

'Let's change the song.' Fiona took the radio from the glove-box and switched on. The transistor began to chatter in French and Spanish, Italian and German. She raised the squeals of a pop group, the bellowing of a tenor and then, suddenly, the final bars of a familiar marching tune. 'This is the World Service of the BBC,' announced a serene voice.

'Thai forces have been placed on alert along the Cambodian frontier as the Vietnamese have begun an onslaught against Khmer Rouge rebels, forcing an exodus of fifty-three thousand refugees into Thailand. . . . According to the Soviet newspaper *Izvestia*,' the newscaster continued, 'the man found murdered in a Swiss hotel two days ago was Leonid Panchenko, a Soviet official who had been working at the International Cocoa Organization . . . The Soviet Union may become militarily involved in the Middle East over oil, Dr Otaiba — Chairman of OPEC — said in Vienna yesterday. He told Chancellor Kreisky that Russia's monthly output of oil was dwindling. He based his conclusions on the curtailment of Russian shipments of oil to Eastern Europe. Dr Otaiba said that the political unrest in Iran was a matter of grave concern as it could cause an unwelcome change in Russia's energy policy . . . The British Prime Minister, Mrs Margaret Thatcher, has arrived in Brussels to discuss her proposed cuts in the British contribution to the EEC budget . . . News is coming in of a major explosion at a factory in the south of France . . . '

'Turn it up,' said John.

' . . . *Companie* Mondial had almost completed the building of two nuclear reactors for Iraq. According to managing director, Monsieur

Jerome, the reactors are a total write-off and there has been extensive damage to adjacent buildings. Thanks to a telephone warning there were no casualties. French police say that the explosion was due to sabotage by highly trained Israeli commandos, who escaped in a helicopter . . .'

34

Shmuel had the momentary impression that he was in King's College Chapel, listening to a Bach fugue. But Vienna's St Stephen's Cathedral was colder, more austere. Unlike the Cambridge church it didn't give one the feeling of being lived in. The droning of the organ had stopped, a discord drifted into the shadowy heights. Kirov came down the transept, his grey Astrakhan hat making him look even taller than usual. He slid into the pew and knelt. Shmuel touched his arm, a gesture of affection and concern.

Kirov said, 'He's outside.'

'I know.' Shmuel had trailed Kirov from the Hotel Bristol, along the snow-powdered boulevard of the Ring, past the two museums, parliament and city hall. Opposite the University they'd cut through the narrow streets of the old town to the cathedral — without losing the KGB officer, who was doggedly following Kirov. They'd established, at least, that the surveillance was confined to one man. It was the Cape Town situation all over again. No one had yet discovered a cure for the distrust between the KGB and GRU. Shmuel cast out the memory of the KGB agent who'd split open his head on the forecourt of the Ritz Plaza.

'What do you think?' asked Kirov.

'Put an end to it.'.

'Thug.'

'*Rega ehad.*'

'Swear in a language I can understand. What do you suggest, Samuel?'

'Follow me along the Graben. Turn left into the Kohlmarkt. We'll make it as near the Michaeler Platz as possible.'

'Your car?'

'Parked in the inner court of the Imperial Palace.'

The shop-windows of the Graben were full of toys for adults — roses in solid silver, gold-plated telephones, mink covers for steering-wheels, marzipan Christmas angels, crystal pigs for new-year luck. The street was packed with shoppers carrying fir trees and parcels. Snow was falling in big, lazy flakes which settled on shoulders and fur hats, on baroque curves, on the spiky memorial to the plague.

Shmuel stopped at Heldwein's display of jewellery. Who could afford the price of a country estate for a diamond bracelet? Certain politicians, for one — if there was any truth in the newspaper reports of Austrian corruption. And the oil-sheiks of course, on their visits to OPEC headquarters. Shmuel caught sight of the grey Astrakhan hat and moved on.

In the Kohlmarkt an icy north wind, trapped between the tall city houses, was assaulting eyes and ears, noses and lips. There was a rush for Dehmel's famous coffee and marzipan potatoes. The more determined shoppers bent their heads and tucked their chins into their fur collars. In the cold blasts from Russia it was every man for himself.

No one noticed Shmuel step into the narrow passage at the side of the art shop. Kirov passed without seeing him. He'd almost reached the square at the back of the Imperial Palace when the KGB agent showed. Shmuel darted out. A lightning chop to the side of the head buckled KGB's knees. Shmuel caught him before he hit the pavement.

'*Was ist los?*' An elderly Viennese had stopped, reluctantly, his impulse of civil responsibility already regretted.

'*Nichts,*' Shmuel assured him. '*Er ist Epileptiker.*'

The man fled.

Kirov had turned back and was supporting the unconscious KGB agent. Passers-by glanced furtively at the two men dragging along a drunk. Drunk in the afternoon, and it wasn't yet Christmas. Improper. Disgusting.

They bundled the agent into the hired BMW. He'd be out cold for another hour or so. Shmuel drove through the inner court of the Hofburg to the main gates and out on the Ring, a short distance to the Russian Embassy.

As they hauled the agent to the locked doors, Kirov said, 'I could deal with it on my own.'

'We've got a good plan. Let's stick to it.'

They stood for a long time before a doorman answered the bell.

'I want Brainin,' Kirov told him. 'Open up, man. We're bringing you one of your friends.'

An official rose from behind a screen of bullet-proof glass. 'Comrade Kirov . . .'

'I remember you. Paris, wasn't it?'

'Yes, Comrade Colonel.'

'Give us a hand.'

Between them they took the body into a waiting-room and put him on a couch.

'Don't worry about him,' said Kirov. 'He'll live. Now, Brainin.'

'Who is . . .'

'My friend? Tell the Trade Attaché, he's Comrade Kuznetsov.'

The reaction was as Kirov had predicted. *Kuznetsov* was too young to be the Vice-President of the Soviet Union; and obviously *he* wouldn't just turn up. A son perhaps? Certainly a relative. It was normal for the leadership to put their relatives into special positions . . . keeping their names from the public. It would be unwise to keep a Kuznetsov waiting. The official scuttled away.

He returned within minutes. 'Comrade Brainin will see you. Please follow me.'

'Stay where you are.' Kirov spoke quietly. 'Sherlock Holmes is coming back to life. Get aspirins and water . . . I know where to find the Trade Attaché.'

The KGB Sector Chief lookd out of place in the Viennese Biedermeier room with its dainty furniture under a painted ceiling. Up high a big-bellied god was chasing succulent pink nymphs through puffball clouds. On the parquet floor, square, bleak-faced Brainin was looking down his long nose, avoiding his visitors' eyes.

'Be seated,' he muttered.

'We won't damage your fragile chairs,' said Kirov.

'You damaged Comrade Klaban.'

'Your mistake, Brainin. You shouldn't be wasting men on me. That's what Comrade Kuznetsov thinks.'

The magic name made the KGB chief twitch. 'We're trying to contain an extremely. . . awkward situation. Your intervention . . .'

'There's no situation *to* contain. It was your job to take care of Professor Balatov . . . just about the most important scientist we have in the Soviet Union. And where is he now?'

'Kirov, we're working on it. We . . .'

'Surely you don't expect the Presidium to sit in the Kremlin and wait . . . while you're *working on it*. You can't have persuaded yourself that Balatov's still in Vienna. The Professor's defected to the West, Brainin. Defected.'

'Gospodin Kuznetsov,' Brainin appealed to Shmuel. 'Let me show you my file on Balatov. You will see . . .'

'*Niet*,' Shmuel turned his back on him and strolled to the window. 'Colonel Kirov's in charge.'

'We've neglected nothing,' protested Brainin, 'short of wiping the Professor's behind. Balatov attended the cocktail party at the Hofburg . . . swilling crème de menthe, as usual. Klaban put him to bed. Next day Balatov took part — as scheduled — in the session on communication satellites and had lunch at the university with the delegates from India and Germany. He went to the lavatory . . .'

'And disappeared without a trace.'

'It was only three days ago.'

260

'Only!'

'The Kriminal Polizei is helping . . . '

Kirov laughed. 'The Austrians! They probably arranged the defection. You must have made them very happy . . . crawling to them for help.'

'Colonel, we have checked the airports. I've got men on every frontier check-post . . . '

'Ah yes . . . the usual.'

'Your GRU won't do better.' Brainin was exasperated, but he glanced at Shmuel's back with apprehension. 'I mean . . . we're faced with the worst crisis since . . . '

'Don't try to explain. I know what's at stake, better than you. You've made a deplorable mess of it . . . so the GRU probably *won't* get anywhere either. Balatov may well be playing chess with Ronald Reagan on his Californian ranch by now . . . But I won't give up just yet.'

'Can I be of assistance?' Brainin abdicated.

'You must use your own judgement. But if I were you I'd put my men back on normal duties and call off the Austrians.'

'But Balatov . . . '

'Exactly. Better leave him to us. And, Brainin . . . don't get in my way again. I'll be doing what I can to find the Professor and— incidentally — save your neck.'

The venue had been arranged by Martin Jabotinsky, whose father had connections in Vienna going back to the Austrian Empire. Until the end of the First World War, Poland had been a part of the Empire; in 1980 a few remnants of the Polish aristocracy still lived in Vienna. Their offspring, efficient professional survivors, had kept out of Austrian politics but were on intimate terms with the top politicians.

It had been no trouble for Count Boguslavsky to put General Jabotinsky in touch with a certain Austrian Cabinet Minister, who usually spent the Christmas recess in the Bahamas. Some American Defense Department funds had been channelled into a Liechtenstein bank account; the Cabinet Minister had departed for his winter vacation, villa and staff had been handed over to General Jabotinsky and his guests.

The twenty-bedroom villa, tucked away in woodland on the outskirts of Vienna, was furnished with splendid English and French antiques. The paintings on the walls included masterpieces by Velazquez and Rubens, Botticelli and several French Impressionists.

'Nazi loot,' Professor Balatov told John and Fiona. He left the Cranach madonna they'd been studying and walked them to the tray of bottles on the verandah. 'The Nazis stripped private homes as well as museums between 1938 and '45.' He poured an inch of crème de menthe into a brandy goblet. 'After the war, the American occupation forces found

261

literally billions' worth of looted art treasures in various hide-outs . . . and handed them to the Austrian government for return to their rightful owners. Austrian officialdom happened to forget all about the hoard until 1969 . . .'

'For twenty-four years?' asked Fiona.

'Yes, for almost a quarter of a century. By then many of the original owners and people who'd witnessed the looting had died. So — very conveniently — the valuable works of art became ownerless again. It seems they've been found new homes.' Balatov sipped the green liqueur and peeled the glass off his bottom lip. 'Adroit politicians, the Austrians.'

'You don't like them,' said John.

'I wouldn't say that. As crooks go, they're charmers. I was a student in Vienna before the war. That's when the mass of Austrians became dedicated Nazis. After the war I landed here with the Soviet army. And that's when the lot of them turned democratic . . . overnight, of course. I have no quarrel with them. They're just a little more cruel and corrupt than the rest of us.'

John looked at the bulky Russian defector with new interest. 'If that's how you feel about humanity, why have you taken such risks?'

'Risks? I've been enjoying myself . . . working at what I wanted to do.'

'Which could have landed you in a prison camp or a psychiatric hospital.'

'Don't make a hero of me, young man. Ever since the Hiroshima bomb I've hated the nuclear filth. And I've believed, for more years than I care to remember, that there must be a cleaner way to keep warm and to kill our fellow-men. I've found it. So have you and your friends. It's logical that we should now work together. I should be able to increase the velocity of your Beam . . . that's all.'

'It's a hell of a lot.'

'I'll get a hell of a lot in return . . . the fleshpots of America. Do you realize what that means to a Russian zombie? who's lived between bare walls — not a fine painting within a thousand miles — in a dark, freezing desert . . . who's lived on the swill that passes for food in Russia . . . whose daughter never owned a smart dress . . . who hasn't been with a beautiful woman for years. Now, at last, I'm going to have it all . . . a house of my own, with two bathrooms and three lavatories. My own car and swimming-pool. A fragrant woman or two . . . or three. Fragrant American fruit and big, soluble steaks. When I snuff it, plenty of money to leave to my daughter Masha. Ah yes . . . and plenty of schmaltz. You know what schmaltz is? Wait!'

Balatov marched through the sliding glass doors into the dining-room, where a maid was clearing the table for the afternoon meeting. 'Alexei! put on my new tape, will you.'

'We'll be starting in a minute.'

'I won't be rushed.'

Kirov shook his head, but he put a cassette into the player.

Balatov rejoined John and Fiona to the sounds of soulful violins and a voice that was sobbing, in German, *Dein ist mein ganzes Herz* . . . and where you are I long to be.

'There,' Balatov finished his drink. 'Beautiful schmaltz.' He turned to the view beyond the picture windows, 'And more schmaltz. Look at it, children! Vienna! city of dreams . . . made of marzipan and whipped cream. A toy-town of snowy roofs against a Breughel-grey sky. And the steeple of St Stephen's reaching up to tickle God under the chin . . . perhaps God can be bribed like everybody else. And over there . . . do you see? the great fairground wheel, going round and round like fate itself . . .'

'Igor,' Kirov came out on the verandah. 'We must start the meeting.'

'What, this minute?'

'Haven't you had enough crème de menthe?'

'It's good for my digestion. Alexei, you have no feeling for sweetness.'

'Come in, you *kulak*. We've still got a lot of work to get through. You're keeping everyone waiting.'

'What do you expect? I'm a genius. Am I supposed to have a conscience as well?'

The scientific sessions had taken up three days and much of their evenings. Now the paintings in the dining-room had been replaced by maps of the world. Political and tactical decisions would have to be made and none of them relished that part of the proceedings.

Looking around the table John recovered the confidence he'd felt at their first meeting. Shmuel, Greg and Fiona — at one with him. The Rav Aluf — associated with Shmuel since his boyhood, a compassionate man without political illusions. Martin Jabotinsky — a scientific modern general with a realistic appreciation of the nuclear menace. Alexei Kirov — a true fighter against war, all his adult years spent in a half-life of lies and fears. And Professor Balatov, the new associate — met briefly at the Cambridge symposium, a genius who had escaped from a Soviet military group so secret that its work was known to none but the Presidium and selected agents of the GRU.

Balatov, flamboyant in many ways, had shown humility and wisdom in discussing his work at Semipalatinsk and Saryshagan. He'd disclaimed any merit in the discovery of speeds greater than light saying, 'There are no barriers to knowledge, except the self-imposed limitations of the human mind.' He'd warned his young colleagues against the dangers of well-established theories, 'because it would be easy to live by them, avoiding great efforts in destroying them.'

And now Balatov was asking the Rav Aluf for his assessment of the recent past and the coming race against time. 'Coming from the Soviet Union,' he said, 'I have a black and white picture of the world in my mind. That can't be right.'

'In the past year there's been an increase in high-risk events. The little commander got up from the table, picked up his pen and went to the largest map. 'In Iran — the end of the Shah's rule and the Ayatollah's revolution, the taking of the American hostages, and President Carter's tragically unsuccessful rescue-attempt. Next, war between Iran and Iraq. The disruptions in the oil industry are increasing the political instability in the area. It's an ideal situation for overt and covert Russian intervention. That Russia invaded Afghanistan didn't come as a surprise, did it? In answer America has sent warships into the Indian ocean and is building up her base on Diego Garcia.

'Unpublicised but effective efforts have been made to prevent the spread of nuclear arms. In France two reactors, destined for Iraq, have been destroyed. And in Paris the head of the Baghdad Atomic Energy Commission — about to conclude the purchase of nuclear warheads — was found murdered in his hotel room. The murder was *not* carried out by Israeli agents; the fact that the man was clubbed to death points to assailants from a more primitive country in the Middle East. Last, but not least, France has decided to go ahead with the development of the neutron bomb. France is outside Nato, let me remind you. There is no legal way by which Nato and America can stop her from developing a lucrative trade in neutron bombs.

'There are incalculable factors which cannot yet be assessed . . . such as the change of Presidents in the States. Jimmy Carter may not have been a brilliant President, but he and his advisers did practice military restraint and initiated the important programme of harvesting energy from space. Ronald Reagan is still an unknown quantity. There's no telling how he and his administrators will react to Soviet provocations. And the most obvious danger-point for such provocation is Poland . . . with its newly formed trade union, Solidarity . . . ten million members at loggerheads with the Communist puppet regime.'

'Polish resistance could be the beginning of the end for the Soviet empire,' said Kirov.

'I think the Polish revolt's started too soon.' The Rav Aluf tapped Warsaw with his pen. 'It's a flashpoint that worries me. We need time. As our scientists here have told us, it's unlikely that our Satellite SRB 2 will be fully operational before 1984. We also need time for helping along the development of the trends in world opinion . . .'

'You'll have your tactical plans, of course,' said Balatov. 'But events *will* help you. The tide is turning already. A few weeks ago eight thousand scientists from forty countries called upon their governments to enforce an embargo on selling technology to Russia. They also demanded an end to the manufacture of nuclear arms. I don't believe it was merely a gesture. Those men won't support us out of highmindedness . . . they'll support us because — as scientists — they're bound to be more frightened of the nuclear monster than the less knowledgeable. Alexei, tell them what's happening in Russia.'

'There's a growing underground,' said Kirov. 'It's been a long, slow development. The man who started it received the decoration *Hero of the Soviet Union*. He was General Piotr Grigorenko. He travelled the country, holding meetings, teaching people their rights under the constitution. He was tortured . . . imprisoned . . . killed, in the end. But he had disciples who've taken over. Now there are millions who are ready to rise against our Communist dictatorship.'

'Alexei's not advocating revolution,' said Balatov. 'He believes, as I do, that the only effective revolution is *evolution*. And this is being helped along by technology-deterioration . . . like one of our twenty-year-old Echo 1 Class nuclear submarines coming to grief with ninety-two men aboard. Tass didn't make a news-story of it . . . yet such news spreads. We Russians keep hearing of leaking nuclear missiles in America . . . and of increasing radio-active pollution. People are beginning to draw logical conclusions. If America's nuclear hardware's rotting and poisoning people, then our Russian nuclear hardware's no less dangerous. Our leadership's aware of the new climate of opinion.'

'Has the Kremlin suddenly become sensitive to climates of opinion?' asked the Rav Aluf.

'Yes . . . when it happens to fit in with Kremlin policy,' Kirov told him. 'Recently Kosygin retired, for *health reasons*; and three top military advisers have been replaced by university professors . . . including an astro-physicist. It's some indication of a new approach. Also . . . Soviet forces haven't gone into Poland . . . yet. I have the distinct impression that Brezhnev and his new caucus are holding back.'

'For what reason?' asked Jabotinsky.

'They're preparing for war in space,' said Balatov. 'And there America is ahead in one area, and one only; it has the Space Shuttle. But Russia may be catching up at this very moment. Three cosmonauts have been sent up to repair the Salyut 6 Space Laboratory, which is three years old. They've been aboard eleven days. Now they're preparing to return to earth in their Soyuz T-3 spaceship. It'll be a crucial test for the craft's new computer system . . . The last Soyuz crew died during re-entry.'

'All the same,' Kirov broke the silence, 'Russia has sophisticated satellites in space. Before long, the particle beam developed at Saryshagan will enable Soviet satellites to destroy *enemy* satellites. I expect America's working along the same lines, because she can't afford to lose her observation and warning systems in space. Such losses would make nonsense of her whole defence system.'

'Back to nuclear war,' said Jabotinsky, 'And the old idea of *first strike*. Whichever side knocks out the enemy's satellites gains the advantage of surprise. Given a surprise nuclear attack, there's every chance that the wholesale destruction, and the nuclear fall-out, will be confined to the

265

attacked side. I'm as convinced as the Russians must be that there would be no retaliation.'

'You're right,' agreed Balatov, 'And yet the Russian shift to satellite-destruction-before-nuclear-attack gives us our chance.'

'How high do you rate it?' asked Greg.

'Yours is a young, extraordinary . . . and passionately determined team. Above all, it's a united team. In Semipalatinsk and Saryshagan there's a disunity . . . discontent among the technicians, who hate living in Kazakhstan and feel they're underpaid. The military, who's guarding the complexes and the civilians, is under very severe pressure. In the race against time . . . that's what you are in . . . I'd put my money on you, John and Fiona, Shmuel and your military back-up. That is, if it were a race between you and the Soviets. But it isn't, is it?'

'The flashpoints,' said John.

'Precisely. I'm old enough to remember the combustion of the flash-points that triggered the two major wars of this century . . . Sarayevo and Poland. In the nineteen-eighties the flashpoints could be Poland — yet again, or Budapest, Tehran or Baghdad, the Strait of Hormuz or Namibia . . .'

Fiona was staring at the world map. 'You're not giving us much hope.'

'Hope, child? You're taking part in the greatest gamble ever under-taken on — and outside — this planet. And you're asking for hope?'

'What else is there?'

'Women!' Balatov covered Fiona's hand with his wrinkled paw. 'How they want nice, tidy homes and lives! I'm not insulting you, child. You're right to want those things. But take my advice and use the recipe that's kept me alive . . . *carpe diem; live for the day*. It's all I remember from the days when people were taught Latin at school. *Carpe diem*. Be kind enough to bring me a new bottle of crème de menthe . . . in case there is no tomorrow.'

From BORIS NIKOLAEVICH PONOMAREV, Chairman International
      Department of the COMMUNIST PARTY
To YURYI ANDROPOV, Chairman KGB

Number ID//KGB 736P273777//0   6 June 1982

The significance of your communication of 2 April 1982 escapes me. If its purpose was to apportion the blame for the prevailing unrest in certain quarters I must remind you of your consistent failures in establishing a proper liaison with Army Intelligence. Your Directorate's paranoiac suspicions of GRU are amply documented in your previous communications on file at my Department. By order of the Presidium the damaging split between your KGB and GRU has recently been the subject of a comprehensive study.

Comrade Galuzin is of the opinion that the security value of GRU has been rising in direct ratio to the decline of your KGB's usefulness. Therefore KGB can no longer live on its past reputation. I hope this clarifies the position of my Department and that your Directorate will now get its priorities right.

Let me remind you of these priorities: the rising discontent over the chronic shortages of consumer goods; the treacherous outspokenness of all too many leading scientists at universities and defence establishments; the almost overt public condemnation of defensive nuclear weapon production as well as nuclear power-plants.

You did not have to inform me of the fact that our labour camps are bursting at the seams. What concerns us here is that for every man sent to a camp, prison or psychiatric ward five new suicide candidates spring up. Your statement that our country is too large to be effectively controlled strikes me as the feeble excuse of an official who is losing his grip. You might remember that the Party has in fact controlled the country ever since the Revolution.

Speaking constructively, I'd advise you to consider very carefully how best to assist the Party in containing what I consider a dangerous state of near-anarchy. In the Presidium's view it is too late for your KGB to retrieve the position it held until the 'eighties. You will therefore have to redeploy your forces, always assuming that your men are capable of co-operating with the most disciplined body at our disposal – the Army and GRU. No one is denying that General Grigorenko caused the Party much embarrassment and anxiety, but your suspicion of the High Command as an organization of equally subversive generals is unjustified and absurd.

My Department considers it useful and timely that the High Command has put forward a scheme for training commandos or shock-troops capable of dealing instantly and effectively with any sudden dissident problem. In my opinion there is nothing fanciful about General Sverdlov's planned exercises of evacuating the Lubyanka Prison, surrounding buildings and streets. Apart from its value as a training exercise, the series of operations will demonstrate to the public that our armed forces are capable of taking total control no matter how apparently impenetrable the target.

In the light of my previous remarks you will appreciate the importance the Presidium and my Department attach to the Lubyanka project as a first step to giving the Armed Forces and the GRU a much greater role in internal security. I take it that you will lose no time in making the necessary adjustments to KGB policy.

Interface V
From Defense Secretary
To Chairman, Senate Appropriation Committee

Reply to Fort K 34 Tac-Squads   9 March 1983

Dear Ed,

Glad to know that you and I had much the same gut reaction to General Jabotinsky's movie. Though he used some library shots of Fort Knox the package he put together appeared to convince everyone who witnessed the screening. Sure, as you pointed out at the Pentagon discussion, the project looks like one of George Keegan's screwy ideas. Yet George, to give him his due, isn't just any retired General who's been sitting on his ass too long.

In any case, it's immaterial whether or not Keegan's been influencing the young guys at the Pentagon. The fact is that Martin Jabotinsky has made out a watertight case in favour of the Fort Knox project and I am going to back him all the way.

I reckon the psychological argument he put forward is indisputable. Unlike the President I don't believe that slackness in the armed forces is widespread, but there comes a time when normal training routines lose credibility in the eyes of the average professional soldier. That's one good reason for the creation of Martin's new tactical squads, guys who're capable of taking control of a fortress like Fort Knox, a tough target by any standard.

The other good reason for such complex exercises, beginning at selected defense sites and running up to the Fort Knox project, is the all-time low in morale right through the country. I guess the military and civilian demoralization began when the special task force and our government failed back in 1980 in liberating American citizens who'd been taken hostage, failed for more than a year. The fact that our country could be held to ransom by primitives like the Iranians set up a deep trauma in the minds of most thinking Americans. Add the effects of recession, the regular reports that the Soviets are ahead of us in the military technology stakes, and the increasingly frequent episodes of missile corrosion with resulting radiation leaks, and you can't blame the citizens of this country for losing all confidence in their governments and in their own future.

Another aspect of the general picture is the attitude of the Pentagon to the theory of Mutually Assured Destruction. No one in the military has spelled it out so far, but it's my opinion that there are mighty few guys left who still believe that the principle of 'you kill me and I kill you' will keep us and the Soviets off the collision-course for ever.

Sure, the Fort Knox project won't cure these ills, but it could be a turning-point. Given the right public relations treatment the new-style training of the Jabotinsky Squads will fire public imagination, make people feel that we are working on creating a defense force second to none, guys capable of operating successfully in the toughest circumstances anywhere in the world.

It is, of course, a pilot scheme. Sure, it will cost money, but General Jabotinsky's estimates don't strike me as extravagant considering the scale of the project, including the ultimate transference of our gold reserves from Fort Knox to alternate top security sites. I am relying on you to convince your Committee that the required funds for the operation will be an investment in the future of our defense system.

       Give my regards to Diana and the boys,
       Yours,
       Bob

From Ambassador, British Embassy Vienna
To Foreign Secretary, London
Instruction: By Messenger

Our Ref. Reisnerstrasse LD/BS   13 February 1984

Dear Foreign Secretary,

The MI reports on what one might call Domestic Military Exercises in USA, Russia, and now Germany are not uninteresting, but the significance of these operations is hard to gauge. I tend to agree with my colleague in Germany that the Americans have started a fashion in non-nuclear spectaculars for home-market consumption. It does look like a psychological ploy, though I fail to see why it should have any startling effects on the American public or the anti-nuclear lobby. That the Russians followed the Fort Knox circus with the Lubyanka show is natural enough. As to NATO, I assume the exercises at the Olympic complex are American-inspired as well as consistent with the German absorption in war-games. Boys will be boys.

The willingness of the Vienna SALT bureaucrats to include selected scientists at the next summit meeting fits in with current rumours. Allowing the attendance of men who have been directly associated with the SRB Energy Satellite could be a sop to the ever increasing numbers of academics and research scientists who are protesting against nuclear stock-piles and civilian reactors.

I can also imagine a harrassed American President welcoming any back-up in his bargaining position. It wouldn't surprise me if the American President arrived in Vienna with a carrot for the Russian donkey: on the lines, 'You keep your bloody particle beams out of Space and we cut you in on our Space-Energy bonanza'. Though there is no obvious bonanza as yet the Russians would want to question experts who have actually worked on the Space-Energy project.

It is gratifying that the Americans have invited the British expert on their team to Vienna. In case he gets in touch with us, I would like to know more about Mr Whitmore. All I have been told is that he came from Kenya, went to the Space Shuttle unveiling at his own expense and then presented HM Government with a useful report. Such generosity is somewhat puzzling.

Like you, I am not happy about the situation in Mongolia. One always feels uneasy when the Russians step up their military activities in an area with a long history of border disputes, particularly if there is a good new reason such as geological reports of gold deposits. In my view there is a distinct possibility that SALT Clause 89A will have to be invoked in the near future. If so, the Americans will certainly go to Vienna within the stipulated time. Whether Comrade Galuzin will comply with the provisions of Clause 89A is anyone's guess.

      Yours sincerely,
      Bonham-Spencer

FREEDOM FROM FEAR II

Satellite SRB 2 - 1984

35

As Greg turned the corner at the last intersection of tunnels the light began to change from silver-white to red-gold. He stopped the electrically powered bug and lay back in his seat until he faced the glass dome of Inspection Chamber Omega. From here the satellite looked like a gigantic but incredibly fragile insect, its steel limbs and antennas reaching deep into unseen space. He'd known every inch of the structure since its inception, yet now he no longer recognized it as his own. It seemed as if the universe, imbuing it with those changing lights, had absorbed it into a system of worlds beyond human imagination. What he was privileged to see was no more than a mirage of the great miracle of divine unendingness.

He waited, savouring the silence, until darkness blotted out the dome itself, and then switched on the intercom. 'Ted, I'm coming in.'

'You OK?'

'Sure.'

A mile on he came to the open docking chamber of the Shuttle. Ted Wagner secured the bug in its bay and helped him out of his overalls. 'How did it go?'

'No problems. They could switch on the power right now.' Greg had worked through the sequences without a hitch. The communication between satellite, computer and terminals had been flawless, the voices of his associates free from interference. For seven days he'd been testing the performance of his forty-five square miles of semiconducting glasses, John's system of aerials and Shmuel's computer. He'd found no snags, yet he was conscious of the myriad malfunctions which could result from a loose nut or a concealed break in a wire.

Ted walked ahead into the crew module. 'The percentage of satellites which have gone wrong is point zero zero three,' he said, over his shoulder.

'Thanks,' Sean's friend, the pilot who'd risked his life in giving him his first aerial view of the Los Alamos complex, *was* being supportive. Translated into unspoken sentiment, the reminder that satellites functioned more reliably than traffic lights was meant to offset depression — a recognized but unpublicized astronaut-reaction to the enormity of space.

Ted began to climb the stairs of the flight deck, 'I'll be down for food in a minute.'

Greg, remaining on the lower deck, went into the port-side living area. Fiona was sitting at the transmission console, writing down a message that was coming through.

She tore off the sheet and handed it to Greg. 'Not so good.'

Underground — query — nuclear explosion in Russia, he read. *Soviets say it was an attempt at unlocking oil deposits trapped in Gobi Desert rocks close to Chinese frontier. Report: nuclear missiles fired at Mongolian dissidents in Sain Shanda area. Report fast rise in radiation levels in China, 300 miles north-west of Kalgan. President Reagan on electioneering tour. Returning to Washington instantly. Harry warns: Vienna arms limitation summit in danger of cancellation on account of USA corporation's delivery of nuclear warheads to China. Suggest: we go ahead as planned.* The recommendation was undoubtedly the outcome of emergency discussions between Shmuel, John and the military. *In force: Highest pressure on USA — USSR Leaders, via media and advisers, to go to Vienna as arranged.*

'What now?' asked Fiona.

'We trust in our organization . . . and luck.'

'John's on his way to South Africa . . .'

'It's a trip that couldn't have been cancelled, no matter what.'

'I wish . . .'

'Fiona, I know. But we needed you here.' Greg put an arm around her. 'It'll be over sooner than you think.'

'Which way? The shooting's begun.'

John had not expected that Research City would look like an integral part of the Kalahari Desert. Yet even those buildings of the great fortress which consisted of steel and other man-made materials had been sprayed to match the walls of the local ferrous-red rock.

Because the complex looked as if it had grown from the soil of the Kalahari, grown as naturally as the bush, it seemed as if it had always meant to stand there like a shrine to an unknown African god. Yet it had risen within the past three years, beginning when Shmuel and his friends in the South African army had selected the site in 1981.

Shmuel's idea for the test site might have been conceived as early as 1975 when the Rav Aluf had sent him to sell Israeli tactical aircraft to the South Africans. The contract had been signed by Joost Grendorp; and Grendorp had finally convinced his government of the twenty-first century alternative to nuclear power.

The early sun was turning the walls of the deserted fortress from pale gold to terracotta. The men, eating breakfast outside their tents, watched in silence. Within half an hour Research City would disappear at the pressing of a button. Perhaps all of them were regretting its end, the hoped-for destruction of pre-stressed concrete and steel, spacecraft alloys, plastics and natural stone.

Andrew poured coffee into John's beaker. 'At least the two of us have made it.'

'I remember.' John had a vision of their last breakfast with their parents. They'd listened to Andrew reading from *The Lost World of the Kalahari . . . For the miraculous thing about the Kalahari is that it is a desert only in the sense that it contains no permanent surface of water. Otherwise its deep fertile sands are covered with grass glistening in the wind like fields of gallant corn . . . After the rains there is a great invasion of life from the outside world into a desert which produces such sweetness out of its winter travail of heat and thirst . . .*

John remembered his father's promise. The Kalahari was a long way from Kisumu but one day they would go there on safari . . . when Andrew was older. Andrew was thirty-four, a physician, father of two children . . . and still an African. He was not seeing the Kalahari at its best. The rains hadn't yet come and the land still looked parched and arid. Yet there were advantages; most living things were still in greener pastures and it was unlikely that birds would get in the way of the test.

The camera crew had mounted their truck and were moving forward, followed by the vehicles that carried the scientific equipment. The truck with the terminal, driven by Joost Grendorp himself, stopped at John's tent. 'Ready when you are.'

'Now.'

Andrew got up. 'I'm coming.'

John didn't argue. He knew that Andrew wouldn't be left behind. 'You're not to leave the car under any circumstances. Understand?'

'Sure.'

Grendorp let in the clutch. 'I can smell water. The rains are not far off. In a couple of days the buck will be coming down.'

Within a quarter of a mile they reached the waist-high stone perimeter of the complex. Grendorp followed it until he could face the truck due north. When he stopped John checked his watch and opened the cover of the terminal. He connected to computer Johannesburg which instantly responded with the count-down.

'Zero minus ten . . . nine . . .'

Suddenly John became aware of a movement by the walls of the fortress. An impala, its tawny coat blending with the stone, was wandering serenly towards a stunted thorn bush. He saw the lyre-shaped black and white marking at its tail, the slow ripple of the rump.

'Eight . . .'

Andrew's eyes were on the terminal. He hadn't yet noticed the animal. In a moment he would.

'Seven . . .'

John leaped from the truck and went racing at the perimeter. He was conscious of shouting words, Swahili words. The gazelle turned, saw the man, sprang forward and leaped over the wall, fleeing past the camera crew into the depth of the desert.

Andrew was out of the truck. 'Back! Go back!'

John was running to him when he heard the gale cut the air, like an express train bearing down on him. He became engulfed in light so brilliant that it hurt his eyes. All around him the Kalahari was exploding. He fell, struck by an unseen force. The ground under him squirmed and heaved in convulsions.

Searing heat. Flames inside his body . . . spreading . . . reaching the pain in his head. Burning out. Not the skin. The husks . . . They'd find his husk. Pain dulling . . . dying down. Nothing more to burn. Weightless. Wind lifting his husk. Floating. Floating up to Andrew's face. Andy . . . sun in his hair. Caressing wind . . . stirring the hair . . . like the down of a fledgling. Andy . . . you . . . you and your gazelle . . .

36

'Mr President,' said the American to the Russian President, 'I suggest we dispense with the interpreters. I know that your English is remarkably good.'

'Gospodin President,' said Galuzin, 'I do not deny that it's very boring to have to listen to the interpreters . . . especially when their English is not as good as mine . . . but we have a tradition that no Soviet leader has ever been heard to speak a language other than Russian.'

'Mr President, I suggest you institute a new tradition that all Soviet presidents must be talented linguists like yourself.'

'Gospodin President, I do not find your idea entirely repellent. History expects one to make one's mark.' Galuzin turned, fixing his little black eyes on Alexei. 'Kirov, I've agreed to reducing the numbers of my advisers for this meeting . . . on the advice of your superior. At top level one can achieve more without experts who hold conflicting views; but I must have someone capable of preparing communiqués. Who's taking care of that?'

'I am, Comrade President.'

'You? Since when is Military Intelligence dealing with press and public relations?'

'My orders are . . .'

'All right, all right; I'll deal with it later. There's more than one unusual feature about this meeting.'

'There's never been a Clause 89A meeting before.'

'Quite. I trust you're acquainted with communiqué formats.'

'Yes Comrade President.' Kirov retreated and joined the group of Shmuel, Greg and Jabotinsky. 'Did you hear?'

Greg nodded. 'He wants the usual amorphous trash for public consumption . . . condemnation of the aggressor — China, of course — and the piece about the world leaders *making progress in their discussions* etcetera.'

Shmuel was studying the long buffet table. The flowers were beginning to droop. The Russians had almost finished stripping the silver platters. 'I think Galuzin's smelled that there's something in the wind. Try rounding them up to the lecture theatre.'

'As soon as they've finished the caviar,' agreed Kirov. 'Greedy bastards.'

Greg went on a round of the reception room. Some fifty men, the Russian security guards in dark grey civilian suits. So far the summit meeting had taken a traditional and predictable course. Having agreed to Vienna as the venue — as all ongoing SALT talks had taken place in Vienna — Galuzin had been bloody-minded about a building for holding this special summit. He'd objected to the Palace of Schoenbrunn on the grounds that it had once been used by the British Occupation Forces. He'd turned down the Imperial Palace in the Inner City, because it was too close to sundry Austrian government offices, and all modern conference suites because air-conditioning aggravated his hayfever.

Finally the American President had personally persuaded Galuzin that the university was the most discreet and prestigious location, especially if the summit meeting should end in an agreement and a signing ceremony which would be watched by five hundred million television viewers.

Public awareness of the nuclear world war danger had become universal. An 'incident', such as the flare-up in the Far East, had been expected throughout the world since the Cuba crisis. Fear had built up with every little war or revolution in South America or Africa, the Middle East or Asia. The one surprising facet of the current Russo-Chinese conflict was that nuclear missiles had not been used in earlier confrontations . . . surprising to most, but not to the scientists who had for years worked closely with decisive sections of the armed forces in Russia and in the West. Greg still believed Kirov's contention that the vast majority in the Russian military had rejected the use of nuclear weapons as positively as the American and Nato commanders.

Jimmy Carter had put Human Rights into his presidential shop-window. Greg had seen the issue as a politician's ploy; and yet the money spent on *selling* the human rights kite had begun to pay dividends. Jimmy

Carter had come and gone. President Reagan had come and would go before long. But the human rights bug had survived, not in an acutely virulent form but viable enough to have maintained a continuing low-grade effect throughout the Russian-American Strategic Arms Limitation Talks. The proof: the Russian Government had not broken the one clause in the SALT agreements which provided for an immediate summit the moment any country used any nuclear weapon.

The flare-up might have broken out in any of a dozen conflicts. That China had been the flashpoint seemed almost accidental now. What mattered above all was that the Russian and American Presidents were honouring SALT Summit Clause 89A. There had been no argument on the principle; both had gone to Vienna within the stipulated twenty-four hours.

Greg saw John, arm in plaster, staring out of a window. 'How are you feeling?'

'Still a bit concussed, but not bad.'

'Why not go back to your hotel? Have a rest.'

'Would you do that?' asked John.

'I guess not.' On the Ring Boulevard below, little red tramcars were tootling along their polished rails and a poodle was lifting a leg against a linden-tree. 'Is it going to work?'

'It has to.'

'Why?'

'You know as well as I do.'

'Must be my concussion . . . I keep thinking in circles . . . trying to remember what we might have forgotten.'

'John, some things had to be left to chance . . . but not a great deal. We know how politicians tick. We didn't always agree with Jabotinsky, Kirov and our other military partners. But now I feel that they've been right; without a practical alternative to nuclear weapons it would have been impossible to achieve the agreement and co-operation of the High Commands or a change in the powers of the Heads of State.'

'We can't yet bank on the reactions of the Presidents.'

'They're politicians above all, aren't they? There's one mistake we haven't made, John. We haven't based our *bloodless revolution* on the intelligence or compassion of man.'

'If we had it would have been doomed from the start. Shmuel's said it; if humans do survive for another couple of hundred years they might well become as sensible and decent as wild animals.'

'They're ready to start.' John watched the exodus from the buffet table to the lecture theatre. 'I think I'll sleep through the first film. I don't need a reminder of the holocausts . . . nor the Kalahari burn-out. But for God's sake, don't let me miss the live transmissions.'

*   *   *

278

The appalling pictures of the human husks in Eritrea and Rhodesia had shocked the two Presidents, but not sufficiently to deter them from speculating.

From their seats in the front row they were firing questions at the scientists and military on the platform in front of the screen.

'Are you admitting', asked President Galuzin, 'that the Americans collected heat from the sun all those years ago . . and developed this criminal burn-up technique?'

'We've demonstrated,' answered Kirov, 'that neither the Americans nor the Russians experimented along these lines. The technique in those days was primitive . . . not much more scientific than catching sunrays in a mirror and beaming them on to an inflammable target. Officialdom in the East and West was too besotted by nuclear options to think of it. It was a team of American corporation scientists and a corrupt general in the West, and a team of Russian scientists — including Professor Balatov — plus military technicians in the East, who *pioneered* the idea. None of them saw a future in the nuclear arms race. They believed they could evolve a war-machine at once more effective and safer than nuclear weapons . . . a war-machine that would cut out the hazards of radiation-boomerangs.'

The Russian President glanced back at his security men. 'Dissidents in the Soviet armed forces.' It was a statement, not a question. 'Countries the size of mine and yours, Gospodin President, are virtually un-governable. Even a security system as efficient as ours cannot control all sectors of every organization.'

'It has to be faced,' agreed the American President. 'But your problem appears to be greater than ours, Mr Galuzin. According to our infor-mation there are millions of dissidents in Russia . . . millions opposed to industrial as well as military nuclear development. Your government's like a big cheese full of holes.'

'You've been given the information you wanted to hear . . . I've seen some of your CIA reports. Clearly, your intelligence network spews rubbish because it wants to stay in power.'

'So did your KGB, Galuzin. But you'll find, I think, that the GRU has taken control of it.'

'You're out of date, Gospodin President. You're harking back . . . it's only to be expected at your age . . . to the historic feud between the two German intelligence organizations in World War Two. A far cry from 1984 Russia.'

'You Russians . . .' The American President sighed with resignation. 'You know, there *are* national characteristics — even in nations full of minorities — and your people must be the most pigheaded in the world. As, indeed, you are. Why not accept that your KGB is dead . . . and that your government has passed into the control of the armed forces?'

'A putsch? A dream, Gospodin President. I can't oblige in sharing it. I don't accept your putsch theory because — however you psychoanalyze us Russians — we *are* realists. I'd advise you to look to your own insurrection problems.'

The sudden silence, in which both leaders seemed engrossed in their doubts and speculations, wakened John. He got up and joined the men on the platform. 'The armed forces *have* taken over,' he told the assembly. 'In the United States and in Russia.'

'Guards!' roared Galuzin. 'Arrest these men! Arrest all the men on the platform! They're madman! Lunatics!'

No one stirred.

'Sit down Galuzin,' said the American President. 'You'd be more on the ball if you'd occasionally talked with ordinary people . . . and read the world press instead of KGB digests and summaries. You've missed out, Galuzin, but that's partly the fault of your system. You've missed out exactly as your last Tsar missed out . . . you never understood the minds of your own people. So I'd better tell you what's happened right now. I reckon the guy up there has just announced the end of the nuclear age. Don't beat your shoe on the table . . . Don't make a scene. Be honest with yourself for a change. You know as well as I do that nuclear weapons have been a sacred cow much too long. These days we don't know what the hell to do with all the nuclear junk. It's rotting and leaking away all over your country and mine. Even without firing missiles at one another the damned junk will kill us . . . unless the bright guys up there have worked out methods of making it safe.'

'We have, sir,' Martin Jabotinsky assured his President. 'In a partnership of civilian scientists, army, airforce and naval research, we have devised methods of mothballing the nuclear junk — of eliminating it once and for all. We . . .'

'Yet another dream,' Galuzin broke in. 'Or have you worked out what you're going to do with your industrial giants and Big Business? Are you going to tell the corporations, "Sorry comrades, the goods you produce are no longer wanted. You've lost your customers for the nice reactors you've been building . . . and all the nozzles, valves, ballbearings, etcetera. Go bankrupt and forget you ever existed. And let's not worry about the fifty million unemployed. We'll pay them social security." Is that what you have in mind?'

'We have in mind', said Greg, 'that the mothballing of the nuclear junk will be, industrially speaking, as vast an operation as the profitable manufacture of past war-materials. Secondly, the industrial power-producing work for space and in space will stretch the corporations — and manpower — to the limits. We have budgeted for a state of full employment in a situation of world peace.'

'That's just great!' the American President applauded. 'And who's

280

going to pay for the modernizing and re-tooling of industry? Not the corporations, I assure you.'

'World resources and accumulated reserves. Corporations for the sake of profitable survival. And governments, acting as business managers for populations.'

'Dictatorships!' shouted Galuzin. 'You'd finish up like . . .'

'Soviet Russia?' asked Alexei Kirov. 'We don't think so. A partnership between practical scientists and the armed forces . . . the most disciplined bodies of men and women in the world . . . stands a good chance. Especially when backed by the cleanest, most selectively efficient weapon ever devised.'

'Ah!' Galuzin smiled, 'The crunch, at last. *Do as we tell you or bang-bang you're dead.* Nothing new, Gospodin President, nothing new at all. They, up there, need a whip for enforcing obedience. They're sensible enough to recognize it as clearly as every kind of sovereign or governor who ever ruled.'

'The whip', said Kirov, 'will be a last resort. We believe that the fear of it — until the plus-factors create world accord — will soon render it obsolete.'

'What plus-factors?' sneered Galuzin.

'The system which will supplant nuclear and other forms of conventional power — such as oil and coal — is now fully operational and ready for expansion. I'm referring to power stations in space. For the past ten years Russian and American governments have spent money on the system — though not nearly enough. Most of our funds came out of university grants, from far-sighted corporations and out of defence budgets. The new weapon is a direct result of the space power stations programme. The demonstration you're about to see will convince you.' Kirov signalled to someone at the back of the lecture theatre.

The overhead lights dimmed. A coloured pattern appeared on the three-by-three metre television screen. It changed to a picture of a Russian officer at a computer console. 'This', he said, 'is an unscheduled interface. Operation SRB posponed in order to give priority to incoming transmission from Satellite Japan 5. Spacial scanning in operation *now* . Multi-channel spectrum analyzers for simultaneous world transmission a-okay. Do not adjust your sets. Repeat: do not adjust your sets . . . Mother of God!'

The screen had filled with images — swirling vapours, weird cloud-shapes, tall buildings snapping like dry twigs, people in flames squirming in the dust, panic-stricken crowds stampeding over the dead and dying. Suddenly, the single figure of a boy — slowly, slowly dragging himself over stark, stony ground; a Mongolian child.

Shmuel felt ice-cold. The bleak wilderness of Kazakhstan raked his body like the pain of a reopened wound. They'd saved him, those

Mongolian deserters from the Soviet army. Forty years ago he had been such a doomed child, and they had salvaged him from the snow and given him his life. Hebrew words flooded into his mind, *Ye shall offer an offering made by fire unto the Lord* . . . He was praying to God to grant the Mongolian child the release of death. But on the boy came, closer and closer, dragging behind him like a blood-soaked rag the skin which had — only moments ago — enclosed his body.

The unscheduled transmission had faded. The blank screen was staring at blank eyes.

'What you've just seen, gentlemen,' came a voice from the platform 'was a fraction of the bestiality caused by firing a nuclear missile. The unfortunate incident which you have witnessed has in no way endangered you, the World Leaders, has it? No, not you. Not yet. But you must be shrewd enough to realize . . . if we don't get rid of nuclear weapons . . . there is a high probability that you will end like the unknown boy in Mongolia. We may safely assume that you'd welcome an escape from the nuclear trap. We are now going to show you the way out. Regrettably — so as to leave no doubt in anyone's mind — our demonstration will have to be violent . . .'

'*Niet!*' shouted Galuzin. 'No! Wait! We must talk!'

'You've been talking for forty years,' said Shmuel. 'Time's running out.'

'Fifteen minutes,' said the American President. 'He and I . . . alone.'

'With one of the scientists,' added Galuzin.

'Not a Russian, Mr President.'

'Not an American, Gospodin President.'

'Very well,' agreed the American, 'Let's have the English guy . . . the one with an arm in plaster.'

The men on the platform conferred. Within moments Jabotinsky stepped down and led the two Presidents, followed by John, through an area which had been turned into an operations room to a book-lined study.

John went to stand by the window, the two Presidents sank into armchairs, facing one another across a writing table. Down below, in the inner court of the University, a young couple was making love.

'Why the adjournment?' asked the American President. 'Is it a breakthrough?'

'More like a break-up,' answered Galuzin.

'I guess so . . . though they're not yet finished with us. We mustn't exclude the possibility that the whole thing's a big confidence trick.'

'Wishful thinking.' Galuzin picked up a paperknife and bent it to near-breaking-point. 'I don't trust Kirov. Let's prepare a joint communiqué now.'

'The old clichés won't do . . . not this time. Wish I had Harry Resnick right here.'

'I wish Litvinov were here. But neither of them is. You!' Galuzin glared at John. 'Can we get international lines on this telephone?'

'Dial 5 for control room.'

'The British Prime Minister?' asked the American President.

'Yes, perfidious Albion. She's the toughest, most ruthless, of the European lot.'

'And the most realistic.' The American President smiled. 'Reckon she's a fanatic.'

'That's why she'd be right for dealing with a situation created by fanatics.'

'Galuzin, what about the communiqué? We have seven minutes.'

'To hell with the communiqué. The strategy's more important. I suggest we push the woman out front . . . through the minefield.'

'Before the demonstration those guys are putting on? Blindfold?'

'As you said, Gospodin President; she's a fanatic. She'll walk into it.'

'We don't know what more the . . . dissidents are planning for Heads of State. Madam Albion will sit on the fence until the situation has been clarified.'

'Mr America, can you think of a better plan?'

'No. One thing about the lady. She's been schooled by generations of improvisers.'

'You!' Galuzin called John. 'Connect us. Look sharp.'

John went to the telephone. 'You have five minutes.'

'What's the hustle?' asked the American President.

'The war in Mongolia,' John told him.

'If you people *are* in control — and so concerned about suffering humanity — why don't you stop the war?'

'No missile's been fired since the attack you've seen. That much has been accomplished. We want to make sure that it ends there, therefore we still need you.'

'I see. So I haven't lost my job.'

'No. We've decided that presidents and prime ministers who are known throughout the world will have their uses.'

'As rubber stamps?' asked Galuzin.

'Front-men, figureheads, rubber stamps. A pattern will emerge.'

' . . . and we shall prove,' said the commentator on the screen, 'that any government . . . any commercial firm . . . that makes any move towards producing or using nuclear equipment can be — and will be — wiped off the face of the earth. Power Satellite SRB 2 is capable of producing life-giving energy or death. We're now linked with the global television networks. The viewers will see — as they happen — three total eliminations. Over to our man in Moscow.'

The screen sharpened into a picture of the Kremlin. The man in Moscow, microphone in hand, wandered through an empty street and stopped in front of the Lubyanka Prison. 'The nuclear era can't be wished away, but it can be burnt away by a beam of cleansing heat. The inmates of this famous prison have been evacuated or released. No living soul will suffer, but the destroyer from space will prove to you that there is a new force that will protect all of us from the nuclear menace.'

There was a roar, like an approaching earthquake, and a flash that made the screen shimmer with piercing lights. It turned opaque and eventually cleared, revealing the commentator beside a gap in the Kremlin buildings — a yawning gap as wide as a toothless grin. 'The Lubyanka Prison . . . elimated in thirty-point-three seconds. And now, over to America. Come in America. Come in Fort Knox!'

'This is . . . this is . . .' stammered Galuzin.

'Fort Knox,' gasped the American President. 'They can't . . . Our gold reserves . . .'

'Gold', said the uniformed man on the screen, 'has been overvalued all too often. But it will have its uses in paying for post-nuclear industrial development. Therefore the ingots which were deposited here — in this tomb — have been transferred to a place of safety.'

The concrete fortress appeared, a bleak monument to fiscal power. The next moment it had disappeared, a heap of soft earth levelled by a gigantic unseen weight.

Over to Munich. Another commentator was standing before the arches and stadiums, the pavilions and flying roofs of the Munich Olympic complex. 'Much ingenuity has gone into building this strange and beautiful place. The operators of the Selective Reflector Beam were reluctant to waste it. Yet it was deemed essential for proving the mobility as well as the power of the Beam.'

Shmuel heard the familiar roar and turned away from the screen. He had argued against the destruction of the Munich Olympic complex, because Israeli athletes had been murdered there, and because he did not want anyone to read political meanings into its elimination. He had been outvoted; he'd accepted the inevitable.

The commentator in Munich faced the cameras. 'We are now taking you to the studio in Vienna, where the Presidents of the Soviet Union and the United States have been watching the elimination of the Lubyanka Prison, of Fort Knox and the Olympic complex in Munich . . . Over to the University in Vienna.'

The doors at the back of the lecture theatre had opened, revealing a battery of television cameras. Powerful lights picked out a corner of the platform where Martin Jabotinsky sat flanked by two unoccupied chairs. On a television screen at the side the British Prime Minister appeared to be gazing directly at the two Presidents.

'May I welcome you, Prime Minister,' General Jabotinsky addressed the image, 'on this day, the twenty-first of August nineteen eighty-four . . . which will surely become the most memorable date in the history of our century.'

'Thank you, General.' The Prime Minister smoothed the royal blue dress over her knees and switched on her composed expression.

'Prime Minister, I believe you have an important announcement to make.'

'Indeed I have, General . . . It gives me much pleasure to be with you; to have the privilege of telling the British people and the world that the Mongolian nuclear war has ended. My government will be a signatory, this very evening, to the World Pact against all uses of nuclear power. Tomorrow Her Majesty the Queen will lead the nation in prayer at a special thanksgiving service at St Paul's . . .'

'Which will be beamed via satellite as part of the World Peace Programme. Prime Minister, we've realized for years that we'll have to kill the nuclear monster before it devours us. But pacts, with due respect, work in times of peace only. In war they tend to get broken.'

'General, it's unnecessary to play devil's advocate.' The Prime Minister spaced her words with the precision of a metronome. 'There will be no more wars. I personally have been engaged in a long, hard struggle. But I've always been absolutely certain that British participation in space research would lead to a lasting peace.'

'May I remind you, Prime Minister, that your participation in space has been a recent development? that your government wasted billions on American nuclear missiles, such as the Cruise . . .'

'General, I could not permit my country to drift into a state of utter defencelessness. Had we not negotiated from strength the World Pact would not have come about. As I have said many times in the past . . .'

'With respect, Prime Minister, you're using a much discredited device in quoting yourself. Having *said so many times* doesn't make anything true . . .'

At the back of the lecture theatre, out of camera range, John turned to Shmuel. 'What's Martin doing?' He felt troubled. The interview was not going as he'd expected. The assignment had been given to Jabotinsky because, as a young general, he had status and media-carisma. He was a fluent speaker and reacted quickly. 'He's not in control, is he?'

'Remember,' murmured Shmuel, 'it was Martin who established the link with the Russian Air force . . . and with the Poles. He won't fall down on strategy.'

The Prime Minister, on the screen, was sitting bolt upright, blue eyes flashing righteous indignation. 'General, as you're not a member of my Cabinet, you don't know how essential our purchases of nuclear defence systems have been . . . *for the creation of a totally new industry.'*

'Prime Minister, are you referring to the wholesale mothballing of nuclear installations and weapons?'

'I am indeed, General. If I may say so . . . ' the PM's elegant nose lifted with inimitable arrogance, 'Great Britain already leads the world in mothballing techniques . . . from superb fifty-foot-thick gravestone platforms to high-rise pyramids which are works of modern art.'

'Prime Minister, with respect . . .' For a moment Jabotinsky did appear to be out of his depth. 'Do you have the audacity . . .' he'd decided on a near-insult delivered with an indulgent smile, 'the nerve to tell the viewers that this new industry — the outcome of today's anti-nuclear pact — has been planned *by you* . . .planned by you personally from A to Z to create work for your six million unemployed?'

The Prime Minister lowered her eyes, all feminine modesty. 'It would be churlish of me not to ackowledge the support given to me by my colleagues in the Cabinet Office and — of course — by the Presidents of Soviet Russia and America. Full employment and the ending of the nuclear menace have always been my first priorities. I do take credit . . .'

'She'll get it too,' muttered the American President, 'Damn her. Big deal . . . sending her through the minefield, Galuzin. How will we get by?'

'Prime Minister,' Jabotinsky interrupted, 'Thank you for your clear and heartening statements. It was right that the lady should come first — especially at the dawn of world peace. But now, over to the Presidents of America and Soviet Russia.'

The lights were sweeping the rows of watchers. Greg, behind the two leaders, prodded them. 'You're on.'

'She's dropped us right in it,' said the American President. 'You asked for it.'

'Don't go paranoiac now.'

'How are you going to handle it?'

'Like a Russian master of chess. How else? You heard . . . we're on.'

The two leaders turned into the performers they were. They walked on, with the little hop and skip which viewers had come to expect of the fit and virile, and took their chairs.

'Sir,' Jabotinsky addressed the American President, 'May I ask you for your reaction to the instant destruction we witnessed earlier?'

'I admit. . . I still feel stunned. And grieved . . . ' the old actor accomplished a catch in his voice, 'to see the marvellous works of man reduced to . . . dust. And yet the world had to see these terrifying eliminations; President Galuzin and I agreed upon it after a series of in-depth discussions. Nothing but that immense visual impact would have served to bring home to all populations the . . . dire necessity of ending the nuclear age.'

'To those of you,' the Russian President took over, in English, 'who have felt fear of the new weapon — as I have — I will say this: yes, there still is a killer abroad; but it will never strike the innocent, nor will anyone ever again die of radiation sickness. But for the guilty there will be no escape from the Beam . . . it will wipe them out whether they are at home or in their offices. They won't be able to run or drive away from the Beam. It will find them wherever they are . . . with inexorable accuracy. With the capable assistance of the American President I've fought with devotion in the cause of peace and prosperity . . . Yes, prosperity. The positive element of the Selective Reflector Beam will be unlimited energy from space . . .'

'Industry,' boomed the American President, projecting his trained voice, 'will, in time, move into space. Our planet will become a Garden of Eden, a place of beauty and . . .'

'John,' murmured Shmuel, 'it doesn't matter what they say. Not now.'

'Performing circus animals.'

'So? People still need circuses with their bread . . . Let's go. Now we can begin our work, step by step.'